Commitments

Also by Devon Scott

Unfaithful
Obsessed
Awakening
Illusions
Complications
Commitments

Published by Kensington Publishing Corp.

Commitments

Book 2 in the Seduction Series

DEVON SCOTT

Kensington Publishing Corp.
http://www.kensingtonbooks.com

DAFINA BOOKS are published by

Kensington Publishing Corp.
119 West 40th Street
New York, NY 10018

Copyright © 2017 by Devon Scott

Published in arrangement with Strebor Books, www.streborbooks.com.
Distributed by Simon & Schuster, Inc., 1230 Avenue of the Americas, New York, NY 10020.
The Forever Game © 2007 by Jonathan Luckett
ISBN-13 978-1-59309-116-3
ISBN-10 1-59309-116-8
LCCN 2007923860
First Strebor Books trade paperback edition August 2007
Originally published June 2004 as *How Ya Livin'*

All Kensington Titles, Imprints, and Distributed Lines are available at special quantity discounts for bulk purchases for sales promotions, premiums, fund-raising, and educational or institutional use. Special book excerpts or customized printings can also be created to fit specific needs. For details, write or phone the office of the Kensington special sales manager: Kensington Publishing Corp., 119 West 40th Street, New York, NY 10018, attn: Special Sales Department, Phone: 1-800-221-2647.

Dafina and the Dafina logo Reg. U.S. Pat. & TM Off.

ISBN-13: 978-1-4967-0245-6
ISBN-10: 1-4967-0245-X
First Kensington Mass Market Edition: October 2017

10 9 8 7 6 5 4 3 2 1

Printed in the United States of America

For Shantel

Author's Note

Hey y'all, since it may have been a minute since you were last acquainted with Trey, Vince, & Erika and all of their shenanigans, let's take a moment to recap what's going on in their world:

Trey Alexander is a thirty-something year old attorney. He's tall, bald, and extremely good-looking (just ask him!). He possesses the vast ego of someone who is used to getting his way. When we first met Trey, he was heading down to Jamaica for a much-needed vacation. Along the way we were introduced to his sexual escapades and his general love of life. His adage: work hard, play even harder, is something that we spy in everything he touches. But he has a weakness: and he thought he saw it while down in Jamaica—Layla, the ex-love of his life, the woman who ruined him. Layla is the one thing that can stop him dead in his tracks. And she does exactly that, when he observes her waltzing in to a restaurant that he happens to be having lunch in, with one of his closest friends, Erika.

But don't get it twisted. Trey doesn't let the thought of his ex stop him from having sex with every woman he meets. Let's see: there's Allison, who turns out to be the attorney for the soon-to-be ex-wife named Aponi Hues of one of his clients, Washington Wizards forward, Quentin Hues.

And speaking of Aponi, Trey ends up sexing her a few weeks after finding himself across the conference room table from her and Allison, although to be fair, he did think twice (or was it three times?) about the hazards of sleeping with her (Trey Rule Number 4—never fuck a client) did cross his mind before he thought, screw it, and directed her to his bed!

On the job front, not everything is blue skies and blue-birds singing. His mentor and boss, Calvin Figgs, is being replaced by a new managing partner, Bernard John Marshall, an evil man who seemingly has it out for Trey. He's got Counselor Alexander in his cross-hairs and is micro-managing the hell out of his work. Trey is about to go off if something doesn't give soon.

It should be mentioned that there is at least one redeeming quality to Trey—he volunteers at the *Nona E. Taylor Women's Center* where he cooks once a month. It's like therapy for Trey, and it's a way for him to give back.

Erika is a single woman who is picky when it comes to men. And why shouldn't she be? She's tired of these knuckle-heads that don't offer her shit. But when she meets James, an anchor on the evening news, she falls hard. What's not to like? He's great-looking, intelligent, can carry on a conver-sation, and oh yes, he knows how to please a woman. Erika is not mad at him! There's just one problem: James can't seem to orgasm when he's with Erika. A seemingly minor problem, but one that begins to taunt her. Is it James or is it Erika? Perhaps she's doing something wrong in the bed-room. These thoughts keep her awake at night. Is it a deal-breaker? She wrestles with this issue, all the while trying to build a lasting relationship with James.

Last, but not least, there's Vince Cannon, Jr. He's Trey's best friend—a renaissance man—artist, author, and motiva-tional speaker. Vince is the kind of man who finds beauty in every woman he meets. When we first meet Vince, he's dating Maxi, a cool, intelligent woman who excites him with her down-to-earth aura. They have fun when they're together. They vibe well, but is she the one? Vince is unsure. While contemplating all of this and his need to find that special person whom he'll spend the rest of his life with, Vince meets Desiree at a local coffee shop. She's young, full of spunk, and catches his eye. She offers to do a lifecasting of her face, and subsequently, her upper body. Vince can't say no to that! Meanwhile, a chance encounter with a woman named Angeliqué while at one of his seminars down in New Orleans takes him on a whirlwind romance and in a new direction. Angeliqué is bold, beautiful, even practices voodoo, and is so utterly different from any woman that Vince has ever met, that he falls instantly for her. And falls hard. But when he tries to surprise her by visiting her down in the Big Easy unannounced, he's the one who gets surprised. For Angeliqué is embracing another woman, and Vince is devastated. He returns home dejected. He reaches back out to Maxi, but it's been several months since she's heard from him and by then she's moved on. What does Vince do now? Whom should he choose to make his life complete?

Trey, Vince, & Erika. Their delicious drama and sexual exploits are laid bare for all to witness. Three best friends. Looking for love. In all the wrong places. I know it's cliché, but hell, in this case, it's so apropos!

And now, onto the second act! Enjoy!

Devon Scott
September 1st, 2015
Alexandria, Virginia

One

A nother dreary day—skies devoid of blue, a steady wind that whipped branches around, announcing the coming of winter. Vince had awakened early; a restless night had forced him from his bed around seven. He had tried to sleep in, attempting to drown himself in the silence and darkness underneath the heavy comforter, but that didn't work. So he rose, and grudgingly went for a run.

He returned an hour later. Glancing around the first floor of his home, a three-story row house a few minutes from Children's Hospital, Vince noticed that there were papers from the previous three Sundays that had yet to be read. Taking in the laptop that lay on the coffee table, he remembered the loads of unanswered e-mails. The cordless phone was positioned snug in the cushion of his couch. Phone calls from several bookstores in Philadelphia and Newark had yet to be returned.

What was he doing?

He was never like this, letting his work pile up.

Last night—a Friday night—he remained at home, even though Trey had begged him to come on out—First Fridays at some spot downtown. You know Trey wouldn't miss those for the world. But Vince declined, saying he had too much work to do—which was true. Only thing, Vince hadn't accomplished anything. Desiree had phoned too, asking if he wanted some company. He had refused her invitation as well, telling her the same lie he had told Trey. Instead, Vince had sat on the couch all by himself, nursing a Corona in front of his television—channel surfing the entire evening, watching stuff he could care less about until midnight rolled around, when he finally gave up and went to bed.

It was now after nine a.m. the following day and his stomach growled something fierce. Unfortunately he hadn't the energy to fix himself something to eat. So he reached for the piled up papers and began to go through them. Vince still wore his tight running pants and a Morehouse sweatshirt. His sneakers remained in the foyer by the door.

The doorbell broke his concentration. Vince glanced at the front door and frowned. He was not expecting anyone. He put down the paper and rose from the couch, smoothing out his hair and reaching to scratch at his beard. He knew he looked like a wild man this early in the morning. He hoped it was just FedEx or somebody like that.

Vince opened the door and found himself face to face with Amber.

She was all smiles.

Behind her stood Angeliqué holding up a bag from Krispy Kreme.

Amber's stare traveled down slowly to his feet before bouncing back up. "Nice pants," she quipped while brushing past him into the house. That left Angeliqué and Vince standing alone.

"Peace offering," she said, handing him the donuts. Angeliqué grinned and Vince felt his heart bake.

* * *

He sat in his kitchen, refreshed from a quick shower, watching them work. Angeliqué was putting on coffee; Amber was slicing cheese for omelets. They had insisted on commandeering his kitchen; and who was Vince to put up a fight?

Angeliqué wore a pair of faded jeans, low riding and tight, with pointy black boots and a thin dark sweater. Adorning her head was a Kangol hat. Amber was clad in a pair of over-sized sweatpants and a form-fitting cotton tee. Her feet were bare. Vince was still reeling from their surprise visit.

"When did you get in?" he asked.

"Last night. We caught a non-stop and was in D.C. by eight p.m."

"And how did you find me?" Vince asked incredulously.

"That was easy," Angeliqué mused, eyeing him from the stove where she stir fried onions, green and red peppers, tomatoes, and garlic. The vapors wafted over Vince and he felt his stomach somersault. "You're on the interwebs—a smart move if you're into stalkers."

"Hmmn," he said. Vince still was unsure of how to play this. Good cop or bad—that was the question. On the one hand, watching them in his kitchen filled his insides with a feeling that he hadn't experienced since New Orleans. But that was tempered by the conversation he and Angeliqué had had a few nights previous. And the images from New Orleans remained . . .

Vince crossed the street, fading deeper into the shadows of the night. Light from the gallery windows flooded the street and he wanted to make sure he wasn't seen—not yet. Sounds from various night creatures were more pronounced here—away from the masses of yelling, inebriated people. Vince came to a stop directly across the street from the broad expanse of glass. He peered in, noticed that the place was empty save for a lone woman who sat at a desk toward the rear of the building, her head down as she attended to some paperwork. He scanned the interior walls, observing from the shadows Angeliqué's art, the veve of the voodoo spirits—the elaborate designs surrounded by colorful hues and shades of the Haitian art.

Vince took a breath and crossed the street, cutting a diagonal line toward the gallery entrance. He spotted the courtyard entrance off to the right, a heavy wrought-iron door that hung open. He headed for that.

Coming upon the entrance, he slowed his gait and peered inside to what lay beyond. The courtyard was bathed in shadows; it was exactly as he remembered. The red brick wall was covered with thick ivy and he could hear the trickling of water from the oval pond. Vince reached for the black metal and then stopped dead. To the left by the table where he had laid his wine stem months before, he saw them—a couple caught in embrace. The shock of frizzy hair was unmistakable. Angeliqué was facing Vince, but shielded from view by the other person whose head she was grasping gingerly between her hands. Angeliqué kissed the person— it was not a long kiss, but what Vince witnessed froze his heart.

Angeliqué was in the arms of a woman.

His thoughts returned to the present.

"And what if I wasn't home?" he asked.

"Oh, I guess we'd be scarfing down these donuts all by ourselves," Amber said, flashing a smile in his direction.

"Right. Well, I am glad to see both of you." Vince stood and went to Amber, who leaned in and gave him a hug. He moved over to the range and slid behind Angeliqué who was busy at work. She tilted her head up and nuzzled her neck against his. They embraced and kissed gingerly.

"Pass those eggs, Vince, and step back," she said. "It's about to get ugly up in here!"

Thirty minutes later their plates were clean. Omelets and fresh coffee, followed by glazed and jelly-filled donuts had each of them holding their stomachs.

"Damn, after a meal like that I need a nap!" Amber exclaimed.

"I hear that," Vince responded as he cleared the dishes.

"Vince," Angeliqué said as they watched Amber stretch, "I was hoping you would show me your studio."

He glanced over at Amber who said, "You two go ahead, I'd like to stay here and crash on the couch for a while. If it's cool with Mr. Cannon, Jr. over there?"

Vince grinned. "Make yourself at home, but excuse the mess—my maid quit just last week; I haven't had time to replace her!"

"Yeah right . . . ," Amber said, ambling toward the couch.

She was silent for a long time. Vince observed her from the futon as she contemplated his wall of masks. Angeliqué moved slowly from one end to the other, studying each one in turn, his masks that each told a story: passion, happiness, anger, sadness. Angeliqué turned to him with a solemn face.

"Vince, these are incredible. I don't know what to say."

"Thank you." He sipped a mug of coffee as he watched her.

"I didn't know what to expect, but you are really good! You have a God-given talent. Are these hanging in any galleries?"

"Not really," Vince said. He'd been thinking long and hard about making some contacts in the art world so that he could begin selling his pieces. At this point, he had one hanging in Cosi on Capitol Hill, and another in Utopia on U Street.

"Well, you definitely should," Angeliqué said, joining him on the couch. She leaned against him, taking a sip from her mug. Her frizzy hair blanketed her shoulders, resting on her sweater. Some of her mane fell on Vince. He eyed her silently as her body pressed into his, concentrating on her straight nose, her rich skin, those cheekbones that rose as she spoke. His mind transported him back to New Orleans, and the very first time—when the two of them had made passionate love that night, the way she had made him feel, out of this world, unparalleled, the passion gushing forth from them both like a geyser. Without fanfare, Vince reached for her face, and placed his lips to hers.

Angeliqué responded by facing him; in a moment their limbs were intertwined like their tongues. They were silent—words did not do justice to what they were feeling. His hands raised to her face, lightly caressing her cheeks and lips, probing her mouth, then feeling her nose, running fingers over her eyelids as he pulled back to gaze upon her. Then he bent forward and kissed her again. Moments later, Angeliqué was atop him, straddling Vince as she squirmed out of her sweater. Her breasts heaved with her breathing, as Vince reached for her pointed nipples.

Cupping her breasts, he felt her warmth transferred between their skins. They kissed ravenously, as if they had been denied sustenance for too long. Glancing upward, Vince watched her from his vantage point below, her eyes that had closed to mere slits, her body that writhed like a serpent as his hands traversed her torso toward her thighs.

Vince lifted her off of him with his powerful arms and returned her to the futon. He stood up and removed his sweater as she watched. Then his jeans slid down his legs, revealing tight briefs that barely contained his engorged state. Angeliqué reached out to stroke him through the fabric of his underwear, taking her time, running a lazy finger up the shaft as the heel of her boot slowly raked itself against his shin.

Reaching out for his buttocks with both hands, she pulled him to her until he was sandwiched between her thighs, his shins pressed up against the futon's skin. After massaging his ass for a moment, Angeliqué slowly peeled off his briefs as her stare locked with his—a devious smile painted on her face. When he had stepped free of his underwear, and stood naked and engorged in front of her, then and only then did she drop her stare, gazing at his member which bobbed inches from her face.

She took him into her mouth, grasping the shaft with an expert hand, tugging on the flesh as she sucked him in, and Vince shut his eyes and threw back his head, reaching out for support because he already felt himself growing weak. She nibbled lightly around the head, using her hand to guide his wand against her teeth and lips, as her tongue flicked against the hole before lowering herself to his sac, lightly squeezing the flesh as she took each testicle into her mouth.

Vince moaned and reached for her breasts, squeezing them between his fingers. His hand snaked down smooth skin to her navel before plunging south, beneath her jeans, searching for the damp cotton of her panties. He flopped out of her mouth, spittle adorning his shaft like a glaze as Angeliqué wriggled out of her jeans. Moments later she was fully nude, and Vince had to stand back and marvel at her form. She lay back on the futon lengthwise and curled her finger at him, beckoning him to enter.

Vince didn't need to be told twice!

He entered her effortlessly as Angeliqué wrapped her ankles around his back, her fingers raking his forearms that flexed as he moved. He began slowly, but increased his rapid thrusting, watching himself go in and out below thin brown pubic hair, as her golden navel seemed to contort with each drive.

She was a constriction around him, her neck nuzzling against his as they made love, panting, eyes closed, both waiting for that feeling to waft over them, those passionate sensations that soaked their essence and consumed them once, twice before, down in New Orleans, when the spirit of voodoo priests and priestesses hovered over them like fog.

But it did not come.

Not for Angeliqué nor for Vince.

Beads of sweat pooled in the valley of her back as Vince took her from behind, her unkempt hair like a scraggy vine as he rushed against her flesh, her thrusts meeting his head-on as their bodies blurred.

But that exquisite feeling, the delicious high that comes from consuming one's sensuality like a drug, remained elusive.

Both of them grunted and groaned as Vince attacked Angeliqué with his fervor, as if accelerating their frenzy might somehow boil their spirits, incite violence inside of them, riot the senses to the point of complete and unadulterated ardor—racing past the point of no return, bursting through the wall, to the end . . .

But as they came simultaneously, streaking through the tunnel toward the sunlight that blazed in, drawing them to the finish line, Vince and Angeliqué separately discovered that it was not what it could have been . . .

Not at all what it *had* been . . .

They disengaged, slowing their quickened heartbeats, and retreated to separate ends of the futon. For several moments neither spoke, as if they needed the silence to complete the tearing down of the cocoon that had shielded each one from the other's view.

Vince rose naked off the couch. Angeliqué did not follow him with her stare. Instead she began to don her clothes.

After several minutes of running water, Vince returned. Angeliqué was fully clothed and studying the wall of masks.

"Can you do me?" she asked softly.

"Hmmn?" Vince had his back to her, his attention at his workbench and the torso life casting of Desiree. The plaster had long since hardened, and yet he studied the rise of her flesh from taut stomach to the peak of her supple breasts, running a hand along its texture as he recalled the real thing: soft, smooth, dark chocolate skin.

"A mask," Angeliqué said, "I was wondering if you can do one of me?"

"I don't know," Vince responded, his mind a million miles away, suddenly feeling the distress that had been heaved onto his shoulders. His fingertips alighted from the plaster as he turned away from the workbench and back to her—reflecting on what just had transpired between them, and all that had *not*. The finality of it all caused him to tremble at his core. "We'll have to see," he said. Angeliqué turned and nodded, but as she gathered up her things to go, she already knew what his answer would be.

Two

Standing in my kitchen off of U Street, staring down at the swirl of coffee, I allowed myself to remember—*her*. I recalled for the first time in many years three singular events—ribbons of celluloid in my mind which had been locked away tight, unable to surface because my psyche would not allow it—for fear of dredging up an ocean of emotions, intense anger and something much worse. But this time, I allowed it to happen. I gave in to the sudden and severe cramps that scraped at my gut after seeing her there in the restaurant, knowing that these thoughts were long overdue. So I sucked in a breath, shut my eyes tightly, and *remembered . . .*

I vividly recall the rain—the steady drone of a downpour, drops as big as bumblebees free-falling vertically, there was no wind, no sideways pressure to cause the deluge to rake across uneven ground—no, it was a simple, yet complete storm. I recall the roar of the showers and the heavy swish-swish of my wipers as they fought gallantly to keep up, yet to no avail. This was no contest, and I remember thinking—God help anyone who is caught in this torrent—I almost laughed out loud as I took a turn with some effort, braking cautiously because I knew my ride could hydroplane at any moment, sending me and my shiny auto careening headlong into the timbers if I wasn't careful, so I concentrated on the yellow lines painted on slick asphalt at 1:17 a.m.—I recall that too—the bright aquamarine LEDs that seemed to wink every minute, as I turned down the stereo in order to gain further concentration—all of these things occurring serially and in rapid succession—my dark hands gripping the wheel tightly as I guided the car into the turn, braking slowly and carefully, the LEDs noting the time, my hand reaching for the volume knob on the stereo, and almost laughing out loud at the absurdity of this storm—and that was when I saw *it* and instinctively jammed on my brakes, causing me to skid to a stop.

Two cars, one by the side of the road, its hazards pulsating into the night, cutting the rain at oblique angles, and headlights shining onto a second vehicle—the other, ten yards away from the first, its body turned at a right angle to the road, an entire third of its body an accordion against a thick dark tree. My eyes flicked rapidly over the scene as my heart raced—then leveled against a form huddled on the ground leaning over something else—I strained my eyes to discern details, but the rain was blotting them out like ink spots. I pulled over and mechanically exited my vehicle without even thinking about what I would do. I was no doctor, but something in me commanded that I help.

I raced around the front of my car, my shoes squishing in the soft earth, mud splattering the cuffs of my suit pants as I came up to the person kneeling on the ground. Beneath her lay a woman—no more than eighteen, eyes closed, as if in deep sleep, mouth hung open slightly. The rain was relentless, and it was clear that no conscious person could stand the force of the raindrops slapping against their warm flesh without flinching. My eyes cut back to the woman hunched over the prone form—the long jet-black hair grabbed my attention first. I recall the way the rain pummeled her head and flowed down her back, causing her hair to shine and glow, but I didn't have time to appreciate the details—she turned her head and stared up at me—and our eyes connected—and this I will *never* forget—I saw something in there that caused my heart to stir—compassion and pain, the yin and yang that radiated out from those dark orbs as she blinked away the rain, communicating more with her stare than mere words ever could. I so wanted to keep my stare locked on hers; marveling at her high cheekbones that were rosy, and drink in the rest of her beautiful features, but the situation would not allow it.

"What can I do?" I belted out, kneeling down as I reached inside my jacket for my cell phone.

"She's unconscious and bleeding," the woman beside me yelled. "I tried my phone but can't get a signal." She was holding the young woman's head between both hands. Underneath, I could see dark red swaths painting grass stems. I glanced around frantically as I pulled out my cell and checked the signal.

Nothing.

"We need to move her," I shouted, already deciding on a plan of action. The woman glared at me, raindrops beating her soft face and shoulders. She flung the water away with a quick shake of her head, and wiped her dark hair backwards. Her eyes never left mine—ours were locked as if in some kind of dance, and even among the storm-chill I felt the warming sensation—the first of many—an oozing of heat that radiated out from my core—just being within arms distance seemed to quiet me. I sensed she felt the same because her glower seemed to soften, as if drawing strength from me, this stranger, forced her to not shut down. She dipped her stare momentarily to the unmoving form before returning it to me. She nodded slowly, and together we lifted the unconscious woman off the sodden ground.

That night was the first time I had laid eyes on Layla, and from that moment I was hooked . . .

There was something about her, something so profoundly different from the other women I had dated, that I found myself completely and utterly *sprung*.

Yeah, y'all, I had fallen *hard* . . .

Layla and I had spent the next five hours together, a first date of sorts in the emergency room as they worked on the young woman, the two of us talking in hushed tones, getting to know one another, until the hours crept onward and I found Layla's head gently resting on my shoulder as she napped on the cold plastic chairs, her feet folded underneath her. I recall how she finally stirred around six a.m., as sunlight slowly crept along the worn carpet toward our row of chairs, Layla leisurely stretching a golden arm before opening her eyes and glancing upward into mine, where our stares once again locked. There was no awkward moment of not knowing where or with whom she was with; no split-second of vertigo where eyes grow wide—no, there was simple purity in her gaze, as if she had awakened knowing exactly where she wanted to be. Instinctively I had reached out to brush her dark hair from her cheek—I can't explain what possessed me to do that—it wasn't so much a physical act as a spiritual one—as if in that moment our souls connected—and Layla watched me silently, her dark eyes unblinking as I whispered that the young girl was out of surgery and in recovery—the doctors were guarded, but thought that she would make it. Layla blinked and smiled weakly before closing her eyes and nuzzling back into the

warmth of my shoulder. An hour later we said our goodbyes
in the parking lot of the hospital.

I recall driving home and using every second to vividly
remember the sweet details of our chance encounter.

How long ago did that fateful event occur that changed
my world? Six, no seven years . . .

In some sense it seems like only yesterday. In another, it
is as if decades have passed by, like when one attempts to recall the details of their childhood and find that the window
that they are glancing through is murky and cracked.

The second set of images that suddenly flooded my psyche caused me to reach out to the counter top for support.
Lately when I glance at that counter top delicious images of
Allison and the wooden spoon leap to mind. But this time,
that did not happen. I felt myself grow weak as if my knees
were about to buckle. My stare was fuzzy. My coffee mug
seemed to swim in and out of focus as if it were alive. I wasn't
looking—I was remembering . . .

Layla and I were at a hotel in New York, Upper West Side
overlooking Central Park. We had come here on a whim; the
weekend rate had set me back over a thousand bucks, but I
didn't give a damn! I was with my lady, and that was all that
mattered.

We had spent the day doing some touristy stuff—shopping on Fifth Avenue, taking in the Museum of Natural History and the Hayden Planetarium, and then back to the hotel
for a quick nap before dinner in Brooklyn Heights overlooking the water and Manhattan skyline. Afterwards, we had
cabbed it back to the hotel where Layla had shooed me into
the bathroom for a long, hot shower. I had come out refreshed; my skin scrubbed clean, my senses singing in anticipation for what was to come. I remember waltzing out of

the steamy bathroom and into a candlelight-filled bedroom. Layla was standing by the large window glancing downward to an expanse of park below. She had her back to me—when she turned, my breath was arrested.

I'll never forget the pose she held—Layla standing there, one hand on her hip, the other reaching out to stroke the wall, clad only in white lingerie: a beautiful laced bra that held her lovely breasts, a pair of matching g-string panties. A thin dark line of pubic hair could be seen through the translucent material. On her feet was a pair of spiked black heels. Her hair was straight down her back and shiny. Her eyes were dazzling orbs that sparkled at me as she smiled. For a moment neither of us said a word. I drank in her features, the sensual stare that cut though me like a blade, and made my entire frame shudder.

I'll never forget that night, for that image, especially that pose is indelibly etched into my psyche. Also is the rush of emotions that I felt that evening—similar to that morning in the emergency room when our eyes locked—more a spiritual and soulful connection than on a physical plane—God yes, my woman was beautiful—but it was her inner beauty that imprisoned my heart that night. And for the first time in my life, I felt something that I had never experienced before. There I was, standing before a breathtaking beauty—her sensuality reaching out to bathe me like a serpent does with its forked tongue, and what I felt deep inside was not the hardening of my sex, but the rush of emotions that made my eyes water. I was completely and utterly inebriated with someone to the point of total immersion . . .

That's when I knew.

I loved this woman, with all that my heart and soul was capable of . . .

* * *

Suddenly the scene shifted. It was like one of those lovely days in Jamaica, ultra blue sky that would suddenly deepen and turn gray. Thick dark clouds rushing in bring torrential rains, but for only a short while . . .

My mind was enjoying the movie it was replaying—it had been a long time since I'd allowed the film to be shown again, but when the images shifted I felt as I had that fateful night on stage in Negril, a throng of partygoers belting out my name in unison as I spotted the woman at the back of the crowd and felt the temperature drop. A sudden chill overtook my body as a new scene replaced the old—one that I was not ready to see again.

I moved quickly to the living room, as if the act of physical movement would cause my brain to refocus.

It did not.

The image remained—Layla standing a foot away from me, hands drawn to her sides, tears streaming down her mascara-smeared face, as she told me her secret. And I remember backing away, as if she were some alien being, a monster that could do me harm, thinking to myself, oh my God this isn't happening to me, this isn't possible, this is a sick joke. A minute from now we'll be laughing and carrying on as we always do. I'll reach out for her, she'll come to me, we'll embrace, becoming one, and everything will be okay . . .

But it didn't end up that way.

I remember reaching up, almost instinctively, and slapping Layla hard across her face, as if in some small measure my action would serve to erase what she had just told me.

But it did not.

To this day, nothing has . . .

* * *

A phone call thankfully saved me. It was Vince.

"Waz up, playa, how ya livin'?" he said.

"Waz up," I responded, but without the usual enthusiasm. Vince, I could tell, immediately picked up on my unusually weak demeanor.

"Hey, bruh, you okay?"

"Yeah."

"Come on, man, this is me you're talking to—what's up?" Vince asked.

"Naw, I'm cool," I said, attempting to muster up the energy that was needed to get through this call.

"A'ight—listen, Angeliqué and Amber are in town. I really want you and Erika to meet them. I know it's short notice, but we're heading over to bluespace later and would love for you to meet us there."

My mind raced. Pushed down into the depths of my brain were the fleeting images of Layla standing before me, swirling downward like a toilet flushed. I prayed they would stay there, but I knew they would not.

"Yeah, uh, that's cool. What time are you thinking?" I asked, wiping away the perspiration that had beaded on my baldhead.

"I don't know," Vince said. "Probably around ten or eleven. Cool?"

"Yeah, that's cool," I said again, my mind still whirling from the blow of that last reflection.

"A'ight, listen, I really want you to meet them, so no excuses, playa!" Vince was trying levity, but I just wasn't feeling it. We clicked off. A moment later the phone rang again. I didn't even bother to check the Caller ID, knowing that it was probably Vince again, forgetting to tell me something.

"Speak!" I said, injecting a bit of the usual Trey-authority.

"Hi, is this Trey?" A woman's voice, heavily accented, vaguely familiar.

"Yes?"

"Hey," she responded, "This is Gabrielle, you probably don't remember me, but we met down in Jamaica a few months ago."

A flood of recognition hit me. Lovely Gabrielle, the honey whom I had boned on the beach to the applause of an entire resort! And in that second, my mind flipped, literally, like a switch being thrown. No longer were there any lingering thoughts of Layla and her secret—those having been replaced by luscious Gabrielle—her rich olive skin, large tits, tight sex, and talented mouth. Oh yeah, y'all, this call was exactly what Trey needed right about now!

"Hey you!" I exclaimed, "of course I remember you; how could I not!" Gabrielle giggled as we chatted for a few minutes, catching up and shit.

"So, listen, the reason I am calling," Gabrielle said in a breathy voice, "is because there's a party tonight at the home of this couple we know—very nice people, Lifestyles folks who just love to party. Anyway, I was thinking it would be great if you could come—come to the party and then hopefully come a few more times tonight, if you know what I mean!" Gabrielle was laughing and I could just envision her straddling my engorged dick. Again . . .

"Baby, I am definitely down for a party—especially if your fine ass is gonna be there!" I said, feeling my jeans go taut as my manhood stirred.

"Oh, Trey, that's great—I can't wait to see you!" Gabrielle gave me the details and I quickly jotted them down. Hanging up, I was giddy again—my old self—racing around the crib, wondering what I was going to wear to a party where mutha suckas got buck naked! I'd have to shave my balls and bring a roll of condoms! Oh yeah, y'all . . . Trey's back in the saddle, y'all, for real!

True dat!

* * *

I found the address easily, thanks to Waze. It was a nice-looking brick Colonial in a well-kept neighborhood just outside the Beltway in Silver Spring. Who would have guessed that mutha suckas were about to get buck wild in this crib, sandwiched between PTA and soccer mom homes. I parked a few houses away and walked leisurely up the stone steps to the door. After much deliberation I had decided on a dark suit, Italian cut, and a fine white silk shirt halfway undone. I didn't know these people save for Gabrielle and Raul, her husband, so I wasn't sure what to expect. But I wasn't one to take chances. You never knew when sexy-ass honeys were gonna show up, so I erred on the side of caution, and dressed contemporary with a bit of Trey-flair as only this dude can do.

Come on, y'all, you know by now how we do!

I rang the doorbell, and glanced down at my black lace ups that I had polished an hour earlier. I checked the Breitling. Ten-eighteen p.m. Gabrielle told me the party started at nine, but bump that! I wasn't one to show up on time for any damn thing. I thought for a moment about Vince and his friends heading to bluespace.

The door opened and I was greeted by a thirty-something blonde with long hair down her back, thin, and nice looking. She smiled straight white teeth. The woman was dressed in a long colorful dress and heels that accentuated her small breasts and shapely ass.

"Hi," I said, flashing her my best Trey-smile. "I'm Trey Alexander, a friend of Raul and Gabrielle," I said, extending my hand.

"Oh yes, we've been expecting you. Gabrielle had some very flattering things to say about you." She invited me in with a sweep of her hand, and I could have sworn that I spotted her gaze take a quick detour to my crotch.

And why not, if girlfriend's already heard about me???

I was led through a hallway, past the dining area and a formal living room, into the main living space. A large family room opened in front of me. It was tastefully decorated in pastels and plenty of eclectic artwork. The room was dim, but I spotted about twenty people at the far end by the floor-to-ceiling glass doors that opened onto an enclosed patio. Beyond was a strand of thick dark trees. The majority of the crowd had their backs to me. Most were half dressed or nude, the former wearing patterned sarongs that immediately took me back to Jamaica. Others were clad in leather— I spotted a few dudes in chaps, and some females in some very sexy black leather bodices with shiny steel rings. At least a handful of those I spotted wore collars.

My host introduced herself to me. She was Terri; her husband she pointed out was Bruce, a muscular guy, clad in brown leather chaps, zebra briefs, and otherwise bare-chested, who was the object of the crowd's attention.

Bruce stood before a nude woman who was bound by thick leather straps to a pair of eyebolts that descended from the ceiling. I could see that her feet too, were tied together, ankles bound with thick rope. He bent down but whatever he was doing was lost on me.

Terri asked if I'd like to get more comfortable. I was contemplating her request, at the same time taking in the intriguing scene before me. Before I could answer, she took hold of my hand with a sly grin and drew me away toward a staircase. I allowed her to lead me, following her as my stare dropped to her well-formed ass that moved seductively underneath fabric, her hips swaying rhythmically as we climbed. I asked if Raul and Gabrielle were here yet—she nodded and said she would take me to them momentarily.

We reached a carpeted landing and turned a corner. Terri led me into a darkened bedroom, which was lighted by a single candle. It cast a ghostly orange flicker about the room.

"Some of our guests find this to be more comfortable," Terri said as she handed me a folded blue sarong with a white fish motif adorning the cotton fabric. "It's up to you, of course, but I'd hate to see you wrinkle a fine suit." Terri grinned and I could see that her eyes were blazing as she looked me over.

"This will be fine," I said, holding the sarong.

"Give me your things then," she said, "I can hang them up for you." Terri made no move to leave. In fact, she promptly sat on the bed and folded her legs in front of me. I stood there for a split second, feeling the rush of adrenaline that was swimming through my veins. Again, thoughts of Vince popped into my head. Oh well, I guess homeboy would have to wait . . . Then I began to undress.

Terri sat there, watching me disrobe. Her eyes were tiny black slits that seemed to dance in their sockets. She didn't try to hide her stare nor avert her eyes. Just the opposite, in fact. It was clear that she took great pleasure in watching me remove my jacket, and lay it flat on the bed. Next, I unlaced my shoes, and as I slid them off my feet I unbuckled my belt and pants. My eyes were locked with Terri's, whose breathing had noticeably increased in intensity. She watched me unbutton the rest of my shirt, and pull it out and away from my trousers before removing it, placing it on the bed beside her. I could feel Terri's stare brush over me as she took in my tattoos, well-defined muscles, and bronze skin. I paused for a moment, counting silently to myself as I laid my hands on my pants.

"Waiting for something?" Terri asked, her voice slightly above a whisper. I responded by slowly allowing my pants to fall to the floor. I stepped out of them, removed my socks and handed them to Terri, who placed them over my jacket. Standing in front of her, clad only in my boxers, my dick became semi-hard under candle-lit illumination. Without further fanfare, I bent down and slid my boxers down my thighs.

Terri let out a sigh as she gazed upon my manhood. I took a step forward and handed my boxers to her. Terri took them silently and tossed them aside.

"Feel better?" she asked, cocking her head upward to meet my stare momentarily before returning to my well-engorged member.

"Much," I responded. I could see Terri's nipples poking through the thin fabric of her dress. I fought the rising temptation to reach out and grab them, not wanting within the first five minutes to blow my load, so to speak. Instead, I let my arms drape by my side.

Terri leaned forward, the neckline of her dress turning downward, allowing a nice shot of her cleavage. She came within a foot of me and I swore she was going to grab my dick.

"Gabrielle told me about your wonderful cock," she said, eyeing it with a smirk. "Perhaps I can get a taste of it myself later on tonight." She licked her lips and then blew gently across the head of my dick that was standing straight upright. It quivered in response to her breath.

I smiled. "I'd like that." Terri handed me the sarong; I wrapped it around and secured it snugly over my hips. I glanced down; my erection was like a Christmas tree draped in tinsel—the sarong did little to cover my meat. I sighed heavily, and Terri laughed.

"Let me take you to your friends," she said, patting the package gingerly before taking my hand and guiding me out of the room.

As Terri and I returned to the main floor, moving slowly toward the mass of people huddled around Bruce, I spotted

Gabrielle. She turned as we made our way over, flashing a huge smile as she noticed me. She rushed over and flung her arms around my neck.

"Hey baby, long time no see," she said, pecking me on the lips before moving in to hug me. I flashed a smile as I held her at arm's distance, looking her over.

"Let me look at you," I said, taking in the white leather bra and g-string she wore along with a matching choke collar. Large holes were cut in the front of the bra allowing her cherry nipples to poke through. Her hair was pulled back and placed in a ponytail. "Damn, this has gotta be D.C.'s finest!" Gabrielle gushed and winked at Terri.

"Just get here?" she asked.

"Yeah. Terri was kind enough to get me situated," I said, showing off my sarong.

"And it looks good on you!" Terri asked me if I wanted anything to drink. I told her a beer would be fine, and she headed off, leaving Gabrielle and I alone. Gabby leaned in and whispered in my ear: "So, Trey, I hope you are well rested—there are a bunch of people here who are anxious to party with you."

"You mean my reputation precedes me?" I asked in mock amazement.

"Oh yes! Some of these couples were in Jamaica when you and I did our thing—remember?" Gabrielle asked with a grin.

"How can I ever forget," I replied, touching the corner of her mouth. She beamed seductively.

Our attention shifted to Bruce. We moved closer—beside his feet was an opened steel case. Bruce knelt and seemed to be rummaging around in it for a minute before he stood up, holding something in his hand—long, thin, and black, with what appeared to be a wide leather tip at the end. The woman in front of Bruce eyed him curiously as he waved it ceremoniously in the air and then placed it on a table nearby. I noticed that the woman's thighs were red. Bruce reached for her ankles and undid each rope. Then he bent down and fastened a cuff to each ankle. The cuff was tied off with rope to two eyelets in the floor behind Bruce. He pulled each rope tight and abruptly the woman was dangling at a forty-five degree angle with both legs spread wide.

The small crowd surged forward.

"Oh, you're gonna love this part," Gabrielle said as she took my arm.

"Where's Raul?" I asked, feeling myself growing hard for a second time as I eyed Gabby's lovely ass cheeks.

"Oh, he's around," she said, casually, "probably found some sweet woman's face to blow his load on!" Gabrielle's hand wrapped around me, and I wasted no time in placing mine around her. My hand found her right hip and descended slowly to cup her ass. I squeezed the flesh and grinned.

DAYUM.

The woman strung out and tied in front of us had a shaved pussy, I noticed. Bruce took his instrument and lightly began to tap around her thighs, using slow yet deliberate taps, not too hard, but enough pressure that everyone could hear the "pop" of leather on flesh.

He used a circular motion, beginning on the right thigh, moving clockwise toward her sex, but bypassing it, moving upwards instead, tapping on her navel before moving on and descending to her inner thigh.

The woman was silent, but she was moving slowly with every tap he made.

Bruce moved closer to her sex, until he began tapping on her slit, using the flat leather tip of the wand to slap against her lips. The woman began to moan, almost imperceptibly at first, but then with increased volume. The crowd around us was silent. They were intently watching Bruce work. He was a master, working his magic for the woman, his slave, and for the crowd behind him. He neither turned nor looked in their direction, his attention totally focused on this woman and his craft.

Bruce moved closer, changing the angle of the wand until the flat head was facing downward—abruptly he slapped her pussy *hard* with an audible whack. The woman let out a short, piercing yell. Bruce moved to her side, facing us for the first time then sent the leather wand back down on her reddening sex-box, causing her to thrash. The woman reflectively closed her legs but quickly opened them again as Bruce laid the wand on her clit, moving it in circles for some seconds before whacking her skin again.

"Oh, I love this," Gabrielle said, reaching down to stroke the front of my sarong. "Seems like you do too!" she exclaimed as we exchanged glances.

"No, baby," I said, looking into her eye, "I'm just happy to see you."

"Yeah, whatever. You'd say anything right now!"

Out of the corner of my eye I spied a black woman heading toward us. She grinned at me and turned her attention quickly to Gabrielle.

"Please tell me this is the chocolate bad ass you've been talking about?" she said. "Tell me this is him!"

Gabrielle nodded. I looked her over—she was a large woman, I'd guess close to 190 pounds, with rich dark skin and full dark lips set in a pretty face that reminded me of that fine-ass Angie Stone, with large full breasts that clung to her colorful sarong. I could see her thighs peeking out from the folds of the fabric. Her ass was huge, jiggling as she genuflected at me.

"Nina, this is Trey," Gabrielle said. "Trey, my girlfriend Nina."

Nina stuck out her hand. "Oh, Trey, I've heard some things about you!" she said, flicking her eyes up and down my frame. I smiled and winked.

"All bad, I'm sure," I said.

"And you know that!"

"Nina," Gabby said, pulling her closer, "Trey and I were just about to go and get more *comfortable,*" she said, eyeing me for a second. "Care to join us?" Before I could interrupt, Nina's mouth was spreading wide in a grin. I was scanning the body of this chick, wondering how I'd manage with all that woman under her sarong! I'd never been with a big girl before. Honestly, y'all know I'm only used to the finest honeys this side of the Atlantic—but then I caught myself and pondered this new thread for a moment—before concluding that, at the end of the day, snatch is snatch—it's all pink inside, ya know . . . so perhaps I'd give this big girl a ride, try her on for size, so to speak!

Yeah, that might work . . .

"Oh hell yeah," Nina said as she quickly grabbed my arm. Gabrielle took the other and I found myself again being led away, Bruce and the woman's shrieks fading from my consciousness as I focused on the next phase of my adventure . . .

Three

Bluespace was packed, even at this time of night, but thankfully, Vince had called ahead. So getting a table didn't require much of a wait. They had arrived around 11:30, Vince and Amber; Erika had called from her cell to say she was on her way and would arrive shortly—Trey hopefully would show any moment now—he said he would stop by, but Vince knew how Trey could be. The only unknown variable was Angeliqué. She had left shortly after they had returned from his studio, saying that she had some errands to run and some people to see—Vince had assumed she would return a few hours later. But she had been missing in action all day. He was feeling a bit of anxiety about that, but figured she, like Trey, would show eventually. She was aware of the get-together later on that evening at their spot.

Amber told him not to worry—Angeliqué was a big girl and could take care of herself.

Vince didn't doubt that for a second.

The colors of bluespace shifted around them as Vince led Amber to their booth upstairs. Dazzling colors—vibrant reds, oranges, greens, purples, and blues—colors that like a lava-lamp coalesced together like some living organism and slid down the curved white walls as the music of Floetry coursed around them. It was an intoxicating slow groove—"Say Yes," that mixed with the lightshow making an emotional statement. And then, as the colors blinked out and the restaurant was bathed in darkness for a moment, the music rose sharply, thumping bass-infused beats of hip-hop replacing the soft sensuous melody, as a half-dozen music videos were displayed on each wall, but out of focus—the fast-cutting imagery lighting up the interior of the space, like lightning, causing folks to clap.

Amber was enthralled as she slid into the curved sofa seat. Vince admired her silently. She was indeed beautiful. Her brown hair was tied back. No makeup adorned her auburn-colored skin. There was no need for it. Her eyes shone as she soaked up the atmosphere. She wore jeans, a thick mocha-colored sweater, and boots—her thighs and ass hugging the denim fabric as if they were family. Vince recalled the way she had looked just a few hours earlier.

She had asked to see his studio. Apparently she and Angeliqué had talked about his collection of masks.

Angeliqué had left Vince and Amber alone—they were hanging lazily around his house when she asked if he could take her to see it. Vince had agreed.

Thirty minutes later, Amber had stood in front of his mask-covered wall. Like the others, she had been spellbound by his art. She found his latest piece—the mask and torso lifecasting of Desiree—vibrant raindrop-splashes of color over an indigo base, most intriguing.

She had asked many questions—who was this person? What was she like? And questions about the actual process. She had stroked the paint-saturated plaster sensuously before spinning on the heels to face him.

"Have you ever done an entire body?" Amber had asked

cautiously as she turned to stare directly at him. Vince had contemplated the question as he put down his coffee mug to return her stare. He felt something fluttering inside of him, excitement and sexual energy that slowly began as an expanding vortex. "No," he replied, "not yet. I've been toying with the idea for many months—but it's fairly involved—lots of material, and of course, lots of time on the part of the model."

Amber had considered this for a moment as her fingers alighted from the plaster of Desiree's breasts.

"Then let me be the first . . ."

Amber had lain comfortably, the futon mattress spread out on the floor of his studio, several blankets covering the fabric as he prepared her for the a full-body lifecasting. She was as beautiful as he had remembered, that first time seeing her in New Orleans, when he hadn't adequately taken the time to really focus on her features, for fear of upsetting Angeliqué, but this time, there was no such trepidation. She laid on her side, nude, one leg bent, the thickness of her smooth, unblemished thigh and tapered legs enthralling. Her hair hung free. Her cheekbones, eyelashes, curved mouth, breasts, and sculpted ass—all works of art. No veve covering her bare skin this time, like a full-body tattoo, nothing standing in the way between him and her splendor.

It was the beauty of her youthfulness that appealed to Vince.

But it wasn't just that—after all, Desiree was young—it was Amber's body. Thick in the right areas—thighs and ass—meat on her bones, as his momma was fond of saying. Curvy sensuous hips that led to a small waist, tapering back out to a voluptuous upper body. Her flesh wasn't taut the way Desiree's was—it wasn't pudgy either, but as he coated her skin with jelly, his fingers found depth everywhere he pressed and massaged—and Vince dug that.

He had taken his time. The process had taken a lot longer than he anticipated—yet, this was a lazy Saturday, he had nowhere to go—and neither did Amber. Painstakingly, he had applied the petroleum jelly to her skin as if he were a professional masseuse; Amber closing her eyes, purring like a kitten as she shifted to ensure every inch of her body was well lubricated. They had talked the entire time, conversation flowing easily, as if they were good friends sitting across from each other at a comfortable Starbucks sipping hot lattes, instead of what they were—a breathtaking woman reclining nude upon his studio floor while his hands caressed the supple flesh of her breasts, neck, shoulder blades, and ankles.

When Vince had completed her upper body and legs he had paused as she shifted to lay flat, parting her legs slightly. Vince gazed down at her sex, a thin line of dark pubic hair above her clit, the rest of that place otherwise manicured clean. He felt himself growing hard again—the fourth or fifth time today, or was it sixth or seventh? Vince had lost count—once again he fought the rising tension between his own thighs.

"Here," he had said, holding out the tub of jelly to her, "perhaps you should finish up . . ."

Amber had stared back at him unblinkingly. "Don't know why, Vince," she had said amusingly, "you seem to be doing such a fine job . . ."

Erika's arrival at bluespace brought Vince back to reality. He hugged Erika, and Amber smiled as they were introduced. Erika sat as drinks were ordered.

"So," Erika said as she removed her leather jacket, settling across from them, "aren't we missing some people?"

"Yeah," Vince said, "Angeliqué is out doing her thing, but promised to meet us here later; and your boy, Trey, well, Lord knows where that fool is!"

"Please—it's a Saturday night—I'm sure His Highness is fondling some hootchie momma this very moment!"

"Shit, he better show—I'm not playing with his dumb ass this time."

Erika turned to Amber. "Don't pay us black folks any mind—we're just messing around. It's good to finally meet you, girl—I've heard a lot about you."

The two began to converse as Vince ordered some hors d'oeuvres for the table. Erika learned that Amber was originally from Texas—born in Houston, and spent most of her life being raised by her great-grandmother.

"I never knew my real parents," Amber said as she sipped a beer. "My mom gave me up when I was barely two weeks old. She had medical problems and couldn't care for me, so I was told. And I never met my father," she added somberly.

Erika patted her arm. "I'm sorry—I'm sure that was very hard on you."

"Yeah," Amber replied, as Vince listened, "it was, but you get used to it." Her voice trailed off. Vince rubbed her shoulder. They had spoken at length about this topic hours ago. Amber smiled weakly. "It's cool, really. I'm not looking for sympathy. As I explained to Vince earlier, I came to the conclusion that this is my life—I can either feel sorry for myself or accept it and move on—I've chosen to live my life. This is the one that God has given me. It could be a whole lot worse."

"Wow," Erika exclaimed, "I love your attitude—so many people choose to feed into the negative aspects of what's been handed to them, but not you! You go girl—a beautiful woman who's got her shit together!" She raised her beer to Amber. The two clinked their glasses together.

"I'm gonna like you!" Amber said with a smile.

"Me too, girlfriend," Erika responded, "me too!"

Four

Wrielle on point, me in the middle, Nina taking up the rear. Gabby came to the landing at the bottom of the stairs and stopped. Terri was at the bottom, stark naked with a frosty Corona in her hand. I took in her features, her small tits, each nipple pierced with a thin silver loop, and hairless pussy. My dick did a quick convulsion. I felt Nina's body pressing against mine. I tried to descend to the bottom step, but Gabby wasn't budging. I felt Nina's hot breath in my ear.

"Sexy-ass mutha fucka," she whispered, and I felt her grind her pelvis into my ass. I half-turned to the left.

"You have a foul mouth," I offered.

"You haven't seen *shit* . . ."

A beer was passed to me, I accepted it, thanked my hostess, and we were moving again. We found ourselves in a narrow hallway, candles suspended from the wall every few yards. We passed by several doorways, some open, others closed. We sauntered on and came to an open door on the right. Gabrielle was peering in and held up her hand, glancing back at us with a grin.

"Looks like I found my husband," she said to Nina and I before moving on. I made my way to the door and peered in. Raul was standing buck naked on a narrow bed, legs spread with a smoldering cigar in his mouth. A demure white woman knelt beneath him as he jerked his cock onto her face. The woman remained motionless but her C-cup tits were jiggling from the bed's and Raul's movement. Raul glanced over and grinned. He took his hand off his cock for a moment, gave me a salute, then went back to what he was doing, slapping the woman's face with his meat. As I moved on I witnessed her smirk before she opened her mouth, readying for Raul's juice to spew.

Gabrielle had gone to the end of the hallway and disappeared into one of the rooms. Nina and I followed, and discovered her stretching out on a queen size bed bathed in candlelight. On the bedside table was a wicker basket filled to the brim with condoms.

"Gonna stand there," Gabby asked in a low voice, "or you gonna join me?" I glanced quickly at my watch, noting the time: it was a few minutes past eleven. A little voice in my head asked if I was supposed to be somewhere else right now? I quickly brushed the thought away—at this point I neither recalled nor gave a shit. I turned my attention to the girls who were settling onto the bed, and let my sarong drop to the floor. I stood there, my dick swaying in front of me like a beacon, letting them feast on the *package*.

Gabrielle had unhooked her bra and placed it on the night table. She then slid her g-string down and stretched out on the bed, spreading her legs. Meanwhile, Nina unwrapped her sarong and let it fall. Her breasts were dark fruits with thick nipples that hung free and looked appetizing as hell. I've got to tell y'all—even though I've never been with a big girl before, the sight of those melons was making my dick harder than it already was. Or maybe it was the sight of Gabrielle's fine ass bod three feet away.

Who knew???

I knelt on the bed and stroked Gabrielle's olive-skinned leg. Ran a finger from her ankle up to her thigh before flattening my hand and gliding it lightly across her shaved sex. I could feel the wetness on my palm. Gabrielle's eyes never left me.

"She's ready for you, Trey," Gabrielle whispered. I responded by kneeling down and letting my tongue connect with the flesh of her knee, kissing it all over sensuously before tracing a wet swath up to her thigh. Gabby spread her legs wider as my hands found her breasts. I kneaded them lightly, then squeezed each one in turn and pulled at her nipples.

"You know what I like, Trey," she whispered again, head thrown back, her eyes closed. Nina was fully nude now, and came around the bed and squatted behind me. Her hands found my back, stroking me up and down before reaching around and grasping my shaft. She began to jerk me off slowly with both hands as she rotated her big titties into my back, sucking on my earlobe. My tongue found Gabby's hole—she held her legs apart and I moved in, tasting her nectar. Her syrup was sweet, just as I had remembered it. I scooped a bit of it up on my tongue and swallowed hungrily, before lowering my face to her pussy. My chin connected with her lips, and I rubbed my face in her box, first my lower jaw, then lips, nose, and eyelids. Gabrielle was squeezing her thighs against my ears, but I didn't care—I increased my tempo, thrashing my head from side to side as I thrust out my tongue, kitty lapping Gabby as I tweaked her nipples. Nina had managed to maneuver beneath me and taken my cock in her mouth. I let out a gasp as her full lips enveloped my entire length—slurping it in and sucking it to the back of her throat as if she were a porno star. This sistah could suck a dick! I glanced down—Nina's eyes were locked onto me as she sucked. I shifted, allowing my hand to find her spongy melons. I palmed each one in turn before returning my attention to Gabrielle. Her sex was drenched now. I returned to her orifice and probed her innards with my nose. Moving it rapidly from side to side, Gabby began to moan.

"Oh yeah, do it like that, damn, that's it!" she said between heavy breaths. "Oooh, Trey, you gonna make me come, damnit!" I increased my tempo, fucking her with my tongue, stabbing her clit with my nose, grasping her lips gingerly between teeth, sucking her in to my mouth, swishing around her entire love hole as I felt her convulse and come.

"Ohhhhhh fuck!" Gabrielle moaned, clamping her thighs tight against my ears as she reached out to grab my shoulders. Her nails dug into my flesh, but I didn't care. I slowed my movement, feeling her orgasm peak then subside, the waves of pleasure receding. I placed my tongue on her still-throbbing flesh at the apex to her core, feeling her pulse and the heat transferred to me. I reveled in making a woman feel good. I glanced up. Gabby was smiling with eyes closed. She opened them, caught me staring, and squeezed my shoulder.

I beamed like the true playa that I am.

Nina shifted and my dick plopped out of her mouth, hard as a rock and glistening with her spit. I moved onto my haunches and sat up, guiding Gabby with my hand. She got on all four as I slipped on a condom. I glanced down. Even in the twinkling candlelight, I could see her asshole glistening with desire. I felt a twitch run the length of my shaft. Gabby's head was turned, watching me. I palmed both ass cheeks, spreading them wide as I entered her still-wet pussy, well lubed from my tongue and her orgasm. I filled her quickly, grabbing her waist with both hands, pummeling her as I watched my cock jackhammer her box. Nina slid underneath us and cupped my balls with a hand as her mouth connected with our flesh—shaft and pussy—her tongue painting a coat of wetness as Gabby and I screwed. The scene was surreal—I tipped my head back, studying the pattern of flickering candlelight on the ceiling for a moment before closing my eyes to concentrate on the feeling alone—Gabrielle's tight sex, Nina's hot tongue, my dark cock—three people coming together in a delicious fashion, the same way a scrumptious pie is prepared, each ingredient added to the bowl and devotedly mixed by hand, creating a creamy batter that drips with goodness.

Reaching forward, I grabbed Gabby's boobs in hand and kneaded her flesh. Glancing down I watched Nina work her magic on Gabby's sex and on me. Deciding it was time to give this sistah some *quality* time, I pulled out of Gabby and maneuvered on top of Nina. Her flesh was heaving as I spread her Hershey thighs, her stomach warm against my own tight body. I grasped my cock in hand, waved it around her sex, spreading those black velvety folds before lowering my weight and thrusting inside of her.

Nina gasped as I entered her. Immediately she lifted her thighs in a motion that surprised me. I felt her draw on my dick and I was amazed at the tightness of this chick's box. I grunted as I banged her, smiling down as Nina thrashed her head from side to side.

"Fuck me, boy!" Nina belted out, as her eyes squeezed shut. Gabby positioned herself over Nina's face and lowered her sex onto her mouth. She reached for me and we tongue kissed as I rocked above Nina's flesh, her stomach and ass vibrating as I thrust in and out. Off to my right I caught a moment and cocked my head to the side. A man had entered the room and was watching us. He, like us was nude, thin, but well toned, his member in hand as he stroked it slowly. He grinned when we made eye contact, but said nothing. For a moment he stood there and I was trying to figure out what he was up to, but Nina was grabbing my ass and digging her fingernails into my skin as I boned her.

"Harder," she commanded, and I forgot the guy by the wall as I lifted her thighs. I reared back and slammed all of my weight into her, hearing her scream with delight as I hit bottom. "Oh yeah, that's what I'm talking 'bout!" she squealed, as I stuffed her, pressing my entire weight against her. I rested for a moment, grabbing both titties between fingers and tracing circles around her nipples with my tongue. They were large, distended things, with dark areolas that looked so freaking good. My mouth found them appetizing and I teased Nina by biting her nipples.

"Do me from behind," she directed. Gabby, who was bobbing to a rhythm all her own disengaged herself from Nina's mouth and I flipped Nina over. I palmed both cheeks. My hands barely covered a quarter of her ass, but something about it drew me near. I felt her pussy, which was hot and throbbing. I ran a finger over her anus, which from this vantage point was puckered at an upturned angle.

I reached for some lube and anointed my condom-covered dick. I slid into her box effortlessly and pummeled it as I contemplated the expanse of ass before me. Gabby had lain down and spread her legs so Nina could feed again. A quick glance to my right showed that the man was still there, his thin dick angled upward as he stroked it. Spreading Nina's ass with my thumb and forefinger, I probed her anus with a lubed finger before pulling out and teasing her backdoor with the head of my dick. Nina glanced back, perspiration adorning her face. Her eyes were on fire as if she were possessed.

"Take my ass, boy," she said, breathlessly, "that ass is yours!"

I positioned myself and barreled forward, feeling her

open up to receive me. Nina let out a squeal; it was loud and high pitched. She lurched forward as I hit ass-bottom, then I felt her meet my thrust with her own, her cheeks a wave that bum rushed to and fro like the tides, a shuddering wall of thigh and ass-flesh as I slapped against her.

Gabby held Nina's head in her hands. Her thighs adorned her face, tremoring along with Nina whose body seemed to convulse in spasms. "Oh God I am coming!" she yelled, before chomping down on Gabby's sex, and reaching back with one hand to spread her ass cheek for me. I gripped her ass as firmly as I could, digging my nails into her flesh as I felt my own orgasms about to spout. I grunted and slapped against her as if there were no tomorrow, pummeling her as if she weren't even human—just an orifice that I was trying to plug, her ass some kind of repulsive, alien thing, and it was my job to snub it out. Nina was alive—I could feel her come, her entire frame shuddering, the waves unleashing from one end of her body to the other, her anus tightening up, as if it would fight to the end, not giving up until this last moment. I heard Gabby pant and then shriek. The pressure was building in me too—my balls, already heavy, sperm-laden, ready to blow. I tilted my head back, eyes squeezed shut, my mind on autopilot, my lower body commanded by a separate microprocessor—one that controlled the simple act of copulating, the quickening in and out—and then I was coming, while I rushed into Nina's ass, filling the condom as I cried out, mingling with the shortening moans from my lovers, Nina and Gabby.

I flopped down on that ass, spent. Resting my entire weight on Nina, I felt the warmth of her body and that of Gabby. The three of us were exhausted. For a long while none of us moved. My breathing was timed to Nina's underneath me.

Hers was in time to Gabrielle's.

"That was so nice . . ." A female voice—that much I registered but beyond it nothing else. My entire focus was on my dick, which was still cocooned inside Nina. It withered, yet she refused to give it up. I felt my sap drain, and as I reached around and palmed Nina's breasts I found myself kissing the back of her neck.

It felt so damn good, I'm not gonna even front!

The candles continued to flicker and the entire scene was so surreal—like Jamaica—I closed my eyes, and concentrated not on the sounds of breathing or heartbeats, but what I was feeling. The rush that comes from passion-filled sex, the excitement from tasting someone new for the first time, entering them, feeling them swell to fit you, riding your sex, doing you, and then coming with you. I opened my eyes and glanced over at Gabby. Her eyelids fluttered briefly, and she smiled at me before extricating herself from underneath Nina's body. I remained inside of Nina, feeling no need to get off of her. I spread my legs and pushed in deeper, feeling Nina's ass quiver with movement as I readjusted. Gabby came behind me, bent down and caressed my ass. I felt her reach for my balls and squeeze before hugging me with her body. I smiled, relishing the feeling of warmth and gratification.

I felt her hands on my ass again. Felt her fingers gliding along the crack of my ass. Felt her stop as she reached my opening. I tensed slightly, but sucked in a breath and reminded myself whom I was with. This scene was cool with me.

Fingers lightly probing my ass. The feeling—tense and exciting at the same time. Breasts rubbing against my back making my dick hard. Nina wiggling underneath me.

Then Gabby was gone, and I felt the air cool on my back. With my eyes closed I waited for her to return.

A pressure on my anus jarred me to open my eyes. As my head did a slow roll, turning in her direction, I felt something penetrate me. I gazed back in horror and jerked off of Nina as I saw the man's face inches from my own.

"WHAT THE FUCK!" I yelled, my forearm raised and pushing him off of me with a strength that I didn't recognize. He flew back and hit the wall with a thud.

I was on my feet, Nina scrambling off the bed as Gabby popped her head in the door.

"You fucking asshole!" I screamed, crossing the few meters of empty space to the guy and knocking him to the ground with a clenched fist. "WHAT THE HELL ARE YOU DOING???" I yelled again. Gabby was on me in an instant, her breasts heaving against my back as she pulled me away and toward the door. My eyes were slits, foam leaping from my mouth—I didn't see or hear anything—I was a bull—out of control.

Then I heard myself utter: "That asshole tried to fuck me . . ." as I was dragged into the hallway. A crowd of people appeared, eyes-wide, Raul brushing past me and into the room. Terri was rushing toward us and then past me. Gabby was pulling me up the stairs, Nina at my back as I thrashed like a caged animal.

"I'm not like that!" I hissed, reaching the top stairs, folks petrified, a black man out of control, backing up instinctively as I passed, fearing I'd lash out. "YOU HEAR ME— I'M NOT LIKE THAT!"

I have no idea how I got my clothes nor how I left the house, but at some point I found myself on the Beltway heading south, the steady drone of tires on asphalt and orange-lit LEDS sobering. The weight of what had just happened came crashing down upon me, causing me to almost wreck.

Everything that had been so good suddenly was erased by a singular event that was all bad . . .

"Shit!" I yelled to the empty interior of my ride, my heart dropping to new depths as images of Layla rushed into my head, fusing with the recent events of tonight, forming a solid twisting mass of repulsiveness that refused to leave me alone.

Five

The remainder of the evening—that is to say, for the next two and a half hours, Erika, Vince, and Amber huddled together, laughing like recently reunited high school friends. Vince enjoyed seeing Amber relaxed and in her element, taking pleasure in the closeness that comes from great conversation among good friends. Erika took to Amber immediately, drawn to her as if she were a long-lost cousin. The bluespace staff left them alone—except for the drinks that continued to arrive with clockwork precision, long after their plates of food had been wiped clean and cleared away.

It was two-fifteen a.m. when they said their goodbyes. Vince and Amber stood outside in the chilled air, their breath rising as she clung to his elbow, huddled together watching Erika's brake lights fade into the stillness of the gray winter morning.

Neither Angeliqué nor Trey had showed . . .

. . . Or called . . .

* * *

It was Erika who made the call.

"Put me through to that *fool,* please!"

India Jasmine Jackson laughed out loud.

"Listen, Trey," Erika began without preamble, "you've got a couple of friends who are extremely pissed at you right now . . ."

"Damn, Sassy—what did I do? It's not even ten a.m.," Trey replied. He glanced at his wristwatch on a dull Wednesday morning—the threat of snow hung in the air.

"Last Saturday, bluespace—you were supposed to show—Vince had *visitors* from out of town—remember?"

"Oh shit! Boo—let me tell you, I had one hell of a night . . ."

"Trey!" Erika exclaimed, cutting him off in mid-sentence, "Save it—we're meeting at bluespace tonight at eight. I strongly suggest you be there—that is *if* friendship means anything to you anymore . . ."

"Erika, come on—"

But she had already hung up.

Trey was already seated at a first-floor booth at bluespace when they arrived. He was nursing a Corona, and had a tired look in his eyes. He stood up; gave Vince dap and Erika a rushed hug.

"You look like shit," were the first words out of her mouth, directed at Trey.

"I love you too . . ."

"I'm serious, Trey. This whoring around is obviously catching up with you. Look at you—I bet you haven't slept in days."

Vince was eyeing his best friend curiously, yet silently. Trey sighed.

"Look—things have been extremely hectic in my life as of late. Work sucks and—"

Erika held up her hand. "Okay—let me stop you right there. See, this is what always happens. We get together, after weeks of not seeing you and the first thing that occurs is that you dominate the entire conversation, and no one can get a word in edgewise. Well, that stops today. We're here because your boy needs you. He needs us. So shut the hell up and listen!"

Trey cut a glance over to Vince who removed his glasses and rubbed his face. They looked at each other for a moment.

"So, Vince," Trey said, "How ya livin'?"

Vince returned a weak smile. "Been better, bruh. I have to tell you, I'm disappointed that you didn't show Saturday night." Vince eyed Trey. "Not only did you not come, but you didn't even call. We were waiting for you."

Trey took a small swig of beer. "Sorry, man. Something came up—I thought you'd understand."

"Yeah—well, that's the thing, Trey. It seems like something's always coming up with you. I mean, I don't feel like a priority in your life anymore." Vince's eyes were unblinking.

"I second that," Erika said, putting down her Corona. "You have high expectations of your friends, Trey, especially from your boy here and from me. When you need us, you call and expect us to come running. Funny thing is, we usually do."

Vince nodded silently.

Erika continued. "But lately, the whole vibe among the three of us has shifted—In recent months, it's all about you. Trey one hundred-fifty percent, instead of the usual ninety. I, for one, am growing tired of it. Seriously tired."

"Damn," Trey uttered.

Vince cleared his throat. "Erika's right, bruh. And you need to hear this. There's a lot of shit that's gone down in the past few weeks regarding both Erika and I—I don't think you have any idea what we've gone through. We need you, dude—we need the old Trey back. You feel me?"

Trey was silent for a moment. His stare moved from one best friend to the other. He wore a down-turned expression on his face.

"I don't know what to say—I guess I've always been a bit selfish. Lately probably more so. I'm sorry, y'all. For real!"

"Yeah," Vince said, "well, to tell you the truth, we've heard all of this before. I guess I need to know whether this is what we can continue to expect from you or not." He glanced over at Erika and then back at Trey. "Whether we can count on you as a true friend."

Trey put his beer down. "Okay, guys. I hear you. Honest I do—and you have my full attention. From now on . . ."

Vince smiled then sighed deeply as he put down his beer.

"I didn't want to tell any of you this but you know several weeks ago when I went down to New Orleans to surprise Angeliqué? Well, I'm the one who ended up getting surprised. I found her in the arms of another person." He paused to stare hard at Trey before shifting his gaze to Erika. "In fact, I found her in the arms of a *woman*."

"What?" Erika exclaimed. Trey opened his mouth to speak, but then thought better of it.

"Yeah. A woman."

"Why didn't you tell us, Vince?" she asked.

"I don't know—I guess I was in shock. I returned home, mad as hell. I needed some time to sort things out. I needed time to think."

Trey shook his head forlornly and said, "Go on."

"Then she and Amber came up last week. It gave us some

time to talk—I thought that perhaps there was a chance between us." Vince paused to down his Corona and signal the waitress for another round. "But now I know that it was not meant to be."

"I'm sorry, Vince," Erika said, rubbing his back with her hand.

"We made love one more time, at my studio, but it wasn't the same. My heart wasn't in it and I could tell neither was hers." Vince sighed as he shook his head. "I mean, it's weird going from what we had—the intensity, the passion down in New Orleans that first time to this. This time it was just physical. Devoid of anything emotional."

Trey cleared his throat. "Did the two of you talk about it? About what happened?"

"We tried," Vince responded, "But it was clear to me that this is who she is. Angeliqué, I guess, has this need to be a free spirited person. Tied down to no one. I don't think she saw us even as a possibility . . ."

Erika asked, "Is that why she didn't show Saturday night?"

Vince nodded. "I'm sure that has everything to do with it. After we made love—correction, make that after we had sex, cause it sure wasn't making love—she left. Amber was still at my house chilling. We ended up spending the entire day and night together. Actually, there's a separate story there."

"Oh, I really like her, Vince."

Vince smiled.

"Don't tell me you tapped that too?" Trey asked.

Erika eyed him and Trey shrugged.

"No, Trey. I'm not like you. But guess what did happen? She asked to see my studio, so I took her. Once she was there, she asked if I'd do a full body casting of her. And I did!"

Vince smiled. Erika was grinning.

"Wait a minute," Trey exclaimed, "You're telling me that one minute you're boning Angeliqué, the next moment you've got her friend butt naked in your studio? Damn, bro, there is hope for you yet!"

"Trey," Erika said, "not everything is about sex, you know. Oh, forget it—you'll never understand. I talked to Amber Saturday and it wasn't like that at all. She felt extremely comfortable being with Vince and actually thought up the idea of doing a full body casting herself. And from the way she described it to me, Vince here was the perfect gentleman, as only I've come to expect from him."

Vince grinned. "What can I say?"

Trey grunted.

"I will say this," Vince continued, turning to Erika, "I'm really feeling Amber. She's so down-to-earth and cool—I mean, don't get me wrong—I'm not trying to jump into anything with her, especially on the coattails of this thing with Angeliqué, but I can't help feeling the way I do. I truly enjoy being with her. I feel as if I can be myself, you know, just let go and say and do what I want.

"When we were in the studio doing her lifecasting she was so relaxed. We talked for hours about everything—her upbringing, her moms giving her up for adoption, her interests, my book, and my passions—all in this manner that I can't put into words, other than to say that there was this *vibe* between us. I could feel it, and I really believe that she felt it too."

"Vince," Erika said, "let me ask you something—where does Desiree fit into all of this? Correct me if I'm wrong, but it seems like you're juggling two to three women, depending on how you count them, in your life right now. Don't you think you should figure out what you want and who you're interested in pursuing?"

"That's the thing, Sassy, I'm trying to do that. I had no intentions of pursuing anything with Desiree—it just kind of happened. And I'm enjoying myself. She's young, smart, got plenty of attitude, but in a good way . . . she looks damn good and sexy, but I don't know, I just don't see her hanging in there for the long term."

Erika nodded, thinking to herself, *I've heard this before . . .*

"Then I met Angeliqué. To be honest, I was swept off my feet; I admit it. I definitely saw myself settling down with her. But it never got off the ground. When I saw her with another woman, I just went cold inside. Whatever I was feeling for her died right then and there."

"I feel you, bruh," Trey said. "See, that's why I don't even front with these honeys . . . I've been down that road before, you know. I tried the whole, let-me-commit-to-you-and-no-one-else thing and I got burned big time! Ya hear? So no more of that shit for me!"

Erika sucked her teeth.

"Negro, please! That was what? Five years ago? What are you saying, Trey, that you're never gonna trust another woman? That you're never gonna give love another chance?"

Trey eyed her but said nothing.

"That's messed up," Erika pronounced.

"Anywho," Vince said, bringing the conversation back to him, "Things are pretty much done with Angeliqué. And then there is Amber. We clicked, we vibed. I don't know how she feels about me or whether she even senses the chemistry that's forming between us or not, but it sure feels different than the ones before her. There's something very special about that woman."

Erika nodded.

"You'd know what I'm talking about Trey if you had shown up . . ." he said.

"Ouch!" Trey responded.

The three were silent for a moment, watching the light show that was erupting around them. A hypnotic refrain from Prince, falsetto vocals wafted over them.

"I wanna be your lover."

Erika broke the silence first. "That reminds me, Vince, Amber mentioned several times in conversation the fact that she has no idea who her parents are. I asked her if she was interested in finding them, and she said she had been thinking about that for the past year. So, I was telling James about her—"

Trey cut a sharp glance her way.

"What? Anywho—James knows this gay couple that runs this service that reconnects adopted children with their parents. Do you think Amber would be interested in finding her birth parents? James seems to think that he could get them to do some research for her gratis, since they've been bugging him to do a story on their firm for months now."

Vince smiled. "Hmmn, I dig that idea. I think she'd be down for that. Let me run it by her and see what she thinks."

"Hold up," Trey exclaimed. "Is James going to plaster her story all over the airwaves? If so, you need to consider whether or not that's in her best interest, or, for that matter, in the best interests of the birth parents, assuming they can be found."

"I asked James about that—he said he wouldn't do anything without getting the approval of Amber first. But I don't think he's interested in this from a news story point of view—he was just offering up a favor to help a friend of mine out."

Vince grinned and said, "Cool."

"Actually, I hope she is interested. I'd kind of like to help, myself," Erika said. "I'm feeling her too, Vince—she's good people, and after James and I spoke it got me excited about the possibilities. At least it's a place to start."

"Thanks, boo, I'll give her a call and holla back."

Vince sat back and sighed, a contented look on his face. Erika smiled back at him.

Trey exhaled loudly. Vince and Erika cut a glance over to him.

"Well?" Erika asked. "We both know you've been dying to open your big fat mouth all evening. I think we've tortured you enough already. What do you think, Vince?"

"Yeah, I say let the man speak!"

"See, y'all ain't right. But since you offered—check this shit out!"

Trey proceeded to give them a blow-by-blow account of the previous Saturday night, working backward from being "assaulted" as he put it, by a "can't-keep-it-in-his-pants guy," to the sexual romping he and Gabrielle had with her home girl Nina!

Vince and Erika were in shock, hearing how the evening had gone down, watching his face turn into a snarl as he described the "assault." Both knew how Trey felt about this kind of thing—Trey not at all comfortable with being approached by men, especially those showing a sexual interest in him. They had witnessed his reaction to gay men coming onto him before, and it wasn't pretty.

"Oh NO!" Erika cried out, but in a soft, whispery voice as if air were being forcibly let out of a punctured tire. Vince snapped his head in the direction of her stare. Trey was the slowest to react. He turned toward the front of the restaurant where two women were being led to a table nearby. His face contorted into pain as the realization of whom he was seeing seeped into his pores, making him sick.

The color drained from his face in an instant.

"Shit!" Vince exclaimed as he made eye contact briefly with Layla, Trey's ex-love of his life . . .

Trey could not speak. He remained motionless as Layla paused for a moment, touching the elbow of the woman with whom she was with. Beads of sweat had popped out on the surface of his baldhead. His mouth was suddenly pasty.

Layla glanced away for a moment, whispered something to the woman, and then approached their booth. Trey attempted to rise, but found his legs and hands would not work.

Layla stopped short a yard from their table. She smiled, white perfect teeth lighting up the room. She was in a word, stunning. From the sleek little black dress she wore which hugged her curves, to her cascading shiny hair, and bright lip-gloss.

Erika was the first to speak.

"Layla."

"Erika. Nice to see you. It's been a long time."

"It has."

"Vince, hello."

"Hey."

Layla turned her attention to Trey who still had not moved or breathed.

"Trey. I just want to say hello. You're looking quite good."

Trey was silent. His stare was riveted to hers. She smiled feebly at him, testing the waters, yet he did not return the gesture.

"You're not going to say anything, Trey, not even a hello?" she asked.

In that moment Trey erupted from the table, his body exploding from the side of the booth like dynamite, frightening Layla to the point that she lurched back instinctively, her hand rushing up to her chest. Vince and Erika flinched in the same moment. The tabletop pivoted, bottles clanking and falling sideways, splashing cold liquid onto the surface, running in a sudden stream toward the wood floor.

Trey was inches from the side of Layla's face when his lips parted. She turned her head ever so slowly, their eyes locking as his expression morphed into a hideous snarl.

"Stay clear of me, *bitch!*" he hissed before pushing past her, toward the front entrance of bluespace.

A throng of folks waiting for their table ceased all conversation and parted quickly as he strode past them, and into the night.

It was over in an instant, a snap of fingers, a mere three blinks of an eye. But when the dust settled, Trey had left Erika, Vince, Layla, and the rest of the bluespace patronage shaking their heads in utter disbelief . . .

"Can I talk to you?"

Layla, visibly flustered, glanced up into the eyes of Erika, and nodded.

Erika turned on her heels and headed for the curved teakwood bar by the side of the main entrance. Layla rose and followed. They found seats and ordered drinks as the light-show facing them was entrancing.

A myriad of sunrises were displayed, rosy pinks and fire reds, following the curved walls as the music rose, and for a moment, neither Layla nor Erika spoke, enthralled with the visual scenery.

Layla took a gulp of her apple martini and turned to Erika.

"Just what the *hell* happened back there?" she asked.

Erika tasted her own martini and nodded silently to the bartender before turning her attention to Layla.

"What are you doing?" she asked.

"What do you mean?" Layla asked, eyes blinking.

"I'll repeat—what are you doing? Here for one. A few weeks ago it was B. Smith's."

Layla's eyes grew wide.

"Oh yeah, you might have thought you weren't spotted, but you were. So come on, girlfriend, don't play me. What are you doing?"

"Nothing."

"I *know* . . . ," Erika whispered.

"What?" Layla stared at her deadpan.

Erika leaned closer. "I said, I know. Trey told me, told us," she said, gesturing back toward Vince who sat alone in their booth.

Layla's lip trembled.

"I'm not sure—"

"Listen, Layla," Erika said, "Once upon a time you and I were friends. You may have forgotten, but I was your biggest supporter, your biggest fan. But that all changed because of what you did to Trey."

"What I did? Let me tell you—"

Erika cut her off.

"And you can sit there with this 'I-don't-have-the-slightest-idea-what-you-are-talking-bout' attitude if that rocks your world, but I'm hear to tell you," Erika said, pausing to slowly glance down the front of her dress, from her full breasts that strained against the silk fabric to her curvy thighs and well-tone legs, "I know, Layla, I *know*."

Layla exhaled slowly and reached for her drink. She looked away, sipped at her drink. Erika watched her silently while she sipped at hers.

"He's changed, you know," Erika said. "Completely. The man you knew left five years ago—destroyed, I'm sorry to say. He will never love again, thanks to you. The old Trey you knew and loved is dead. Gone and buried."

Layla took a gulp and swallowed hard. Erika witnessed her wince as the liquor shot down her throat.

"I still love him," she whispered, turning to face Erika, her eyes wet with tears. "Haven't stopped, even after all these years . . ."

Erika set down her martini and gripped her hand.

"It's too late, Layla, believe me when I tell you this." Flecks of sunrise flashed in Erika's eyes as she stared at Layla. "The Trey you knew is dead. Leave it alone. And leave him alone. No good can come from this."

A lone tear meandered down Layla's right cheek. "But I still love him . . ."

"Please," Erika begged, "Layla, please don't do this to him. Don't do this to him or to yourself all over again."

Layla cried silently.

Erika turned away with a sigh. She downed her drink and shook her head, thinking just how bad things were about to get . . .

Six

Erika lowered herself into the steaming bath, her eyes fluttering with delight as the jasmine-scented hot water infused into her tired pores.

It had been a rough day. *Another* twelve-hour shift. The third one this week. Covering for Janice, whose child was out with the chicken pox.

Thankfully, it would end soon.

It better . . .

She had come home at nine, microwaved some leftovers, threw on her worn sweats, and slumped onto the couch, too exhausted to even give herself a pedicure.

Perhaps this weekend.

James had called thirty minutes later saying he wanted to come over. Erika politely refused, citing sleep deprivation, but James was insistent. Erika, being too tired to argue, gave in. He was now lying on her bed in the next room, channel surfing.

Glancing around, Erika had to smile. Her Bose Bluetooth speaker was on top of the vanity sink—her favorite Luther songs providing comfort. Several candles were positioned around the tub. A stick of incense burned not far from her feet, sending delicate tendrils of perfumed smoke wafting over her.

Erika leaned back and closed her eyes, lowering herself further until her shoulder blades dipped beneath a sea of bubbles.

Ah yessssssssssss! Her bath tonight felt wonderful. As she shifted in the tub, little waves caressed her neck and breasts, soothing her.

All in all, it was a perfect end to an otherwise shitty day.

Then without warning James burst in, a tormented scowl on his normally smooth face, ruining all that Erika had fashioned in an instant . . .

"Just what the hell is *this*?" he yelled, holding up a large dildo the color of a Snickers bar.

Her dildo.

Her *buddy*.

Erika sighed. At that instant there were a thousand separate thoughts that lit up the living matrix of her cortex. She sucked in a breath. "Where did you find that?" she uttered slowly, eyes glaring with sudden intensity.

"That's not the point," James said, a bit flustered, "the point is—"

Erika stood as rivers of foamy suds cascaded down her taut body. She extended a finger toward the door.

"GET OUT!" Erika screamed, her eyes blazing. "Get the hell out of my apartment. NOW!"

James did not move—his stare dropped momentarily, eyes scanning her wet body, slick and shiny from the jasmine bath gel. "Erika, wait," he said, gulping air as he weighed the dildo in his palm, "we need to talk about this—"

Erika placed a hand on her hip and pursed her lips.

"Let me tell you something," she said. "You come into my house, rifle through my shit, and then have the nerve to throw what you find in my face? Oh hell no! I don't think so!"

Erika sat down abruptly, immersing her entire torso in the bathwater as a wave of bubbly suds rose up and over the lip of the tub, spilling onto the bathroom floor. James retreated like a toddler afraid of a frothy wave rushing toward the shore. "You need to leave!"

"Erika," he said in a kinder, gentler voice, "just explain to me why . . . why do you need this?"

Erika turned her head to stare at him in disbelief. James wore a sorrow-filled expression; as if he were constipated or suffering from deep abdominal pain. His eyes roamed over the jelly dong, considering it the purest form of evil.

"Why do I need that? Why do I need that?" she asked incredulously. Erika laughed. "Because it feels freaking good, you nitwit!"

James swallowed as his eyes lowered to the floor.

"You know what, James?" she said, "You have a lot of nerve coming in here with your porno tapes and your . . . how do I put this delicately . . . your sexual idiosyncrasies—"

"Wait, hold up," James exclaimed, raising a hand, *"idio-syncrasies?"*

"Well, James, some might call them 'dysfunctions' . . ."

"I beg your pardon?"

"Please, don't get me started, because you don't want to go there, trust me!"

"No," James said, shouting as he moved closer to the edge of the tub, a fierce look about him, "Let's go *there* . . . say your piece, Erika."

She sneered, nodding. "Okay. . . . Let's just say that people who live in glass houses shouldn't throw stones. Translation—dudes who possess weird sexual hang-ups don't have the right to say shit to dildo-toting sistahs! Now GET THE HECK OUT!"

"Ah shit, Sassy!" I exclaimed, while grinning from ear to ear, "You da mutha sucking man, ya hear me?" Erika cut a sharp glance my way, but I continued to laugh anyway. I took a quick sip of my Grey Goose apple martini—oh hell yeah, y'all—the firm was picking up the Christmas party's tab—open bar, dinner and shit, so you know this boy wasn't about to drink anything but top shelf!

Here we were, two weeks before Christmas, I, clad in a decadent black tux, looking sexy as hell, if I may say so myself, staring on in disbelief at my date for the evening, Erika, my boo, dressed as only she can in this sexy-ass red dress that came down two inches above her knee, plunging back, ribbons of silk crisscrossing down the front of her torso, holding her perky breasts in place. White pearls, hair down and done to a T, diamond studs, eyes glimmering. I kid you not—if Erika wasn't like family—I'd wax that ass for sure right now!

"Tell me you're shitting me!" I yelled as a table of partners and their wives nearby glanced our way.

"Trey! *Please*!" Erika whispered. "You need to keep your ghetto-talking ass down—those are your co-workers, in case you've forgotten." Erika took me by the elbow and ushered me away from the wood bar toward the railing overlooking the main dining room of Sequoia.

Together we glanced downward at the horde of people— the firm's finest—partners, associates, support staff, and their spouses, girlfriends and whatnot, all feasting on beef tenderloins, baked turkey, and candied yams. I spotted a few of my boys—office mates who I hung with when at the office—we exchanged smiles and chin nods.

Erika was by my side. I placed my hand on the small of her back.

"For real, girl, you look so damn good tonight," I said with a smile.

I meant every word.

Most of the women here were wearing formal gowns. Politically correct to-the-floor ensembles that were safe, yet fashionably boring. Erika stood out like a beacon of pulsating light.

"Whatever, Trey. You're just horny. And don't think I won't slap you silly if you try some stupid shit with me!" She grinned and I had to shake my head.

"So," I said, "Getting back to the story at hand. Are you telling me this dude went through your shit and found your vibrator?"

"Trey, please, keep your voice down," Erika scolded. "Yeah, can you believe it? The asshole tried to say he was looking for some Scotch tape!" Erika shook her head slowly. "Please, do I look like a fool?"

I laughed. "So?"

"You haven't heard the good part yet," Erika said, and I noticed that the smile on her face faded. She took a sip of her martini and became somber in her expression.

"James told me he loved me." Erika paused to let that sink in.

"What?" I exclaimed. "That boy's so pussy whipped it ain't even funny!"

Erika became silent for a moment. She bit her bottom lip before continuing. "I don't know Trey—all kidding around aside, I am really confused by this whole situation."

I led Erika over to a small table by her elbow away from prying eyes. We sat. "Go on," I said.

"I don't know, Trey. On the one hand, I've got this wonderful guy in James. He is very attentive to me, worships the ground I walk on, and is a very good lover. I am getting satisfied, you hear me. I've got no complaints. Well, if only that was true."

"Yeah, I mean, the guy has a fucking problem. And I mean literally, a *fucking* problem!" I had to snicker at my own humor.

Erika smiled weakly. "No, you are right—he does have a problem. Or maybe problem is not the right word. James can come. He has on a few occasions. But it is the circumstances of his climax that has me worried."

"Sassy," I said, taking her hand in mine, "I'm gonna tell you this straight up, Trey-style. James is gay. No two ways about it. He gets off by having shit up his ass!" I eyed her seriously for a quick second. "Okay, poor choice of words, but you know what I mean."

"Trey, he's not gay. James is attracted to women."

"Please, boo. I call it as I see it. The boy's got problems, okay? There are so many dudes out here who don't have issues with their plumbing—take me for example. You don't see me making excuses for why I can't come. Please—the day my dick doesn't work is the day I slit my own throat. Believe that!"

Erika shook her head sadly. "You are so messed up, Trey, do you know that?"

I feigned hurt.

"Can we get serious for a moment?" she asked. "I've got a great man in James who adores and loves me. And I'm sitting here being nitpicky over some shit that perhaps doesn't even matter. I mean, who out there is perfect? Who do you know that doesn't have issues?"

"Me!" I said quickly, unblinking.

"Boy, you are straight tripping, you hear me? I'm serious,

Trey. I think that people spend their entire lives searching for Mr. or Ms. Perfect, when the fact of the matter is they don't exist. We need to learn to accept people for who they are—imperfect human beings, with faults and idiosyncrasies. Perhaps, I should accept James for whom and what he is—a great guy who has some hang-ups. I mean, who doesn't?"

"Trick, did I stutter? I said me!"

Erika smirked. "Please! You've got more issues than Imelda's got shoes. Look at you—you can't commit because you're all screwed up inside!"

"Damn, Sassy, don't sugarcoat it, girl . . ."

Erika ignored me. "Psst. You jump from bed to bed, as if boning every Toni, Dina, and Harriet will make you more of a man. When what you really need to do is settle down—find yourself a good woman and get married!"

I looked at Erika as if I'd just been shot.

"Trick, you are the one who's straight trippin'! This kid ain't never getting married. And I'm never settling down. You forget that I tried going down that road once, and looked where it got me. Hell no, Sassy, screw *that* and screw *you*!"

I sucked down the last remnants of my martini and quickly glanced around for a waitress to bring me another.

"Whatever, Trey. You can say what you want, but I know you. I know you are hurting inside." Erika leaned closer. "I know that because I see how you react when Layla's around . . ."

"Please!" I said, loudly. "That ho can come and go—it don't mean shit to me!"

"That's why you ran out of bluespace the other night like a dog with its tail between its legs. Dude, don't play me."

I glared at Erika but remained silent.

"She still loves you, you know?" Erika said, lowering her voice a notch. "Layla told me so."

"What?" I shook my head in astonishment. "It's been five freaking years. The bitch needs to get over me. Dayum!" I stood up abruptly. "I'm getting another drink. You need one?"

Erika nodded once, as her stare never left mine. I blinked once before turning away.

"No," Erika said quietly, "it is you who needs to get over her . . ."

I was washing my hands in the men's room sink when I heard the door open. I glanced up as I grabbed a towel to dry my hands. In waltzed Bernard John Marshall. I felt the temperature slither down several degrees.

Through the mirror we made brief eye contact. He was silent as he moved to a urinal. I quickly checked my tux and bow tie, ran a hand over my baldhead, and headed for the door. I made it six paces when I heard him speak.

"I'm very impressed . . ."

I paused and turned slightly to glance his way.

"Excuse me?" I asked.

Bernard flushed and went to the sink. He turned on the water while eyeing me through the mirror.

"I said I'm impressed. Your date, Mr. Alexander. She is not at all what I expected." He smiled and I felt my face flush. I clenched my right fist and wanted nothing more than to bash his face in. I hated this mutha sucka with a passion.

"Excuse me?" I replied again, turning fully to face him.

"She's quite lovely. I guess I was expecting something else." Bernard pulled out a comb, ran water through it, and methodically slicked back his hair.

"Meaning what?" I said, a taste of venom on my lips.

He stopped combing, and turned to face me. "No need to get hostile, counselor. I thought your tastes ran in, shall we say, different waters . . ." Bernard smiled, showing me his teeth. His eyes were dead orbs that spoke volumes about the man.

I advanced toward him, my teeth clenched. "If you have something to say to me, Bernie, why don't you go ahead and stop pussyfooting around."

"It's Bernard, and I don't like your tone." He wiped away the grease from his comb with his fingers, ran them under the water as he eyed me. "I guess that opposing counsel from the Hues case wasn't interested, right?"

I stood with a deadpan expression; the only thing moving was my jaw.

"Oh, come now, Trey, you know what I mean—what was her name? Allison somebody, if my memory serves me." He grinned again.

"You're an—" I said quickly, and then caught myself. I silently counted to five before exhaling through my nose.

Bernard crossed the distance between him and I quickly, stopping a mere foot from me.

"A *what*, Mr. Alexander? If you have something to say then say it. To paraphrase you, 'stop pussyfooting around.'"

I remained silent.

"That's what I thought," he said with a sneer.

Bernard brushed imaginary lint off of his tuxedo. "In case you haven't figured it out yet, Trey, I don't like you. I think your vast ego far outshines your mediocre work."

I blinked rapidly.

"And I so do hope you show me your true colors soon. I trust it won't be too long a wait. People like you can't help themselves . . ."

"People like me???" I said incredulously. "Just what—"

"Enjoy the party, counselor," he said as he breezed past me, his shoulder grazing the fabric of my expensive tux.

The conversation was over.

I remained alone, staring down at the bathroom tile, attempting to control my breathing . . . and my surging anger . . .

Vince Cannon Jr. was helping clear the dishes when his cell phone chirped.

"Go ahead, honey," his mother said to him smiling, "your father can finish up here." Vince's dad gave his mother a brooding stare as she walked away.

It had been a while since Vince had spent time with his folks. For years he had never missed a Sunday dinner at their home in Northwest D.C. But over the past few months Vince's visits had begun to slip, missing the weekly meal on a more frequent basis. His parents understood—lately his book tour and seminars had been kicking up a notch or two. Just recently, he'd spent time in Philadelphia, New York, and Trenton doing one-day seminars and book signings. He had Boston, Atlanta, and Tampa booked for next month.

Vince glanced at his cell and felt his heart rate spike.

"Hello?"

"Hey you." It was Angeliqué.

"What's up?" he said, moving from the dining room with the massive oak hutch that had been in the family as long as Vince could remember, to the living room. He sat on a love seat by the window, hearing the clanking of plates in the background as his father moved around the kitchen grudgingly.

"I'm fine," Angeliqué said. "I just wanted to say hi, since you and I haven't spoken since we got back."

"Yeah, well, I'm sure you've been as busy as I have."

"Perhaps—I have to tell you, I was pissed that you did the casting of Amber."

Vince was silent.

"But I'm over that now."

"Okay," Vince said unsurely.

"And I hear it came out really nice. You'll have to send us a photo when it's complete."

"Will do," Vince responded.

"So, what has kept you from calling?" she said, with a touch of sarcasm.

Vince emitted a short laugh. "What can I say? I've been busy. This past week I was out of town doing some one-day seminars."

"Cool, how did they go?" she asked.

"Very well. I conducted a few book signings as well. It's always nice to get out and meet the folks who support you."

"I hear that. Well, I just wanted to make sure that you and I were still cool."

"Yeah," Vince said, "why wouldn't we be?"

"You know—that weekend in D.C. didn't exactly go as planned, did it?"

Vince considered that for a moment.

"No, I guess not."

"Our time spent together didn't match what we had in New Orleans. I had hoped to rekindle what we felt when you and I first met, but it didn't work out that way. I know that now, and so do you."

"Correct." What else was there to say?

"I guess what I'm trying to say Vince is this: I want us to remain friends. You are an exceptional person, and you touched me in a special way. I don't want to lose that, Vince. I don't want to lose you as a friend."

Vince sighed. "You won't, Angeliqué. You won't."

He heard Angeliqué expel a breath. "I'm so glad to hear you say that. I was worried." Vince heard her giggle and his thoughts were transported back to that first time, when they walked the Quarter after a tantalizing dinner at Brennan's, their shoulders and arms brushing against each other as they sauntered past antique shops and blues clubs, fingers inter-twined like vines. Vince recalled with vivid clarity that first time they made love in her studio, colors splashing across their bodies as they painted each other, creating art, making vibrant, passionate love. It was a moment Vince would soon not forget.

They talked for fifteen minutes more, getting caught up in each other's lives. The conversation grew friendlier by the minute, as if crossing this hurdle, deciding to remain friends, now enabled them to continue their friendship unen-cumbered.

Vince asked about Amber.

"She's been asking about you. I take it the two of you hit it off in Washington?"

Vince felt himself flush.

"She's good people—like you, Angeliqué, she's got soul."

"You trying to butter me up, Vince?"

"Naw, girl . . . not me."

"Alrighty then. Well, I'll be sure to tell Amber you asked about her. And Vince, don't be a stranger, okay? I dig talking to you on the regular."

"I feel the same, Angel, I feel the same . . ."

His cell rang thirty minutes later. Vince was sitting in the living room, shooting the breeze with his parents.

"I don't get this many calls," his father quipped while shaking his head, "and I'm a damn physician!"

Vince rolled his eyes at his mother as he glanced at the Caller ID number.

A 718 area code.

A number he did not recognize.

"Hello?" he said.

"Hi, may I speak to Mr. Vince Cannon, Jr.?" a female voice said.

"Speaking."

"Hi. I got your number from the coffee shop on Capitol Hill. I was inquiring about your artwork. Is it for sale?"

Vince smiled.

"Well, as a matter of fact it is. I've been working with some local galleries in the area, and should have most of my art on view shortly."

"That sounds great. I have to tell you, I was very impressed with the piece you have hanging in the Cosi shop. I don't think I've seen anything quite like it before." Vince listened to her voice—smooth, sensuous in its delivery.

"Thank you. That is one of my favorite pieces."

"Let me tell you my situation. I'm moving into a new home and am looking for eclectic art to furnish it with. The more colorful and passionate, the better."

"I hear that," Vince exclaimed.

"And, I'm particularly interested in art done by those of color. You understand me?"

"Very much so," Vince said, grinning. He focused on her voice again—a quiet timber, but one which exuded power—a woman who knew what she wanted, and was used to getting it . . . Who was this woman???

"Great. I'd like to see your other work. I'll be in the market for some pieces fairly soon."

"That's fine. What is your schedule like? I have a studio located in D.C."

"I'm flexible this coming week. How about tomorrow, sometime during the day?"

"Fine by me. Shall we say two p.m.?"

"Works for me. Give me the address."

Vince did.

"So, I will see you tomorrow at two o'clock. Looking

forward to it, Mr. Cannon. Or may I call you Vince?" she asked in a voice that took Vince's breath away.

"Please call me Vince," he said in his rich, motivational speaker voice that drove the women wild. "And what may I call you?" he asked.

"You may call me what my friends call me," she responded in a singsong voice. "You may call me Raven . . ."

Calvin Figgs, Esq., spotted the change in my demeanor immediately. He and his lovely wife were huddled around a batch of senior partners and their wives, Calvin doing what he did best, playing the game, showing these white folks that he still knew how to hang with the best of them. It was good to see Calvin; lately he'd been in the office on average only three days a week. We hadn't had an in-depth conversation in a while. He stood there, looking dapper as usual, wearing that tuxedo like he was a damn model; his wife of twenty-five years by his side, looking like a spitting image of Lena Horne, with her fine self. I was not mad at either of them!

He excused himself and came over, kissing Erika on the cheek.

"It is so good to see you again, Erika," he said. Calvin's hair and thin beard were manicured to perfection, and it pleased me greatly to see another black man who took pride in his looks as much as I did. He shook my hand and smiled as he said, "Counselor, looking good as usual!"

"Thank you, but I don't hold a candle to you, sir. Check you out! The O.G.—Original Gangster!"

Calvin grinned. "As my daughter is fond of saying, 'don't hate the playa!'"

His smile turned serious. "What's the matter, Trey, I can

see that something's on your mind. Not enjoying yourself this evening?"

"The party's fine, Calvin. It's that asshole Bernard. I'm about to put my size twelve foot up his ass, for real!"

Calvin grinned at Erika. "Would you excuse us for a moment? I need to school this youngster for a minute."

Erika smiled. "Please do. You know he needs all the schooling he can get."

"Ain't that the truth," Calvin quipped as he led me away.

Together we walked to an outside section that had been enclosed in a huge white tent. Due to the cold weather, few people were sitting there, even though the restaurant had provided tall gas heaters spaced every few yards apart. We found a table under one, unbuttoned our jackets, and sat down.

"What's going on?" Calvin asked.

"It's Bernard. He's a world-class asshole."

"Tell me something I don't already know!"

"Calvin, this guy is something else—he's all over my shit—putting his nose into every case I'm working on, questioning my judgment and everything."

"He is the managing partner of the firm, Trey. As such he does have the right to monitor the progress of partners and associates."

"Calvin, please!" I exclaimed. "Monitoring is one thing—but this guy takes 'micromanagement' to a whole new level!"

Calvin nodded.

"And that's not all. Tonight in the men's room he made a comment about Erika not being my type. Then he tells me that he doesn't like me, that my work is just 'mediocre,' and that he's just waiting for me to mess up."

Calvin shook his head.

"Here's the clincher, Calvin—the a-hole then says to me:

'I can't wait to see your true colors soon. People like you can't help themselves.'"

Calvin scratched slowly at his beard, but said nothing. I waited for him to speak.

"Well?" I said, irritably.

"Trey, listen, my advice to you is to keep your head down and watch your back. Bernard is gunning for you, there is no doubt about that. I'm not sure why you've gotten under his skin, but you have."

"Can't something be done about him? Can't you do something? I mean, come on, Calvin. I've been busting my ass for five years around here. I'm valuable. I bill more than some of these lily white partners, and I'm freaking in demand, you know that."

"I do."

"But???" I said, trying to maintain my composure.

"Trey, things are changing around here in case you haven't noticed. The management is taking the firm in a new direction. That's why they brought Bernard in. That's why I'm out."

Calvin paused to let that sink in.

I stared at him in disbelief.

"What do you mean, you're out?"

"Just what I said. I've served my purpose here. It's time to move on."

"Are they forcing you out?" I asked, my voice barely above a whisper.

"Trey, it's complicated. They acknowledge my value to the firm over the years. And with my contacts around town, they'd be committing suicide if they just cut me loose. So no, they aren't forcing me out. But it's been made clear that my time is up—it's a new day around here."

"Damn . . ." I said. What else could be said?

"Calvin, I'm so sorry this is happening to you. Of all people," I said with more sincerity then I've shown in months. "Are they going to take care of you at least?"

"Yes, they are. It would be insulting if they asked me to leave without making it worth my while. Between you and me, I'm being handsomely compensated. But you know what the best part is?" he asked smiling.

I shook my head.

"My wife is ecstatic. She gets to spend time with me again. To be truthful, my long hours have been straining our relationship for too long to remember."

"What? You can't be serious?"

"As serious as a heart attack. You know the life of a partner—you have no life. Try being a managing partner. You must bump it up by an order of magnitude or you don't survive. I did what I had to do—I loved this firm. I put my heart and soul into it. It became my family, my life. In doing so, I sacrificed what I had had with Linda."

I sat there, staring off into space.

"Damn," I repeated.

"You know what they say, Trey. When one door closes, another one opens. That adage is so true, I can't begin to tell you. Frankly, this is the best thing that could have happened to me. I was feeling stagnant for years, not knowing that I was in a funk, not knowing how to get out of this mess that I had built for myself. Now I'm free. Unchained, unencumbered."

Calvin grinned. "I'm pursuing new endeavors, like teaching. Georgetown Law is very interested. I've met with the dean and he's offered me an adjunct faculty position. I'm also thinking about doing some writing for some law journals."

"DAYUM, Calvin!" I shouted, slapping his shoulder. "You are da man! Good for you. Damn good for you." I dropped my voice a notch. "Screw these mutha suckas, you hear me. Walk away with your head held high. You don't need these bitches. You will come out on top!"

Calvin's smile evaporated as he leaned closer to me. "Trey, listen to me. I know things are hard right now. But you need to watch yourself. Things are different now—I'm not going to be able to shield you from Bernard and his wrath. He's connected, senior management believes in him, and as I said, he's gunning for you. You need to keep your nose clean, and make sure you are on point 24/7. And Trey, above all—don't give him the satisfaction of losing your cool in front of him. That's what he's waiting for. Waiting for you to act like a nigger . . ."

Calvin stared at me.

Silently I stared back, swallowing as I nodded my head slowly, contemplating his words and their meaning.

Like a nigger, Calvin had said.

Yeah, I thought, Calvin had Bernard pegged . . .

Seven

Vince glanced at his watch: 1:45 p.m., fifteen minutes remaining until the woman named Raven would arrive at his studio. What would she be like? Vince didn't know. But the conversation last night gave him a sense of what to expect.

He had put on a pair of jeans still warm from the iron, lavender button-down shirt, and a pair of leather boots he normally reserved for riding. He took extra care to trim his beard and mustache, not wanting to look like a wild man. Not that Vince ever did. Not even on a bad day . . .

She arrived promptly at 2. Vince buzzed her in and heard the knock on the door a minute later. He opened it, and what he saw took his breath away.

Raven stood there, clad in a red wool coat, matching wool hat and mittens, holding a steaming Starbucks cup.

"Vince?" she asked.

"Yes, you must be Raven," he said with a smile.

He opened the door wider and stepped aside so she could walk in, glancing at her as she strode by.

He felt his heart beat faster as he witnessed her hips

move. Raven stopped mid-center of his studio, glancing around. Her attention was immediately focused on his wall of masks.

"Very impressive."

"Thanks. Let me take your things." Raven unbuttoned her coat and slid out of it. She removed her hat and mittens and handed them over with her purse. Vince took the opportunity to look her over.

Raven had long dark hair that was tied back. Brown eyes were piercing and always moving. She wore tight jeans that showed off her long legs, firm hips and ass, a rusty brown sweater containing full breasts, and tan boots. Her smile was what captivated Vince the most. Her lips curved up in a sensuous kind of way as she extended her hand to him.

"It's nice to meet you and put a face with the name."

"Same here," he said. "Can I offer you something?"

"I'm good," she said, holding up her cup.

"Cool. So, welcome to my humble studio," he said, holding his arms wide. "Feel free to look around."

"Thanks." She moved over to the wall, studied the pieces hanging there for a few minutes before moving across the room to the worktable that held the unfinished full-body casting of Amber. It lay on the table like a half-finished mummy, the plaster of Paris already smoothed by Vince's hands, awaiting paint.

"My goodness," Raven said, walking over and lightly touching the casting, "this is amazing."

"Thank you. I did that particular piece just a week or so ago. I'm still trying to decide on a color scheme. As you can see, it's my first full body casting."

Raven nodded.

"So," Vince said, "You mentioned on the phone that you recently purchased a home and are looking to furnish it with some art."

"Yes. I'm looking for pieces that stir my emotions every time I gaze upon them."

"I feel you."

Vince observed Raven as she returned to the wall of masks. She moved slowly, examining each one, shifting closer until her nose almost touched the paint-covered plaster, taking in each piece, letting the colors invade her space. Vince was silent as he sat on the futon sipping at hot coffee.

"These are wonderful," Raven mused. Vince was silently watching her. His stare took in her features—long black hair, parted in the middle, and tied back with multi-colored rubber bands, caramel cheekbones, sensuous lips that parted ever so slightly to reveal a pink tongue as she concentrated on his art. A good half dozen silver bracelets adorned her left wrists, glinting as she moved to sit on the futon beside him.

"Have you priced out each piece?" she asked.

"Well," Vince said, "these masks go for between seven hundred fifty and twelve hundred dollars apiece." He paused to watch her, then added: "I hope you find them reasonable."

Raven was silent as she moved forward. Her hand went to her mouth, the bracelets jingling as she moved. After a moment she moved back from the wall.

Vince cleared his throat and spoke. "Art prices are always so subjective, don't you think? I mean, what the artist sees as value—"

Raven held up a hand, her bracelets clanking as they moved up her forearm. "No need for explanations, Vince. I believe artists should be paid for their craft."

Vince watched her, not trying to eye her directly, but enjoying the closeness as she studied his art. A number of thoughts went through his mind as his stare flicked over her features. She was indeed a beautiful woman. Her dark hair shone and Vince dug the way she had it tied down her back. Her jeans were tight, revealing nice curves, the rise of her breasts hypnotic. Her lips were wet from her tongue. How old was she? Raven appeared to be around his age, but one could never tell. Was she dating? Married? He glanced down—numerous rings covered both hands, so it was difficult to tell. Vince caught her sipping at her coffee. "Mmmmn . . ." she exclaimed almost absentmindedly. Vince grinned.

"I take it you are a coffee connoisseur."

Raven eyed him with a smile.

"Ain't nothing coming between me and my coffee," she said.

Vince nodded, feeling the temperature rise a few degrees.

Raven turned abruptly. She went to the wall and pointed to four masks. "I'm interested in these," she said, decisively.

Vince stood excitedly. "Let me take those down and put them together so you can decide."

Raven shook her head. "I'm interested in all four. That's not a problem, is it?"

Vince swallowed hard. "No. Of course not."

"Will four grand cover it?"

Vince blinked. "Why yes," he said, not knowing what else to say.

"I thought so," Raven said, and Vince swore he saw her eyes twinkle. She turned back to the wall of masks while Vince pulled them off the wall one by one, leaning them in a row on the floor. Raven studied her acquisitions carefully, bending down onto her haunches so she could get eye level with the masks.

Vince was silent as he stood back. She stood, turning to him, and sighing heavily.

"Shopping always makes me hungry," Raven said with a teasing smile.

Vince beamed.

"There's a damn good Chinese place nearby . . ."

"You treating?" she asked with a sly grin.

* * *

They sat across from each other, silently enjoying their food. Vince had ordered the Hot Crispy Beef. Raven had selected the Szechwan Shrimp. He forked a sliver of the crunchy beef into his mouth, eyeing Raven as she helped herself to a helping of his entrée.

"Hungry?" he teased.

"What? A girl can't get her eat on?"

Vince smiled. They sat at a small table for two by the window overlooking a busy intersection. Automobiles whizzed past, spewing exhaust. People huddled together in an open bus stop across the street, bundled up against the cold. The threat of snow hung in the air like cigarette smoke.

Forty minutes earlier Vince had wrapped up each mask in newsprint while Raven had run to the bank. She had returned twenty minutes later with a cashier's check for the entire amount. Vince carried the packages to her black Range Rover before they locked the car and walked the three blocks to the restaurant.

"So," Vince said, wiping his mouth with a cloth napkin, "tell me about yourself. What do you do, where are you from?" he asked, "The whole nine!"

Raven reached for the cup of green tea and sipped slowly. She placed the cup down gingerly and shook her head with a sigh.

"What?"

"Let me ask you something, Vince," she said. "Do you ever get tired of the back-and-forth games people play, this ruse, for lack of a better term, this self-marketing hype where I tell you of my significant accomplishments, and you nod your head vigorously while telling me yours? And it goes back and forth, deeper and deeper as the bullshit mounts:

'I did my undergraduate at Vassar!'

'Oh really? My post-doc work was done at U Berkeley.'

'Oh my, one of my frat brothers is a U Berkeley graduate—perhaps you know of him. Chad?'"

Raven shook her head sullenly. "At the end of the day, what does it all amount to, Vince? Nothing. People meet, they dance, they perform this ritual whose sole purpose is to search for their perfect mate. And when they don't find him or her what do they do? They move on to the next person, regurgitating their résumé all over again to the next poor slob who will listen."

Vince had been eating slowly, digesting what she had said. He put his fork down, a bit taken aback.

"I didn't mean to hit a sore point, Raven. I was just wondering—"

"Vince," she said, interrupting as she stabbed a piece of shrimp and baby corn, gesturing in his direction. "Let me ask you this: What are we all searching for?"

"Vince eyed her. "What do you mean?"

"Just what I said—what is it that men (and women) are searching for?"

Vince reflected. He knew the answer to this one. He'd written a book about it, for God's sake!

"Love. I think in a nutshell folks want to be loved. They want to fall in love, and remain in a long, nurturing relationship, where they can feel safe and be themselves."

"Well stated. But answer me this. How do we find love?"

Vince smiled as he glanced at his watch. "Well, I'm not sure if there are enough hours in the day to answer that one."

"Why not? It's a simple question," she quipped, eyeing him closely.

"I think not. Love is complex. It's mysterious. It may be simple, but it remains extremely elusive to most, and therein lies the rub."

Raven reached across the table to grab another helping of

Crispy Beef. She slipped a piece of the crunchy meat into her mouth and chewed while her stare never left his.

"I'm not sure how we went from 'tell me about yourself' to 'what is this thing called love?' " Vince said. "I was just interested in getting to know you—"

"Vince," Raven said, putting her fork down, "Are you listening? I know you hear me, but are you really *listening*?"

Vince sat back, feeling a trace of annoyance filter into his bloodstream. "I *thought* I was listening, Raven."

She beamed, erasing any ill will he was feeling at that moment. "May I school you?" She didn't wait for a response. "See, love is not, contrary to popular opinion, an emotion, which can be turned on and off, like a switch. No. It's not something that grows, like a dandelion. Nope. Love is innate. Love, my new friend, is *chemical*."

Vince looked surprised. "Chemical?"

"Yes," Raven said, smiling. "Do you really think that when two people meet and exchange their bios it brings them any closer to falling in love?"

"Yes, I do," Vince said. "Call me old-fashioned, but I believe in connections. I believe in the power of communication, of people connecting on a plane of mutual respect and understanding, and—"

"Vince—it's chemical, plain and simple. Spending time with someone, getting to know them better—that's all well and good—but at the end of the day, it's like it's been preordained. Whether two people fall in love has everything to do with chemistry. Some elements mix. Others don't. And all the forcing in the world won't change that simple fact. It's high school chemistry."

Vince stared at her. "So, what are you saying, Raven? Don't waste your time getting to know someone? Stop communicating because there is no point?"

"No—"

Vince barreled forward. "I should think not. No, Raven. Love may be chemical—and I'm not convinced that it is, but I'm not one to throw our tried and proven, yet perhaps old-fashioned ways to the curb. For me, I still treasure sitting down and talking to a woman, getting to know her, finding out what makes her tick. To me, Raven, there is a certain feeling I get, deep in my gut, when I'm sitting across from someone I fancy, and I'm still learning about what their likes and dislikes are, that overwhelming sensation that is hard to describe—happiness, excitement, anxiety, and passion, all fused into one, making your stomach twist into a knot because of the infinite possibilities you see sitting across from you. That feeling, that first inkling that you may be in *love* . . ."

Raven sat back, folding her arms across her chest. She stared silently at Vince for a bit, nodding absentmindedly. She reached for her tea and took a sip, placing the cup down before speaking.

"Obviously I'm sitting across from a romantic . . ."

"Card carrying member for life, baby!" Vince grinned.

"I'm not mad at you, Vince. I guess I'm just tired of the whole scene—answering myriad questions about this and that when, fundamentally, it doesn't matter."

"Then I won't ask any more questions."

"Yeah, right. Like I know you're dying to know more about me!"

"Please, honey," Vince quipped, "Do I look pressed?"

"You're a man, right? Then you're pressed!"

Vince laughed. "You've been watching too much of The View!"

"You know what I dig, Vince? I live to be unconventional. Out of the ordinary. Like, instead of sitting here going through the motions, I want to think outside of the box.

Dare to be different, regardless of what society says the rules should be. You feel me?"

Vince nodded, unsteadily.

"Let's you and I become the people we've dreamed of being. Let's not talk about it, let's just do it! Show me, Vince, who you can be!" Raven's eyes lit up and Vince found himself aroused at the prospect.

"Go on," he said.

"Don't you sometimes want to be somebody else? Take on a new persona? Well, here's your chance. I don't know you; you don't know me. What a perfect opportunity to start with a clean slate."

Vince paid the check and escorted Raven out the door. The cold hit them in the face, hard. Raven wove her arm through Vince's and nuzzled close to keep warm.

"I've got an idea, if you're game," she said as they turned the corner, away from the traffic noise.

"Shoot."

"Let's hang out tomorrow night, if you don't have plans. The rules are simple: You aren't Vince and I'm not Raven. Tomorrow night, we reinvent ourselves, and we see where this chemistry thing takes us."

"I'm down," Vince replied enthusiastically.

"Cool. How about I pick you up at seven?

Vince raised his eyebrows. "Okay. Where are we going?"

"It's a surprise, but don't worry, I don't bite. Unless of course you want me to . . ."

Vince smiled, but said: "I have to admit I'm a bit confused . . ."

"It's simple, Vince. I don't want to hear about us—you and me—who we are or where we've come from. I'm not interested in accomplishments. Frankly, resumes bore me. Instead, I want to see where this can take us. Think of this as a grand adventure where the wind is nipping at your heels, and you have no idea where this safari will lead."

"So, if we don't talk then what do we do?"

Raven's eyes sparkled like diamonds. "It's an adventure, man. We do whatever we choose to do . . ."

"Hey you, it's Vince. Is his Highness in?"

"Oh Vince," India Jasmine Jackson said in an enthusiastic voice, "What is up, my fine Nubian brutha? How are you?"

"Can't complain. You?"

"Still waiting for you to propose . . ."

"It's in the mail, baby!" Vince exclaimed.

"Yeah right. Let me connect you."

Trey got on a moment later.

"How ya livin'?" he asked.

"Large and in charge. You know how we do!" Vince responded.

"Cool. So what's up, my bruh?" Trey asked.

"You got a minute?"

"For you? Always . . ."

Vince thought about the irony of that—perhaps one could teach old dogs new tricks . . .

"Listen, I met this woman today. She came over to purchase some of my art."

"Congrats!"

"Yeah. So, check this out. We're sitting together afterwards having lunch, and I ask her the usual questions—where she's from, what she does, etcetera., and she like bugs out! Starts talking all this crazy shit about how she's not interested in any of that—how that's tired and played out. How she lives to be unconventional and shit. How she likes to think outside of the box."

"Hmmmn," Trey said, thinking out loud. "How's this chick looking?"

"Trey, she's amazing," Vince said. "Long legs, long dark hair, curves in all the right places."

"Solid. So, give me the specifics. What exactly did she say?"

Vince recounted the details of their conversation. Trey interrupted frequently, asking questions; Vince clarified as best he could.

When Vince was done with his explanation he sighed deeply. "Tell me what this shit means, bruh."

"See—it's a good thing you called the master. Cause your dumb ass would be floundering if it weren't for me."

"Yeah, whatever, Master Bator . . ."

Trey chuckled at that one. "It's simple, really. This chick is sending you a message—and you best pay attention. She wants you, man, and she wants you bad. But she can't come out and say it—not that she seems that shy, based on what you told me, but she doesn't want to come off sounding like a ho. Oh yeah, she wants you in the worst way. She's messing with you, telling you all this 'think outside of the box' and 'I'm unconventional' shit!" Trey laughed. "Negro please! She's signaling just how bad she wants you to bone her!" Trey giggled. "What you need to do is show up in a pair of tight leather pants and some boots, with a riding crop in hand and spank that ass as soon as she glances your way. That'll teach her to fuck with a dude!"

"Trey, I don't know . . ."

"Bruh, please don't make me school you again! This chick is signaling to you exactly what she wants. She's looking for a man who is unconventional, she's practically begging you to be that man, cause she's tired of mutha suckas with the same old tired-ass lines—translation—take the bull by the horns and screw that horny little beast!"

"Trey, not everything is about sex."

"Oh Lord! Am I speaking to Erika or my boy? Dang, what am I going to do with you, Vince? I'll tell you what. Let me go on this date tomorrow and I'll give her a ride she'll never forget."

"That's okay, partner, I can handle this one myself."

"Make sure you do. Seriously, dude, this woman is asking for you to amaze her—show her what you are made of. So show her a man that she's yet to see. Vince Cannon, Jr., what you gonna do?"

"I don't know, Trey. I mean, I don't know if I can waltz in there, acting like some rap star or someone whom I'm not, acting like I take no prisoners, just to impress her. That's really not me—I've got my own approach, and it's a bit less . . . *flamboyant* . . ."

"Vince," Trey said, raising his voice, "Bump that! We see all the time how women pass up the smooth romantic types for those ruffneck bad boys. That's why I'm so successful with the ladies, man, 'cause I give them what they really want—a sense of excitement and the freedom that they've yet to experience. As only I can do—Trey style!"

"I don't know . . . ," Vince repeated.

"Listen Vince, I gotta go. I've got a client coming up in five. But take my advice. Don't mess this one up. She sounds like she's a hell of a ride. So ride that shit—go in there like you own that mutha sucka! That shit is already yours. So, sweep her off her feet. Take her and spank her ass without asking permission. I guarantee you won't be disappointed. Just don't forget in the midst of all your enthusiasm to videotape that shit for me and the rest of the fellas to see! For real, playa!"

* * *

His next call was to Erika. She picked up on the third ring.

"What up, Sassy? How ya livin'?"

"You tell me, you're the man."

"I'm good, but I need some advice."

"Shoot."

Vince described his dilemma for Erika. He told her of his encounter with Raven and her challenge to him.

"I'm digging this woman, Sassy, and I want to impress her. But I don't know if I can be someone I'm not, you know what I mean?"

"Yes, I do. I don't get why she's got you going in circles anyway. It seems as if she's just playing a game with you, and you've got to decide if that's a good thing or not."

"If I understand her correctly, she's tired of the same old thing—tired of meeting men and recounting for them her life story over and over again."

"Yeah, well, welcome to the club, man. I mean, we all go through that stuff. It's part of the mating ritual; you know that as well as any of us. How does she expect to get to know someone? By osmosis?" Erika laughed.

"Yeah, I think so. She says it's all chemistry."

"Whatever," Erika exclaimed. "You can do what you want, but my advice to you is this: don't start off a relationship with game playing. That's not healthy. You don't need to be anyone but yourself. Vince, you are already cool with being who you are. You are comfortable in your own skin, and you've got nothing to be ashamed of. You're good looking, intelligent, creative, and have a great career. So, why spend time trying to be someone that you're not?"

"Good point. I tend to agree with you, Boo. That was my first thought—why should I play this game and try to be someone else? But at the same time, she seems very cool, and I think she just is looking for something different. And I think I can give her that."

"Hmmmn," Erika said, with not a lot of conviction in her voice.

Vince was silent for a moment. "Trey says I should—"

"Hold it, Vince. Why you listening to his monkey-ass? It'd be one thing if he had a lock on love and relationships, but he's the last guy you should be listening to!"

Vince could imagine her shaking her head. He smiled.

"Yeah, you got that one right."

"I mean, please—when was the last time Trey had a meaningful relationship with anyone? A year ago? Two? Try five!"

"I hear you . . ."

"Vince, this woman may be cool and all, but tread lightly. Don't commit yourself until you know more about her. Something sounds fishy to me, and us girls have got a sixth sense about these things."

"Okay, Ma, you're the expert . . . by the way, how are things between you and James?" he asked.

"Who? Oh please! Don't get me started, okay???"

A dozen separate scenarios occupied Vince's psyche. For the next eighteen hours he thought of little else. How to impress the mysterious and sensual Raven?

That was the question.

Show up, clad in a lime green pimp outfit with matching wide brim hat and platform shoes, courtesy of (who else?) Trey Alexander?

Pretend he was a rapper, and arrive in a limo with a pair of ghetto fabulous girls on either arm?

Perhaps he could take on the persona of a plastic surgeon who does all the elite locals and politicians' wives?

Or a movie star in town for a film shoot?

No. Vince wasn't feeling any of these.

The problem was simple. Vince wasn't like Trey. He couldn't just waltz into a room and take charge, pretending he was someone else. It wasn't in him. Never had been.

His cell chirped around noon as he contemplated his options.

"Vince," a vaguely familiar female voice said.

"Yes?"

"It's Raven."

Vince smiled. "Hey you."

"Change of plans," she said, in a voice that chilled him with its sensuality. "I've got to take care of something. Why don't you just meet me at the spot later on tonight? Around tenish would be cool."

Vince frowned, but then realized that arriving by himself would give him some options he had yet to consider.

"Yeah, that's fine. Where shall we meet?"

Raven gave him the address.

"Did you say Philly?" Vince asked suddenly sitting upright, "as in Philadelphia, PA?"

"That's right." These words were delivered in a singsong upswept voice that hinted of deviousness. "I trust that won't present a problem, will it?"

Vince's mind raced. "No . . . not at all, Raven. The adventure, then, begins at ten . . ."

"Looking forward to it," she said.

"Likewise," was Vince's response.

Eight

The spot was named Infusion Lounge. Vince found it shortly after ten thirty. It was a small place, sandwiched between a bar and grill named Nick's Cuban restaurant. As he drove by slowly, he could see the bar and adjacent space was filled to capacity with patrons sharing holiday cheer. He drove on and found parking two blocks over.

Was he ready to see Raven?

Yes.

Vince knew exactly what he was going to do.

Reaching behind him, he pulled out a thin walking stick.

He checked himself in the rearview mirror before readying to head out. Vince had opted for a dark single-breasted suit with a contrasting turtleneck underneath. His dark gray overcoat was buttoned against the deepening cold. He eyed his hair and beard; everything looked good, so he exited his car.

There was a large glass door leading to the entrance of Infusion Lounge. Vince paused by it, reached into his breast pocket and pulled out a pair of black designer shades. He donned them, checked to make sure his sight was completely impaired, and slowly went inside.

The warmth and sounds assaulted him. He stopped as soon as he felt the door shut behind him. There was music—acid jazz that invaded his senses, up-tempo bass lines, funky synths that gave it a kind of techno groove. Vince moved his head slowly to the beat while his body remained motionless, the cane steady by his side. He could hear bits and pieces of conversations—a table of women directly to his right, black women, there was no doubt about that. A smattering of talk to his left also, yet most of the chatter came directly from in front of him. The bar area, from what he remembered when he did his quick drive-by.

Someone came up to him and touched his elbow.

"Hello," a warm, friendly female voice said. "Welcome to Infusion Lounge. Do you need, ah, a table?"

Vince smiled and nodded. "Yes, that would be nice. I'm supposed to be meeting someone here, but don't seem to *see* her."

There was a short pause.

"That was a joke," Vince said, softly, leaning in the direction of the woman. He grinned, and heard her laugh. "Can you assist me? I'm *blind*."

"Of course," the woman said quickly. "We have tables both here and upstairs. Do you have a preference?"

"Not really. I'm feeling the music, so wherever I can hear it best," he said. The woman took Vince by the arm and led him forward.

"Let me take you upstairs then. The live band's there."

"Wonderful," Vince said. "Lead on, pretty lady." Vince could sense her smile.

He was led past the bar, up the stairs, and then reversing direction toward the front of the building.

"I've never been here before," Vince said to the woman.

"Oh, you'll really like it. We're actually well known for our signature cocktails, and we have the best martinis this side of the Mississippi, if I may say so myself."

"I hear that."

"And I think you'll like the band. They're a combination of neo-soul, smooth jazz, and spoken word. They're called The Verve."

"Sounds good," Vince exclaimed.

The band, Vince could tell was positioned in front of him. He was led to a table off to the left side of the stage. The woman helped him into his seat and bent close to his ear. "Your waitress will be with you shortly. I hope you enjoy your evening."

"Thank you for your kindness," Vince responded, glancing up in her direction.

Vince sat back into his chair and concentrated on his surroundings. It was extremely difficult not being able to see . . . he, like most people, took for granted being able to use his visual faculties to their fullest. But tonight he would be forced to refocus his energy into what was left of his available senses—his touch, his hearing, and his smell. It would be difficult. Just walking past the bar and up the stairs took effort. He was conscious of every step he made, cautious not to bump into anyone, or hit them with his cane. He found that he was already mentally tired, his brain being forced to process much more data than normally, and from less used sources—the other senses abruptly tuned up high.

A waitress brushed past his shoulder. He could sense her standing on his right. Vince glanced up, not being able to see a thing in front of him.

"What can I get you?" she asked, her voice a deeper, richer sound than the first woman who had led him here.

"I hear you've got great martinis."

"We do indeed."

"Can you make a mean apple martini?" he asked.

"Trust me, ours are the best! You won't be disappointed."

"Then I'll take one."

The music was rising as a keyboard solo went into overdrive. Vince bopped his head to the beat. He loved listening to live music. He loved the energy. Too bad that tonight he couldn't watch the band do their thing . . .

His drink arrived five minutes later. The waitress put it down beside him. Vince glanced up. "Tell me your name," he asked.

"It's Nechelle."

"Pretty name, Nechelle. I'm Vince. Listen I'm supposed to be meeting a woman here, her name is Raven. She has long dark hair, very striking. If you spot her, can you send her my way?"

"I'd be delighted to."

The waitress left and Vince tasted his drink. Damn good!

He detected shadows and slivers of light that seeped into the sides of his glasses. Vince glanced left then right as the music died and claps erupted around him. He joined in, moving his head to try and discern the shapes and patterns that hovered around his head. There was hushed conversation around him; his senses clearly picked up the clanking of bottles and glasses; chairs being scuffed along the hard floor. The scent of apples was strong, as was something light and perfumed. Vince took it all in, amazed at how much one could pick up if you just concentrated on the senses available to you.

The music began again. A slow, steady groove, this time, just drum and bass. Vince turned his attention toward the source. Folks around him began to clap in time to the beat. He took another sip of his martini, placed his glass down and joined in. A woman began to sing. Her voice was sweet, low pitched, and pure. It reminded him of India Arie. He leaned forward, concentrating on the sound. She wasn't speaking any words, but just scatting along with the melody, her voice like a surfboard, riding the wave, the highs and lows, and Vince was tempted to yank off his glasses and peer out at this woman, but fought the urge to do so. What did she look like? If her voice was any indication, she was a goddess . . .

The music shifted, abruptly upbeat as the rest of the band joined in, and suddenly the woman was rapping, her voice lifting up above the din of the music—sharp lyrics talking about strong black women, the foundation of the family. Folks were yelling as if in church. Vince was moved. He smiled to no one in particular. Cocking his head to the side, Vince suddenly realized something.

The voice on stage was familiar. Very familiar. Could that be Raven up there?

Vince fought the urge to peek above his shades.

The music downshifted and slowed, and the woman's voice became soft and light again. This time she began to sing, and Vince was blown away by the purity of her voice. Like others around him, he was mesmerized by her song. When she was done, the crowd erupted with thunderous applause, and Vince found himself out of his chair and standing, not sure if he was the only one giving her and the band a standing ovation or not, but not caring what others around him thought. He was moved, and he wanted this woman and the band to know it.

As the applause died, smooth jazz came on, while the band took their break. Vince sat down, gingerly feeling his way across the table for his drink. He took a sip, realizing that his martini glass was empty. He felt something between his lips, reached for it and mouthed the sweet cherry, swallowing it down heartily.

"Is this seat taken?" a soft, sensuous voice asked.

"That depends," Vince responded with a tilt of his head. "I'm actually saving this seat for a very beautiful woman. So," Vince said, with a smile, "are you beautiful?"

"You tell me."

"Well," he said, straightening up, "we'll have to see . . . sit down for a moment, please."

The scent of perfume wafted over him. The woman leaned close, something of hers brushing against Vince's forearm. "So, what do you think?"

Vince's hands crept over the table surface until he found her arm. He traced a finger along her skin toward her wrist. When he came to her hand he took it in his. Then he began moving his hands up her bare forearms feeling her skin on his fingers. She did not resist his touch.

"Nice skin," he said, leaning toward her. "Let's see about the rest of you . . ."

Vince grinned. His fingers reached her shoulders, feeling the fabric soft underneath his touch. Using both hands, he reached for her clavicles, and followed the contours of her neck upward until he came to her face. His fingers traced the outline of her jaw and chin, glazing over the soft tissue of her mouth. Remembering Raven when she visited him for the first time at his studio, he touched the flesh of her lips, feeling her upswept smile.

Moving upward, he ran a finger over the bridge of her nose, cheekbones, and eyes, upward still, tracing the crease in her forehead.

The waitress arrived, touching his shoulder. Vince turned his head to her, but did not take his hands away from the woman beside him.

"Nechelle, I'll take another apple martini. And whatever this lovely young lady desires."

"The same."

Vince heard her footfalls as she moved away.

"Reached any conclusions?" the seated woman asked.

"Too early to tell. I mean, you are indeed beautiful, that much is clear—but whether or not you're the one I'm looking for remains to be seen."

"Oh really?"

"Don't take it personal, but I am waiting for someone special . . ."

"And just who is this chick, the object of your affection and attention?"

"Are you listening to me?" Vince mused. "I know you hear me, but are you actually *listening*?" Vince grinned.

"I see . . ."

His hands reached the top of her head, gliding over hair, smooth and silky. Downward, a single, thick braid ran halfway down her back.

"Ummmn," Vince moaned, "very nice."

"So can I stay?"

"Answer a question first? Was that you up on stage? Tell me that sultry, sexy voice belongs to you."

She leaned closer, taking his hands in hers, fingers interlocking.

"You're very perceptive. I dig that."

Vince smiled. "One of my many talents."

"And the others?" She leaned in, close enough for Vince to feel her breath on his neck. Her perfume invaded his olfactory senses, causing him to inhale deeply. His fingers rested in hers, both sets of hands lying on her lap. Vince could feel the warmth of her skin radiating into his.

Chemistry . . .

"Well, let's see . . ."

Vince's mind raced back to the conversation he had shared with Trey. He could hear him now—take charge, bruh, be completely in control, and above all else, take no prisoners . . .

"I've been told," Vince said, with a sly grin, "that my tongue possesses a mind of its own."

"You don't say?"

"I do."

Vince released his fingers from hers and traced the contours of her legs downward, cupping her calves in his hands, feeling the power contained there.

"A good-looking man with a talented tongue—damn, I'm sure you're in demand."

"Naw, it ain't like that. I have an exacting palate. It's very particular about who and what I eat . . ."

"I see."

"Nice legs, by the way. Well toned, but not too muscular. I like that."

"I'm glad you approve."

"Let's review—you're a beautiful woman, obviously talented. So, I guess you can stay . . ."

"Thank goodness."

"Tell me. Is singing your main profession?" Vince asked.

"Like you, I've got many talents . . ."

Vince smirked. "I'm sure you do."

She leaned closer, taking his head in her hands, and kissed Vince gingerly on the mouth.

When she pulled back a moment later, Vince asked, "What was that for?"

She replied, "For being *unconventional* . . ."

Raven led Vince outside. The cold assaulted them, and they reached to each other for warmth.

"Take the glasses off." It was a command, issued without malice.

Vince had no problem complying. He stared at her for a moment, not saying anything, reveling in the closeness that they shared. Her eyes sparkled, and her hair shined, even in the streetlights of evening.

Raven was draped in a luxurious fur coat that hung inches from the ground. It was thick-haired and deep brown. Vince estimated its worth fifteen thousand dollars *minimum*.

"It's good to see you again," he said softly.

"It is good to be seen," she replied, reaching for his arm and wrapping hers in his. "There's someplace I want to take you to. Since we're in this mode of thinking outside of the box, and on this grand adventure."

"I'm game wherever you take me."

Twenty minutes later he parked on a side street and followed Raven for a short walk. They came to a building with a neon sign in the window announcing live dancers. Vince glanced at Raven who merely smiled as she paused in her step so Vince could get the door.

The interior of the club was small, but cozy. It actually had atmosphere. Vince had been to a number of strip clubs in his day, but this was a first. Missing was that seedy, almost dirty feel—this place had class. Most of the thirty or so patrons were seated at low couches or on love seats. There was actually art on the walls. Funky music emanated from ceiling hung speakers.

"This your day job?" Vince asked jokingly.

"You wish." They found an empty couch with a low coffee table positioned in front. They sat and glanced around. There were a few other couples enjoying the show. A number of women, clad in various stages of undress, meandered through the crowd, talking to patrons. Vince spied the main stage, up front, a raised square platform with mirrors behind and on the ceiling. A tall, thin, dark-skinned woman gyrated her hips to 50 Cent, "In Da Club." She was fully nude, and her body was exceptional.

A waitress came and they ordered a round of Coronas. Raven sat back and glanced at Vince.

"You gonna keep that coat on all night?" he asked.

Raven smiled, her lips curving upward into a sensuous grin. She removed her coat and Vince's eyes almost popped out of their sockets.

She wore a black with white trim half shirt and matching panties. The top was stretched across her breasts, displaying perky nipples underneath. The panties were tight and short, baring ample amounts of flesh. Vince looked her over. Her stomach was flat, and her legs shined. Vince was speechless.

"You don't mind, do you?"

"You're kidding, right?" he responded, moving closer until their shoulders touched. "Damn, woman, you are fine!"

"Thank you."

Her eyes flirted over to the patrons, and observed the other dancers for a moment. A few had taken to dancing on the low tables in front of the patrons. Vince watched Raven silently. He sensed something in her, a bit of anxiety mixed with excitement.

"Everything okay?" he asked.

"Everything's cool." The beers arrived, and Raven took a long swig.

"You sure?" he asked, eying her as she took another wild gulp.

Her eyes sparkled as she nodded. Placing the bottle down, she stood up, pressing her hands to her torso and stomach. Vince couldn't help but admire her beauty. She placed one pump-clad foot on the coffee table and reached out with her hand. Vince leaned forward, taking her hand as she climbed up, using him for support. Raven glanced down at him and smiled. Vince was in shock.

The music shifted, 50 Cent to Beyonce, as Raven began

to move. There may have been other activity going on in the club, but at that exact moment, no one seemed to notice. It was as if all attention had shifted to Raven. Vince could feel the temperature change. Conversation had been cut short that quickly!

Raven began a slow dance, moving her hips seductively as her arms went over her head. Eyes closed, head angled upward, she moved not like a stripper, but a woman who was in tune with her sexuality, enjoying the thrill that one receives from displaying her wares for all those hungry to see. Vince was alive. Although she hadn't removed anything yet, he was thoroughly enjoying the scene unfolding before him.

A brunette with fake breasts and an assuming smile came up to the table, holding something in her hand. Raven glanced downward and smiled; the woman reached for her ankle and slipped a lacy garter belt up to her thigh. She then placed two crisp dollar bills between the lace and her skin. They exchanged a few words that were lost on Vince. As she moved away, Vince stood, reaching for his wallet.

Slipping a twenty into her garter belt, Vince stood back and enjoyed the show. Raven pirouetted on her high heels, giving him her back. She tilted her head upwards, letting her hair free fall down her back. Vince marveled at the sculpted back muscles that led to a perfectly shaped ass. Orbs of flesh peeked out from the edges of the fabric; she spun around before he could study it further, and moved in, until mere inches separated them. Raven flipped her hair forward, letting it fall over Vince's head and face. He glanced upward, their eyes and smiles locked.

"Enjoying the show?" Raven asked seductively.

"More than you know . . ."

"Should I keep going?" she asked, her hands gliding over her breasts and resting at the bottom edge of her top.

"Only if you want to."

Raven smiled. "I'm feeling particularly *frisky* tonight . . ."

"Then do your thang, girl. No one here is mad at you, least of all me!"

Raven turned away from him, and Vince sucked in a breath as her arms crossed over her stomach and in an instant her top was lifting up over her head. She glanced back, eyes sparkling, teeth flashing before she turned, and Vince got to see her in all of her unadulterated loveliness.

Her breasts were solid orbs of jiggling flesh that shook as she moved. Vince resisted the urge to reach for them. It was something he wanted to do very badly. Instead he sat back down.

Immediately, a graying man in his fifties approached the table. He smiled up at Raven, words were spoken, and he handed a folded bill to her. She curtsied and placed the bill in her belt.

More patrons lined up. Vince smiled at Raven as her eyes widened for a brief moment before tending patiently to each customer. For some she held on to their shoulder as she waved her hair in their faces, for others she presented them with her ass inches from their face.

After about fifteen minutes, Raven had a nice wad of cash protruding from the lace around one thigh. Vince stood again, the table finally to himself, and approached Raven. The music shifted from hip-hop to reggae. The thumping bass lines were hitting Vince squarely in his chest. Raven held onto his shoulders as she gazed downwards. Her nipples were hard, a thin sheen of sweat adorned her skin. Vince couldn't remember being more turned on.

He sucked in a breath and exhaled forcefully.

"Take your panties off," he said surely. He eyed her; unblinking as she stared back.

A moment passed.

Then another.

Slowly, methodically, she slid down her panties while Vince remained inches away from the core of her sexuality, the place where toned thighs came together, a half-inch thick track of pubic hair on otherwise shaved skin. Without thought, Vince licked his lips. He glanced up, smiling, before returning his gaze to her sex. Raven backed away, fully nude now, the music infusing renewed passion and energy into her being.

She spun on her heels, and bent over, her ass and thighs a mastery of craftsmanship. She spread her legs slightly, and Vince sucked in a breath, marveling at her bare sex and the rest of her package, a work of art that spoke to him with her pure lines and soft curves.

Vince turned to see a throng of patrons, folded bills in hand lining up. He sighed as he returned to his seat, thankful for being able to hide his growing erection.

Thirty minutes later when Raven stepped down and donned her clothes she had earned slightly fewer than four hundred dollars.

Vince grinned as she sat back, their shoulders touching as she placed a cold Corona to her lips and chugged the entire bottle.

Vince placed his hand on her thigh and whispered in her ear.

"That was truly incredible. You are incredible."

She turned to him and grinned.

"I can't believe I actually went through with it. I've wanted to do that for so long, but never could summon the nerve until tonight."

"What changed?"

"Seeing you in Infusion tonight. You were unconventional. Never in my wildest dreams did I think you'd come up with what you did."

"You said, 'think outside of the box . . .'"

"You amazed me," she said, her hair falling onto his shoulder. Vince made no effort to move away.

"The feeling is very much mutual, I assure you." Vince downed his beer. "Listen, as much as I love watching you, I'm tired of sharing your beauty with these other patrons. Let's get out of here—call me selfish, but I want you all to myself!"

Raven stood and donned her fur coat as the graying gentleman returned.

"Leaving so soon, Miss?" he asked, clutching a sheaf of bills in his hand.

Vince stood, taking her hand.

"Show's over, my man. Thank you for your patronage . . ."

Raven grinned as the gentleman handed her the bills; she stuffed them into her purse; all eyes were upon them as Vince led the elusive dancer from the club.

They were silent as Vince drove. It was a quarter past one in the morning. The heat was turned up high; the volume in the car on low.

An old Joe Sample song was playing. Raven closed her eyes briefly and let the melody carry her.

"Where to, sexy lady?" Vince asked, breaking the silence.

"Turn right at the next light."

"Cool." Vince's mind whirled. He wondered where this evening would lead. Raven was subdued, and that worried him. He wasn't sure if it was the lateness of the night or something else.

"Another right," she said.

Vince steered his car up Chestnut Street as directed. They went three-quarters up the block before Raven said: "Pull up in front of that awning."

Vince did as he was told.

He put the car in park and glanced to his left. The Omni was a five-star hotel in the midst of Society Hill not far from Independence Hall and the river.

Raven was stepping out of the car as a bellhop approached Vince's window.

"Checking in, Sir?"

Vince glanced quickly between him and Raven, who turned to the man and said cheerfully, "Room 1004."

The bellhop nodded as Raven took to the revolving doors, escaping the cold quickly as Vince followed mutely.

The ornate foyer was desolate of people this time of night. Off to the left, behind the registration desk, a lone attendant nodded to Vince. Raven's heels echoed on cold marble as she walked ahead of him. She cut to the right, toward a bank of elevators. Vince caught up as the doors hissed open.

"Everything okay?" he asked, when they were safely inside. Raven, who was clutching her fur with one hand, let it fall open. She smiled at him.

"Why wouldn't it be?" she replied with a devilish grin.

Vince exhaled, feeling his heart beat loudly in his chest. "You were incredible tonight. I don't think I've ever been more impressed."

Raven eyed him curiously but said nothing. She turned to the elevator controls and their reflection that shone back at them from the mirrored doors. Her hand reached up, pressing a button, and the elevator jolted to a stop. Vince felt his heart flutter as Raven turned to him. She took a step forward.

"I'm feeling *unconventional* right about now. How about you?" Before Vince could respond, her lips were pressed onto his, their mouths opening in unison as tongues fluttered against each other for the very first time. Vince reached for her, wrapping an arm around her body and pulling her to him. She let out a gasp as their bodies connected. His hands went to her face, grasping her gingerly as he kissed her ravenously, as if they were lovers reunited after a very long stay apart. Vince pulled back, holding her at arms' length as he stared at her longingly.

"You are so beautiful," he said, and he kissed her again. Slipping out of his coat, he let it fall to the floor. Raven backed up, Vince interlocked his fingers in hers, and their arms rose over her head as they bumped into the elevator wall. He released her, his hands finding her waist, and moving upward, following her curves until his fingers slipped underneath the fabric of her top, gliding over smooth flat meadows until he reached her mountainous breasts. Palming them gently, he squeezed her lovely mounds while Raven groaned.

Vince attached her neck, first kissing, then sucking at the flesh of her clavicle, as one hand snaked down her torso and stomach. Downward it went, slipping underneath the fabric of her panties, until his fingers felt the rising flesh of her clit. Downward still, his fingers spread over her pubic hair and lips of her sex, before curling upward, finding her center, wet to his touch.

"Oh God!" Raven whispered, clutching at his neck as their mouths attacked each other. Panties slid down her thighs, her top bunched up until Vince retreated backwards to view her in all of her magnificence.

Bending forward, Vince traced a line of wet kisses from her neck on down until he reached the top of her breast. He cupped each one in hand, circling the rising flesh with his wet tongue, before taking each nipple in his mouth, biting down lightly, tugging at each one in a teasing kind of manner, as Raven moaned and grasped his head tightly, scrunching her eyes shut in tortuous pleasure.

His tongue meandered downward—circling her navel, painting a decreasingly wide swath until he met her sex, probing the hole lightly with a curled tongue.

Raven was a snake wriggling with delight as Vince kneeled down on his coat. Grasping her ankles, he ran his fingers lightly upwards to the top of her thighs before quickly retreating the way he came, stroking her flesh with his fingernails. Vince moved his palms to her inner ankles and applied pressure, gently spreading her legs, before beginning his upstroke with his digits, but this time on the insides of her legs. His fingers traveled until they met at the apex of where her legs came together, that lovely spot of flesh that Vince drew himself to. Placing one hand on her pussy, Vince spread his fingers, and without fanfare, bent in, his tongue connecting with her gaping chasm as he sucked her into his waiting mouth in one giant gulp.

Raven clutched at his head and moaned as Vince fed, licking the lips of her sex and clit before swirling his tongue between her fleshes in a frenzy of activity that left Raven dizzy. He glanced upwards and smiled, his tongue still connected to her saliva-coated clit, tickling it before swooping down, probing her insides deeply as he heard Raven gasp.

"Oh God, that tongue, yes! Don't stop," she moaned. Vince moved backwards, pulling her with him until he was prone atop his coat on the elevator floor, while Raven knelt over his face. He reached for her ass, took hold of her cheeks and forced them apart while sticking his nose into the interior of her cunt. He thrashed his head back and forth, side to side, his nose, lips, and teeth connecting with her wet pussy lips and engorged clit. He felt her spasm, as Raven sucked in a breath, clenching her thighs around his ears.

Vince continued his feeding without let-up, briefly allowing thoughts of Trey to bubble to the surface. Lord, his boy would be damn proud of him, if only he could witness him in action this very minute. The thought remained uncompleted, because Raven grabbed his hair, digging her fingernails into his scalp.

Vince spread her ass further apart, clutching at her flesh and pulling her downward as his tongue arced upward, slicing against the twitching opening of her anus. As his tongue flashed against it, Raven shuddered; her thighs tightened then opened. Vince curled his tongue and darted it against the puckered opening. Raven screamed: a short, high-pitched yell that reverberated along the steel walls of the elevator car.

Making his tongue flat, Vince licked her lengthwise, anus to pussy, and pussy back to anus, hearing her shriek and feeling her explode against his mouth with a force that pushed him into the car floor. Yet he held on, squeezing her ass cheeks and taking her drenched lips between his teeth, slurping her sex into his mouth before turning attention to her clit and stimulating it with his teeth, gums, and frenzied tongue.

Her syrup oozed, warm and sticky on his face. After one final shudder that ended with Raven falling on top of him, exhausted, Vince reached for her breasts and tugged at her nipples, feeling the last of her orgasmic wave subside. After what seemed like several minutes of minimal silence and movement, save for the rise and fall of her breasts on his stomach, her head resting in the cleft of his thighs, his penis fully engorged and waiting to be unsheathed, Raven stirred. Silently, she unzipped him, extracting his thick member from the confines of his pants as Vince let his head fall to the floor. His eyes were unfocused as he glanced upwards, past the curves of her ass, and dabs of love juice that was drying on her inner thighs. Vince sucked in a breath as Raven took him into her mouth, licking the shaft with her hot tongue as Vince squeezed his eyes tight, and tried to slow his breathing.

Fingers wrapped themselves around his meat, jerking up and down methodically as she took him deeper into her mouth. Vince fought the rising tide within as he felt the first inklings of an orgasm begin deep in his belly. He desperately wanted to implant himself inside of the sweetness he had just tasted, entomb his cock in her tight little sex, fuck her from behind in the elevator of this five-star Omni. Vince longed to bend Raven over as her lovely ass cheeks quivered, his member slipping in and out of her rapidly, dizzying her (and him) with the intensity of his love making.

But it was not meant to be!

Vince groaned, feeling the dam burst, as he erupted into Raven's waiting mouth, trying as hard as he could to hold out, attempting to command his body to yield.

But Raven was too good, her mouth a lovely cavern that fit him like a form-fitting glove. Raven moaned, feeling Vince shudder underneath her. Vince shouted, "Oh God!" as every fiber of his being tightened simultaneously, and his toes, without being told, curled back like a wicked grin.

When he was done, when Vince was completely spent, he opened his eyes, as she rose, smiling as she came to him, her mouth an expanding orifice as their tongues intertwined. After a minute, Raven pulled back and stood up, releasing the STOP button as the car jerked upwards in sudden movement.

"*Unconventional,*" she whispered as the elevator chimed; the doors opened and Raven strode out, a satisfied smile adorning her pretty face.

Vince remained for a moment more on the floor before springing to his feet, grabbing his coat, and exiting the car. Raven sauntered down the hotel corridor naked, her decadent fur dragging on the floor behind her, Raven's bare ass and hips shaking seductively as she moved. When she had gone twenty yards, Raven turned her head back and smiled, a grin so hyper erotic that Vince found himself growing hard again. She glanced down at his crotch and then back up at him, winked as she curled her finger beckoning him near. In that second, as Vince began to move, the elevator doors snapped shut behind him . . .

Nine

They were led to a quiet table in the back, away from the din of the bar. Erika was grateful. She beamed at Naomi, while removing her coat and handing it to the maitre d'.

Two weeks into the New Year. They were dining at D.C. Coast, an upscale restaurant located at K and 14th Streets.

"Girl, you look *good*!" Erika exclaimed, while wiping flakes of moisture from her hair. A thin layer of snow blanketed the streets, making driving conditions hazardous. It always amazed Erika how a little bit of snow could shut down this metropolitan city.

Naomi grinned while smoothing back her short brown locks. She crossed her legs and folded her hands on the table. "Thank you, Erika—you ain't looking half bad yourself!"

"Please, this do is tired, ya hear me? I need to do something with it."

"Well, you could always cut it all off like I did!"

"Girl, I'm too scared to try that. But it looks damn good on you." Erika glanced at the menu. "Seriously though, you've got a glow to you, sistah. What are you doing? Getting some on the regular?"

"Please, I wish!" Naomi exclaimed. "Just the opposite with me," she said softly.

"What do you mean?"

"Well, I told you the last time we hooked up that Michael and I had broken up."

"Yeah," Erika said, "I'm sorry to hear that."

"Don't be. That sorry specimen of a man was cheating on me—says he wasn't but you know what? I don't have time for that mess—having other women calling his cell or texting him at all hours of the night. I'm too old to be putting up with that shit!"

"I hear you, girl."

"I decided that it was time to focus on me—make me the number one priority instead of these crazy-ass dudes out here."

Erika nodded.

"It's only been a month or so, but I feel wonderful. I'm focusing on my relationship with God; I joined a gym, and am working out on the regular. And, check this out, I joined this really cool book club, and am taking an art history class!"

"A what?"

"You heard me right: an art history class. I wanted to stay busy and keep myself focused. So I signed up for this class. It's something I've always wanted to learn about, so I said, why not go for it. Let me tell you, girl, I love it! I spend my weekends going around town taking in the various museums, checking out the works of the Masters—it's intense."

"Dayum!"

"Yeah, it's all that. And this book club is the bomb. It's a bunch of professional sistahs who meet every few weeks to talk about black literature. Not this ghetto fabulous drama that's out there, but real literature. Like Baldwin, Toomer, and Hurston."

"Wow. Well, you're doing your thing, girl, and it shows, cause you got this serious glow going on. You look rested and refreshed," Erika said.

"Thank you. I feel good. I'm putting it all into perspective—men are wonderful, but you've got to keep your priorities straight. Too many of us get it twisted and forget what's really important. We run ourselves ragged trying to keep our men so damn happy, that we lose a piece of ourselves in the process."

"I hear that!"

"So, what's new with you? I take it that you and James are still together?"

Erika nodded solemnly.

The waitress arrived with drinks. Naomi ordered the Caesar salad topped with grilled shrimp, Erika the broiled Atlantic salmon.

"Do tell . . . ," Naomi encouraged.

Erika sighed. "Where do I begin?" She paused to sip at her chocolate martini, grimaced, and pushed the glass away. "Honestly, Naomi, I feel funny talking about it, because I'm not sure if I shouldn't be feeling this way."

"What do you mean?"

"Well, I've told you before about what's up."

"You mean about the sex?"

"Yeah—James is a wonderful man. And we have fun together. I shouldn't be complaining at all. So many women would give their left breast to be in my shoes. With a fine man like that? Shoot!"

"Looks ain't everything, you know."

"I know."

"Are things improving—in the bedroom?" Naomi asked.

"I don't know. I guess I'm having fun, but each time we make love and he doesn't come, it becomes even more difficult for me to relax and enjoy myself. I'm lying there, enjoying the sensations, but in the back of my mind, I can't help but wondering if he's going to come tonight. It preoccupies my mind and frankly, now it's beginning to interfere with *me* coming!"

"That's not good."

Erika shook her head.

"Then a few weeks ago, he comes over, I'm taking a bath, and he storms in with my favorite dildo in his hand, freaking out and whatnot! 'What the freak are you doing with this? Why do you need this?' he yells. 'I'm not enough?' Girl—I told him to get the hell out of my damn apartment!"

"Good for you. The boy shouldn't be rifling through your shit anyway. Serves his ass right for finding it!"

"Yup. But then he breaks down and tells me how much he loves me; how he's afraid of losing me . . ."

"Damn . . . ," Naomi said, shaking her head.

"Yeah, damn is right. I mean, I dig James. He's a cool dude. We are having fun together. I'm comfortable with him. But lately, I can't help thinking about our relationship. I've been wondering if I'm being too judgmental—no one is perfect, right? Women spend half their lives looking for Mr. Right. Well, perhaps James is Mr. Right, imperfections and all, and I'm just being unreasonable, insisting that my man be perfect, when I'm not."

Naomi nodded. "On the other hand, some imperfections are deal breakers. Some quirks you just can't get past. Only you can decide if James is one of those men."

"I know. Am I being too persnickety? I mean, who has a perfect relationship without issues? Every woman I know complains on some level about her man and his shit. Everyone!"

"Right."

"And what if I let James go because of his 'sexual' problems and then regret it. I mean, another man of James' caliber may not come along anytime soon, if ever."

"True," Naomi said. "I guess you need to just weigh both sides carefully. And take your time—cause you don't need to rush things . . . especially when it comes to love."

"I wish that were true," Erika said. "But James is bugging me every other day. Calling me, e-mailing me, wanting to know how I feel. You know how it is when one person says 'I love you' and the other one remains silent . . ."

"Yeah I do."

The food arrived. Erika was grateful for the lapse so she could collect her thoughts. She told the waitress to take away her chocolate martini and bring her an apple one. So much for daring to be different!

Erika took a bite of the salmon. It was delicious. Naomi attacked her salad with zeal.

"I just wish I could figure this shit out, girl!" Erika exclaimed. "It's driving me crazy."

"I know, but don't let it. You'll figure out what's best, in time," she said, patting her hand.

"Yeah, but in the meantime, it's bugging me big time!" She glanced up. "Can't I just get a sign? God, can't you show me the way to go?" she asked, gazing upward to the ceiling. "Is that asking too much? 'Cause I sure could use your counsel right now . . ."

I heard the sharp rap at the door, and glanced up from working on my brief. That's when Bernard John Marshall waltzed in. I set down my fountain pen with an audible sigh.

"Bernard," I said, not wanting to deal with his shit first thing this morning.

"Trey. I have an assignment for you," he said, without preamble.

I stared at this mutha sucka in his starched white button down shirt, yellow and blue striped power tie, hair wet with that slick-back shit he uses too much of, and let my expression remain flat and emotionless, not wanting him to sense my discontentment.

"I need you to meet with a client in New York. Day after tomorrow."

I didn't even blink.

"Can't, Bernie, I've got a deposition scheduled for Thursday at—"

"Cancel it."

"That's not how I do business—"

"Counselor, this isn't a request and I'm not seeking your permission!" He stood, smoothed out his slacks and turned for the door. "India has the details. I'll expect a full brief on your return." He reached the door and placed a hand on the knob. "This is an important client, Mr. Alexander. I'll expect your best work on this one."

"Last time I checked, we didn't have offices in New York City."

Bernard sighed. "I'll see you back here on Friday."

"Yessah mastah," I hissed.

Bernard turned.

"What did you say?" he barked.

I blinked but said nothing.

"You are this close," he said, showing me a quarter inch between thumb and forefinger, "from disciplinary action. Keep it up, counselor, and I will personally have the pleasure of escorting you from this office . . ."

The door slammed shut and I sat there, shaking my head morosely.

*　*　*

The flight to LaGuardia was uneventful. Left on time, arrived on time.

Imagine that!

I grabbed my garment bag and laptop, left the terminal quickly, and hailed a taxi for the thirty-five minute ride into mid-town Manhattan. India had booked a room for me at the Marriott in Times Square. She had contacted the client, and made arrangements for her to meet me at the hotel for a breakfast meeting at ten. I glanced at my Breitling. Plenty of time to check in and even relax for a few minutes before we got started.

I recounted the conversation I had had with Calvin the previous evening. I had phoned him, pissed about my trip to New York, this interruption to my schedule, and the general way Bernard's style of micro-*fucking* management was creeping into my personal life.

Calvin counseled me to chill.

"Trey, I told you, you need to relax and stay focused. This guy is gunning for you; so don't give him the satisfaction of seeing you angry. That's what he wants—he desires to see you all up in a tizzy. So don't feed into it."

I grunted.

"Besides, is New York so bad? We all could use a diversion every so often. Think of this as a mini-vacation. You get out of here for a quick minute, you get to stay in a posh hotel on the firm's nickel—hell, go have a great dinner, take in a show or something, and come back refreshed, with a new attitude."

I grunted again . . .

"Trey, you need to stop letting him get to you. Here is my advice: Screw Bernard John Marshall and the horse he rode in on . . . forget about him and move on with your life . . ."

I smiled at the thought of Calvin Figgs, Esq., and Extraordinaire, cursing my boss' name. It made me feel better. Calvin was right. New York wasn't so bad. Hell, there was always something to do in this city, even in the midst of winter. Shit, if trouble wasn't around here somewhere, Trey Alexander would find it his damn self!

That's right. Flip the script, make this an outing. I hadn't gotten away from the office in a hot minute anyway. So now was my chance. Take advantage, as Calvin had suggested. Well, take advantage I would. Beginning this minute. Oh hell yeah, y'all!

Less than an hour later I was sitting at a table overlooking Broadway. I had checked in, finished reading the Post, and even watched a few minutes of Live! Kelly & Michael before heading downstairs to the restaurant.

I sipped at my coffee while watching the people meander down the street. Cars and cabs (cabs mostly) whizzed past my view as obscenely large neon signs advertised everything from Calvin Klein underwear to Nike kicks. A folded Times in hand, turned to the sports section, occupied most of my attention. I didn't hear her walk up until she cleared her throat.

"Mr. Alexander?" a sweet voice pronounced.

I placed my paper down and glanced up, almost dropping my cup in my lap.

DAYUM. I stood abruptly.

"Giovanna Marquis?"

"Yes." She smiled briefly. "May I sit down?"

"Of course. Please," I said, gesturing her to the seat across from me. She sat, and folded her legs. Her skin was caramel colored and as smooth as syrup. She wore a dark pinstripe business suit, form-fitting jacket that displayed a hint of shapely cleavage, and a short skirt that showcased lovely long legs. Her hair was dark, and tied up in a bun. Her makeup was flawless. She was in a word, stunning.

My dick was growing hard by the second, and instantly I found myself forgetting about business, instead plotting a way into her soon-to-be-drenched-thanks-to-you-know-who panties.

"Have you been waiting long?" she asked, making eye contact with me. She was so freaking beautiful it almost hurt my eyes to stare back.

But I held her gaze.

"Not really, I checked in about a half-hour ago and just sat down a few minutes ago."

"How was your flight?" she asked while looking over the menu.

"Quick and uneventful. Just the way it's supposed to be." My hand instinctively went to my tie and readjusted the knot. I was so damn thankful for wearing this particular ensemble. Dark gray Italian sports-cut suit, polished shoes, and powder-blue tie! Funky fresh as only yours truly can do . . . I just know this honey was impressed.

The waiter came and we ordered breakfast.

"Where do we start?" she inquired when he had left.

"From the beginning, if you would," I said, all business-like, yet still wondering about how this chick would look straddling my dick. But then, like a blow striking the abdomen, I winced with the thought of Trey's Rules.

Those damn rules . . .

Trey's Rule Number 4—never *ever* fuck a client.

And so far, to date, I hadn't violated that rule. But damn, this chick was so *foine*, I was having trouble just sitting still.

Yet I persevered . . .

"Well, let's see," Giovanna said, "I was married seven years ago. Ali is a high-ranking diplomat working for the Qatar embassy. We separated about two months ago."

"Where were you married?" I asked.

"In Paris."

"And the marriage license is from—"

"New York."

"Go on," I said, reaching for my legal pad so I could scribble some notes.

"We divided our time mostly between New York City and Washington, maintaining two residences, sometimes traveling abroad. Since our separation, I've moved into an apartment on the Upper West Side, and use the Washington home on occasion."

I nodded, as I scribbled. "Have the two of you worked up any agreement concerning division of property?"

Giovanna shook her head.

"Good. Let me handle that. I'll need for you to put together a list of all marital assets and property amassed during the marriage so we can work up something for his attorney. Any idea whom that might be?"

She reached into her purse and pulled out a business card. Giovanna slid it across the table, and I took the opportunity to focus my attention on her slender fingers, nails polished to perfection. I swallowed involuntarily, suppressing the urge to suck those fingers into my waiting mouth.

"Thank you," I said, glancing at the card and copying the information onto my legal pad. "So, you've been together seven years, then you split. Who made the decision?"

"I did."

"And can I assume you are seeking the divorce?"

She nodded.

"How is your husband reacting to all of this?" I asked delicately.

"Not well."

I nodded. "So I can assume he will not react well when we file for divorce?"

"Correct." She stared straight at me, an even expression, devoid of smiles or frowns.

"I can understand that," I replied.

"Why do you say that?" she exclaimed, her shoulders perking up.

My eyes grew wide for a split second. "No reason," I said, blinking. "I didn't mean anything by it."

"You had something on your mind when you uttered those words," she said coolly.

I smiled, holding up my hands as in surrender. "You've misunderstood what I said. I only meant that you're a beautiful woman," I said, flashing her my pearly whites, "and that it is understandable for your husband to be hurt by your actions."

Giovanna sat back, arms folded across her chest as she glared at me. Suddenly I realized that things were not going well, and I couldn't, for the life of me, understand why.

"So, let me understand you," she replied. "You've known me for all of what—five minutes, you've never laid eyes on my husband, yet you profess to understand how he must have felt after I left him? That doesn't make sense."

"No, no, Mrs. Marquis—I didn't mean any disrespect. This is a difficult time—"

"Please, Mr. Alexander, don't patronize me. I know first-hand how difficult divorce can be. Can we get back on track?

"Of course," I said, swallowing hard. "You are seeking to dissolve your marriage because of—?"

"I am no longer in love with my husband, Mr. Alexander. I was once, but not anymore. Therefore, I see no reason for the continued charade." Her eyes were brown unblinking orbs. I stared, unmoving for a moment before nodding quietly.

"Okay. Let's move on. Tell me, do you work? Any income?"

"No, Mr. Alexander, I do not work. I haven't since college."

I nodded and made a few notes. "So, I can assume we will be asking for alimony since—"

"That won't be necessary."

I looked up, pen poised above the yellow paper of my pad.

"And why not?" I asked, cocking my head to the side and eyeing her curiously.

"Because my family comes from wealth. So money is not the issue here."

"Okay," I said. I put my pen down and held both elbows close to my chest.

"Mrs. Marquis, I think we have gotten off on the wrong foot. I want to apologize for that." I stared hard at her eyes. "I want to be your attorney, and I want you to get everything that you deserve. To do that, we need to trust in each other and feel comfortable together."

She nodded but said nothing.

"I don't know what you've heard about me, but I am a damn good attorney. Divorce is all that I do—call it a specialty. I've handled all kind of clients from—"

"Mr. Alexander, let me stop you right there," Giovanna said, holding up a chiseled hand. "There is no need for you to relate the details of your accomplishments, for I can assure you that they are already known to me." She smiled, I think for the first time since we got started, and I felt my face flush.

"Alrighty then. What I'm trying to say, Mrs. Marquis, is that I don't want this to feel forced. I want you to relax and feed me any pertinent details about your married life and the financial situation of you and your husband, so that I can do the best job I can for you."

"I have no doubt in your abilities, Mr. Alexander, or you wouldn't be here . . ." she said, cracking a slight grin.

I smiled back. Thank you, Lord! There's hope yet for getting into those panties.

"Okay!" I sighed heavily while picking up my pen. "So tell me, Mrs. Marquis, what is it that you want out of this divorce?"

Giovanna glanced toward the window for a second, lost in thought. Even in profile this woman was beautiful. I rubbed my thighs together, attempting without success to quell the sexual tension I was feeling.

"I want my freedom back. I've been restrained for far too long. I don't like the way it makes me feel. It isn't me, Mr. Alexander. Can you understand that?"

"Yes," I replied, giving her my rapt attention, "of course I can." I have to confess that my "darker" side was thinking— if it's release you want, baby, come on upstairs to my room right now—I will set your sexy ass free!

"Material things are not important to me," she said, continuing. "We amassed some items of value during the marriage that I'd like to keep. I'm unsure about the properties and how they should be handled. I'm moving permanently to Washington, but have no desire to live in our home there."

"That's fine," I said, as thoughts of seeing Giovanna back on my home turf expanded my insides with desire. "I'll need a list of marital property so we can go over that. Item values, as best you can determine them, and all relevant information so that I can proceed." Giovanna nodded. "How quickly can you put this together?"

"How long are you in town?"

"I return to Washington tomorrow."

"Then I'll have it ready in the morning." She pulled out a day timer and jotted down some notes.

"Wonderful," I replied, "I'm looking forward to working with you." She nodded. "I'll try to make this as painless as possible, so you can get on track with your life . . . get your freedom back." I flashed a smile, and she returned a weak one.

The food arrived. We ate silently. My attempt at small talk was rebutted by more silence. Giovanna answered my questions, but didn't volunteer anything further. I was, in a word, perplexed. Frankly, I wasn't used to fine-ass, soon-to-be-single women acting this way toward me. I was getting restless, wanting something to kick-start this thing between us into high gear. But it wasn't going to happen . . . not today anyway.

Giovanna pushed her half-eaten fruit plate away and dabbed her lips with a silk napkin.

I finished my omelet and took another sip of coffee before putting my mug down.

"Mrs. Marquis, can I get your contact information? I'm here the rest of the day and am anxious to begin working on your case. If something occurs to me, I'd like to be able to reach you."

She reached for her purse again and extracted an embossed card.

"You will find all my numbers on there."

"Wonderful," I said, again, taking the card and glancing at it quickly.

She stood, buttoning her jacket as she reached for her purse. I took the opportunity to scan the curves of her lovely form, the rise of her breasts, the fullness of her ass against the tight fabric of her skirt. Long, silky legs, high-heel fuck me pumps . . . the entire package was speaking to me . . .

I swallowed . . . *hard* . . .

DAYUM

"Thank you for breakfast, Mr. Alexander. I guess we will be in touch," Giovanna said pleasantly before turning on her heel and beginning to walk away.

I had to think fast—I cleared my throat audibly.

"Oh Mrs. Marquis?"

She paused in mid-step and turned. "Yes?"

"If you don't have plans tonight, I'd love to buy you dinner. We don't have to talk shop if you're not up to it. We can just kick it somewhere nice, and—"

"Mr. Alexander," she said, with a pained expression on her otherwise beautiful face, "I'm afraid that won't work." She stared at me for a long second as I felt my sails deflate and my mind whirl, contemplating my next response. I sucked in a breath and grinned.

"Perhaps another time . . ."

"Mr. Alexander," Giovanna said, buttoning her jacket with one hand. "I'd like to keep this strictly professional. I'm sure you can see the wisdom in that."

I swallowed and nodded slowly. Giovanna threw me a fake smile and walked away without further comment.

And I was left there, a stupid expression on my normally confident-looking face.

Ten

"Naomi, hold that thought for a second," Erika said with a sigh, while reaching into her bag for her cell phone. This was the fourth ring in the past thirty minutes. She had let the others go to voice mail. Checking the Caller ID quickly, she huffed. "Damn, this boy is getting ridiculous!"

"Perhaps you should answer it . . . ," Naomi said with a serious expression.

They had finished their dinner, their plates had been cleared away, and they were sitting enjoying the conversation and their espressos.

"James," she said into her cell sternly.

"Baby, I've been calling you for the past hour," he said, his voice harried.

"Stop exaggerating."

"So you purposely haven't been taking my calls?" he responded, incredulously.

"James, I'm out with a friend having dinner. I'll call you later."

"Who's the friend?" he said, quickly. "I don't recall you saying anything about having dinner tonight with any *friend*."

Erika stared at her phone as if it were a disgusting bug. "And I don't recall having to check in with your high-nASS. Now, if you will excuse me." Erika hung up before James could respond. She dropped the phone into her purse and looked up. "Can you believe this shit? Now the dude's checking up on me, wanting to know my itinerary. Oh HELL NO!"

Naomi chuckled. "Can you blame him—the boy's sprung—and hurting big time—first he finds your dildo, then he tells you he loves you and gets no response. Now his woman is out having dinner, for all he knows with some other guy—come on—cut him some slack!"

"Trick, please!" Erika exclaimed. "Don't you dare take his side—"

"I'm not, Erika, I'm just saying—look at it from his perspective . . ."

Erika grew silent for a moment as she sipped at her espresso.

"ERIKA?" a low male voice was rising in pitch from her nine o'clock position. Both women glanced up.

"OH MY GOODNESS, Erika!"

Erika dropped her jaw as the color drained from her normally rosy cheeks.

"Marcus?" she asked cautiously. A tall, athletic-built man appeared, dressed in an impeccable dark suit and grey tie. His hair was cut close to the scalp. He wore no facial hair and his baby face made him appear like a college student. He reached for Erika and gave her a bear hug. Behind him another man stood patiently, sharing his grin between the table of onlookers.

"I can't believe it—Erika," Marcus said, holding her at

arms' length. "Look at you, girl. Damn, you look wonderful. It's so good to see you!"

Erika was blushing. She shook her head slowly from side to side, her lips pressed together as if attempting, without much success to suppress a grin that threatened to erupt. Her hands remained in Marcus', who massaged her fingertips slowly. She pulled them away, pressed her hands to her jeans, and glanced at Naomi.

"Oh, my bad—Naomi—this is Marcus. Dr. Marcus Washington." Marcus reached out to take Naomi's hand in his.

"A pleasure," he said, showing her his straight white teeth. "And this is my boy, Dr. Harold Beasley."

Harold shook hands with the women.

Naomi was glancing rapidly between Marcus and Erika. "So where do you two know each other from?" she asked.

Erika was silent for a moment. Marcus was about to say something; he actually opened his mouth to speak but then thought better of it.

"I'll let Erika answer that," he said a split second later.

Erika smiled. "Well," she began, "Marcus and I dated for a while," she said, "but that was back in the day . . ." she added quickly.

Marcus turned to Erika and smiled. And at that moment, it seemed to Erika as if they were the only two people in this room. She smiled back, numerous thoughts and emotions welling to the surface. She felt herself grow weak, and sat down quickly to hide her disorientation. Marcus? She couldn't believe her own eyes . . .

"It is so good to see you, Erika," Marcus said again, and suddenly the thought occurred to her: was this the sign she'd been praying for???

* * *

"Hey you!" Vince exclaimed while sitting back in the low futon in his studio, facing his wall of masks.

"Hey yourself," Amber replied in an upbeat and welcoming voice. "Happy New Year!"

"Same to ya! I figured I better call you before half of the New Year flies by!"

"No chance of that happening," Amber said. "So what's up? How have you been?"

Vince could hear the enthusiasm filter through the connection loud and clear.

"Fine, can't complain—Not a whole lot going on." Vince paused for a moment. "Actually, that's not true—a whole lot's been happening!"

"So, hook a girl up!"

Vince laughed. "How's Angeliqué doing?" he asked.

"Fine," Amber responded. "She's been all busy getting ready for a new show. You need to make plans to come to the opening down here in March."

"We'll see—are you going to be in it?" he asked.

"Yup, bare ass and all!" Amber mused.

Vince grinned. His thoughts were transported back to the first time he spied Amber reclined on the floor of Angeliqué's studio, the hypnotic veve covering her nude form like lattice.

"In that case, count me in. I never turn down an opportunity to see a beautiful woman strut her bare ass!"

Amber laughed. "Hmmn," she said, "I wasn't sure you noticed . . ."

Vince got serious. "Excuse me? You don't need me to tell you that you're as fine as they come. I'm sure this isn't the first time you've heard that."

"Perhaps," Amber said, quietly, "But it's nice to hear it from *you*."

Vince was silent for a moment.

"So, tell me what's been up, man?"

His thoughts shifted to Raven and the incredible time they had shared just a few weeks ago. Should he tell Amber? Vince was like a little kid in a candy store. He needed to tell anyone who would listen to his adventure. The thing he really dug about Amber was the way they jived—the two of them—being able to just talk about anything—conversation free-flowing. But could he talk to Amber about Raven, he wondered?

"Well, the holidays were nice. I spent them with my folks here in town. That was cool. No drama!"

"Yeah, us too. Except we didn't get any snow—we never get any snow around here! Christmas and its seventy-five degrees—that ain't right!" she said, pouting.

"Be happy you don't," Vince replied.

"So, Vince, now that you and Angeliqué are just friends, are you seeing anyone?"

Vince smiled. Here's the opening he'd been waiting for.

"Actually," he began, "I met this pretty cool lady a few weeks ago."

"Yeah? So, spill the tea. And don't leave out any details."

For the next fifteen minutes Vince recounted the story of how he met the mysterious and invigorating Raven, their initial encounter at his studio and the subsequent lunch where they discussed their adventure, to that fateful night in Philly, where he became a blind man, only to see her in a completely different light.

"Let me get this straight," Amber said, "Girlfriend pulls you into an empty elevator, presses the stop button and proceeds to seduce you?"

Vince laughed. "Yeah, something like that. But once I figured out what was going on, I took control of the situation . . ."

"Yeah, I bet. Vince—this chick was planning on seducing you from the moment she laid eyes on you. I've got to give home girl credit—she's got skills!"

Vince had to agree with her on that point.

"So what happened next?" Amber asked.

"Well, we spent an incredible night in this very posh hotel. I have to say it was one of the most romantic moments of my life . . ." Vince said quietly.

"Boy, you know you did nothing more than wax that ass till daybreak. Please! Ain't no romancing involved . . ."

"Oh you an expert now?" Vince yelled.

"Please—girlfriend ain't the only one with skills," she mused.

"Is that right?"

"That's a fact."

Vince chuckled along with Amber.

"So, you spent a romantic evening with Cat woman— yada yada—okay, I'm with you so far. So, you popped the question yet? Sound's like you popped everything else, man!"

"You ain't right." Vince became serious for a moment. "Here's the thing that I'm not understanding. The next morning, I woke up alone. Raven wasn't there . . ."

"Where'd she go?"

"Not sure. She left a note thanking me for the wonderful evening and telling me to order up whatever my heart desired from room service."

"What did you do?" Amber asked.

"What could I do—I had breakfast, showered, and left." Vince paused. "I haven't heard from her since . . ."

"WHAT?" Amber yelled, "How can that be? Did you at least call her?"

"Here's the thing. I don't have her number."

"Wait a minute—you guys kick it like that—spend the

night swapping spit and God knows what else, and you didn't even exchange numbers???"

"Amber—I didn't expect to wake up alone," Vince replied a bit defensively.

"Okay, don't cut my head off—I hear you. But it's been what? Two weeks. She hasn't called?"

"Nope. Explain that one to me," Vince said dejectedly. "I don't get it. We spent this incredible night together. She wanted unconventional—well, I damn sure gave it to her, if I may say so myself. I blew her away—she told me herself. So why spend that kind of night with someone, becoming intimate, just to run away the next day? It just doesn't make any damn sense."

"To me neither. You can't get her number from information?"

"She called me on her cell phone—twice. I inadvertently erased my recent calls. Like I said, I didn't expect for her to just *vanish*."

"Vince, perhaps with you guys hooking up so close to the holidays she just got busy with family and friends. I have a feeling she's gonna come around. Don't give up hope. She doesn't sound like the type to just play with a guy like that."

"I hope not."

Vince's cell phone beeped. At first he thought it was Amber's line, but when it happened again, he glanced at his phone and paused in mid-breath.

"Amber—hold on, hold on." He clicked over.

"Hello?"

"Happy New Year," a smooth, sultry voice said.

"Raven." It was not a question, but a statement.

"Yes, baby—how are you? I've missed you." Vince felt his heart skip a beat. The mixture of frustration and passion collided inside his veins, making him tipsy. Vince was glad to be sitting down.

Ignoring the question, Vince replied: "Been a while, hasn't it?"

"Don't be mad at me."

Vince shut his eyes and said, "Raven, hold on, I'm on the other line." He clicked over before she could reply. "Amber—I'm back—you'll never guess who that is on the other line . . ."

Amber laughed. "Cat woman? As we live and breathe???"

"Yup."

"Thank you, Lord Jesus!" she replied, in her best phony church deacon voice, "Mah prayers have been answered!"

"You ain't right. I gotta go. Let me find out what this chick's been up to—why she's been dissin' me so!"

"Do your thang—I ain't mad at ya."

Vince turned serious. "Thank you, Amber—I consider you a true friend."

The warmth from Amber's smile could be felt through the phone close to a thousand miles away. She sung softly, "That's what friends are for . . ."

Vince grinned as he clicked over.

"I'm back."

"I'm glad."

Vince sucked in a breath. "So, Raven—it's been, what? Two weeks? No phone call, no nothing. Is that how you roll?"

"Vince, baby, don't be mad—okay?"

"And why shouldn't I?" Vince asked, purposely letting his irritation seep into his voice.

"Because, I'm gonna make it up to you. Gonna make it up to my man," she cooed.

That got Vince to pause.

"And how do you propose to do that?" he asked, the ice slowly thawing.

"I'm unconventional *and* resourceful. By now you should have no doubt in my abilities."

Vince grinned, but was careful not to let Raven hear him laugh.

"Whatever, Raven. At this point in time I am not impressed."

"That's too bad," Raven responded in a low, seductive voice. "I guess I made the trip here for nothing."

"Trip here *where*?" Vince asked, feeling the pressure rise in his bowels.

"Look out your window, *baby* . . ."

Eleven

Glancing at her wristwatch, Erika was amazed at how time flies . . .

One minute she was greeting her ex-beau, Marcus Washington, a pediatrician whom she'd met when they both were doing their residency at Howard University Hospital, the next minute she, Naomi, Marcus, and his boy Harold were kicking it round a table at D.C. Coast, allowing the libations to flow freely as they conversed and caught up.

And damn, there was much catching up to be had!

It had been, what? More than four years . . .

Erika tempered her enthusiasm for seeing Marcus with thoughts of how he had left her, somewhat abruptly, with only so much as a half-hearted goodbye . . .

But that was a long time ago . . .

She'd grown up since then.

Meanwhile, Naomi and Harold were getting well acquainted. The two were both fresh from a breakup and not looking for anything serious beyond good conversation. So it was a nice surprise to find that each was enjoying the other being real and non-pretentious. What a surprise these days!

Erika didn't waste any time. As soon as the pleasantries were dispensed, she proceeded to grill Marcus point blank, her low voice, discontent dripping from every syllable.

"So, Marcus," Erika said, eyeing him with disdain, "It's messed up when a girl has to find out from your mother that your sorry ass has left the country!"

Marcus looked at her sheepishly.

"Erika," he began, baring palms in forgiveness, "that was a long time ago—we were both young and naive."

"Yeah, especially me," Erika declared. "Young and stupid. For thinking that you would act like a man . . ."

Marcus smiled, his white teeth a stark contrast to his rich dark skin. His closely cropped hair and smooth features caused Erika to shudder. But she would be damned if she'd let this man see her sweat . . .

He moved closer to the table, his elbows perched atop his knees so he could be eye level with her.

"I screwed up, Erika, no two ways about it," Marcus said, his eyes unblinking. "I should have come to you earlier. I should have told you of my plans."

"Oh you told me, Marcus—yeah, you mentioned on several occasions your desire to go to Africa. I just never believed that it would happen so soon."

Marcus swallowed hard.

"Erika, believe me when I say I'm sorry. I know I should have discussed it with you. I was so wrong to up and leave like that. I don't know what else to say. I've never forgiven myself for that."

Erika stared at him, her insides warming. She could see the compassion and warmth that had originally attracted her to him.

That and his chocolate-covered smile.

"Well, I hope it was worth it—I hope your work in Africa was fruitful . . ."

Marcus and Erika had dated about nine months. Not a long time as far relationships go, but there was something special about him that struck Erika deep to the core. His convictions. His passions. And his faith.

Unfortunately, she had never gotten the opportunity to truly know him well.

Their romance had come at a time when both of them were working insanely long hours, reeling from the intense stress that comes from working in a hospital, with little to no time for release. But when they found each other, they took those precious moments and made them last, relieving their stress together, the way young passionate lovers do—and what a wonderful release it had been . . .

Marcus smiled at her again, and Erika instinctively brought her hand to her forehead.

As Nelly would say, "It's getting hot in here . . ."

"Africa was a wonderful experience, Erika. Living and working among our people, experiencing them on their terms and not ours—what can I say? It was *intense*. But I have to be honest. I grew to really miss the things Americans take for granted—cable TV, Internet access, late-night lattes, McDonald's Big Macs . . . all those things began to weigh heavy on my mind. After four years, I knew I had had enough."

Erika nodded.

"It was a very difficult decision for me to leave—in the same way as it was incredibly hard for me to leave you . . . but ultimately I had to go, I felt as if I was losing myself and needed to regain my soul.

"So, enough about me, what is up with you? You look fantastic, have I told you that?"

She grinned. "About three times already, but don't slow your roll on my account!"

They talked for another hour and a half, as if their time

apart had been compressed into a few weeks instead of a few years, the two settling easily into the rhythm of back-and-forth communication. Glancing to her left, Erika could see that Naomi and Harold were as into their discussion as much as they were. Naomi and Erika exchanged a quick grin. Erika took the opportunity to rise.

"Will you excuse me, I need to use the ladies room." Naomi took the cue and left her seat too.

"I'll be back, Harold," she said seductively.

"I'll be waiting . . . ," he cooed in response.

Once in the restroom, both women high-fived each other.

"Girl," Naomi exclaimed, "that Harold is fine. You hear me? I am loving his style—the way he actually gives a damn about what I'm saying! And a doctor no less??? SHOOT!"

Erika grinned. "Good for you, girl. Do your thing. Ain't nobody here mad at ya . . ."

"And how about you? Damn, Erika, Marcus with his fine self! I take it you two are catching up?"

"Yeah, girl, we are." Erika smiled but her mind was racing. So many different thoughts and emotions were rushing through her right now.

How to feel?

She was happy to see Marcus—actually, "happy" didn't do what she was feeling justice. There was a sentiment, deep inside of her that she didn't wish to acknowledge just yet.

On the other hand, Marcus had hurt her when he had left for Africa in search of a dream. Did she have a right to feel the way she had felt? It wasn't as if they had entered into a committed or exclusive relationship. That was something the two of them had never really talked about.

Why?

Because she had never felt the need to do so.

From her perspective, when Erika had had free time and wasn't working, she was spending it with Marcus.

Period.

Marcus had showed his true colors when he upped and left four years ago.

Then again, people change . . . folks make mistakes and then they learn from their mistakes.

Sometimes . . .

Some dogs can be taught new tricks, her mama used to say . . .

"I don't know, Naomi, this shit is too complicated even for me to consider. I mean, I don't even know how I should feel!" Erika glanced down into her open purse and her cell that lay there. James had called numerous times . . .

She'd powered off the phone after the fourth call, not wanting any further interruptions.

Not tonight.

Naomi touched her shoulder tenderly.

"Let me ask you something. Are you happy to see Marcus?"

Erika nodded.

"Did you feel something stir inside of you when you first sighted him tonight?"

Erika exhaled.

"Yes, definitely."

"Then my advice is to enjoy the moment and go with the flow. You're entitled to rekindle an old flame. Nothing wrong with that. Nothing in the rule book that says you can't do that . . ."

"True, true," Erika responded, nodding, thinking.

"Besides," Naomi said softly, "this might be the sign you've been waiting for . . ."

Fast forward two hours. Naomi yawned as she nuzzled against Harold. The two ladies exchanged a quick glance and a devilish smile. There were unspoken words that were lost, of course, on the men beside them.

The two couples had absconded to Busboys and Poets one block north of U Street on 14th. They were sitting on a plush couch and love-seat set against brick walls in mottled light, not far from the window. The DJ, a friend of a friend of Harold's was spinning acid-house-trance, whatever the hell that was, but it sounded damn good. The vibe was right, their drinks were on point, and the conversation bubbling along like a rain-laden stream.

Naomi yawned again as she covered her mouth. Erika laughed as Harold shook her shoulder. It was after one a.m. on a weekday . . .

"Wake up, baby girl," he said in a soothing voice. Erika and Marcus exchanged silent looks. For the past hour and a half, the conversation between them had intensified to the level where it felt as if they were the only ones there, regardless of the fact that Naomi and Harold were chatting away three feet away.

Naomi and Harold didn't seem to mind a bit.

They, too, were lost in their own little world. Naomi, it was obvious, had become enamored with Harold. Their bodies were pressed together on the love seat as if they had been intimate for months now.

Erika had to grin at her girl. It was all good!

Harold maneuvered Naomi off of his lap and stood up, attempting without much success to press out his wrinkled suit pants.

"I think I need to take this lady home," he said, pulling Naomi to her feet. She complied without so much as a grunt. "It's getting late."

Erika eyed her friend.

"You gonna be okay?"

"Yup, I'm fine," Naomi said. The two stared at each other

as more unspoken words were transmitted between them. Naomi nodded silently to her friend. Erika nodded back.

"Okay."

A few minutes later, when they were gone, Erika turned to Marcus and smiled.

"I think it's time for me to leave too."

Marcus nodded.

"Let me drive you," he said.

Erika smiled, but shook her head. "No, it's late, Marcus. I can catch a cab—I have no problem with that."

Marcus stood. "I won't have that. Not at this time of night. I'll take you home." He reached for her arm and slipped on her coat. "It's settled and I won't hear anything else." He smiled as she brushed against him, his powerful athletic body soothing against her own.

"Okay."

They rode together in silence, the only sound coming from a smooth jazz satellite radio channel. The early morning air was frigid, yet crystal clear. A piercing three-quarter moon shown down, illuminating the roadway where there was no light. At this time of morning, most of the downtown streets were completely desolate. It was an eerie feeling to be whizzing along 9th Street, past Chinatown and the F.B.I. Headquarters, and not see folks milling about.

"Can I interest you in a nightcap?" he asked in a low voice, parting the silence the way a sharp knife does a stick of butter.

Erika was silent for a moment.

"I don't know, Marcus," she uttered, indecision etched into her normally smooth face.

"I do," he replied, "And I'm not ready to say goodnight just yet." He turned to her, just for a brief moment, and smiled. The interior of the car was dark, but his smile lit up the space, warming her heart.

Erika nodded silently, feeling a pang of guilt paw at her skin. She thought of James, knowing by now that he was beside himself with fear and raw jealousy. More than several hours had gone by without her returning his calls.

Marcus made a right and steered his vehicle over the bridge toward Rosslyn as she thought about the fact that she had never done this before.

James was a good man. What was she doing now, in an ex-lover's car, heading to his place at one something in the morning?

Erika didn't even know where he lived.

But then a calm overtook her as she closed her eyes, and let the music's haunting melody rock her to sleep.

He shook her gently awake minutes later.

"We're here," he said, taking her arm and leading her from the car. The wind bit at her face and neck as she intertwined her arms within his, attempting to fight the bitter cold.

They rode the elevator in silence, holding hands, Erika totally conscious of how his palm felt in hers, and the warmth that seemed to emanate from his hand and suffuse into hers. She tried to let go, but found she lacked the strength to do so.

No. It wasn't a weakness that interlocked their fingers together. It was desire.

Safely inside of his apartment, a tastefully decorated one-level overlooking the river and Georgetown, he removed her coat, set her on the couch facing the windows, and went to the kitchen to fire up some hot water for coffee.

When he returned with two steaming mugs, she rubbed her eyes and grinned.

Her eyes scanned the room, noticing the modern furniture, and eclectic artwork. "No way you did all of this yourself, Marcus. You had to have help!" She sniffed about, almost instinctively, for a female scent, noticing the coordination of colors. "No freaking way . . ."

Marcus grinned.

"You got me. It's a furnished place, courtesy of Georgetown Hospital until I get settled in my own place."

"Must be nice . . ."

"It is. Here, let me warm things up." He reached for a remote and pointed it at the stone fireplace between the two large panes of windows. Flames instantly erupted, coating the logs with a bluish/yellowish glow.

"Oh my!" Erika exclaimed. "You trying to impress a girl, Dr. Washington?"

Marcus turned to her. "Why, is it working?"

He led her over to the fireplace where they lay down on the soft, cream-colored carpet. He reached for her boot and slipped it off, then did the same to the other one. Peeling her socks down until her toes wiggled free, Erika sipped at her mug of coffee.

"Be right back," Marcus said, rising from the ground. Erika watched him, feeling a dual pang of guilt/passion spike inside her. She glanced at her watch.

Close to two a.m.

She should leave.

Immediately.

Okay, you just got here—how about right after you finish your coffee???

But watching Marcus, the way he slipped in a Christian McBride CD, the manner in which he removed his jacket and flung it to the sofa in a slow, fluid motion, then removing his shoes and socks, the dark makeup of his feet in stark contrast to the bright carpet, she imagining his muscles flexing underneath his clothes as he moved, and Erika had trouble deciding between what is right and what is wrong.

Marcus returned a few moments later. Gone was the suit.

Replacing it—a pair of worn jeans, holes strategically placed, barefooted as before, a collared, button-down white shirt, un-ironed, hanging open, showing dark, supple skin and tight, fit muscle.

Erika couldn't help but stare as she sucked in a breath.

Leave . . .

Now.

Marcus was holding a tube of something in his hand.

He dropped down onto the floor, his white shirt fluttering as he moved. Erika took a gulp to hide her growing anxiety.

"Warming up?" he asked.

"Oh *yes* . . ."

Marcus held out his palm and squeezed a large dab of a clear, oily substance onto his skin.

"Give me your foot," he said, and Erika complied without so much as a second thought. He began to massage her, concentrating first on her toes, then moving to the underside, the ball of her foot and backwards to her heel before covering the top of her foot with the gel. When it was fully coated, he bent down and lightly blew on her skin. Instantly, Erika could feel the warmth; her eyes widened as her skin began to glow for a moment before fading.

An illusion?

Marcus did it again.

No, this was real.

"Oh my," she exclaimed, "that is wild!"

Marcus cocked his head in her direction, grinned before bending toward her toes and blowing on each one. Erika was beside herself—her skin was tingling and actually glowing. She wiggled her toes almost instinctively as Marcus continued his expert massage.

Erika sucked in a sharp breath and with one hand fanned herself. "Are you licensed to perform this procedure, Doctor?"

Marcus eyed her with a devilish grin.

"Why yes, Nurse. Of course I am."

Completing one foot, he reached for her other and repeated the entire process, massaging toes and flesh, the ball and heel of her foot before bending down and blowing lightly, setting her skin aglow.

Erika could feel herself becoming aroused.

Marcus lay prone beside her, his head to her feet, his open shirt fanned out on either side of him, the heat from the fireplace washing over them. She sipped at her coffee—the combination of experiences—the soft, yet hypnotic jazz, firelight and fire warmth, Marcus' expert hands, and his breath on her skin, utterly wondrous.

He reached for her shins and pushed the fabric of her jeans upward. Lathering up her calves, he massaged them with long strokes of his fingers, kneading the flesh before hovering his dark lips inches from her flesh and blowing gently, watching the skin come alive with color. Erika twitched involuntarily then lay back, her head resting on the carpet near the fireplace. Her eyelids fluttered momentarily before she shut her eyes with a sigh.

And opened them with alarm as Erika felt a set of hands tug at the clasp to her jeans.

The lights had been extinguished. The only illumination came from the open windows and the fireplace. Shadows danced over their prone forms. The music lingered.

"It's okay, Erika," Marcus whispered, his face suspended inches away from hers, "I can't do your legs with your jeans in the way . . ."

Erika stared for a moment, her heart racing, eyes darting across his soft features.

"Besides," he continued softly, "I'm a doctor, so there's nothing to fear . . ."

Erika shut her eyes without so much as a murmur as Marcus slipped down her jeans. For a brief moment her skin was cold, but Marcus' hands grazed her skin from ankle to thigh, instantly warming her.

"Turn over," he commanded.

Erika opened her eyes briefly, their eyes locked for a second or two before she silently obeyed.

He applied a liberal amount of the gel to her leg beginning at the back of her ankle and traced a line upward to the ridge where her ass cheek met her thigh. Erika was wearing a pair of black panties. Simple yet elegant. She thanked God that she had chosen clean, un-tattered drawers.

Marcus began at her ankles, massaging the goo into her flesh as he worked her muscles. That feeling, in and of itself, would have been enough, but when he paused to blow on her skin, Erika felt herself ignite with heat and passion. Head resting gently on the carpet, eyes fluttering as firelight danced off of her smooth features, she let out a soft moan. Erika was now moist between her legs—in short time she would be damn near drenched, and Marcus, damn it, would know it too!

Applying another line of gel from thigh to ankle, Marcus attacked the other leg with renewed vigor, massaging the goo into her skin with broad, strong strokes from his fingers and palms. This time, he straddled her below the knees, positioning each one of his hands by the insides of his thighs and pressing upward, his palms creating a wide trench in her skin as he moved toward her ass. When he reached the top of her thighs, he paused to apply more gel to his fingers, before palming both cheeks and commencing a slow massage of that area. Erika opened her eyes and glanced back at him, observing the fire in his eyes. When he bent forward, his fingers still attached to the flesh of her ass, and blew on her skin, Erika groaned out loud, and without thought parted her legs.

"Damn, boy . . ." she managed to say in between her accelerated breathing. Erika found she couldn't find the strength to say much more.

Marcus didn't pause—he continued to blow across the soft curve of her ass, his nose inches from the cleft, blowing an arc of moist, hot air downward toward her core. Erika spread her legs farther, feeling Marcus coat the insides of her thighs, and work his magic there, closer and closer to her moistened sex, her moaning becoming incessant and a separate distinct melody to the soft jazz emanating around them, until his fingers brushed against the gate to her canal, the soft folds of her lips, the now drenched entrance to her sex.

Erika sucked in a breath, knowing his fingers would enter her momentarily. Every sense was tuned to that single upcoming event. Her insides contracted, a quick spasm that sent a spike of electricity down her spinal cord, ending at the center of being, the locus of her passion, the entrance to her tunnel that ached for his passionate touch. Her torso even rose off the carpet and arched backward, another shudder of pleasure rippling down her spine as she felt his fingers brush lightly against her wetness down there, anticipation driving her absolutely crazy.

But Marcus slid his hands upward instead, gliding over gel-lubricated skin as his fingers crept underneath the cotton of her top, feeling the power of her lower back muscles contract to his touch, as Erika nuzzled down against the carpet and let out a low lengthy sigh.

Her shirt was removed without words, his fingers reaching around and undoing the buttons. Erika's fingers assisted his own quietly; moments later, she was reclining on the bare rug, the curves of her opulent form silhouetted against the carpet as Marcus straddled her thighs, kneading her shoulders and arms, taking his time, ensuring every muscle received its share of his attention. He even worked her fingers, first applying the gel before massaging it in to her skin and blowing on it, setting it momentarily aglow, just as sensually as before.

Erika lost track of the time—could fifteen minutes have passed by?

Twenty?

Thirty or forty?

She didn't know.

One thing for sure—her body was energized like never before, Marcus tuning the muscles and tendons of her insides to the point that she was smoldering and on fire, ready to ignite. He was purposely avoiding her sex, using broad brush strokes of his palms and fingers to go back over territory already touched by his talented hands, rushing downward toward the lovely rise of her ass and thighs, plunging down into the cleft of her ass cheeks, gliding by her now-wet inner thighs as Erika moaned with passion, no longer concerned by the volume of her outburst or what Marcus' reaction might be.

When she could no longer take it any further, when Erika reached the point of no return—when she knew what it was that she desired, and that, unequivocally meant Marcus inside of her, his sex deeply entombed in hers, she turned on her back, allowing Marcus an unencumbered view of her perked breasts.

Taking Marcus' hand in hers, Erika guided it to that sweet spot between her legs.

This time, it was Marcus' turn to moan.

They made love on the carpet.

And in the bedroom.

And later, much later, in the bathtub, the sudsy water sloshing around them as they danced.

Erika lost count of how many times she came.

But she knew with precision accuracy just how many times Marcus came.

Yes.

Marcus came.

And came.

And came . . .

Erika felt a wave of calm overtake her.

For the first time in months, she felt at ease with herself and her sexuality.

It wasn't her.

It wasn't *anything* that she was doing wrong.

Marcus had come hard.

Three times by her count that night.

By four thirty they lay exhausted on his bed, their skin reddened from the bathwater and the fervor of sexual passion that coursed between them.

She had enjoyed herself.

No question about that.

But now, as she shot a glance at the clock on the nightstand, she felt a pang of guilt attack her solar plexus. Erika had turned off her phone hours ago, not needing James or anyone else to interfere with her evening.

She needed this, she told herself.

She had prayed for a sign.

Well, she'd gotten one, that's for damn sure.

Except, now, Erika felt more confused then ever.

What to do?

First with James, and now with Marcus.

Perhaps it was too early to tell. Too early to make any lasting decisions. Let some time pass—and all things will become clear.

Erika untangled herself from Marcus' sleeping form—his arms and legs that bound her to him in a wondrous kind of way. She crept out of bed, not that she needed to do so—Marcus was so far gone, so deeply wrapped up in a slumber, that a jackhammer would not have awoken him.

Naked, she sauntered down the hall to the living room, where she stood by the large pane of cool glass and stared out at the expanse of river and city. Her nipples climbed to attention as she recounted the previous moments in Marcus' arms, the delicious way he had made her feel, his thick member thrusting inside of her, filling her insides up with his well-oiled manhood, the two of them grooving to their own syncopated beat, their own music, their own kind of jazz, as she rode him hard, contracting around him, making Marcus feel her, as if for the very first time.

Making him remember what he had sorely missed . . .

Powering up her cell phone, she was not in the least bit alarmed to find her voice mail icon blinking, a swift reminder that brought her crashing back to reality. She positioned the phone to her ear and listened to the single message, her heart plummeting to the ground as she heard his voice and his words, which like an artic wind blowing through a line of icy glaciers, cut straight to the bone.

"Erika, it's James. It is now two thirty-eight a.m. and I guess you do not intend to return my call tonight. That's fine. I trust you enjoyed your dinner with your *friend*. I'm sure you did—since I've been sitting outside your apartment, in your parking space actually, for over three hours now, and I see you have no intention of returning home. At least not tonight . . ."

James paused, before letting a long, harried sigh escape from his lips.

"I hope it was worth it, Erika . . ."

Twelve

Vince exploded inside of her with a grunt, with each and every muscle fiber of his being tensing in unison as his seed filled the latex. He held himself up as he squinted his eyes tightly shut, feeling the brush of flesh against flesh as he pulled out slowly, Raven's hands kneading his chest and stomach as she wriggled underneath him in joyful ecstasy.

He rolled off onto the bed, and lay face up toward the ceiling, totally drained and exhausted. His left ankle found hers and they rubbed against one another, the flesh of his shoulder connecting against hers as well, feeling the perspiration slide from her flushed skin to his.

"Dayum, Raven," Vince exclaimed once his heart rate had returned to a comfortable level. He eyed his sheathed penis, which was withering like a flower in brilliant sunshine.

"So," she purred, "does this make up for me not calling?" Raven asked sardonically.

Vince turned to face her, searching her eyes for meaning behind her words.

"Perhaps," he replied. Vince sighed as he felt the rush of

sensual satisfaction course through his veins. "But truthfully, I'd need another dose to be sure . . ."

Raven held herself up on one elbow as she eyed Vince curiously. Her breast hung boldly in the air as Vince traced around her nipple with his fingernail.

"Another dose?" she asked, seductively, while reaching for his shriveling penis, and slipping off the used condom. "Hmmn, perhaps it can be arranged . . ." Raven cooed as she clasped his member between her fingers, taking his warm flesh into her hungry mouth.

Minutes later, Vince's lower half was slapping against hers, her long dark hair clutched tightly in one hand as he palmed her ass cheek in the other. Pummeling her from behind, Raven glanced backwards as their eyes met and locked, a look of pure delight drawn on her mouth, breasts swaying to his cadence while Vince made love to her hard.

The doorbell broke through the clamor and intensity of their lovemaking.

Vince paused in his movement, allowing himself to come to a rest deep inside of Raven's womb, posting his head to one side, unsure of the sound that he had just heard.

Then it resonated again.

Raven moved forward, Vince's member slipping out of her as his lips twisted downward as if in pain.

"You expecting company?" she asked.

Vince swallowed hard, stealing a quick glance at the clock.

Ignoring Raven, Vince moved to the bathroom where he grabbed his bathrobe and donned it. He checked his reflection in the mirror and sniffed. A blind person could see that he'd been having sex . . .

Oh well. Serves them right for disturbing me . . .

Vince moved to the door and opened it.

There stood Desiree.

Vince gulped.

Hard.

"Desiree," he said, awkwardly.

She nodded.

"I see you remember my name. Good start." She stared him up and down for a moment before continuing. "Now why don't you invite me in?" she asked. "It ain't summertime out here, you know!"

"Umm, look, now is not a good time—"

"Seems you've been quite busy these days, right, Vince? No time to call a sistah or to return her call, never mind stopping by to see a friend." Desiree had one hand on her hip. Vince wore an uncomfortable expression on his face.

"It's not like we're in a relationship," she continued, waving her hand in front of his harried face. "I mean, we're only *fucking*, right, Vince?"

A movement behind him caught Vince's attention. He turned his head and dropped his jaw. Raven slid up to the door, completely naked, eyes glistening with that just-sexed look. She moved to the right of Vince and glanced quietly at Desiree whose eyes grew into quarters when she spotted the nude form.

"Oh, excuse me," Desiree said defensively. "Now I see why you haven't called." Her eyes traveled the length of Raven's body with disdain in her stare. Raven said nothing but smiled, her own stare unblinking.

"You know, Miss Thing," Desiree belted out, clearly angered by Raven's presence and silence, "he's fucking me *too*!"

Raven took her time responding. She nodded once.

"You mean he *was*, honey. 'Cause he just finished doing me!" Raven smiled at Desiree briefly whose eyes were wide with hatred. She glanced back at Vince and said: "don't keep me waiting too long, this kitty ain't finished with you yet . . ."

Raven reached down to his crotch and gave Vince a quick squeeze before turning away. Desiree huffed deeply before belting out: "Fuck you, bitch!"

Raven stopped dead in her tracks, pivoted on the balls of her bare feet and turned to face Desiree.

"Sorry, honey, but I like dicks not chicks!"

Raven flashed Desiree a fake smile and turned away, leaving them both in shock, totally speechless.

I was knee-deep in legal briefs, up to my ass in judicial bullshit between myself and opposing counsel, preparing for this big case that went to trial next month, but as they say, that's why I make the big bucks! It didn't bother me one bit—I live for this shit—the opportunity to stand in front of a judge and jury and pontificate for the court, weaving lurid tales of infidelity and injustice for all who will listen, garnishing as much support, and of course, money, for my clients as humanely possible. For in the end, it all comes down to cheddar, baby!

A knock at my door interrupted my concentration. I glanced up, and in strode Calvin Figgs.

I put down my fountain pen and grinned.

"To what do I owe this honor," I said, enthusiastically, but my smile died on my lips as quickly as it had spread. I spotted his disconcerting look. I thought to myself, *Oh shit, what have you done this time, Trey*???

"Trey," Calvin said, without preamble, "we have a problem."

I swallowed hard. "Okay," I said while gesturing to the couch, "have a seat." Calvin did.

"I received a disturbing call today. From one Giovanna Marquis. I believe she is your client."

My heart spiked. I freaking knew it!

Goddamn it!

Damn her!

"Trey—Mrs. Marquis was not amused by your gesture of sending flowers. Frankly, I'm quite surprised by your actions—you have to know that this is out of line, even for you, and potentially damaging to your career."

I held up my hands.

"Calvin—listen, I think you are taking my actions out of context," I said, thinking fast. "Mrs. Marquis is under an intense amount of stress. She is having a hard time with the separation, and it is affecting her thought process. I merely was trying to cheer her up, to show her that not all men are the bad guys, and that in my case, I'm on her side."

Calvin steepled his fingers together while nodding silently.

"Perhaps, but most folks won't see it that way. Surely not Bernard John Marshall."

He let the weight of that remark settle in.

"Trey—listen up—you probably don't know this, but I'm the one who suggested you to Mrs. Marquis."

I registered genuine shock.

"Yes, it was me. Her husband and I go way back. We've met socially a number of times, with her, of course. I heard that she was shopping for a good divorce attorney and gave her a call."

I shook my head.

"Damn, Calvin. All this time I thought it was Bernie."

"I made the suggestion to him also—figured I'd work both sides. You needed a change of pace. I knew Giovanna was a beautiful woman, but I figured that you could handle your emotions and keep it in your pants."

He glared at me.

"You have kept it in your pants, haven't you?"

"Yes, Calvin. Damn!" I replied again. "This feels like a setup."

Calvin shook his head forcefully.

"No setup, son. Believe that. I was trying to get you to focus on something new. You're in a rut—your output is down, and frankly, you're no longer in the zone. Trey—you're disenchanted with this place, which is understandable, given the circumstances. That is exactly why I was throwing you a bone. Something fresh, something new and exciting to stir your interest, get you back where you belong. But I didn't expect for you to break all the rules."

"Calvin," I said, my eyes pleading, "This is being blown way out of proportion. I've met with the woman once. I've talked to her on the phone several times. She's messengered documents over to me and I back to her. My conduct has been at all times professional. I am doing my job. However, I want my client to feel comfortable, and she is having a tough time. So I showed her some compassion. Is that really such a crime?"

Calvin stood up and went to the window. I followed him with my eyes.

"Does Bernard know?" I asked quickly, my anxiety evident.

"No, and he won't find out, unless you tell him. I counseled Mrs. Marquis to let me handle this, and she gave me her word that she would. I trust her to leave this in my hands." I nodded as Calvin clasped his hands behind him, staring out at the Capitol.

"Trey, you know as well as I do that if Bernard or any of the partners get wind of this, they will roast you alive. She's a beautiful woman, and you have, let's just say, a reputation with the ladies."

I exhaled a breath sharply. There wasn't any use taking

my frustration out on Calvin. After all, he was covering for me. He was my friend.

Calvin turned to stare sharply at me.

"You need to tread lightly, Trey. Don't be messing this up, or Bernard will have all the ammunition he needs to boot you out of here. I'm serious. My advice is to give this woman a wide berth. Yes, she is gorgeous. Any man can see that! But she's not worth losing your job over."

Calvin was standing by my chair. Placing a hand on my shoulder he squeezed as he glanced down and smiled.

"You'll get through this—just keep your head clear and focused on the task at hand. You hear me?"

I swallowed hard, but nodded silently.

Calvin reached for the door.

"Good. I consider this case closed." He grinned like the old-school playa that he was, a man of class and distinction. He opened the door.

"Thank you, Calvin," I muttered morosely.

He turned. "Don't mention it. Just make sure you keep that thing of yours in your pants," he said, his voice dropping in pitch, "or I'll personally whip your ass my damn self!"

He waggled a finger at me.

"And you don't need this O.G. on your ass, you feel me???"

I was so freaking pissed, I could barely see straight. I wanted to pick up the phone and scream at that goddamned woman for almost ruining my life, but thought better of it. I paced the office, staring obscenely at the phone as if I wanted to kill the thing with my fist. But it had done me no wrong.

Still . . .

Why had Giovanna misconstrued my intentions?

Hold up . . . whom the hell was I kidding? I knew damn well what I was doing when I sent her those dozen roses two days ago! I was trying to get something going, since she'd been as cold as a fish from the first moment I'd laid eyes on her.

Every time I thought about Giovanna—her smooth dark skin, those haunting eyes, and ripe curves, I wanted to explode in sheer ecstasy.

That woman was screwing with me, big time!

I shook my head as I slumped down into my chair. I didn't freaking get it. Women are always complaining about not getting roses, but when a good-intentioned man tries to send them some, all of a sudden they get all jiggy on him!

Go figure!

My first reaction was to call her, and tell her that the shit with Calvin was completely uncalled for. But that would have made matters worse. I felt like I needed to speak to her, and talk with her about what I was feeling.

But probably not the best thing to do right now.

My hand poised over the phone a hundred times but didn't actually lift the receiver.

India came in to check on me, and I sent her away with a fling of my hand.

She vanished in a huff, her long braids waving behind her.

I skipped lunch. This shit was eating away at me.

Should I call her?

I had reason to. Business reasons . . .

I picked up the phone, dialed her cell (from memory) and listened to it ring.

My heart was thumping, but it relaxed a bit when I heard it switch over to voice mail.

Does anyone answer their phone these days???

"Mrs. Marquis, this is Trey Alexander." I took a deep

breath. "I wanted to apologize for my behavior. Sending you flowers was inappropriate and out of line. It was not my intention to upset you. Merely, I wanted to cheer you up. Obviously, my actions were misconstrued. I'm sorry for that, and assure you that it won't happen again."

I took another deep breath.

"Good day, Mrs. Marquis." I hung up the phone.

A sudden thought occurred to me that gnawed at my skin.

I had just left incriminating evidence on the phone. If Giovanna wanted to really screw me, all she had to do was play the message . . .

How damn stupid of me.

A lawyer no less . . .

I swore loudly as I picked up the receiver again and buzzed India.

"I'm leaving for the day. Cancel my appointments."

"Good idea," I heard her say as I slammed down the phone . . .

I spent the next eight hours alone. Driving around for several hours in my coal-black Escalade, heat up, CD changer whirling as I rode up and down streets and neighborhoods I hadn't been on in years. Georgia Avenue, Takoma Park, New Hampshire Avenue, Glover Park, until that got boring. So I went home, only to stare at the walls of my condo. I sat on the couch, remote in hand, scanning channel after channel—it's screwed up when you've got over three hundred digital channels, and can't find a goddamn thing to watch on T.V.!

I wasn't used to sitting at home by myself. Especially not during the day. I was getting angrier by the minute. It seemed like everyone around me was getting more play than me. I couldn't understand it. I mean, I'm an intelligent guy,

I'm good looking, and usually I never *ever* have a problem attracting the ladies. Usually, I get more pussy than I can shake a dick at . . . (Get it? Shake a dick at? I crack myself up sometimes)!

My thoughts went back to Jamaica. Too much fun in the sun for a mere mortal. Rum, reggae, and tons of naked women . . .

But lately . . .

Vince was getting more play than me.

That was a first.

And even Erika was juggling James and getting some new strange!

Go figure that one!

A tremor shook my head.

This shit wasn't right. Ever since I'd gotten back from Jamaica things had been going downhill. It was as if God was mocking me—saying, oh yeah, you thought you were the big man down there, the H.N.I.C, but back here among the normal folk you ain't shit!

That's what it was—he was taunting me, all cause a dude had got his groove back.

Even God was hating!

Dayum . . . that's messed up . . .

By nine, I was totally annoyed and fed up. Not to mention famished. I had kept calling my voice mail at work, hoping and thinking that perhaps Giovanna had returned my call, thanking me for my phone call and the flowers, saying it was all a big mistake, and if she could come over and suck my dick . . .

Make it all feel better . . .

I even VPN'd to grab Aponi's contact info from my Outlook, giving her celly a ring. Hoping and dreaming that perhaps she was in town and in the mood for some Trey-steak . . .

She answered on the third ring.

"Who's this?" Aponi asked irritably.

"Trey Alexander, Esquire—your husband's lawyer, your lover, remember?" I was trying to sound cute, but I don't think she was in the mood to play.

"Yeah, what's up?" Total dismissal.

"Uh, well, I was wondering if you were in town. I thought perhaps we could get together. For dinner or something." I was so damn glad she couldn't see me sweat.

"No, Trey, I'm home."

Silence.

"Okay . . ."

Hanging up, I tried to remember the last time I'd gotten laid. I was horny, like a freaking toad, I kid you not, and finally decided that it was time to take matters into my own hands.

No, not that—I mean, I was gonna go out and get me some.

Wednesday night, mid-January, cold as hell. But screw it. Trey was gonna get his cum-on.

Damn it, I was gonna get myself laid tonight! Come hell or high water. I refused to take this shit lying down.

Watch me work . . .

My first stop was F Street. I pulled the Escalade up to Eden DC, but quickly frowned as I spied their windows dark. Down the street, Home was in the same sorry-ass state.

Onward up Connecticut Avenue, stopping briefly at Dirty Martini. I valeted my ride, and told the parking attendant to chill for a second while I ran in.

Not shit going on in there, so I handed the Mexican a ten-spot and moved on. Glancing up the street Lucky Bar looked dead and lame too!

Damn, was any place open tonight???

I mean, come on now, this dude was on a mission . . .

HELLO????

I knew bluespace would be open. I could always count on that place to be on point. Plus, by now I was famished and felt no need to be searching all over Chocolate City for food and companionship. So I steered my ride over to my favorite spot.

I pulled up in front of the awning. Me and the valet boys were on a first name basis, much as I frequented this place.

I got out, gave one of them, Hector, dap. We exchanged pleasantries, "How ya livin'?"

"You know how we do!"

"Right, right . . ."

I handed him a twenty and told him as always to keep the change.

Nikki, the stunning Ethiopian, met me at the door. We exchanged hugs and I kissed her on both cheeks, as her country custom dictates. I stepped back, holding her at arms' length.

"Check you out, girl!" I said, all animated, "Looking like a pork chop, good enough to eat!"

Nikki chuckled while displaying perfect white teeth. She was so fine I had to bite my knuckles.

Me love some Ethiopian women, ya hear me!

As with every time I came in, we exchanged small talk, and I attempted, once again without success to get her digits.

"What's the matter, Nikki, you don't like Americans?"

She waggled her finger in my face while shaking her head.

"For the thousandth time, Trey Alexander, I'm not giving you any."

I radiated my infamous Trey smile.

"That's okey doke with me, bab-ee. See, I'm gonna keep bugging you until them panties are mine, you hear me!"

Nikki smacked me on the arm and I moved on.

Inside, the restaurant was a kaleidoscope of colors. My man, Scott Chase, the owner, had, as of late, been bitten by the social consciousness bug. He'd been working on a new joint, a symphony of sorts—the theme being homelessness. He had solicited the help of black artists and photographers from up and down the East Coast: New York, Philly, Baltimore, Atlanta, Boston, and gotten them to photograph or paint images of homeless folk. These images were filtered through lenses of red, brown, orange, and blue/greens, the colors constantly shifting from bright to dark as jazzy/blues melodies of despair and heartbreak tracked along with the pictures.

I had to admit that the scenery made me pause. I stared up into the images, thinking to myself, these people looked just like me—a bit more worry lines in their brow, a touch of sweat mixed with ground-in dirt around the edges of their eyes, but fundamentally, they were the same as me.

The idea was sobering indeed.

My thoughts went to the Nona E. Taylor Women's Center and the women whom had passed through there. I had to watch the haunting images for a moment, making a mental note—I needed to get back there and cook for those ladies real soon.

The bar wasn't crowded. A scattering of folks, well-dressed men and women nursed their drinks. The mood was somber. I ordered a Hennessy and sat down as the cognac was poured into an oversized snifter. Can somebody explain to me why black folks order this shit? Not that I don't dig it, but it must be some heavy-duty subliminal marketing going on cause I didn't even blink when I sashayed up to the bar to order.

I took a sip, listening to Mary J. Blige's melodic voice, observing the grainy image of a woman pushing a shopping cart past the steps of the Lincoln Memorial, her two dirty children in tow. No words were needed—no subtitles required—the meaning was clear.

I glanced around. Most of the patrons were coupled up—a few women traveling in packs of two and three.

Like wolves . . .

I didn't see anything worth pursuing, although I was very horny and considered dropping my standards for one night until just after I secured some tang . . .

But that's always risky . . . I mean, someone could see me . . . and then my secret would be out!

Playa card confiscated . . .

NOT!

I watched the light show for a moment, sipping slowly at the X.O. as it glided down my throat, smooth. Finally, I felt myself unwinding, courtesy of Hennessy and Scott Chase—his images and accompanying sounds made me relax and realize that life wasn't all that bad.

Lately, today in particular, I had been dwelling on my own situation—my deteriorating work environment, a dysfunctional asshole for a boss, my non-existent love life, my drying up sex life . . . dayum . . .

My stomach churned.

I grabbed my drink and pushed off the bar, in search of a quiet table upstairs, hoping that a decent meal would bring me out of this funk.

Pan-seared salmon with fresh asparagus, and mashed potatoes.

I tore into that bad boy like it was the Last Supper. The pink meat, all hot and moist reminded me of—well, never mind, but trust me, I was enjoying the hell out of that fish! It was cooked to perfection, the mashed potatoes and asparagus so damn tasty that I was tempted to head to the kitchen just to pat Scott on the back.

I finished my dinner and pushed the plate away, the waiter cleared the table and offered up a dessert menu, which I half-heartedly looked over. I was sipping at my cognac when I heard someone utter my name.

"Mr. Alexander."

I glanced up into the beautiful face of Layla.

A cold wind suddenly whirled around my face, neck, and shoulders, instantly freezing my skin into hardened leather. Frowning, I said nothing.

I could feel my muscles tensing, my stomach, which was full with food suddenly replaced with a swarm of African killer bees. A range of emotions flooded through me, but I blinked them back as I sucked in a breath.

"Layla," I said, low-pitched.

"Happy New Year," she said.

I nodded.

Layla hovered over my table, but not crossing into my personal space . . . yet. She was dressed in hip hugger jeans that flared at the bottom, black boots, a short midriff sweater that accentuated her large breasts. Her hair was tied back into a thick braid that ran down her back. It shone with blue and purple hues, reflecting stray light from the lightshow overhead. I gulped as I looked away. I hated to admit how damn good she looked—fine was an understatement—the thought alone, however, made me nauseous.

"It's been a while," she said, making no move to come closer.

I nodded again.

"You look well, Trey. You always did, no matter what the circumstance."

I grunted. "Good genes, I guess."

Layla smiled. "May I sit for a moment?"

I frowned. "No, Layla, that's not a good idea."

Layla ignored my remark and moved into the booth.

"I don't bite you know. I just want to catch up, Trey. Is that so bad? Two old friends catching up on the times."

"No, Layla, it's not okay. I'm asking you nicely, and I don't want to make a scene. Okay?"

"Trey, please—"

"Look, Layla—not everything is about you. You can't always get your way. I don't want you at my table. And that's my right!" I was hissing, trying to keep my voice low as so not to alert the other patrons, but it was getting difficult. I did not want her at my table.

"I just want you to talk to me . . ."

The look on her face was one of complete dismay.

"No, Layla. I said no!" My fists suddenly clenched. "Can't you get this through your thick head? I've had a shitty day, a shitty week, basically an entirely shitty freaking couple of months. My job sucks, I want to kill my freaking boss, and the only woman who turns me on is acting like I don't exist. Okay? I've stooped to screwing my own clients' wives, or ex-wives, I don't even give a shit any more, and to top it off, Vince and Erika are getting busy more than I am! Now if that doesn't signal an imbalance in the universe I don't know what does. I have my own problems, Layla, real problems, so I neither need nor do I want your support, guidance, or counsel. What I want, and what I am going to fucking insist on is that you to stop showing up conveniently at every damn spot I choose to dine in, and stop for God's sake these lame-ass games. Layla—" and suddenly I could care less who heard my voice accelerate in pitch and in volume, "In summary, I want you to leave me the hell ALONE!"

I pushed myself up from the table, glaring down at her.

She was weeping silently. Two tracks of tears ran down her cheeks. She did not look at me.

I clenched my fist, sighing deeply.

"Layla," I said quietly, glancing around. Thankfully, the place was darkened by the lightshow. I was grateful. "No need to cry. Please. Don't cry."

I couldn't help it. I hated to see her cry. After everything we had been through, I just couldn't find the strength to walk away, leaving her like this. Regardless of what she had done to me, I could no longer hate her.

This was a woman whom I had truly loved.

I hated to see her cry.

So, I shook my head and sat back down.

Handed Layla a cloth napkin from the booth behind us.

She wiped at her eyes.

"I'm not looking for your pity," she said softly. "I just miss what we had, Trey. Our friendship is what I miss the most."

I was silent.

She was staring into my eyes.

"I'm not stalking you, Trey; I'm not attempting to regain a place in your heart—I know that is impossible now. But it would be a crime if two people who used to be this close," she said, holding up two fingers curled together, "can't even have a drink and talk."

"Please, Trey," her voice had dropped to a whisper. "Do it for old-time's sake . . ."

I exhaled slowly. I felt dueling emotions tear at my heartstrings. Glancing downward, finding it difficult for me to hold her gaze with my own, I stared at my cognac. The golden liquid was still, no ripple upon its surface. It was like a quiet lake at sunset, peaceful and serene.

I took a sip, grateful for its invading warmth.

"One drink, Layla," I heard myself say in a voice that shocked me with its compassion.

Layla nodded silently. It took a moment, but her face gradually lit up, like a sunrise announcing a new day, and I found that I was trembling from the cold within.

Layla was back . . . and I was very much afraid . . .

Thirteen

Closing my eyes, I allowed the vapors to envelop me. The sweet smells of cooking penetrated my pores and circulated through blood vessels and nerve endings, entering my very being. It made me smile. This was me at my best— away from the pressures of the office, allowing my mind to free-fall, not prickled by minor distractions or daily annoyances—instead being free to create, the way a sculptor or painter does. Thin strips of freshly-cut steak, marinating in my own spicy sauce I picked up from the natives in Jamaica; succulent lamb that was slow-cooking on a thirty-year old rotisserie; stir-fry vegetables in my seasoned wok; fresh bread that I was baking myself; and of course, the piece de resistance—two pies—a chocolate bourbon pecan pie (I had never made this before, but had been dying to try)—sweet, chocolaty, crunchy, and down-right decadent—and a cherry cheese pie made with cream cheese, cherries, and loads of whipped cream! My apron had been dusted with flour and stained with jerk sauce, my fingers and palms greased with virgin olive oil, my baldhead streaked with brown sugar flecks—but it was all good. My friends were coming over tonight. After what seemed like a stretch of months without being seen, it was time for Vince, Erika, and yours truly to all crawl out of their respective caves and hook up!

It had been a while. A lot of shit had gone down. We'd all heard bits and pieces over the phone . . .

About Vince and his new beau, Raven.

About Erika and her old-fling, Marcus.

About yours truly and Layla . . . and the woman who kept me lying awake at night with perverse thoughts of her incredible form and splendor—Giovanna . . .

We'd talked about getting together at our usual spot—bluespace. But work and personal schedules conflicted. So, tonight, we were hooking up at my crib.

Tonight, I was gonna throw down for the family.

By now y'all know how we do!

Erika arrived first.

She showed up looking fly, as usual, carrying an aluminum foil-covered pie she had baked. I had told them not to bring anything, but of course, these mutha suckas never listen to me! Erika was in the kitchen checking out my goods, and relishing in the vapors when the doorbell rang. It was Vince, dressed casual yet dapper, as he always did, carrying two bottles of wine. We hugged, longer than usual. It had been a while—we had all seen each other briefly a few days before Christmas—but that had been it. Now, weeks later, it was good to see old friends again.

"Damn, bruh, I can smell the cooking!" Vince exclaimed.

"You know how this playa do!" I responded, giving him dap. "Shoot, I'm not playing tonight—y'all my friends, and I don't half-step it with my friends." Erika raised her eyebrows but said nothing.

"How's everybody?" I asked.

Erika nodded. "Busy at work," she replied, "but it's all good. If I can keep my personal life straight I think I'll make it."

"Yeah, I heard about that shit," I said, laughingly. "You just a regular ole tramp, plain and simple—you getting more play than Vince and I combined!"

Vince shook his head.

"I'm not so sure about that," he added with a grin.

"Oh, so it's like that?" Erika inquired.

"Yeah, it's like that!" Vince said. "Don't hate the playa . . ."

I had to shake my head.

"Hate the game."

The table was already set. Vince opened the wines—one Merlot, the other a Chilean Chardonnay, while I pan-fried the steak. The aroma wafted out into the living room where Erika sat barefoot on the couch.

"Damn that smells good," she said.

I served dinner and we ate.

(Pigged out was more like it!)

The conversation flowed as easily as the wine being poured. We were best friends, and it felt damn good to be in their presence again. After a way too-long hiatus, it truly warmed my heart to reconnect again.

"Where the hell to begin!" Erika exclaimed while dabbing at the corner of her mouth with a cloth napkin, wiping away a fleck of my jerk sauce.

"Language!" I noted, eyeing Vince. He nodded, sucking his teeth. She told us about her chance encounter with Marcus, a person all too familiar to us. See, we had been there during their brief relationship, and dealt with his abrupt departure, leaving Erika to handle her emotions alone.

I, of course, couldn't believe that she had slept with him that same evening.

"Damn, Sassy, couldn't you have waited like one freaking day? I mean, why give him the keys to the castle so soon." I sat there shaking my head.

"Trey please! We've been through this shit before. This is

a new millennium—women are doing it just like men. I'm allowed to do my own thing, and if that means going to bed with an ex-lover, well, then that's my prerogative."

I held up my hands. "Okay. Whatever you say, ho."

Erika eyed me with disdain. In the background Evelyn "Champagne" King's "Shame" was blaring through my Boston Acoustics speakers. Vince told us to pass the lamb down his way. That man was on a mission!

"You know what?" Erika exclaimed. "I enjoyed the hell out of myself. I mean, that shit was off the chain! Seriously though," she said, pausing to take a sip of her Merlot as she forked a piece of the lamb, "for the longest time I'd been thinking that something was wrong with me. That I couldn't please my man." She glanced up, making eye contact with both of us individually. "That is sobering—the fact that you may not have what it takes to please your lover . . ."

"Sassy—you know it wasn't you," Vince interjected, with food in his mouth.

"Yeah, in an intellectual sense you know. But when you're lying there and your man doesn't come, night after night, you begin to wonder. You can't help but not wonder . . ."

I nodded. "Well, now you know," I said, somberly.

Vince smiled. "So, I hear James isn't taking it too well . . ."

"That's an understatement," Erika said. She smiled, but it was a weak one, devoid of any color, or any potency.

"He actually sat outside my apartment half the night—at some point he figured out that I wasn't coming home . . ."

"Ouch!" I responded, my shoulders flinching.

"So what did you say to him?" Vince asked.

"Well, I called him the next morning. It was the hardest thing I've ever done. Frankly I was scared shitless."

"How did he respond?"

Erika shook her head.

"He didn't—he didn't speak to me for three days. When he finally did return my call he was very short. I guess that's to be expected."

Vince and I nodded in unison.

I helped myself to another helping of piquant, cooked-to-perfection steak and the lamb that would make a Middle Eastern eatery proud. Vince tore off another piece of piping hot bread and dipped it in a saucer filled with virgin olive oil.

"I toyed with making up some lie," Erika continued. "Telling him that it got late and I just stayed over one of my girlfriend's, but then realized that that story would eventually come back to haunt me. So I told the truth—that I had met Marcus, that one thing had led to another, and that I had slept with him." She paused. "And most importantly, that Marcus had come."

Erika nodded her head to the surprised looks from us.

"Yeah, Marcus came—and that he, James didn't—couldn't! James had a problem that I could no longer sweep under the rug."

"Oh no you didn't!" I said, shockingly.

"Oh yes I did. I figured that the damage had already been done. So why not go ahead and spill all the damn tea!" She paused to remember the conversation. "Besides, it was time for James to hear the truth."

"Ouch!" I repeated, shaking my head forlornly.

"Yeah," Vince said, pitifully, "very ouch . . ."

"So," I said, trying to change the pitch and direction this conversation was taking, "what's next? I mean—are you going to see Marcus again? And what about James?"

Erika sighed heavily.

"I'm seeing Marcus, yes." She paused to the shocked stares around the table.

"You're kidding," Vince said, dropping his fork and

putting down his glass of Chardonnay almost simultaneously.

"No, I'm not." Erika set her fork down, more perfuncto-
rily than Vince had. "I'm enjoying seeing Marcus again.
He's grown up—I think his stint in Africa changed him—
made him more respectful of the things that are near and
dear to his heart. I don't know if we have a future together or
not—but right now, I don't care. There's too much uncer-
tainty surrounding James and I. I don't know where the two
of us are going. I don't know if my future includes him or
not. And frankly, my head has been hurting from all the
thinking going on."

Vince and I nodded silently.

"You know I was having a hard time with all of this—
then Marcus appears—almost like a godsend. Sometimes I
think he came into my life for a reason—like a test—to see
if what James and I have is real. I don't know the answer to
that, guys."

Erika paused, forked some of the stir-fry veggies into her
mouth and chewed, the delight on her pallet evident from
her smile. I shook my head.

"So, let me get this straight—you're just gonna let Marcus back into your panties and what? Kick James to the
curb? After what that mutha sucka did to you?"

Erika gave me a hard look.

"Man, please. This girl is older and wiser. I'm not trippin'
over Marcus—and I'm not expecting anything from him. To
be honest, I don't know what I even want from him—if anything. I'll tell you this, though—being with him makes me
feel good—there's something between us—call it chemistry,
that makes me feel alive. I dig being in his arms. And home
boy rocks in bed, so don't hate!"

"And James?" Vince asked cautiously.

"I guess we will have to see. James has a choice to

make—whether he wants to continue seeing me, knowing that I am spending some time with Marcus or . . ."

"Hold up," I said. "He *knows* that you're gonna keep seeing Marcus?" I shook my head with distaste.

"Yeah, I figured that I would be completely honest with him. So I told him that I had no plans to stop seeing Marcus. James knows that I'm feeling torn—and that at this point I don't know what to do."

"What about the problem?" Vince asked. "Is he going to take some action to address his sexual issues?"

"Well," Erika said, holding up her glass so the light reflected red hues against the dark wood of the table, "I guess that remains to be seen. He is no longer denying there's a problem between us, but he has yet to admit his malady outright." She took a sip of her merlot. "According to James, his 'issue' is not a problem, but a fetish. Some people, according to him, are turned on by various things—for example, some folks get off on sucking other folks' toes, or having a large object shoved up their ass. James has a *fascination*, for lack of a better term, with his asshole." Erika shook her head. "That didn't come out right—what I meant is that James gets extremely turned on by anal stimulation."

Erika paused at my raised eyebrow.

"What?"

"Nothing—continue, please," I uttered.

"Some men can't come from a blowjob. Others need a particular type of stimulation to orgasm. James falls into this category."

This time if was me who put my fork down with a clank.

"Hold up—who do you know who can't come from a blowjob? Even gay dudes can come that way!"

"Trey, sometimes you are so ignorant, it ain't even funny." She turned her attention back to Vince who was watching her closely. "James says that there is nothing wrong with him.

He just happens to need this kind of stimulation in order to come. When he's stimulated in the right way, he comes. That's his story and he's sticking to it."

Vince nodded. He reached for his wine and took a sip, staring for a moment at the ceiling. Then he leveled his gaze at Erika.

"I would say that in one sense James is correct."

I threw up my hands. "Oh *Lord*!" I exclaimed.

"Trey—you have to admit that people are into all kinds of shit these days—I mean, just spend a few minutes on the Internet checking out the wide variety of porno sites—folks into all kinds of kinky shit—from bestiality, anal sex, and golden showers, to teens, fisting, and S&M—"

"Fisting???" Erika bellowed, interrupting. "Just what the hell is fisting?"

Vince smiled. "That's when someone puts their entire hand in a woman's vagina—for some women it's an incredible turn-on."

"Damn, bruh, you sound like a damn expert rattling off all that shit!"

Vince ignored me.

Erika sat there shaking her head, the image of an entire hand, up to a wrist, or worse, rooted deep inside her. She winced uncontrollably.

"My point, Erika, is that there's a lot of variety out there. James is indeed correct when he points out that some people derive stimulation from sources that others might find objectionable. That fact that some men need an underage child or teen just to get off proves my point."

"Yeah, but that's just plain sick," Erika exclaimed. She grabbed at a piece of bread, and soaked it in the olive oil before taking a huge bite.

"Of course it is. But let me serve up another example. How about someone who has a foot fetish? There are men (and women) who get off on seeing, stroking, and licking another's toes. While we might find this kind of behavior distasteful—I, for one, don't want anyone's toes, not even Halle's, in my mouth—that doesn't make it wrong."

I snapped my head at Vince.

"Are you out your God damned mind? Bruh—Halle can put her funky ass toes between my teeth any goddamn day, ya heard me!"

Both Erika and Vince sighed audibly.

"To continue," Vince said, shifting his gaze to me for a moment before settling back on Erika, "the point is that folks respond to a variety of stimuli. I think that's what makes lovemaking between different couples so individual and unique. I mean, looking back on my share of lovers, no two have ever made love the same way. Each one had a different way of pleasing and being pleased—each one responding to different stimuli. That's what makes it so exciting and refreshing every single time . . ."

I shook my head vigorously.

"I can't believe you're taking up for the mutha sucka. Sassy—you need to drop-kick both of these knuckleheads and move on! For real!"

"Trey—I'm not taking up for him," Vince said. "But if James gets off from having his ass licked or from someone sticking a banana up that there, then more power to him. My philosophy is, and has always been, simple—as long as it doesn't hurt anybody, and it is consensual, then go for it. Life's too short to have certain folks telling other folks how to live their lives—and how to get off."

Vince picked up his fork and reached across the table for the last piece of steak that sat alone in its juices. He put it on his plate and attacked it with his steak knife. Half of the meat disappeared into his mouth within thirty seconds.

Erika was nodding slowly, digesting what he had said.

She sipped at her wine as she draped her cloth napkin over her plate, signaling that she was done.

"I guess that's why you're the motivational speaker in the bunch," she said, "and the most cerebral one here—you always give us a fresh perspective, Vince—something to think about. That's why I love you."

Vince beamed as he chewed his food, reaching over to pat her hand.

"Do your thing, Ma," he said, as soon as he had finished swallowing. "If Marcus makes you feel good, then feel good with Marcus. But my advice to you is to not kick James to the curb just yet. You two have good history together. It would be a shame to throw it all away, especially over something that perhaps could be fixed—or at least dealt with."

Erika nodded solemnly. I glanced rapidly from Erika to Vince, and back again to my boo.

I had no choice but to nod solemnly as well . . .

We retired to my living room after a scrumptious meal for coffee before dessert.

Everyone was stuffed. Erika held her stomach as she lay on my buffalo brown couch, head back, eyes closed as if exhausted. Vince was by the stereo, cranking up the volume on an old Con Funk Shun jam, "Fun." For three minutes, we all sang along with that old school song, like it was yesterday's number one hit. I was by the window, glancing downward, holding a steaming mug of coffee as I moved my head to the beat, completely satisfied at the way the evening's meal had turned out.

The song died, segueing into another old school classic from the Ohio Players—"Skin Tight." I had burned a CD of my favorite songs from back in the day. Lately I had that shit playing on a loop in my ride to the delight of my passengers . . .

"So," Erika purred with her eyes closed, "that's definitely enough of me and my drama for one evening. I believe the gentleman from the District of Columbia is next . . ."

"Oh hell!" I exclaimed, turning away from the window and glancing upward at the slanted ceiling and dual skylights. "I always go last . . ."

Erika and Vince exchanged a quick glance before giggling like schoolchildren.

"Y'all ain't right," I said, as I sat by Erika, dejectedly.

"Well," Vince said, sitting down across from us in the big dawg's love seat. He settled his frame around until he was comfortable, took a sip of his coffee, closed his eyes as if that act would assist in savoring the already luscious flavor, before placing the mug down in the palm of his other hand.

"Man, I am blessed! Let me just say that."

"Okay," I said, feigning annoyance. "I can see where this conversation is going."

Erika's eyes snapped open. She cocked her head toward me, staring me up and down.

"What? When you are gloating about your latest wild-ass monkey sex conquest, we sit there and take it. Therefore, so will you!"

"Dayum, Sassy, cut a dude some slack . . ."

"Whatever," she hissed. "Go on, playa—we're all ears . . ."

Vince cleared his throat. "As I was saying," he uttered with a grin. "Things are going *wonderfully* with Raven and me. I find it hard to even put into words what I've been experiencing. Raven is not like anyone I've ever been with before."

"So, I take it that she's been making up for not calling you those weeks," Erika said.

"Yeah, you can say that. I was pissed as all hell, and frankly, had written her off. But then, out of nowhere, she appeared, and what can I say? She made me forget any and all frustration that I was feeling. And trust me, it was all goodness!"

"I bet," I replied in an exasperated tone.

"Trey," Erika said, turning toward me, "Can it be that you're jealous of your own boy? Say it ain't so!"

"Trick, please! I just wish I were getting as much as y'all seem to be getting. I hate it when you mutha suckas get more stank than I do. That shit just ain't right. It ain't supposed to be like that, and y'all know it. Something is screwed up big-time in the universe, the damn planets are way out of alignment, you hear me?"

Vince laughed.

"Listen, I refuse to feel sorry for your crusty ass—as much pussy as you command. But anywho—back to Raven. This chick is something else. I mean, she is strange—she keeps the details of her personal life close to her vest. I think there's been some drama in her life recently that she's desperately trying to run from. I'm not pushing her to open up. Not yet. In time, I believe she will confide in me. In the meantime, we are having one hell of a time! This woman loves to do anything out of the ordinary. Whether it's meeting at a bar pretending to be complete strangers, or acting out these elaborate sexual fantasies of hers, she keeps things totally refreshing and passionate. I am loving life right now!"

"Good for you!" Erika exclaimed, raising her coffee mug to Vince. "Just be careful, Vince. I don't want you to put too much of yourself into this woman without knowing where she's coming from. Call me old-fashioned, but I tend not to trust a lover who isn't completely open with me from day one."

"Yeah, I hear you. But I get a very good vibe from this woman. I don't think she's out to deceive me. She's going through something right now, yet it is clear that she wants to spend her free time with me. And when she's around, she's mine—I get all of her attention."

"Cool. So when are we going to meet her? I figure if home girl is doing this kind of number on you, the least you can do is introduce her."

"Oh yeah—I've been trying to set that up for several weeks now. She's been pretty busy, running in and out of town on a frequent basis, plus I told you about her singing. She has an incredible voice and has this gig in Philly once a week."

"Well, girlfriend best make time to meet us, or I'm gonna put her on the shit-list! She doesn't want to be there, trust me."

"I will pass the word on—I expect to see her tomorrow night."

"Please do."

There was a pause in conversation. Vince glanced over at me and grinned.

"You okay, bruh?"

"Never better," I responded.

"By the way, how are things between you, Angeliqué and Amber?" Erika inquired.

Vince's face glowed.

"Oh man, I've been talking to Amber on the regular. In fact, we're becoming quite close."

"Yeah?" I said. "And how's Angeliqué taking all of this?"

"In stride. She and I are cool—we've moved on to being just friends. She's doing her thing and I'm doing mine."

"So you and Amber are growing closer?" Erika asked, raised eyebrows and all.

"Yeah, she is good people—man I dig her. So down to earth. It's amazing how I can talk to her about anything. When Raven first did this disappearing act after our night in

Philly, I talked to Amber about it. She was so cool—she gave me a different perspective, and allowed me to vent without being judgmental."

"Doesn't surprise me," Erika said, "I picked up on her vibe when we were at bluespace—you wouldn't know about that, Trey—'cause your black ass was a no-show, as I recall . . ."

"Ouch," I said, a hurtful look painted across my face. "Is tonight 'mess with Trey night'? I'm just wondering?"

"That reminds me," Erika said, all excitedly, "I spoke to James about getting in touch with those people who help others find their birth parents. He called them and they said they'd be happy to assist." She put down her mug and directed her attention to Vince. "So you need to call your girl and tell her that if she's ready to do this, then to give me a call so I can get the ball rolling—get her in touch with these folks."

"Very cool!" Vince exclaimed. I'll let her know. I'm sure she's anxious to get started. It sounds like this is something that's been on her mind for a while."

"So, big daddy," Vince said to me, "I think you're finally up. What's new, playa? Fill us in on your world."

I raised my hands in a mock shrug.

"Ah, you know me—I'm just a squirrel trying to get a nut . . ."

"Oh lawd," Erika exclaimed, "it's gonna be a long-ass night!"

Back in my dining room with my guests seated around me, I waved my knife ceremoniously over dessert as if I were presiding over some Masai warrior initiation—Erika's homemade apple pie and my chocolate bourbon pecan and cherry cheese pies laid out majestically in front of us. The vapors wafted over the table, and for a moment I had to close my eyes to focus every nerve ending on what reached my nostrils. I could feel my dick swelling as my olfactory senses kicked into overdrive. DAYUM, those desserts smelled so freaking good!

Slicing into them, I handed over gleaming china filled to the brim with chocolate, cherry, apple, whipped cream, sugar, and pecans heavily doused with bourbon. Erika and Vince didn't wait for me, attacking their plates with a vengeance. There was pure unadulterated passion in their eyes as they licked their forks—you could see their crazed look, their don't-mess-with-me-right-now-I'm-in-the-midst-of-ecstasy painted on *thick*. These weren't any old kind of pies—these mutha suckas were to die for!

Pouring more coffee, I sat down and took a bite, relishing my own handiwork.

"You my man!" Vince said, in between bites, "This shit is the bomb!"

"For real, Trey—I take back every bad thing I've ever said 'bout you!"

I eyed her as I forked another bite.

"So, bruh," Vince said, pausing to slurp at his mug of coffee, "stop dillydallying and give us the 4-1-1 on your shit. How's the love life? Been kicking it with anyone new?"

"Dude, please—I fucking wish!" I shouted. "This dry spell of mine is lasting way too long. This shit keeps up, my dick is gonna shrivel up and fall off, I kid you not!"

"You know, Trey," Erika said, seriously, "it's not a bad thing to abstain from sex for a time or two. Every now and then we need to clean the system out, so to speak—let our bodies rest from all of the impurities that come from intercourse."

"Trick, please—this coming from you? A woman who's boning two dudes at once? Take your own damn advice!"

Erika chuckled.

I continued.

"Things are so messed up, I actually had a drink with Layla the other night."

Erika's jaw dropped; Vince bent forward explosively as if being shot in the back.

"WHAT?" they both barked simultaneously.

"What's the big deal?" I replied, nonchalantly. I paused to fork another bite of pie into my mouth. Erika and Vince watched my every move, their mouths hanging open in shock.

"You can't be serious," Erika muttered.

"As a heart attack. Listen, I can take care of myself. Besides," I added, boisterously, "Layla doesn't scare me . . ."

Vince and Erika exchanged looks, as they remained silent.

"What? She came into bluespace while I was there having dinner alone. She came over to my booth to speak, and we ended up having a drink or two. No big deal."

I took a sip of coffee and glanced rapidly between Erika and Vince.

"WHAT?" I yelled.

It was Vince who spoke. Slowly, and with purpose.

"And you're okay with this—Layla back in your life?"

"She's not back in my life, Vince, just because I had a drink with her. Y'all are trippin'!"

Erika sighed.

"Okay, you're a big boy. Don't let us stop you."

"Thank you, momma!"

"One question though. What are your intentions with regard to her?" she asked.

I didn't even blink.

"Sassy—I have no freaking intentions when it comes to Layla. She walked over, we had a drink. End of discussion.

Ain't nothing going down. Not then, not now, not in the future. Believe that!"

"Okay . . ."

"Besides," I said, scraping my plate clean with my shiny fork, before popping the warm sliver into my mouth, savoring the last bite, "I've got this other honey in my gun sights—Giovanna, my new client, with her sexy ass. I know, I know," I said, holding up a hand. "I might lose my job over that fine heifer, but I'll tell you what, I swear I don't even care anymore—she's making me crazy, I can't tell you just how much. I am stone cold in lust with the thought of getting between those sultry-smooth thighs, and I refuse to stop the pursuit of little Ms. Thing until the fat lady sings!"

I glared at Erika and Vince, raising a finger in their faces before continuing.

"Bernard John freaking Marshall be damned! Y'all can put that in your peace pipe and smoke it! That *honey* is mine . . ."

Fourteen

I was sitting next to an angel. And nothing else in the world mattered . . .

There was this long table of dark wood, polished to perfection. I was like a child, cognizant of my handprints leaving marks. So I folded, then unfolded my hands repeatedly, attempting to hover above the grain, feeling the sweat drip between palms, before finally giving in and resting my hands flat on the table, fingers outstretched, as if in surrender.

Next to me, Mrs. Giovanna Marquis sat rigid, the tendons in her face clenching as if they owned a pulse—otherwise she remained still. Her hair was pulled back into a single long braid that wound down her back. Not one strand of hair was out of place. She wore makeup, flawless: boysenberry lip-gloss that made her entire mouth shine, some rouge that roseyed up her high cheekbones, and a touch of eyeliner and shadow. An impeccable light green pantsuit—taut against flesh, was showing off sensuous curves, and tight-ass matching heels. I found myself stealing a glance over to my left every other minute or so. The outline of her breasts was hypnotic, the way they rose and fell with her steady breathing. I imagined where her nipples lay, and felt my craving for them burn inside of me. A fire was brewing; a volcano about to spew, and it took every ounce of strength to tear my gaze away. Shutting my eyes briefly during a lull in the conversation, I was transported to a place where her husband, a sand-colored man named Mr. Mubar, who sat directly across from me in a flawless double-breasted blue wool suit with a fiery look in his eyes, did not exist. Neither did his attorney, who also sat across the moat of dark, polished wood—a tall, gaunt man of Middle-Eastern descent, slightly balding on top, bespeckled, with the look of an authoritarian. Trying to scare me . . .

But I don't scare easily . . .

We were here, two days after the night of food and drink among friends at my crib, in a warmly lit conference room on the fourth floor of an office building a stone's throw from the United Nations. I had soured at the idea of meeting Giovanna's husband and attorney on their turf. But I wasn't going to argue, especially since I didn't have an office in New York.

The purpose of the meeting was to initiate a property settlement agreement. It hadn't gone well up to this point. Her husband, a high-ranking diplomat in the Qatar government, was pissed off and not afraid to show it. He leered at his soon-to-be ex-wife, raising his hands into the air every time I made a point about their impending divorce. Old boy wasn't taking it too well—that much was clear . . .

I had been corresponding with his attorney for over a week now. I was under the assumption that we were on the same page. Apparently, however, Mr. Mubar hadn't gotten the email . . .

"As I was saying," I began, glancing between Mr. Mubar and his attorney, "At this point we just need to come to closure with regard to the main residence here in New York, and the secondary home in Washington. We have provided counsel with a proposal that we think is amicable."

Mr. Mubar threw up his hands again, a string of spittle flying from his mouth as he glared at his wife.

"I cannot for the life of me believe that you are actually going through with this!"

He turned to his attorney and began speaking rapidly in some language that was foreign to me. Slapping his hand hard on the table, he stood abruptly and went to the window. Pivoting, he glared for a moment at Giovanna before pointing in her direction.

"No!" he shouted, boisterously. "I will not agree to this proposal. The apartment here in the city was furnished by my government and therefore not negotiable. As far as the Washington residence, I still use it when I'm in D.C. and therefore have no plans to give it up. *She*," he said with discontent dripping from his lips, "can find somewhere else to live, if she's not happy in our marriage!"

Giovanna's jaws clenched, I could see the muscles working beneath skin. She said nothing. I had counseled her to let me handle it.

I cleared my throat.

"Well, Mr. Mubar, I assure you that Mrs. Marquis is as distressed as you are—in fact, more so. Regardless, we need to reach an agreement on the property. Unfortunately this is a necessary step—"

"I am done with this!" he said, glaring at his attorney. "I am leaving this meeting and going home. To *our* home if she so chooses."

The attorney stood. Bent forward and whispered in the ear of his client. I took the opportunity to pat the hand of Giovanna, letting my hand stay on hers a microsecond more than custom would dictate. She glanced my way but remained silent. She was so beautiful, even when she was fuming. I fought the sudden urge to tongue kiss her.

The two men's whispers pierced the air with their harsh language. I once again cleared my throat as I stood up.

"Excuse me. I have a question. Is it true that you will be returning to your native country for good next week?"

That got *everyone's* attention in the room . . . but quick . . .

Giovanna's husband spun around to glare at me. His eyes bore into my skull, yet I remained motionless, a smile painted on my face, unhurried in my breathing. I was not afraid. Just the opposite. I was galvanized with exhilaration.

Giovanna was getting out of her seat, a look of utter disbelief on her face. I used my palm to rest it on her shoulder, and apply slight pressure. I shook my head and she sat back down.

"How do you—"

"A simple yes or no will suffice," I said casually. I reached for my cell on the polished wood, eyed it as I held it in my hand. "If yes, then we have nothing further to discuss—your actions will unfortunately be interpreted as fleeing the country in order to hide assets and—"

"That is preposterous!" his attorney yelled, his hands raised in the air. "I've never heard anything so ridiculous in all of my life!"

My eyebrow rose.

"I think not. Anyway, we will let the court decide. My job is to ensure that my client is not harmed in any way by his actions."

I pressed a few buttons, placing the phone to my ear. The two men stared at me in disbelief, jaws hanging open as if they could not believe what was transpiring.

"Yes, it's me. File the emergency injunction I drafted earlier per my instructions and have Mr. Mubar served within the hour. Yes. That is correct. Thank you. Goodbye."

I shut the call down yet kept the phone held between my fingers where they could see it.

"Our business has concluded, gentlemen," I said, reaching for Mrs. Marquis's shoulder. "Let's go," I whispered to her, "I'm sorry it had to come to this . . ."

Giovanna rose, her features stunned into slow motion as she wrestled to understand what was going on. Mr. Mubar was shrieking at his attorney, whose entire body was shaking with incredulity. I pressed my navy blue and mauve tie with a hand and buttoned the top two buttons of my suit.

"WAIT!" Mr. Mubar exclaimed, more froth alighting from his lips. "Wait—can we discuss this as civilized men?" he yelled, arms outstretched. The look on his face was priceless, and for a moment I actually felt sorry for him—first losing his wife, and now this.

I cocked my head sideways and said, "Yes?"

"Please!" he uttered, almost out of breath. "Let us sit and come to an agreement. I am not trying to hide anything. And I do not want to drag this out."

I motioned for Giovanna to sit.

Then I gestured for Mr. Mubar and his attorney to do the same.

My cell remained in my hand. I noticed that Mubar couldn't take his eyes off of it—as if it were a piece of steak that a Doberman was eyeing, or a petite young stripper on stage in front of a throng of anxious inebriated freshmen.

"Mr. Mubar—I hope you understand that my client has no desire to hold you here, especially if your official business has concluded." I paused for effect and to glance at Giovanna who stared straight ahead, her eyes boring laser holes into her husband. "But we will need to conclude all business related to the property settlement and the divorce, since as I'm sure your attorney here will tell you, once you leave the country, well, it will be difficult, if not impossible for any jurisdiction here to enforce a ruling that the court may impose."

Mubar's jaw rattled, but he said nothing. He eyed his attorney as sweat broke out on his forehead. I took the opportunity to continue.

"Therefore, Mr. Mubar, I propose that, with your approval, we draft papers turning over ownership of the Washington residence to Mrs. Marquis immediately. And these other items that were highlighted here . . ." I slipped three typewritten pages across to them, "will need to be dealt with as well. ASAP, since we don't want to hold you up . . ."

I opened my hands, palms up. The cell lay in my right hand. I took the opportunity to lay it gently on the polished table. "If this is agreeable to you, then we can forgo any further inconvenience to you and I will, of course, cancel any pending motions or emergency injunctions."

An audible sigh escaped from the lips of Mr. Mubar.

Forty-five minutes later, our business was concluded and Mrs. Marquis and I were escorted out. We stood on the corner, the curvature of the United Nations building to our backs, as Giovanna stood lost in thought.

"Walk with me. The fresh air will do you good."

I glanced at my watch. It was after three and my stomach was growling. I wondered if Giovanna could sense my hunger.

For food and something more primal . . .

She glared at me for a moment. I held out my hand, yet she refused to take it. I looked at her in earnest.

"What did I do?" I asked disbelievingly.

Giovanna fumed.

"You . . . have a . . ." She fought to find the right words. I stopped, letting well-dressed people meander around me, as I opened up my hands, palms up.

"What?"

"A certain *way* about you . . ."

I cocked my head to the side as I stood on a corner, cabs and pedestrians whizzing past me as if we were the only ones standing still.

"Meaning?" I asked with the birth of a smile.

Giovanna ignored me and began walking; I jogged to catch up. She glanced my way and said: "you can be one son of a bitch when you want to."

"*Excuse me*???"

I stopped dead in my tracks, my irritation clearly evident.

"Don't get all up in a tizzy," she said, "I just meant that you were tough as nails in there."

I shook my head slowly.

"And how would you have me act?" I asked.

"Trey, calm down—I don't have a problem with what you did today. Actually I'm grateful. The son of a bitch had it coming. I can't believe he's actually leaving . . . ," she said, fuming.

Giovanna was shaking her head morosely as the lines around her mouth deepened.

"Listen, try not to dwell on that—the most important thing is that you've won—you got what you wanted and now you can go on with your life, free and clear from him. From this point forward, everything else will be just a technicality."

She nodded silently.

"I thank you for that," she said softly.

"It's what I do," I said, as if my performance in there was no big deal.

I could see the faint beginnings of a smile; her lines softening and her eyes beginning to brighten. I flashed a grin, and Giovanna grinned back.

"That's what I'm talking 'bout!" I exclaimed, watching her radiant smile. A wave of pleasure coursed through me and I'm sure she witnessed me shudder. I checked the Breitling again as my stomach groaned. "Listen, I'm famished; I'm sure you are too. Let's grab some lunch, my treat, and celebrate."

Giovanna slowed her roll. We were half way up a block of stately apartment buildings when she stopped and turned to me.

"Rain check—I need to be on my way."

I frowned.

"Hey, come on. You deserve this—you got what you wanted—to be free. And I want to take you out. It's just lunch, Giovanna—it's not a date, just lunch." I smiled, but I could feel the tension rising in my gut. There was no wind, but the temperature was cold. Regardless, I could feel beads of sweat below the surface of my forehead readying to appear. I hoped Giovanna couldn't see what I felt.

"Trey, I don't think so, but thank you just the same." She headed for the curb. "Actually, I think I'll catch a cab here." She raised her arm.

"Hey, wait a minute, am I missing something?" I asked, the frustration that had been bubbling to the surface finally erupting. I made no attempt to hide my resentment. "I really don't understand you, Giovanna. Have I done something to offend you? I mean, please tell me if I have, because ever since we've met, it seems like you've gone out of your way to avoid me. What is up with that?"

Giovanna sighed heavily.

"Correct me if I'm wrong, but our business had concluded. It's over. So, why can't two grown people get together and have lunch." I took a breath and moved forward into her space. "You're a beautiful woman," I said, my voice low as I eyed her, "and I'm not going to lie—I'm interested in you. I'd like to get to know you better. Is there something wrong with that? Tell me if there is . . . What am I missing here?"

Giovanna sighed again as her eyes locked onto mine. She made not a move to retreat, our bodies deliciously close.

"Trey, you're a nice guy. Intelligent, successful, and very handsome. But . . ." Her words faltered as she glanced downward.

I felt my sails deflate.

"But what? You're not attracted to me?"

"Trey—let's not do this. I'm not feeling this, okay? I don't know how else to say it."

"*Okay . . .*"

She glanced back at the curb, raising her hand as a cab ground to a halt. I stared sheepishly at the driver. Giovanna stepped off the curb and into the cab. Once sequestered inside, she glanced my way.

"I never thanked you properly for the roses," she said with a timid smile. My pulse was racing as I stared into those eyes feeling my heart plummet. "They were lovely."

The cab sped up, leaving me on the sidewalk uttering, "glad you liked them," to myself . . .

Two eighteen a.m. I know because the glaring ring of the telephone stung in my ears, yanking me away from a deep slumber. I struggled onto my side, glancing at the alarm clock as I reached for the phone, my eyes swimming inside my head.

"Hello?"

"Sorry to disturb you, Mr. Alexander, it's the front desk."

I sat up, rubbing my eyes as I fumbled for the light switch.

"Yes?" I responded, alarms going off in my head. What possibly could the front desk want with me at this late hour?

For a split second a horrific thought flooded through me—

a terrorist attack was unfolding floors below, and I had minutes or even mere seconds to react before the mayhem and
carnage kicked into high gear.

"You have a visitor, Mr. Alexander. I need to know
whether to send her up."

Her.

My stomach tightened.

"Who is it?" I asked barely above a whisper, feeling my
heart bounce.

"A Mrs. Marquis. She says she's a client of yours."

My mind hit a wall. For a moment I was speechless, unable to process what the desk clerk had just told me. Hours
ago, the very same Mrs. Marquis had left me standing on a
picturesque curb in midtown Manhattan, a sour look painted
on my face as the epitome of perfection had left me standing
there like a fool. Alone.

And now she was here . . . downstairs . . .

"Send her up," I said, my mind clearing.

"Right away, sir," the clerk responded, replacing the
phone.

I stared at the receiver for a moment then down at my
half-naked form. I was clad only in a pair of black French
Connection boxer briefs, FCUK written across the waist-
band in bold, block lettering, the fabric tight and form fitting, showing off the package.

My package.

My mind continued to race—what to do, how to act?

But then a calm overtook me. I let my breathing return to
normal. What was there to be concerned about? I was Trey
Alexander, the *man*, and I needed to damn near start acting
like him. I was in control—always had been. The fact that a
fine-ass woman was in my sights should *never* throw me for
a loop. I guess I was slipping . . . the past few months had

taken a toll on me. With work and shit—not that that was any excuse, but I had slipped and lost sight of who I was for a moment . . .

But Trey was back in control!

And tonight, I would take no prisoners.

A rap at my door cut through the din of my concentration. I rose from the bed, went to the door, and opened it.

Giovanna stood there in a red terry cloth sweat suit, a pair of Nikes, and an oversized leather coat that hung to her midsection. A Baltimore Orioles baseball cap adorned her head. I felt myself stirring, and did nothing to contain my swelling state.

I let my gaze scan over her body, my stare lingering at the curves of her hips.

"Did I wake you?" she asked, her voice not far above a whisper.

"You did," I answered.

She smiled seductively.

"Can you find it in your heart to forgive me?" she asked.

"Time will tell . . ."

Opening the door wider, she brushed past me, glancing down at my stomach and what lay below. I had not taken steps to cover my near-nakedness.

"Nice . . . abs," she said.

"Thank you," I said, following her as she sashayed into my room. "You will forgive the untidiness, but I wasn't expecting company this late."

Giovanna turned and eyed me as she threw off her cap and let her jacket fall to the bed. "I can leave if you'd prefer—come back another time when you're more . . . prepared."

"That won't be necessary."

She sat on the edge of the bed and I took the opportunity to view her ample breasts that strained against the terrycloth fabric. She had her top unzipped enough to show a hint of flesh and cleavage—I took it all in, her long, tight legs, and the cleft between her legs.

"So," I continued, "to what do I owe this pleasure?"

Giovanna stared at me without responding. Instead, she scanned me up and down in the same way as I had done moments before, paying close attention to my boxer/briefs, and to my chest. A grin was painted on her face. She nodded approvingly.

"Well," she finally said, after a moment of tense silence, "I didn't come here for small talk, I can tell you that."

I was standing a mere three feet from her, glancing downward at that most sacred of places—the point where her thighs met—when her hand went to her chest, manicured fingers hovering dangerously close to the zipper. She toyed with the thing as she closely monitored me. I was silent. Giovanna commanded me to sit. I took a seat on a couch that was positioned in front of the closed drapes. As I sat back she stood, coming within a foot of me and glancing down, wearing a seductive smile.

"Trey Alexander," she began, with one hand on her hip. The other remained poised on the zipper to her top. My eyes were glued to that hand. I did not blink. "Esquire," she continued, "A man who commands attention whenever he speaks. Whenever he enters a room." Giovanna smiled. "I can just imagine how you command a courtroom—not a whisper nor sigh when Mr. Alexander is cross-examining a defendant!"

I nodded.

"Oh, but I wonder if you are man enough to command this," she said, with a gleam in her eye.

Ever so slowly she began unzipping her top.

I was utterly speechless.

When it was down to her navel, she separated the two

halves and let the top fall from her shoulders. I swallowed hard as my eyes bugged out. She was nude underneath. Her breasts were airbrush perfect, full, with small brown areolas—lovely pointed nipples that beckoned me, like a curled finger. I placed both hands on the couch, beginning to rise but Giovanna gestured for me to remain where I was.

I sat back down, as I was told.

Giovanna licked her lips seductively before kicking off her sneakers. Her palms went to her waist, hooking her fingers underneath the fabric of her sweatpants as she began to pull downward. I remained transfixed as her bare flesh came into view: a thin patch of hair between smooth, caramel thighs as her sex was unveiled. I sucked in a breath, my cock fully hard now, fighting against the fabric of my boxer/briefs. An audible moan escaped from my lips.

"Goddamn, Giovanna," was all I could muster.

"Are you, Trey?" she murmured, with a raised eyebrow. "Man enough to take this, making it yours?"

"God *yes*!"

The sweatpants pooled at her feet. She kicked them away as if they were a mere irritation.

Giovanna stood before me fully nude, the glory of her body a sight to behold.

"You best be sure. Because I don't need a man who's content just following along. I don't need a man who needs to be told. I could go to my husband if that's all I'm after."

She took a step closer. My hands reached forward, finding the soft curves of her waist. I pulled her into me, her breasts inches from my face. A nipple grazed my cheek. I closed my eyes, inhaled the essence of her being, the scent of her womanhood, as I exhaled forcefully.

"Why all the charades the past month?" I asked.

"Because I couldn't make it too easy—that would make me a slut, which I am not!"

I nodded, my insides burning. My head ached—but it was one of those damn good feelings . . .

"Tonight, Trey, I want a man who can take charge, command me with his power. I need this to be yours. I think you are that man. Don't prove me wrong . . ."

I enveloped the soft tissue of her breast with my mouth, reaching for her ass, palming each cheek as I massaged the taut flesh, circling each nipple with an erect tongue before some internal force consumed me, overtaking me with its fury, forcing both hands to ride the crease of her ass downward to her opening, finding her cavern, already moist, and plunging in, two fingers simultaneously attacking her slit as Giovanna arched her head back and cried out, "Oh *yes*, that's what I'm talking 'bout!"

My fingers shimmered with her juices; I spun her around, heart shaped ass inches from my face as I bent her forward forcefully, hair flying as I used the palm of my hand against the flat of her back, commanding her to spread her thighs, plunging my fingers in and out of her cave. Leaning forward, my tongue lashed out against the smooth darkness of her ass, tracing a swath downward, finding the cleft and riding it like a wave, downward still, past the tight puckering of flesh, licking that hole as she squirmed and groaned, inching downward still until tongue hit the fleshy folds of her sex.

"God *yes*!" Giovanna moaned, as I tongued her insides, tasting the sweet nectar that glistened against her pussy juice-laden skin.

Her head was almost to the ground, legs spread wider as I invaded her opening, using two fingers to spread her wings, attacking her clit with my teeth and gums, letting her feel my power and precision as I ran the length of her engorged sex, her lips glistening like fresh morning dew, the fleshy bulb of her clit pulsating as I sucked it into my waiting mouth, feeling the passion overtake me, giving in to my desire of wanting to devour her whole, sex and all, leaving nothing but a wasteland in my wake.

As suddenly as I had begun, I shut it down, gently guiding her down onto the couch as I groped her breasts. Giovanna's chest was heaving, and her thighs were on fire. I could feel the heat on her skin.

I kissed her longingly.

Removing my briefs, I stood, naked, engorged, full of life, my thick cock dancing slothfully in front of me, as Giovanna tracked my every moment with glinting eyes. She licked her lips seductively as I brought my dick within feeding distance. Giovanna's hand raised up, her palms on my chest, twisting at my nipples, then gliding her hands down against the tautness of my stomach, one hand circling around to my tight ass that she gripped between clenched fingers as her other hand descended to the top of my sex, feeling the base of my stalk, running a hand up the shaft, encircling the girth then tightening her grip, sliding upward, jerking as she went, until she reached the head, giving it a light squeeze before dropping her hand to my balls, which she cupped, squeezed, letting me know who was in charge . . .

There was a high-back chair—one of those old fashioned things one found in rich folk's homes—with a cream color seat set against richly stained wood. It sat off to the side, diagonally from the bed. I was eyeing it as Giovanna pulled me toward her, the pressure on my ass revving up, her lips parting, mouth opening, eyes closing as she prepared to consume my meat. But at the last second, just as the tip of my head, already speckled with precum, breached her opening and was grazing lightly against her teeth, I abruptly pulled out and went to the chair, leaving Giovanna bewildered and panting, a sour look on her face as she wondered just what I was up to!

Two neckties were draped across the back of the chair—

the navy blue/mauve one that I had worn earlier in the day, and an aquamarine one with small rectangles that had been my alternate for the day—I grabbed them in one fist, the chair in the other as I dragged it over to Giovanna. I placed it in front of her, facing the draped windows, led her to it, and sat her down. Giovanna was silent as she stared at me. I took her hands and raised them over her head, following the lines of her arms with my fingers, stroking her smooth, caramel flesh in a seductive way, before I brought both of her hands down and behind the back of the chair. Interlocking her fingers, I used the blue and mauve tie to affix her wrists to the legs of the chair. Her eyes widened as she watched me, not with fear, but with delicious anticipation of things to come. Next, I spread her legs, slowly, purposefully, using the other tie to lash one ankle to the front leg of the chair. Her other leg remained free—I quickly glanced around the room and spied my Kenneth Cole belt on the floor. I scooped it up, and in a minute, Giovanna was completely bound to the chair—legs splayed, eyes wide, breasts heaving and skin quivering while her attorney stood nude before her.

I was silent for a moment, my cock swinging inches from her face. She was eyeing me before her gaze dropped to my member. Once again she licked her lips, but once again I moved away, this time behind her. Giovanna struggled to keep me in her sights, but she could not. Extinguishing the lights, the room was plunged into total darkness. For a moment neither of us moved. I listened to her breathing, my toes curling into the firm carpet as I tugged at the bulbous head of my cock and smiled.

Trey was back in the saddle, y'all.

For real!

Moving to the window in the obscurity of darkness, fingers stroking the edge of the bed for guidance, I found and grasped at the drapes. The fabric parted, revealing floor to ceiling windows and a spectacular view of the Hudson River with New Jersey beyond. Twinkling lights from streetlights, automobiles, and apartment buildings winked at us. A heavy rain had commenced. It pelted the glass, the sound therapeutic, as lightning flashed every few moments. I glanced back at Giovanna who was bound to the chair. She stared on in awe, the scene in front of her hauntingly beautiful. The river was an undulating mass of blackness. It was hypnotic. It was eerie. Had it not been for the sex-starved woman lashed to my chair, I would have taken a moment to take in the entire scene . . . with all of its splendor and glory.

Perhaps another time . . .

Returning back to Giovanna, I stood before her, hands on my hips. For a moment neither of us spoke. I tugged at my cock, using full long strokes, inches from her face. I waved it in front of her, my shaft tracing figure eights above her cheek.

I allowed it to come to a rest above her lip, my fingers still wrapped around the shaft as I sucked in a deep breath. My stare bore into hers as I felt myself boiling. I could not put into words what I was feeling—everything these past months—the good, the bad, and the ugly—had rolled up into one considerable event that suddenly had been tossed away like an outdated magazine. Suddenly, tonight—this moment—*this* woman—overshadowed everything else. My eyes burned—with the anticipation of sexual release—it was right there, so close I swear to God I could taste it.

Reaching down with my free hand, my fingers grazed her opening. I rubbed her clit, then shot a finger deep inside, feeling her suck me in, my flesh swishing against her own moist flesh.

She was wet.

She was ready.

And so was I . . .

But there was unfinished business between us.

"Whose pussy is this?" I asked, my voice slightly above a whisper. Yet there was no dithering in my pitch, no vacillation to my cadence.

Glancing upward into my face, Giovanna swallowed hard.

"Yours. No question . . ."

Her lips remained parted. She licked them nervously, the fleshy part of her mouth glistening. I entered her mouth slowly with the fullness of my cock, reaching for the back of her head as I guided my missile home, not stopping until the entire length of my shaft was entombed in her throat. Giovanna's eyes widened, and her body shifted unsteadily in the chair. But my hands remained locked onto her head. When I could feel the back of her throat rubbing against my tip, I ceased my thrust, gripping her head more tightly as I felt the pressure within me rise. Giovanna's eyes were locked onto mine.

"Are you ready?" I asked in a harried voice.

She could only nod.

She clamped down her jaws and I began a rhythmic thrusting of my cock in her mouth. I marveled at the way my length disappeared between her moist lips, only to reappear an instant later, shiny with saliva. I thrust harder and deeper, feeling the smoldering lava within me rise . . .

And then, almost without warning, my entire body convulsed and I was screaming and simultaneously coming, flooding her with my seed, my eyeballs rolling back into my head, toes forcing me to stand on end as lightning flashed through my eyelids, thunder pounding around us, Giovanna lapping up my juice, not having any other choice, and I not giving her the chance for any other course of action. My cock quivered in her mouth, balls patting against her chin and neck as my orgasm rocked me.

"Oh FUCK!" I groaned before the wave subsided. After what seemed like perpetuity, my chest ceased to heavy, and I opened my eyes. Giovanna's stare was locked onto mine.

I slowly pulled out, watching my glistening shaft slide between her luscious lips, as I opened my mouth to speak.

"Swallow it," I murmured, and then as an afterthought I added with authority, "*bitch*!"

For a split second her eyes widened, but then grew soft, seeing my thin smile. So Giovanna did what I asked of her, silently and obediently . . .

I suddenly grinned, for she and this scene reminded me of that dairy commercial. Giovanna must have sensed the same because she grinned back too. She glanced upward, and said with an infectious beam: "Got *more* milk???"

Fourteen days later, yours truly was in the office, head down, mug of steaming coffee by my side when the intercom buzzed.

It was India Jasmine Jackson.

"Mrs. Marquis is holding on line one."

I smiled eloquently as I laid down my fountain pen.

"Hey you!" I sat back in my leather chair, swiveling around to my window as I grinned at the office buildings and Capitol in the distance. I could feel my dick tingling in my pants. *He* always stirred when there was any mention of Giovanna . . .

"Hey baby," she cooed in response. "The roses are sooooo wonderful, Trey! I can't believe you sent me two dozen!"

I clenched my fist in victory.

"You are quite welcome and you're more than worth it! Anywho—I was just thinking about you," I said, closing my eyes and re-running the delicious scenes of Giovanna and I in New York two weeks ago—her heart-shaped ass slapping against my pelvis, screwing her doggy style as thunder and lightning pounded the hotel. Outside, it was a storm of hurricane proportions—inside, the steamy passions were reaching similar magnitude . . .

"Oh really?" she said. "Do tell."

"I was wondering what color of panties you were wearing today?" I mused.

"Oh baby," she replied playfully, "you *know* I don't wear panties . . ."

I grinned like Stevie fucking Wonder.

"That's my girl!" I exclaimed.

For the past two weeks, I had been like a kid in a candy store—no, scratch that—like a child in the hood who's celebrating Christmas for the very first time! I was hooked on this woman like I don't know what. My friends hadn't seen me. My office mates were wondering if I was seriously ill with all the time off I had been taking. Even Bernard John Marshall had inquired as to my health.

But really, mutha suckas were just jealous as hell cause they could see the glow in my mug . . .

Oh yeah.

They just *knew* I was getting some on the regular.

Giovanna and I had gotten together four more times since New York—twice more in Manhattan, and another two times here on my home turf. I was burning up those frequent flyer miles, but it was all good!

She was all I thought about—I was like someone with ADD—I couldn't wait to see her again.

Speaking of which . . .

"When am I gonna see you again?" I asked, my voice breathless.

"Listen to you. You sound like one of these men who are pressed as hell. I LIKE THAT!"

"I *am* pressed. Shoot, this dude's not afraid to admit it. I'm stuck on you like glue, bay-bee . . ."

She laughed.

"Well, Trey, I have some business to finish up tonight, but I'll be back in town tomorrow afternoon. We can get together anytime after that."

My mind was whirling. It conjured up a mouthwatering four-course meal; I would pull out all stops to impress the hell out of this gal!

"Can't wait! I'm gonna—oooh, I can't even begin to tell you what I'm gonna do to you when I see you again!" I said, holding my clenched fist to my mouth.

The thoughts swirling inside my brain made me wince.

Giovanna laughed.

"Promises promises. Just make sure you do that thing with your tongue I love so much."

"Anything you say, baby . . ."

"Oh, and tie me up again—I loved that!"

"If you're good . . ."

Giovanna purred.

"So, baby—what's on the agenda for tonight?" she asked.

"Oh, I don't know—I'm really not feeling work at the moment—what can I say, but I can't seem to keep my mind focused on anything related to the office—anywho—I think I'll run to the gym and grab some takeout and see what's on Netflix tonight."

"Sounds like a plan!" she said. "Wish I could join you."

"You will," I said. "Tomorrow . . ."

She hung up and I grasped the phone for a moment more,

as if holding the receiver, even after she had gone, would allow me some kind of continued connection with her.

There was a sudden rap at my door and Mitch Wagner waltzed in.

Mitch, like me, was an Associate Attorney, another fast-track guy who worked his white ass off, hoping to make partner before he was 40.

He was one of those guys who loved black people—he dated black women exclusively, he dressed like a brutha, and wore his hair combed forwarded to look like one of us, and he constantly was in my office looking for tips on everything from how black people talk to how we act in certain situations—we had a name for people like him—wigger!

But Mitch was good people.

And don't let the looks and lingo fool you—Mitch was one of the best litigators this firm had.

He was one of the good guys.

"Waz up, playa?" I said, returning the phone to its cradle.

"Same ole, same ole, Trey, how ya livin'?" he said.

I chuckled 'cause I'd taught him that shit too!

"Large and in charge!" I replied, as he sat on the edge of my desk. Mitch was wearing a black pinstriped, single-breasted, four-button suit that was fly as hell. I told him so.

"So what can I do you for?"

"Last-minute thing, Trey—I got this ticket to this function tonight, but I can't go. Bernard's got me humping on this prelim—thought you could go in my stead. It's at the Mexican Embassy. Lots of fine-ass Latino honeys gonna be there, my man!" Mitch arched his eyebrows as if to say, "Bruh, you know how we do!"

"Yeah?"

My mind whirled. I didn't have anything going on tonight—it was a Thursday night and miraculously, I was free. Giovanna wasn't due in until tomorrow, and even though I missed her terribly, I still was the head-Negro-in-charge in this city—and the thought of surrounding myself with some Latino pussy did have a certain appeal . . .

"What's this thing?" I asked, giving Mitch my full attention.

"You gonna love this—the Ivy League Black & Latino MBA Society is holding their annual gala tonight. Gonna be some intelligent pussy up in there!"

I grinned.

"And how the hell did you get an invite?"

Mitch feigned hurt.

"Trey, you know I'm an honorary member, cuz!"

I held out my hand.

"I'll go—and let you know how it turned out tomorrow!"

Mitch handed me an envelope as he waggled his tongue.

"Eat some of that hot spicy pussy for me, bruh, ya hear me?"

I just laughed as Mitch left me to my work . . .

Nine hours later—I should have been tired, but instead I felt energized. I had spent an hour at the gym getting my workout on, and then swung by this really great West African place on 18th Street in Adams Morgan that did takeout. I came home, showered, ate, and chilled for a minute before putting on a fresh new suit that I had just picked up from Barneys the week before last while in New York, and headed out to the embassy. The invitation stated that the gala began at 7 pm. So I figured I'd waltz in there at 9 and stop freaking traffic!

You know how we do!!!

Nine oh nine, to be exact (according to the Breitling). I showed my invitation to the doorman, a curly-headed, short, squat Latino with a badly tailored suit—but I wasn't mad at him. At least Juan was trying . . .

He waved me through and I took the stairs to the main reception hall.

The place was packed.

I grabbed a flute of champagne from a passing waiter (another Latino—a friendly-faced middle-aged woman with dark hair and piercing eyes), stopped to nibble on some hors d'oeuvres—some smoked salmon rolled in cream cheese that was quite tasty, and miniature crab cakes—delicious, if I may say so myself, and began to mingle.

There were a lot of college-aged faces, but a good number of thirtysomething folks like myself. I was scanning the crowd, searching for fuckable honeys when I heard my name being raised above the din.

I swung around and wound up face to face with Vince Cannon, Jr.

"What's up, my dawg?" I exclaimed, slapping him on the shoulder.

Vince looked back at me with this stunned look on his face.

"What are you doing here? You know Hoyas ain't exactly Ivy League," he replied.

"Ouch," I said, "That truly hurts."

I gave him dap anyway.

"Seriously, bruh," he said, "I didn't expect to see you here."

"Yeah, well an associate gave me his invite—he was working late—I had no plans so I said, what the hell!"

"I hear you. This is great, man—this is wonderful!"

Vince's eyes were blazing—he was on fire, and excitement oozed from his pores.

"What's up?" I asked, nodding to a pair of dark-skinned

honeys that walked by, checking us out. They wore name-
tags with their school affiliation written with bright blue
marker. Both of theirs read, "Cornell '02." I did the math
and shook my head with a grin.

I bet that pussy is *tight* . . .

"You get to meet Raven tonight," Vince was saying.

"What?" I asked. Vince's words flew by me, my mind
elsewhere, on the hunt.

"Raven—she's here, man—finally, after what seems like
an eternity, you get to meet her—Oh I can't wait to introduce
you. Your dick is gonna jump to attention when you—"

Vince lowered his voice as a movement off to his left
caught his eye. He ceased speaking—instead a wide grin
formed at his mouth. I stared at him for a second and then
turned to search out the object of his affection.

I was taking a sip from my champagne stem when I spotted her.

I think she saw me at the exact same time.

Time suddenly ground to a halt.

Burgundy and gold print dress, knee-high brown leather
boots—sexy as all get up—hair down free, diamond ear-
rings that sparkled, flawless makeup, unmistakable beauty
and sensuality.

I almost choked on my drink.

Giovanna stopped dead in her tracks when she spied me.

The smile that she had worn a microsecond ago was gone
in the blink of an eye.

Her stare panned from Vince to me, and back again.

I saw her mouth the words, "Oh *shit*!"

Vince saw it too.

His smile died on his face as he struggled to figure out
what was happening.

We stood side by side, the two of us, men purporting to

intermingle and socialize, as we wondered why this beauty wasn't advancing any closer.

I stared at her.

She stared at me.

Vince glared at her.

She seemed to be glaring back at Vince.

I called out her name.

"Giovanna," I yelled, gesturing at her to come closer.

Vince shot me a look.

"Raven," he called, gesturing the same.

"I'm sorry," she mouthed, as she crept closer.

And then, in an instant, all things became crystal freaking clear.

I glanced at Vince, my eyes wide. He wore the same comprehending look.

Raven and Giovanna were one and the same . . .

Fifteen

"May I speak to Amber?"

"Speaking."

"Hey girl! It's Erika!" she said, leaning back into the folds of her comfortable chair. It was a frigid Sunday morning, but a beautiful one, blue sky, no wind, just down right cold. Glancing outside of her picture window to the waiting street below, she just knew that looks were deceiving—that in fact it was freezing. But inside of her apartment with the heat cranked up, and wearing her flannel long johns and an oversized University of Southern California at Berkeley sweatshirt, she was feeling no pain . . .

"What's up, sistah?" Amber said enthusiastically, "It's been a while."

"Sure has. I hope I'm not catching you at a bad time."

"Not at all. It's good to hear from you. How's my buddy Vince doing?"

Erika grinned. "That fool is the same. Doing his thing. He tells me you two have been keeping in contact."

"Yeah, we have. I really dig Vince. He's got such a big heart. And so easy to talk to. I swear, sometimes we are on the phone for like hours, and I don't even know that the time is flying."

"I hear you. That's why Vince is so damn good at what he does. He has a gift for speaking and for listening. I think that's why we've been friends as long as we have."

"And how about you? What's new in your life?" Amber asked.

"Girl, I don't even know where to begin! My job is going really well, except for the long hours, but that's to be expected. It's just the male drama in my life that's got me jumping. Otherwise, I really can't complain."

"See, that's why I have to leave these Southern knuckleheads alone. 'Cause all they bring to the table is drama and more damn drama!"

"I hear ya! Sometimes I wish I was a damn lesbian!" The words slipped out effortlessly, and Erika instantly regretted it. "Ooops, I didn't mean it like that."

Amber chuckled.

"Hey, you're preaching to the choir."

"Yeah . . . well . . ."

Erika suddenly found herself thinking about Angeliqué. "Anywho—I called because I wanted to talk to you about something we briefly discussed when we all first met."

"I'm all ears," Amber replied.

"I remember that you mentioned you were raised by your great-grandmother and that you never knew your father."

"Right." A pause.

"Well, perhaps Vince mentioned to you that my boyfriend, James, works at a local television station here in town, and he knows someone whose business it is to reconnect lost children with their parents. I thought you might be interested in pursuing this."

"Yes, Vince mentioned it to me a few weeks ago. And I told him I was very interested."

"Good. I thought you would be. Something about the way you spoke about not knowing your father told me that you were anxious to find him."

"I don't know if anxious is the right word," Amber said. "But I'm definitely interested in knowing who he is and whether or not he'd like to meet me. Growing up not knowing your father, what he looked like, or even his name, was extremely difficult, to say the least."

"I can't even imagine," Erika said.

"Yeah. I remember when I was little, probably no more than five or six, and being in school—this was in Houston. And we'd have these school activities where fathers and mothers would be invited to participate. And most of the kids would show with their parents proudly in tow, except for this white girl and me. I'll never forget her name—Amy—she was just like me. She never knew her father. She didn't even know his name . . ." Amber paused in remembrance.

"I'm sorry," Erika offered.

"Don't be. That's life. After repeatedly questioning people about your father and not getting a response, you finally stop asking. But you never stop wondering . . ."

"Here's your opportunity to find out. These two people—they are a gay couple living in Washington—have started this foundation to reunite kids with the parents they never knew. They've approached James in the past about doing a piece for TV, in order to garner some financial support, but James put them off. When I told him your story he said he'd be willing to pursue it. So he spoke to the men, and they are more than willing to help."

Erika was getting excited about the prospects of assisting in Amber's search.

"That sounds great—but one thing," Amber said cautiously. "I don't have a lot of money—I've never had a steady income so I can't pay a lot."

"You don't have to worry about that at all," Erika exclaimed. "These folks are taking this case gratis, because James has said that he'll produce a segment on them if they do!"

"Wow—I don't know what to say!"

"Why don't you just start at the beginning? Tell me what you know about your family—and let's get this ball rolling!"

Amber sucked in a breath, then exhaled.

"Well, you know I was born in Houston. My mother is from New York. I'm not sure if she met my dad there or not. Anyway, she had me when she was real young—like fifteen. Her parents, my grandparents, sent her away to Texas to have me. From what I've been told, they were extremely upset by her getting pregnant so young. After my mother had me, she basically up and left. My great-grandmother, Stella, wound up caring for me. I don't know where my mother off and went to—I assume back to New York. All I know is that Stella raised me—*she* was the only mother I ever knew."

Erika nodded to herself as she reached for a legal pad and began to scribble furiously. "Okay. Can I ask a question?"

"Of course!"

"Why didn't your mother stay and raise you?"

"That's something I've wondered all my life," Amber said. "According to my great-grandmother, my mother wasn't really fit as a parent. She had issues of her own. And her family just wanted to pretend as if the whole thing never happened—as if I was never born . . ."

"I don't know what to say . . . ," Erika said softly.

"Yeah, to say it was messed up is an understatement." Amber paused for a moment, as if in deep reflection. Erika let the silence waft over them both.

"Anyway, Stella was my mother. She was the one who put a roof over my head; she was the one who raised me. She and she alone put me in school down in Houston."

"What about your great-grandfather?"

"He had died of a heart attack years before I was born, so I never got a chance to meet him."

"And your grandparents? Did you interact with them?" Erika asked.

"Very little. They came basically once a year to visit Stella. Most times my mother didn't even accompany them. They always said she was preoccupied with something, like she was off doing something important—but Stella would tell me the truth—that she was down on her luck, moving from one loser to the next. My grandparents always blamed my father for the downturn in her behavior—as if it was his fault that she turned out the way she did."

Erika noted that Amber didn't use her mother's name.

"Amber, what did Stella say about your father?"

"Very little—supposedly, she had never met him. Whenever I asked about him, she just told me that he was a nobody. After a while, I stopped asking."

Erika scribbled.

"What happened to your mother?"

Amber sighed. "She died in a car accident when I was eight. She fell asleep at the wheel after leaving out of some guy's house at three in the morning; she hit a telephone pole and was killed instantly."

There was no bitterness in her voice. But it lacked any measure of emotion. She was reciting facts, nothing more.

"Amber, I'm sorry."

"Don't be. I refused to go to the funeral. That was one of the few times in my life that Stella and I really got into it. God, I'll never forget that!"

Erika remarked, "Go on."

"There's nothing more to tell—I continued to live with my great-grandmother until two years ago when she died."

"Damn, Amber, I'm really sorry about your loss."

She was silent for a moment. Erika could hear her controlling back the tears. After a moment she cleared her throat.

"Yeah, now *that* was hard on me. Losing Stella meant losing the only family I'd ever known."

"I understand."

"I went to the funeral. I had no choice but to go—I mean, she was my mother, right? My flesh and blood. Afterward, I upped and left. There was nothing keeping me in Houston. I was done. I packed a suitcase and took a Greyhound out. Headed to New Orleans . . . but that's a whole 'nother story . . ."

"I hear you, girl," Erika exclaimed as she put the legal pad down.

"I'll need everyone's full name and addresses if you have them," she said.

Amber recited what she knew. They chatted for a few moments more.

"I can't promise you anything, I hope you know that—but these folks are good at what they do. It's very possible that a name will turn up—and then we can go from there," Erika said.

"I know. I'm not getting my hopes up. But I do hope it happens. I've been waiting what seems like my entire life to meet my father—to look him in the eyes and hear his voice—I've spent years imagining what it would be like." Amber paused for a moment before continuing. "I just hope it's not too late," she said, quietly.

"Me neither, girl," Erika responded, "me neither . . ."

*   *   *

"Hey you, it's me." Erika let the words sink in before venturing further.

"Hey . . ." There was a long pause as James processed what he was hearing, and what he would say next. "Long time no hear," he said.

That wasn't exactly true. It had only been four days. But it was like an eternity to him.

"How are you doing, James?" she asked tenderly. A big part of her missed him terribly. And she knew that her actions were hurting him deeply.

"Can't complain. Work's got me humping, as usual. You?"

"Same." Erika paused, waiting for him to chastise her for delaying four days to call—and letting most of the weekend pass without contact. But he remained silent. She was impressed.

Erika ventured forward. "I called, James, because I need to talk to you about my friend, Amber. Remember her? Vince's friend—the woman from New Orleans?"

"Yeah, the one who is searching for her father?"

"Right. I was hoping you could get things rolling. I've got the information you'll need from Amber."

James was silent. Erika knew his critical thinking mind was turning over like a twelve-cylinder engine.

"So, that's the only reason you called? Is this what its come to? Just business between us?"

"Of course not, James. You know me better than that. I'm sorry—would it make a difference if I told you how much I missed you?"

James let out a breath.

"Yes."

"A lot. I've *definitely* missed you," she said, and she meant it.

There was several seconds of dead silence.

"Perhaps you can come over and show me just how much."

Erika was prepared for this.

"Is that an invite?" she teased.

"What does it sound like?" he replied.

"A booty call."

"You know me better than that, Erika. I miss you. Badly. Remember, I'm the one who said, 'I love you'."

Erika found she couldn't respond.

James, thankfully, continued. "Why don't you come by around seven for dinner—I'll whip up something special; meanwhile, you can brief me on your friend Amber. Cool?"

Erika smiled.

"Way cool."

"Hey you!" Erika exclaimed. She waited for the familiar response, but got none. "You there, Vince?" she asked.

"Yeah, Sassy, I'm here. What's up?" The way he said those six words made her heart sink.

"Hey, just checking on you. How you holding up?" she asked gingerly.

"I'm living."

Erika listened to the silence that seemed to envelop them. She took a breath and continued.

"I take it you haven't heard from Raven."

"Nope." The word popped off the top of his teeth. Erika cringed.

"Wow, I don't know what to say."

Vince emitted a grunt. "Haven't heard from Trey either." He let the weight of that statement fill the silence between them. Erika's mind raced.

"Now that's surprising. What's his problem?" she asked.

"Guess he doesn't want to fraternize with the enemy . . ."

He spit a short laugh and then grew silent, contemplating the full meaning of those words.

Erika shook her head, making a mental note to call that fool and set his ass straight but quick. But first she needed to console Vince.

"I doubt that, Vince. I'm sure he's just busy. Working on some case, that's all." The words seemed hollow, however, even to her. "Listen, this thing is going to work out in the end, you'll see. You just need to have faith."

"Sassy, I just can't believe that I'm even in this mess in the first place. I mean, how does this shit happen? Raven is the first woman who's come along in a while that messed me up. This woman's got me hooked, and now look what's happened. She's screwing my best friend!"

"I know, Vince. I know. But as I said, things will work out for the best. You just have to have faith in what the two of you shared. If it's meant to be, then it will be . . ." Erika didn't know what else to say.

Ever since Vince had called her in a panic, she had been in a state of shock—how the hell did two best friends end up dating the same woman, without even knowing it? This chick was playing a game on them; there was no doubt about that. And what the hell was Trey thinking? She had spoken to him only briefly a few days ago. He had sounded genuinely perplexed, as much as Vince, if not more so. He had ranted and raved for a good fifteen minutes, talking about how Giovanna, as she was known to him, was the best lay he'd had in a solid year! Trey wasn't about to give up that shit without a fight!

The whole mess made Erika sick.

Vince continued to air his thoughts. "Part of me doesn't even want to see her again, knowing that she's been with him. I mean, how can I continue to see Raven knowing that she's been doing things with Trey. God knows what things! Come on!"

"Have you tried to talk to her?" Erika ventured.

"Yeah, I had one really short conversation with her that night. She said she was sorry and that she needed some time and space to figure things out."

"I'm sure she does," Erika shouted. What did she think she was doing?"

"I don't know, Sassy. I honestly don't know."

"Well, I think the first priority has to be making sure your head is together; and that your friendship with your boy remains intact. No one should lose a friendship over a woman. No one."

"True dat! I just hope Trey feels the same," Vince responded.

"Me too, Vince. Me too . . ."

Dinner was pan-fried tilapia with sweet potatoes and a fresh Caesar salad—Erika was extremely impressed. James was no Trey, that was for sure, but he tried hard, and got mega points for his efforts.

He served dinner in his oversized dining room. Conversation was relaxed and not forced. Erika was thankful. Over the past few weeks, their relationship had taken such a twisted, violent turn that Erika was unsure of where they stood now. And she knew James felt the same. But for some reason, James wasn't acting the way she had expected him to—gone was the incessant questioning of weeks before, and the condescending tone that had forced her to lash out at him when he burst into her bathroom that one evening, holding her prized chocolate dildo in hand!

James was holding a glass of Kendall Jackson Chardonnay as he spoke about the various assignments he was working on. He listened diligently as she recounted her work days and nights at the hospital—the critical cases that kept her late into the night, the patients who had gotten under her skin. James nodded as he forked the tilapia into his mouth, savoring the flavor of the sweet potatoes, and the crunchiness of the fresh Romaine lettuce.

The conversation shifted to Amber. James cleared the table as she talked, before retiring to the living room for coffee. Dessert would wait a bit further.

"You sound engaged about this whole thing," James remarked. "It's nice to see you getting involved."

"Yeah, I'm psyched, to tell you the truth. I don't know Amber all that well, but I feel a certain connection to her—I can't tell you why. Vince and I spoke about it—he had the same feeling when he first met her—as if they had met in a previous life or something. I can't put my finger on it, but something about her says 'family.'"

James nodded. He sat opposite her on the sofa—Erika placed her legs gently on his lap. James reached for her feet and began to massage them in turn.

"I'll give the foundation a call first thing tomorrow morning. They are anxious to begin working—I've already briefed them on the situation."

Erika smiled. She loved James' go get-em attitude.

"I really hope they can help," she said. "I hear the despair in Amber's voice when she talks about him. She truly wants to find her father. If only to bring some closure to her life."

They conversed for a few moments more. James continued his massage—his hands moving upward, gliding over her jeans to massage her calve muscles, knees, then thighs. He had put on some Brahms—it played softly and lazily in the background. By the time James reached for her breasts, Erika was moist beyond words. She hungrily took his tongue into her mouth, drinking in his familiar taste, like wine.

They groped each other for a moment further, mouths twisting about until James pulled back and looked at her longingly.

"Let me make love to you," he said, not bothering to hide his solid erection.

"What are you waiting for," Erika replied softly, with a glint in her hazel-colored eyes.

Flickers of candlelight danced over her prone form as she lay snuggled in James' terrycloth robe. Erika's head was in her hands, her smooth, relaxed face turned to the side, cheek pressed against the thick blue-green comforter. She had come to love that thing—loved the way it felt on her skin, loved the way it shimmered and shined as they moved against it—she felt as if she were gliding underwater, the muted sea greens and blues comforting. The shower was raging in the next room. James had been in there for ten minutes now. He had invited her in, to wash away the remnants of their lovemaking, but Erika had declined. She wanted to savor this moment, alone.

Their lovemaking had been wonderful. Tender in the beginning, accelerating to a frenzied ending, like waves whipped up by gale-force winds; raw, primeval, and animal like. James had surprised her with his actions. Normally so in control, so refined in everything he did, this night he seemed to lose control as the heat erupted between them. Perhaps he had lost himself within her slippery folds.

"Coming, baby?" he called from the next room.

Erika smiled but said nothing.

Her toes wiggled. As she shifted on the sea-green comforter, Erika could feel something stir inside her. She tightened the core of her being as it began to move. An imperceptible feeling, almost a silent thing, but she knew it was there—a trickle that began to seep, James's seed—slowly draining out of her, and that was what mattered to her most.

Driving home, Erika reviewed their lovemaking in her mind as she checked messages. There was only one—from Marcus.

"Hey Missy—it's me. I was hoping you didn't have plans tonight and would do me the honor of having dinner with me. I took the liberty of running by Redbox and picking out three must-see classics—hopefully one will catch your eye. Remember how we used to stay in for hours at a time watching movies, eating popcorn and pizza, and making what seemed back then like endless love? Well, I do. I suspect, and hope you do too. (Laughing). Okay, well, call me when you get this. I was thinking we could hook up around sixish . . ."

Erika's heart sank. The message was over five hours old. She glanced at the time: eleven forty. Too late to call? Probably. She felt terrible, imagining Marcus, alone in his apartment with his movies, popcorn, and cold pizza.

For a few moments, indecision froze her. Then she hit speed-dial as she switched ears. He picked up on the fourth ring.

"Hey you—I'm sorry for calling so late."

"That's okay," he responded, and she could hear him yawn as he stretched.

"I just got your message—I guess I missed dinner and a movie," she joked.

"That you did. Boy—I must have dozed off. What time is it?"

"Almost a quarter to midnight."

"So, what movies did you get, not that it matters now?" Erika asked.

"Well," she could hear the excitement in his voice. "I got a comedy, an action-adventure-thriller, and a drama, because I didn't know what you'd be in the mood for. First there's *Romancing the Stone* with Michael Douglas, Kathleen Turner, and Danny DeVito—I just love that movie. Number two was *Top Gun*, with Tom Cruise, and the third was *Ben-Hur*."

"Ben-Hur?"

"Yeah, *Ben-Hur*. That movie's the bomb. Charlton Heston is da man, you hear me?" Marcus said, laughing. He sighed before continuing. "It's too bad—I had a great evening planned—dinner, a movie, and a *special* massage for a special lady," he mused.

"Damn, damn, damn! So, what did you end up watching?"

"Two—*Romancing the Stone* and *Top Gun*."

"No *Ben-Hur*?" Erika mused.

"Not enough time—I only had *five* hours . . ."

"I'm sorry, Marcus," she said softly, "Can a girl get a rain check?" Erika pleaded.

"Nope."

"Marcus?"

"What?"

"I'll make it worth your while . . ."

Erika could feel his smile. She sighed heavily, thinking about her life at this very moment—having two good men who cared for her, both treating her right. She shook her head in amazement.

When it rains it sure does pour . . .

Marcus' voice interrupted her thoughts.

"Come sleep with me?"

"What?" She didn't think she had heard him correctly.

"Come sleep with me. I need to go to bed, and I suspect

you do too. But I'd love nothing more than to fall asleep with you in my arms. So come and sleep with me."

Erika thought about those powerful black arms surrounding her like a cocoon, holding her hostage, keeping her warm. She felt a shiver travel down her spine.

"Give me about twenty minutes," she heard herself say as she cut right, toward Rosslyn.

When it rains it sure does pour . . .

I paced my office, jacket off, clad in my finest starched white cotton shirt with tiny black and purple stripes, dark wool suit pants, black onyx cuffs, suspenders, dressed to the nines, one thought coursing through my head:

How the hell did I get myself into this mess?

I was pissed.

No. That was an understatement.

I was ready to put my size twelve up someone's ass, but quick.

An ass that I'd had the pleasure of getting to know intimately before this whole mess blew up in my face.

I cut a sharp glance at the phone. It sat on the edge of my desk, silent. I resisted the urge to bash its plastic shell with the underside of my hand. But that wouldn't accomplish anything. It wasn't the phone's fault.

Several more minutes of pacing before I stopped dead in front of my desk, glaring at the phone before snatching it up. Three days had gone by—I'd tried numerous times to reach Giovanna—on her cell, and at home. But my calls had been unanswered. I finally stopped calling, not wanting to seem like I was one of these dudes who was sweating a woman. Shit, I sweated no one!

Fuck it, I thought as I punched in those numbers so hard I

almost busted the damn phone. She picked up on the fourth ring.

"Trey," she said breathily.

"Oh, you're finally gonna take my call? How nice . . ." I let the sarcasm hang thick in the air. I was fuming and had no intentions of hiding it.

"I know you're angry with me—"

"Excuse me, Ms. Giovanna, or whatever the hell your name is, but I only want to know one thing—is it gonna be him or me? The rest of what you have to say is excess baggage—frankly, I'm not at all interested."

There was silence on the phone, and my heart spiked. I knew I was gambling with the best sex I'd had in a long time. This was no way to talk to a lady. On the other hand, she had messed with my boy, Vince and with me. And I wasn't having it. Trey was not about to go out like that!

"I was going to call you. Vince too. I've arrived at a decision and need to tell you both. Can we meet?"

"Why don't you dispense with this formality bullshit and give it to me straight. I'm a big boy; I can handle it."

"Trey please—you're not making this any easier. I didn't mean to hurt you or Vince."

"Well, I guess you should have thought about that before you began boning my best friend."

"Trey, if I could take it back, I swear I would. I never would have done what I did knowing that the two of you had a friendship."

"Whatever. I just want to know what is up. 'Cause I sure as hell don't plan on sharing my lady with anyone, least of all my best friend. I don't have to, you hear me?"

Silence.

I could feel my head throbbing, and my fists tightening. I don't know what was worse—finding out that the woman who you've been bedding down has been sexing someone else or finding out that that very person is your best friend. No, that wasn't true—it was far worse to learn that the pussy you'd thought belonged to you also belonged to your best friend. I loved Vince like a brother, but the thought of his dick sliding in and out of *my* baby's shit caused me to see red. I quickly reached out to my desk for support.

"Trey, this is difficult. For all of us," she replied. "Meet me tonight at eight. The bar in the Four Seasons, Georgetown. I'll let Vince know . . ."

I sighed, feeling the rush of blood as it pounded my forehead. "This shit better be worth my while . . ." I hissed.

But Giovanna's silence was unnerving . . .

"Mr. Lenitz will see you now," the stone-faced executive assistant uttered. I smoothed out my tie, buttoned the top two buttons of my jacket and strode inside.

Mr. Lenitz, the senior partner of the firm, was behind his mammoth desk. It was a huge thing, close to ten feet long and half that in width. Behind him were spacious floor to ceiling windows, with an amazing view of downtown Washington and the Capitol.

He rose, flung his bifocals to the table, and reached out his hand.

"Counselor, always good to see you," he said with an infectious grin. I smiled, took his hand and shook it, leveling my eyes with his.

"You too, sir."

"Sit," he directed. I took a seat on a plush leather couch that seemed to envelop my entire lower half. I sat forward as the senior partner pulled up a chair directly across from me. "Coffee?"

"No thank you, sir," I responded. I could feel the beads of

sweat begin to form on my brow, but resisted the urge to wipe my forehead and baldhead. That would show weakness, and I didn't want to convey that to the top dog.

"So," he said, spreading his hands wide, as his eyes took on a menacing glare, "What brings you here to the top floor?"

I smiled, briefly, as I reached into the interior breast pocket of my jacket. I grasped a folded document between my slender fingers.

I had contemplated this action for a while. Had even tried to get Calvin's take on the whole mess, but found out that old boy was on vacation.

Vacation???

Shit, Calvin Figgs *never* took a vacation. Things were indeed changing . . .

I took a breath, and spoke. "Sir, I'm filing an Equal Employment Opportunity complaint against the firm. I wanted to personally deliver a copy of the complaint to you, and answer any questions that you might have before I filed it."

"I see," Mr. Lenitz replied. His expression did not change and he mulled this over for a split second. "May I see the complaint?"

"Of course, sir," I said, handing over the folded document.

He took several minutes to read it. What I had given him was three single-spaced typewritten pages that outlined my complaint against my superior, Bernard John Marshall, and the firm. In it, I alleged discrimination based on race.

"Sir," I ventured to break the silence between us, "I've labored over this for quite some time now. As I'm sure you are aware, I have been a loyal servant to this firm for close to six years. I've worked hard, built up my clientele while bringing this firm a substantial amount of referral business, and most importantly, I'm very good at what I do. I love working here, and have every intention of remaining at the firm. But the actions of Bernard John Marshall are discriminatory and creating what I can only describe as a hostile work environment. I have never had a problem with a supervisor—either at this firm, or in any prior work situation before Mr. Marshall. Simply put, he refuses to let me do my job. He harasses me, takes assignments away from me, questions my legal tactics, and interferes in my dealings with my clients. I cannot, for the life of me, understand why he would do this to me. It is not, I assure you, my work performance. The only explanation I'm left with is that he has a problem with my skin color, and that he is letting his discriminatory beliefs interfere with him managing me."

Mr. Lenitz steepled his hands as he listened intensely. When I grew silent he nodded once and put down my memorandum to the EEOC. He sighed before speaking.

"Mr. Alexander, these are serious charges."

I nodded.

"Thank you for bringing this to my attention. I am shocked by these allegations, and want to assure you that this firm does not tolerate discriminatory practices of any kind." He paused as if to consider how to proceed next. Glancing up at the ceiling for a moment before leveling his gaze at me, he continued. "Let me ask you a question."

"Of course, sir."

"You've always known me to be a straight shooter, correct?"

"Absolutely, sir."

"Good. I would ask this of you. Give me seventy-two hours to personally investigate these allegations of racial discrimination before you go to the EEOC. Let me conduct my own discovery of the facts; let me talk to our managing partner and review whatever pertinent information you deem material to the case. Give me seventy-two hours to get back to you. I'm not asking you to forgo taking your complaint to the EEOC. Instead, I'm asking that you delay it, so that I can give it my full attention. First."

I considered his words. His eyes bore into me as I mulled over his proposal. I nodded once.

"Fair enough," I said, standing and attempting a half smile. "I'll await your call on how to proceed next."

We shook hands.

"Thank you again, Trey, for bringing this to my attention. By all accounts you are a fine attorney with an exemplary work record. I'm sure that we can get to the bottom of this *misunderstanding*." Mr. Lenitz smiled as he let go of my hand. Unexpectedly, I was left with an uncomfortable feeling that began oozing through my veins. I was a black man in a white man's world. I was rocking the boat and the partners would definitely not appreciate that. I was messing with one of the top dogs—the new managing partner.

Did Mr. Lenitz care about me? Probably not. His allegiance was to the firm, first and foremost, ensuring that its pristine reputation remained intact.

Would he do anything regarding my complaint? Perhaps. But probably not.

Was I just being cynical?

No, I was black man in a white man's world. I was just being *real* . . .

Suddenly, my anger flared. At my job, my boss, my personal life, my ex-girlfriend, my so-called-woman, and even my best friend. I felt my face flush, boiling rage meshed with red-hot heat.

Screw them, I thought as I stood impatiently waiting for the down elevator.

Screw them *all* . . .

Sixteen

Seven forty-five p.m. The lounge of the Four Seasons Hotel in Georgetown was moderately filled with patrons—out-of-towners and locals alike enjoying a cocktail, while Dennis, clad in his tuxedo, played softly on a Baldwin Grand piano. Trey swept in, the coattails of his long camel-hair coat flaring behind him as he walked briskly, his eyes scanning the tables for his party. He slowed as he spied his best friend, Vince, who was already seated at a table off from mid-center. Trey wore a tight expression on his face as he reached the table. Vince didn't bother to stand up.

"Vince," Trey said.

"Trey." Gone was the normal back and forth banter between these two. The tension hung in the air, thick like cigarette smoke. Vince motioned for his friend to sit down.

"Waiting long?" Trey asked as he removed his coat and flung it on the chair beside him.

"Not really." Vince nursed a Corona. Trey could see that he had barely touched it. A waitress appeared to take Trey's drink order.

"I'll have the same," he said, motioning to Vince's beer.

He rubbed his hands together vigorously to remove the chill as he flashed a fake smile.

"So, bruh, here we are," Trey mused. Vince eyed him but did not smile.

"You think this is funny?" Vince asked, cocking his head to the side.

"Not at all. Actually, I think this is seriously messed up." Vince nodded.

"And you?" Trey asked. "What's your take on this whole thing?"

Vince glared at his best friend for a moment before clearing his throat.

"What I'm trying to figure out is a) how we let this woman do this to us—two grown-ass men, and b) where do we go from here?"

Trey steepled his fingers together and nodded silently. Vince continued.

"I mean, I met Raven several months ago and made no secret about it. I was pursuing her and let you and everyone know about it. So how is it that you end up with my woman?"

Trey's drink had arrived. He was placing the bottle to his lips when he stopped in mid-reach, putting the bottle down on the table. He looked at his friend incredulously.

"What are you saying, Vince? That I pursued this chick knowing she was dating you?"

"I'm trying to figure that out."

Trey forcefully exhaled.

"Man, please! Is that how you think I roll?"

"I don't know, Trey, you tell me . . ."

Vince's gaze was unwavering as he stared at Trey.

Trey fumed. "You know what, this shit is whacked. And you're whacked if you think that I somehow planned this. Vince, we go way back. I may have done a lot of messed up things in my day, but screwing my best friend's woman ain't one of them!"

Vince took a swig of his beer and put the bottle down. He nodded to himself.

"That's good to hear, Trey. I needed to know."

"Yeah, well now you know." Trey took a swig of his own beer and shook his head.

"So, where do we go from here?" Vince repeated.

"That is a question you need to pose to Giovanna, or excuse me, Raven, as she's known to you."

Vince shook his head.

"I don't know, Trey. Do you think we should let her continue to control this situation, given what we've gone through? I've given this a lot of thought over the past few days and I'm very uncomfortable with having this woman who, obviously neither of us knows very well, pit two best friends against each other."

"How is she pitting us against each other?" Trey asked.

"Isn't it obvious?" Vince responded. "Here we are, sitting in this bar, waiting for her to render a verdict—it's either you or me. Don't you have a problem with that? Doesn't it bother you that we're letting a woman get between our friendship?"

Trey sighed.

"Vince, listen, I don't like this any more than you do. But I'm not sure what the proper course of action is. I mean, we can both walk away, but what would that solve? If we do that, we both lose out on a relationship that up to this point was pretty damn satisfying for both of us."

Vince exploded.

"I can't freaking believe what I'm hearing, although I shouldn't be surprised. Trey, what fucking relationship? The woman conned us. You and me. She played us. We thought she was someone else—"

"Hey," Trey said, raising his hands in self-defense, "I'm not condoning her behavior, I'm just saying, do we cut off our nose to spite our face, or—"

Vince waved him away as he leaned in, lowering his voice to a near whisper.

"You know what? This comes down to pussy, plain and simple. At the end of the day, you don't want to give up any fine snatch without a fight, your friendship be damned!" Vince took a swig of his beer while locking his gaze onto Trey. He shook his head slowly. "Well, I'm here to tell you Trey Alexander, that that, my *so called* friend, is messed up!" Vince emptied his beer as someone cleared their throat. It caught both Vince's and Trey's attention. They both turned simultaneously and glanced up into the lovely face of Raven/Giovanna.

"May I sit down, gentlemen," she uttered softly. Raven/Giovanna was covered in a luxurious fur wrap, which she draped over an empty chair. Vince eyed her silently. She wore a beautiful print dress, in various shades of brown that hugged the contours of her voluptuous body. Trey nodded to her once as she sat next to him, across from Vince, whose lips were pressed together, draining all color from his flesh.

It was difficult to imagine that just a week ago this icon of beauty was his lover. Vince took a millisecond to remember their last lovemaking session—the passion; the fury that accompanied their conjoining was unlike anything he had ever experienced. This woman was something else, that's what he had told himself over and over again.

A gift from God.

Yes, he had been *that* blessed.

And then, like a heavy foot disturbing a puddle after a rain, all of what they had shared was shattered, like a fist hitting a pane of glass, and Vince was left with this deep-seated feeling of revulsion. He stared at her lips, thinking to himself, Trey has kissed those same lips. His eyes dropped unconsciously to her breasts as he thought, Trey has caressed those very same breasts . . .

Raven/Giovanna stared at each man for a moment before speaking.

"I honestly don't know what to say other than I am so very sorry for what I have done to both of you. I know my words must sound hollow, but I hope you will believe me when I say I never meant to hurt either of you."

"Question," Vince uttered, glaring at her. "Tell me your name, your real name—since I obviously don't know you."

Raven/Giovanna swallowed hard.

"It's Giovanna Marquis. I'm so sorry, Vince." She reached for his arm, but he pulled away.

"So, Giovanna, tell me. Why? Why run to another man, my best friend, no less? Was what we had not special?"

Vince's eyes seemed to water. Giovanna's lips quivered.

"Vince, what you and I had was special. Please believe me—"

"How the hell do you expect me to believe anything you say now?" Vince bellowed.

"And turning to me, Giovanna," Trey quipped, "why the game playing? Why not come straight? Why not just tell me the real deal? Did you think you could just continue playing me like that? Playing the two of *us*?"

Giovanna was silent.

"You know what?" Vince exclaimed. "This is bullshit. There is no explanation. Nothing she can say will change anything. She dogged us. She dogged us both and now she stands here begging forgiveness. Well, she can't have it. Not from me."

There were several seconds of silence while all three

stared each other down. The waitress arrived, Giovanna ordered a Johnnie Walker Black and Coke on the rocks, while Vince and Trey waved her away.

"Vince is right," Trey said, as he fondled his bottle. "This is bullshit. So why don't you tell us what you came here to tell us—and dispense with the rest of the formalities."

Giovanna nodded.

"Okay." She sucked in a deep breath. "Both of you are wonderful men in your own right. I'm lucky to have met both of you. Vince, what you and I had was indeed special—you took me to new heights that I'd never been to before, and for that I am immensely grateful. Trey," she said, turning to him, "I'm still getting to know you, but you have a side to you that I find extremely desirable."

Vince exhaled forcefully, but said nothing.

"As I stated, you both are wonderful men—but I can't date both of you," she remarked before pausing to gaze at each man in turn before leveling her stare at Vince, "Therefore, I would like to pursue things with, that is, if you'll have me," she said, eyes dropping momentarily to the table before flicking over to Trey and then resting on Vince, "what I'm trying to say, is that, Vince, you're a wonderful guy, but, I think I'm more compatible with—"

Vince was rising, reaching for his coat as he shook his head slowly. He refused to meet Giovanna's stare. Instead, he locked eyes with his best friend.

"Trey, you do what you want, man, but I'm done here. If you choose to allow this woman to get in the way of our friendship, then that's your prerogative. I can't stop you."

He glared at Giovanna for a moment.

"I've got *nothing* to say to you . . ."

Vince walked away briskly as Trey rose, calling out to him.

"Vince, bruh, hold up a second," he yelled, but Vince

continued along, ignoring him. Trey sat, glowered at Giovanna for a moment as she followed Vince's retreat with her own gaze.

"You did a messed-up thing, you hear me?" Trey exclaimed, leaning in to her.

She nodded silently. A minute passed.

"A real messed-up thing. So, the question becomes, what am I gonna do with your sorry ass?" Trey grabbed the bottle in front of him and downed the last of his beer. Giovanna reached for his arm and stroked it. She smiled weakly.

"Trey, I'm busted. What else can I say? I fucked up. But I want to be with you. And I hope you'll have me back." She made eye contact with him and smiled seductively as she dropped her voice to a near whisper. "I took the liberty of getting a suite here for the night. I thought that perhaps I could persuade you to come up for a . . . nightcap. Listen, I know I've been bad—very bad . . . and I'm hoping that you're willing to correct my dreadful behavior. I'm ready to be punished, Trey, anyway you see fit. Just come upstairs with me, okay, baby? Teach mommy a lesson, Trey? The way you do so good . . ."

Trey sat back and frowned at her. He could feel his flesh stirring as he took in her lovely features. His thoughts were instantly transported back to those multitudes of moments where they shared each other intimately. He smiled, unconsciously, thinking about how freaking good she was. Giovanna set him free, like very few women before her had—brought him to that place where he was a sexual beast, a prince among men. Yes, Trey smiled at Giovanna as he eyed her seductively. Then his smile was erased.

"Key," he said.

"What?" she asked, her eyes blinking in confusion.

"I didn't stutter," he mused. "I said, 'key'."

Giovanna rummaged through her purse. "It's suite 1211,"

she said before taking a deep breath. "Thank you, Trey, I'm—"

Trey cut her off with a wave of his hand as he leaned in and whispered, "Just do what I say, okay?"

Giovanna blinked and nodded once.

"Go upstairs, remove your clothes, and get on the bed, on all fours, *doggie-style*, and wait for me to come. Are we clear?" His face was inches from hers. His eyes bore laser beams into her retinas. Giovanna swallowed and nodded silently.

"Good. Go on then," he said. "All I wanna see is ass and pussy when I come through that door. Comprendè?"

Giovanna rose, grabbed her wrap, and turned to leave. Trey watched her retreat as he slapped some bills onto the table. He motioned for the waitress. "A celebration is in order," he mused, all teeth as he grinned. "So, bring me a glass of your finest scotch, on the rocks, with a beer chaser."

"Of course, Sir. I'd recommend the Ardbeg Provenance. It's the Holy Grail of scotches, with a sweet smoke flavor, and a multitude of layers."

"Perfect," Trey replied. "Bring me the bottle, if you would, thanks."

The waitress blinked. "I believe, sir, that the bottle is $875."

Trey didn't even blink. "I'll be charging it to Suite 1211 . . ."

He hummed to himself as he watched her give his drink order to the bartender. Trey smiled before whispering, "Trey back in the saddle, y'all, for *real*!"

The night was frigid, but Vince seemed not to feel it. Perhaps his body was on shutdown, after walking for over thirty minutes now, his extremities no longer feeling the cold, as if his limbs were lifeless, immune to the bone-chilling cold.

He had taken a cab out of Georgetown; had hailed one immediately from the front entrance of the hotel, as if he were suffocating and could no longer stand being in this neck of the woods a minute longer.

He was now blocks from his home, and it was getting late. He knew better than to be out at this time of night—but the thought of getting mugged didn't even enter Vince's thoughts. Tonight, he had other things on his mind.

He had called Erika as soon as he had been deposited on the cold, dark sidewalk. Had reached for his cell and speed-dialed her number. Thankfully, she had answered on the third ring.

"Hey Sassy."

Erika could hear the misery in his voice.

"Vince. I take it things didn't go too well."

"An understatement. She chose Trey—no real surprise there. I upped and left the two lovebirds. I'm done with her and with *him* . . ."

"Oh, Vince," she exclaimed into the phone, "I'm real sorry to hear that." Her tone changed from soothing to hard. "But what the hell is up with your boy? He can't be seriously contemplating dating her—not after everything she's put the two of you through."

"Sassy, please! This is Trey we're talking about. You know that dude is only thinking with one head—and I ain't referring to the one on his shoulders . . ."

"I feel you, but damn! I'm gonna call his trifling ass—"

"You can do what you want, Erika, but I'm telling you. I'm done with his dumb-ass. Tonight was an eye opener for me. Tonight I saw my best friend choose pussy over me . . ."

They had exchanged a few more minutes of conversation; Erika repeatedly told him that this was for the best— that she had gotten a bad feeling the first time he'd talked about Raven. There was something that wasn't quite right.

And now, Raven's true colors had shone through, and the best thing Vince could do was move on and not look back.

Vince agreed.

But that didn't mean it wouldn't hurt for a while . . .

Immediately after hanging up with Vince, Erika called Trey on his cell. He answered on the second ring.

"What up, Boo?" he said, in a cocky, upbeat voice. Erika could hear the sound of a piano playing and distant chatter in the background.

"Oh, you're all full of yourself now that you've won your prize," she said, not bothering with pleasantries.

"Sassy, don't be calling up here with one of your lectures, 'cause I don't need it right now," he spat back.

"Oh, I see. You're in the zone right now, so nobody can tell you shit, is that it?"

"Na, it ain't—"

"You listen to me, Trey. I don't care what that bitch is saying to you, and I don't care how good her cootchie is, the shit ain't worth losing a friendship over! Use your head, man! She's gonna dog you until she's done with your sorry-ass, and then she's gonna up and leave. Where will you be then?"

Trey looked at the phone incredulously.

"I really don't know who you think you're talking to, but I'm tired of you trying to tell me how to lead my damn life. It makes no sense to me that both Vince and I should come out losers in this game. Why not take advantage, Erika? Hell, one of us should, and guess what—I'm the chosen one! So sorry to disappoint you, but damn it, I'm gonna take advantage. To *not* do so would be ludicrous!"

"And what about Vince? Do you care about his feelings, Trey? Or is it, as long as you get yours, its every man for himself?" Erika exclaimed.

"Yeah," Trey snorted, "I care about him *and* his feelings.

But he needs to take this shit like a man—if I was the loser I wouldn't be running off like a dog with its tail between its legs, and having my girlfriend call the winner to complain. I'd go out the way I came in—like the man that I am, not a bitch!"

Erika shook her head.

"So that's what Vince is to you—a bitch? You know what? Vince is done with you and so am I. You are one sorry-ass excuse for a man."

Trey chuckled.

"And I'm going to tell you something else, smart-ass, whether you want to hear it or not," Erika continued. "You've changed. Your priorities are all screwed up. You used to be all about the friendship and family *first*. Now it's all about you—Trey getting his, regardless of the cost. Damn—now every freaking action of yours revolves around your dick—and that's messed up. Your life is so one fucking dimensional, yet you can't see the forest for the trees. I just hope when things finally come crashing down you'll have someone to reach out to for support. Because it won't be Vince or me."

Trey sucked in a breath, felt his heart racing, and went off.

"And now let me tell you something, Sassy. You and your boy are just envious of the way I live. I'm living large, on my terms, by my own rules. And you know what—y'all are just jealous, because your lives don't match mine. I don't have your problems. My dick works—I come. Yeah, Sassy— I said it. You know what your problem is, and that of your boys? You need to stop riding my jock!"

Erika fumed.

"You know what, Trey? Fuck you and the horse you rode in on!" she yelled, her thumb jamming the End button force-fully.

"Not if I don't screw you first," he replied as he ended the call.

Thankfully, Erika was no longer there to hear his reply.

Vince was back in the confines of his warm house when he reached for the phone. He glanced at the clock—saw it was a little after eleven-thirty at night. He knew it was late, but he had to talk to her. And so he dialed and waited for the familiar voice to warm his heart.

"Hey you," he said easily into the receiver when she answered.

"Hey," Amber replied, sitting up in her bed. She immediately detected that something was wrong. Gone was the normal jovial tone in her friend's voice. "Vince, you okay?" she asked. The TV was on, volume muted as she listened to an Erykah Badu cut. She pointed the remote at the stereo to cut the power. The silence was abrupt. She waited for Vince to respond.

"Sorry for calling so late," he said. Vince sounded winded, almost out of breath, like he was sick.

"You know it's cool. Always a pleasure to talk to you. So, what's up? You aren't your usual self—I can tell that."

"Yeah, I can't front with you, Amber." Vince paused.

"It's about that woman. Raven, right?"

"Damn, you're good." He attempted a smile, but it came out flat and subdued.

"Talk to me . . ."

Vince brought her up to speed on his situation. Amber listened patiently and without comment until he was finished. When he took a deep breath and sighed, Amber spoke.

"Oh, Vince, I am so sorry. Damn, that's messed up. I wish there was something I could do to make you feel better."

"Hearing your voice does that," he mused.

"Does Erika know?"

"Yeah, I spoke to her earlier. She was sorry too, but told me to move on. And that it's for the best."

"Smart woman. Heed her words, young man!"

"I figured you'd say that."

There was an awkward moment of silence. Vince sighed heavily.

"So, what's new in N'awlins?" he asked, trying to change the subject.

"Same old, same old."

"How's the artist doing?" he asked, referring to Angeliqué.

"She's good. I haven't seen much of her lately—she's always on the go, doing something, you know how your girl is, all flighty and shit. Can't keep still for a minute! But she's always asking about you."

Vince smiled. "Tell her I said, 'waz up!'"

Another pregnant pause.

"Vince," Amber said, "I've got an idea. Why don't you come down here for a few days? I know its middle of the week and all, but it would be great to see you. We could hang out, do some stuff to get your mind off of this woman, or whatever. You promised you'd come down soon anyway. Well, now you've got a reason . . ."

Vince smiled.

"I don't know, Amber . . ."

"What's not to know? You need to get away. Staying in D.C. is only going to remind you of her and all you've been through. If you come down here, I'll play doctor and take care of you . . . make you forget all about that crazy-ass woman and her messed up antics!"

Amber laughed, and Vince was filled with a feeling he wasn't yet prepared to comprehend. He smiled, laughed along with her, and heard himself saying, "Yeah, Amber, perhaps you're just what the doctor ordered . . ."

Vince strolled up the incline of the jetway, lugging his carryon bag over his left shoulder as he made his way to the waiting area. He was tired and ill tempered. He hadn't slept well at all the previous evening. Vince had tossed and turned all night—images of Trey and Raven floated in and out of his consciousness, no matter how hard he tried to shoo them away. But thankfully, dawn had brought on a new day. Vince had risen at seven, showered and shaved, and grabbed a coffee and a bagel before heading to Reagan National Airport for his two-hour and fifty-two-minute flight to New Orleans.

He entered the bright terminal and his eyes squinted as they took a moment to get used to the light. His gaze fell on a form to the left of the check-in counter. A woman was holding a placard with a name written in thick black magic marker.

Vince Cannon, Jr.

His name . . .

A lovely creature wearing a green-and-white Tulane University hooded sweatshirt, white sweatpants, and an engaging smile.

Vince smiled for the first time in twelve hours.

"Hey you!" he said, enthusiastically, sweeping Amber up into his arms and kissing her on the cheek, "what are you doing here?"

"I'm your official welcoming committee!" she replied, stroking his face with a fingernail before moving in and quickly kissing his lips. "Wanted to make sure there were no issues with your arrival."

She flashed Vince a smile as he thought: Amber is a sight for sore eyes. Her skin had a natural glow to its texture, and her eyes sparkled as they fell on his face. An aura presided over her, and Vince knew he had made the right decision in coming down here. He found himself staring once again at her facial appearance and her auburn-coated skin—not only beautiful on the outside, but her inner being as well—something familiar yet elusive stabbed at his insides—and as he did the first time he'd laid eyes on her lovely form, he tried to decipher where—but the answer alluded him.

"I took the liberty of picking up some java for you—that shit they serve on the plane is nasty . . ."

Vince beamed as she handed him a steaming cup of Starbucks.

"Bless you, my child," he said before pulling her to him and hugging her again. "Damn, it's good to see you, Amber. I feel better already."

"I guess my work here is done," she mused, feigning leaving.

"Not so fast," Vince replied, "I'm not done with you yet . . . we've only just begun . . ."

Vince noticed how her eyes sparkled when he uttered those words.

The ride into town went quickly. There was no traffic; besides Amber knew these streets like a native—Vince was impressed as she bypassed the interstate to cut through the city.

"Nice ride," he commented.

"It's Angeliqué's," Amber said, "You know I can't afford anything but a hooptie right now, and my ride's in the damn shop!" she mused.

"Hell, a hooptie gets you where you need to go, so don't knock it."

"I hear you . . . anyway, I just want you to sit back and

relax—for the next few days it's all about you—it's your world, Vince. My job is to serve you," she said with a devil-ish grin. "I'm gonna make you forget all about your troubles up north—think of it as a soul cleansing," she said, eyeing him as she steered though the narrow streets of the Quarter, "washing away those negative toxins, leaving only positive energy in its place." She grinned over at him as he nodded to her. "You feel me, Vince?" she asked, in a tone that belied any seductive intent. Yet, as Vince stared back at her, he couldn't help but feel a fire being stoked.

"Yeah, for real, Amber," Vince replied, finding that he was having trouble breaking away from her stare.

"The woman up north is *history*," Amber said. "Poof—be gone, bitch," she uttered with a single flick of her wrist.

"You're *all* mine now . . ."

How to describe the rest of the day?

One word said it all—*extraordinary*.

With the temperature hovering in the mid-fifties, and with no wind to create a discomfort, it began with a walk through the Quarter to a salon where Vince received his first manicure and pedicure; he found the whole process energiz-ing, and vowed to continue the practice once he returned home.

Next, they walked Jackson Square, taking in the Pontalba Buildings with their cast iron galley railings and hanging ferns; the St. Louis Cathedral, which, Vince learned, was originally built in 1724, and was the oldest Cathedral in North America; and The Cablildo, the site of the signing of the historic Louisiana Purchase.

Walking down Pirate's Alley, Amber led Vince to Faulkner House, where William Faulkner rented a room on the ground floor close to eighty years ago. They perused the bookstore for thirty minutes before heading over to Café Du Monde on Decatur where they partook in dark roasted coffee and beignets. Vince was impressed with her knowledge of the city's history and it's heritage.

"That's one thing I love about this place," she said while cupping her hands around the hot ceramic mug, "is that it has a richness that very few places can touch. And it is that abundance of culture that hangs in the air here—you can sense it when you walk the Quarter, and I never grow tired of inhaling that scent."

A streetcar with mahogany seats and brass fittings took them along St. Charles Street to the Garden District, where Amber led Vince through Lafayette Cemetery No. 1 and the impressive aboveground tombs of the dead. Vince marveled at many of the eighteenth century monuments, and the haunting emotions they evoked. After what seemed like hours, they hailed a cab back to the serene tranquility of St. Philip. There, they took a much-needed nap, Amber in her second-floor bedroom, while Vince made ready to recline on a futon in a room behind the gallery that overlooked the courtyard.

Vince felt a stab of guilt when he stared out from behind the wooden shutters, remembering with too much clarity, spying Angeliqué, the woman whom he had fallen hard for, in mid-embrace. That night seemed like eons ago. Yet, that night had changed him. He closed the shutters, muting the light, and sunk into the confines of the comfortable futon, like the arms of a beautiful woman, seeming to embrace and hold him captive. And he slept, dreaming of a time when things seemed less complicated and confused, and of Raven, the mysterious woman who had betrayed him.

* * *

It was after dark when Vince was awakened. Angeliqué stood over him, hands folded across her breasts.

"Living the life of Riley, I see," she mused.

Vince jumped up and hugged her.

"How ya livin'?" he asked.

"Can't complain, Vince. Life is good," she said, all smiles. "I'm sorry to hear about your . . . *situation*," she added.

"Life goes on, Angeliqué," Vince responded as he stretched. Amber bounced in looking radiant in a pair of form-fitting black pants and an off-white sweater that highlighted her perky breasts. "Dayum—look at *you*!" he exclaimed.

Amber pirouetted for the pair as she grinned. "Don't hate the playa, Vince," she said with a gleam in her eye, "hate the *game . . .*"

"Are you hungry, Mister?" Angeliqué asked him. "Amber and I thought we'd take you out to eat, since you're gracing us with your presence."

"Bring it on, ladies!" he replied.

Vince took a quick shower and changed into a pair of corduroy slacks, dark sweater, tweed jacket, and boots. Amber told him he looked like a college professor, "but I mean that in a good sort of way!" Angeliqué looked like the artist that she was in a pair of brown leather pants, boots, and a funky Sixties top.

The trio dined at Emeril's on Tchoupitoulas Street, a hop and a skip from Riverwalk and the Mississippi River. Vince had the crawfish ravioli with sun-dried tomato pesto butter sauce. Amber selected the Foie Gras pizza topped with roasted Portobello mushrooms, caramelized Chianti onions, and house-made mozzarella cheese, while Angeliqué had the pistachio crusted salmon. They shared a bottle of Kendall Jackson Grand Reserve Chardonnay while they chatted and got caught up.

The food was excellent; the conversation even better. Vince was so glad to have taken Amber up on her offer. And he was pleasantly surprised to see that there wasn't any tension between Angeliqué and him. She treated him like a good friend, with warmth and compassion.

Afterwards, they strolled the Quarter, stopping in at House of Blues to listen to some live music. By midnight, Angeliqué excused herself, and hailed a cab home. Amber and Vince stayed until 1:30 a.m., continuing to enjoy the libations and the conversation.

Vince followed up on their previous discussions surrounding Amber's goals, ambitions, and future plans. She always had many questions for Vince, considering this was his field of expertise.

"I don't know, Vince. I know I'm still young and all, but I feel as if I should be focusing on my passion and not the normal nine-to-five."

"I hear you, but don't beat up on yourself. Many people don't even know what their passion is, let alone how to turn it into a money-making endeavor," he replied. "You're doing what you need to do—one step at a time."

For months now, Amber had been talking to Vince about her love of writing—poetry, short-fiction, and of one day tackling the great American novel. Through her conversations with Vince, he had convinced her to keep a journal, and focus on honing her craft. She still held her administrative job at Tulane, largely so she could take classes at no cost to her.

Vince was proud of her, and let her know it every chance he got.

They took the stroll back hand-in-hand, taking their time, letting their silence envelop them, and enjoying the early morning chill and the night sounds. Vince was cognizant of the fact that not so long ago he and Angeliqué had walked the Quarter hand-in-hand as he did now. But he didn't dwell on the past. Amber made that impossible. There was only the here and now, and what was to come. Vince enjoyed her company—the closeness that they shared was something that had caught him off guard. But the more time he spent in her presence, the greater he felt the bond between them hardening.

They spoke little of Raven and Trey back in D.C. Vince found that he could go for hours before a thought of them whisked into his consciousness. But then, like one of those oversized horse flies, he waved the annoying thought away.

They made their way to the silent block of St. Philip and Angeliqué's home. It was close to 2 a.m. Amber opened the wrought-iron door and led Vince inside. They were quiet since they didn't want to disturb Angeliqué. On a hallway table was a note to Amber from Angeliqué. It said that she would be spending the night at a friend's, and would be home the following afternoon.

Amber grinned. "Ut-Oh, Vince, you better watch your-self, cause big momma's gone away. We've got the crib to ourselves!"

Vince yawned.

"Whatever, I ain't scared of you."

They laughed as they took the stairs.

"Thank you so much," Vince beamed when they reached the second floor landing. He faced her and placed his hands on her shoulders. "This day has been something I can't put into words. You talked about healing. Well, I swear, I almost feel like my old self again."

"You're quite welcome. And it was my pleasure. That's what good friends do for their friends in need . . ."

He turned toward his room facing the courtyard. "Well, I'm gonna bid you goodnight," he said.

"Not so fast," Amber replied, following closely behind. "The night's not done yet."

Vince turned and stared at her, trying to read her expression. She wore a grin, but he couldn't decipher the meaning behind it. He raised an eyebrow.

"One more thing, before we both turn in. Something that I've planned for you. Part of the healing process, Mr. Cannon, Jr."

"Really?" Vince replied, suddenly feeling wide-awake.

"Trust me," she said, turning to head in the opposite direction. "Give me a few minutes, will you?" she said, with a gleam in her eye.

Just what is this woman up to, Vince pondered silently.

He was about to find out.

Vince's legs were splayed across the open futon. Gone were his clothes—instead, he wore a pair of blue scrubs, courtesy of his dad, Dr. Vince Cannon, Sr., and Children's Hospital in D.C. His chest was bare. His gaze swept over the darkened ceiling, as Amber knocked on the door.

"Come," he said.

She strolled in. Gone were her earlier clothes too—instead she wore a pair of gray sweat shorts, and a wifebeater. Her hair was pulled back and held with a scrunchie. Vince thought she looked wonderful, no matter what the attire.

"Your bath is ready, Sir!" she said, without preamble.

"Excuse me?" he said, rising quickly from the futon.

"Just follow me," she said, exiting the room.

She led him down the hallway to a small bathroom at the end. Vince entered, and was in awe at what awaited him.

The entire room was ablaze in candlelight—there must have been close to thirty candles placed on the black and white tile floor, on the lip of the old porcelain tub, and on the windowsill and commode top. His eyes swept to the filled tub—red and pink petals danced lazily among scented bubbles. There was no shower stall—just this ancient tub, a commode, and a small sink. Vince was, for a brief moment, speechless.

"Oh my God!" he exclaimed. He didn't know what else to say.

Amber grinned. "I take it you like?" she asked.

"Are you kidding?"

There was a folding chair leaning against the back wall. Amber unfolded it and scooted it up to the head of the tub. She sat down, tested the waters with her forearm as she locked her stare onto Vince.

"What are you waiting for? Get in!" It was a command.

Vince stood there, a look of incomprehension on his face. He swallowed involuntarily.

"Don't tell me you're scared?" Amber teased. "Big strapping hunk of a man like you? Say it ain't so . . ."

"Na . . ."

"As I recall, Mr. Cannon, Jr., you've already seen me in my birthday suit, and I didn't pitch a fit then, so neither should you." Amber splashed some water on her forearms and reached for a loofah and the soap, lathering up. "Come on, mister, don't want the water to get cold now, do we?"

Vince smiled. As he turned away to remove his pants, he felt his heart rate spike. He exhaled slowly, as the scrubs went down past his knees and onto the floor.

"Nice buns," Amber teased. "I love me a mans with nice buns!"

Vince lowered himself into the water, grateful for the thick bubbles that covered his growing erection. He sat back, letting the water envelop him, the scent of jasmine, Egyptian musk, and sandalwood, invading his senses. For a brief moment he shut his eyes, allowing the candlelight to flicker across his closed eyelids. Then Amber's hands were on his head, pouring water over his hair and massaging shampoo into his scalp. The feeling was indescribable, Vince lying in a tub of hot, scented water, rose petals lapping against his chest, being pampered like this as the flames from dozens of candles flickered around him. He began to speak, but Amber stopped him.

"Don't say anything," she said, continuing as she ran her fingers through his wet, soapy hair, "let the essence of this experience cleanse you."

Vince closed his eyes and focused on her hands.

She washed his hair with shampoo that smelled of lemongrass and eucalyptus. Let her fingers roam over his neck and shoulders, leaning him forward in order to soap up his back. She took her time, massaging the muscles in his skin with soap and hot water, cupping her hands and rinsing the flesh before moving onward, and down.

She told him to stand. Vince rose from the tub, his body dripping myriads of bubbles that meandered down his dark skin like a winding river. She took the loofah and soaped it up again, held it against his ass, coated his cheeks with a layer of soapy bubbles before using strong fingers to knead the flesh. Vince was fully hard now, his thick member facing away from her, but bobbing to its own rhythm as flickers of candlelight danced off the veined shaft. When she was done with his ass, she moved downward still, to his thighs, the back of his knees and onto his shins. Amber finished up by rinsing him clean with hot water, before urging him to turn around.

Vince did so, with only a single moment of hesitation, until his fully engorged state was in full view, directly in front of her.

Amber said nothing, eyeing him for a moment, her hands

dipping lazily in the water, before she grabbed the loofah and soap, and stood.

Still silent, her eyes locked onto his dark skin, Amber washed his chest and stomach, lathering him up until not one inch of darkened flesh shone through. Then she rinsed him, slowly and methodically, watching the water flow cascade down and between his legs.

Vince remained silent, closing his eyes to the scene, allowing her touch and sound of her sighing to guide him.

Amber lathered his thighs and knees before rinsing. Vince remained standing, his eyes closed. He was breathing deeply, pulling air into his nostrils and letting it flow through his body before exhaling the same way it had come.

When she reached for him, Vince cut his breathing short.

Her fingers tentatively wrapped themselves around his penis, using her palm to stroke him from testicles to head. When she reached the tip, her fingers constricted, applying pressure, molding the bulbous flesh, almost twisting it out of shape.

Vince was about to lose his mind.

His eyes opened as she used her other hand to cup his balls lightly, pressing upward and around them, as if encasing them in her own wet cocoon. Vince groaned. Her eyes flicked upward for a brief moment, their eyes met and locked before dropping her gaze back down, concentrating on the task at hand . . .

He closed his eyes again as Amber washed him, using her hands, fingers, and the soap, alternating between gently stroking the sides of his shaft, and gripping the entire girth in her hand and squeezing.

Hard.

Feeling him pulse.

When Vince opened his eyes, she had joined him in the tub.

Gone were the shorts . . .

Gone was the wifebeater . . .

And her hair hung free.

She gazed into his eyes for a moment, one hand encircling his penis, the tip nudging between her well-toned thighs, inching forward. She tilted her head up, parted her lips, as Vince's mouth came down onto hers.

There were no words.

Only sounds as they explored each other with their tongues.

Their bodies pressed against one another, fingers and hands finding breasts and nipples, then descending down slender soap-covered backs to each other's asses, gripping the flesh, holding it firm, feeling the weight of the one rock against the other as candlelight flickered over their pulsating forms.

She rolled a condom onto him silently.

There were no words.

Only sounds as she gripped his head and neck tightly, climbing him the way an insect does a grass stem, rising before settling down, exhaling with a forceful sigh as Vince entered her cavern, plunging into the depths of her molten core.

There were no words.

Only sounds.

No foreplay.

The entire day had been just that—a preview of things to come.

Vince thrust into Amber with ambition.

As they rocked against one another, their bodies fusing as one, Vince thought about the first time he'd laid eyes on Amber's lovely prone form. It was at that moment, he mused, that the foreplay between them had begun—he hadn't considered it consciously, but he vividly recalled a quiver of excitement that ran down his spine as he watched her veve-covered flesh then.

And now, they were making love; passionately, completely, and without reservations, giving all to the other, as their tongues encircled the other like a slick vine.

And when they came, Amber and Vince came together.

Amber shouted, "Oh God!" and moaned before sucking his tongue into the recesses of her mouth. And for Vince, the explosion in his loins was the most powerful he'd ever experienced, like a wave of fireworks that roll overhead, a kaleidoscope of colors, cleansing his insides of anything that was bad, leaving only goodness remaining . . .

And as he held her quaking form in his arms, legs encircling his ass, her chest heaving against his own, petal-laced water splashing around them, Vince found he had no choice but to give in to his emotions and let the tears flow down . . .

Seventeen

Y'all don't know how damn good it felt to fire up the old Indian once April rolled around. I mean, February had been a mutha sucka—and March was just as bad. Windy, snowy, and downright bone-chilling cold, as if God was punishing us for a sin-filled year. It felt like we were living in Minneapolis and not the Nation's Capital. Dayum!

But once April hit, it was as if a light switch had been flipped. I swear! One day it was nasty-gray-cold. The next, April second to be exact, the sky turned ultra-blue, cloudless, with temperatures rising into the forties. The following day—a bit warmer. The day after that—fifties! Can you believe it? Just like that! Me and everyone else in D.C. thought we'd died and gone to heaven!

For real!

So I pulled the Indian out, hosed her down for the first time in over six months, and spent the good part of a Saturday polishing that girl's chrome until she shined like I don't know what. That bad boy was looking so fly, I felt myself getting hard. Oh yeah, y'all, I couldn't wait to get on the bike. And that's exactly what I did.

Took Giovanna out for a spin that turned into an all-day affair. Rode out Route 50 to Annapolis, spent some time walking Main Street before heading over the Chesapeake Bay Bridge and to the Red Eye's Dock Bar on Kent Island where we chilled, had lunch, and a few Coronas overlooking the bay. Finished off by heading up Route 13 into Delaware and looping back down into Baltimore, stopping for dinner at the Inner Harbor. It turned out to be a wonderful day, and it felt so good to have the Indian once again between my legs.

Giovanna loved it too.

For that day, I forgot all the trouble that seemed to have seeped into my life as of late. I can't even begin to explain where everything broke down, but damn it, things were, in a word, screwed the hell up!

Ever since . . .

Vince and I had become strangers the night Giovanna chose me over him. I'd given him some time to chill and get over it; had even called him a week later to see what was up, but he refused to take or return my calls. And I'm not one to beg, so I left it alone . . .

Same thing with Erika.

I know she's my boo and all, but damn, that last conversation really messed with my head. I figured that like a woman, once she regained her composure she'd come around.

Wrong.

I guess both she and Vince still had a stick up their ass . . .

Well, I wasn't going to lose any sleep over it.

At least that's what I told myself.

The truth is, I missed them both.

Missed them terribly.

But what was I to do?

Should I give up on a perfectly good relationship with a

woman whom I was feeling just because my friends were in a tizzy?

I don't think so.

Then there was the situation at work. You will recall the initial meeting I had had with the Senior Partner, Mr. Lenitz. Although the follow-up meeting had occurred almost two months ago, it felt just like yesterday.

I clenched my jaws as I recalled that event . . .

Mr. Lenitz's executive assistant had buzzed India asking me to come up. No matter that I was in the midst of preparing a brief. This was the Senior Partner, and when he called, you jumped.

I grabbed my jacket off the back of my chair and headed for the elevator, heart thumping in my chest. A thousand thoughts flashed through my mind. What was he going to say to me? A part of me thought that Mr. Lenitz was as fair as they came—and that he would cut through the bureaucracy and bullshit of the firm and vindicate me.

I was a damn good attorney.

I kept my nose clean (for the most part, I told myself), and did what they asked of me.

I billed as many hours as most partners (okay, this was definitely the case *before* they ushered in Bernard John Marshall).

And I was held in high regard by my clients and associates alike (true).

Yet I couldn't shake the brooding feeling that had swept over me. Mr. Lenitz was going to blow me off. He was going to side with the managing partner, and that was that. How could he not do that? And then, what would I do? Move forward with my complaint to the EEOC? And let the chips fall where they may?

I arrived at the top floor and strode with a purposeful step toward his office. His exec assistant eyed me and told me to go on in.

I knocked once and entered.

Mr. Lenitz was already seated in a chair across from his couch. His legs were crossed and he was reading a document. He flung off his bifocals, as he was known for doing and glanced up.

"Do come in, Counselor," he said, gesturing for me to take a seat.

"Thank you, sir," I replied, taking a seat as I unbuttoned my jacket and flattened my tie.

"Trey," he began without preamble, "I've had a chance to investigate your allegations of racial discrimination as outlined in your memorandum," he said, staring directly at me. "I take these allegations extremely seriously, and want you to know that I appreciate you bringing this to my attention."

I nodded. "Yes sir," I said, urging him to continue.

"I've spoken at length with the managing partner of this firm. I also talked with other partners and associates who are familiar with your work and work environment. Of course, these discussions were conducted in the strictest of confidence, I assure you."

"Okay," I said, and then held my breath.

"Trey, it is my conclusion that there is a lack of evidence of racial discrimination by Mr. Marshall and this firm."

I exhaled slowly, the color draining from my face.

Mr. Lenitz sat forward.

"I will tell you what I see, counselor—we have a new managing partner here. Bernard is damn good at what he does, but his methods may be construed by some as, how should I say this, *different*. Yes, that's a good word. I've spoken with him and with others—we are all in agreement that you are a damn fine attorney. And we don't want to lose you.

I will tell you this—Bernard thinks that you're not working up to your potential—that you've," he paused for a brief moment to search for the right words, "you've slacked off a bit—I don't mean to imply that you aren't doing anything. No, that's not true at all. But the Trey Alexander that we've come to know and count on has taken a hiatus . . . and Bernard is working with you to bring that person back."

I was in a daze. I was having trouble focusing on the words that were being spoken.

"Trey, Bernard can be a bit bullish at times, I'll admit that (in confidence to you, of course). He pushes, hard sometimes, and he's pushing you. Is it racially motivated? No, not in my opinion. Is he creating a hostile work environment? No, I don't think so. He's attempting to get the best performance from one of our finest attorneys."

He sat back. Paused for a minute to let me take stock of what had been said. Then he leaned forward again and said to me, "Trey, does any of this make sense?"

I nodded slowly, silently.

Lenitz continued. "You know, Trey, sometimes we need to simply *adjust* the way we interact with our boss—even if the way we've dealt with him or her in the past has worked. I know it's not fair, but Bernard's a different kettle of fish, and it might make things a whole lot easier if you would just approach him differently. He is, I don't have to remind you, your supervisor . . ."

I took in a deep breath, letting the air swirl around my insides for a moment before exhaling. Lenitz watched me silently.

"Sir," I started and then shut down. There was so much I wanted to say, but suddenly I found that I had no words to say what I was actually feeling. My shoulders hunched. I exhaled again. "Okay," I began, "This is all—I don't know. I need some time to digest all of what you've said."

Mr. Lenitz was nodding as he rose from the chair, signaling that our meeting was over.

"Of course, counselor. Take the time you need. Remember what I've said. You are a damn fine attorney. Do consider changing the way you interact with Bernard. Perhaps then you'll see that he's really out to help, not hinder you, son."

"Okay," I said, rising and quickly turning on my heels so that Lenitz wouldn't see the redness that had enveloped my face. I was so angry I wanted to kill that fucking guy. Instead I nodded once and exited his office quietly. No sense in making a scene.

Where would that get me?

Seven ten p.m. on a Tuesday night at the office, and my freaking head throbbed. I popped two Aleve with water and pushed back from my desk. Behind me the evening sky was subdued. The stars were just beginning to shine. The moon would be rising soon, I knew, bathing the D.C. skyline with light.

What a day, I thought with despair. When would it end? Would it ever?

Doubtful.

I toyed with the idea of packing up for the night, but lacked the energy to do so. In a minute, I decided, once my head cleared.

For the millionth time, I pondered why I even bothered with this shit anymore. Bernard John Marshall had not let up on me one single iota. I would have thought that my discrimination complaint would have, at the very least, slowed him down a bit. But not that mutha sucka. He was relentless. I think it amused him to think that he was getting to me. For a few days after my meeting with Lenitz I had no idea how to act. So I took some time off—called in sick, which I rarely did. In the end, I went back to work, and filed my god-damned complaint. Take that you pig, I thought—and waited and waited for the EEOC to get back to me.

I was still waiting . . .

So what was I still doing here, working late?

Because it was my nature—besides, what else was there for me to do?

I had bills to pay like every other sorry-ass mutha sucka on earth!

Giovanna was busy tonight doing something, which was cool with me. We'd hook up later on this week—I knew that—at this point we were spending like three to four times a week together, which was damn near a record for yours truly. I mean, usually after I hit the punany a time or two, I got bored and moved on. Not so with Giovanna. She kept me occupied. Truth be told—that pussy was damn good! I kid you not! But the other reason was that I simply lacked the energy of my old self—the old Trey was in hibernation for the winter, or that's what it damn near felt like. Vince and Erika weren't around; I wasn't going out much, other than hanging with Giovanna . . .

I kneaded my temples while I contemplated my situation. I was the kind of guy who was used to staying busy. And, face it, I didn't do well just lounging around the crib, watching cable or waiting for some shit to happen. If I wasn't chasing tang, well then I was working or hanging with my friends—that's the way it had always been. But with my friends out of the picture as of late, well . . .

A sudden knock at my door burst through my psyche, causing me to flinch.

India had jetted, leaving me to fend for myself.

I glanced up, expecting to see Bernard John Marshall waltz in.

Instead, Layla flowed in, like mercury, and I felt myself wince.

"Hello Trey."

She wore a to-the-knee wrap-around black and gray dress that tied on her left side. Shiny black knee-high boots. Her overcoat was draped over an arm. Hair worn down long as usual, sexy as all get up. Her eyes sparkled as she locked her gaze with me.

I felt myself flush.

"Layla," I responded, my palms reaching for my desk top as my fingers extended outward. I could feel the perspiration on my skin. It was that quick.

"Been a while, Trey. You're a hard man to track down." Layla took a step forward, flinging down her coat onto my couch. "I hope you don't mind," she mused. I watched her silently, wondering to myself, mind what? The fact that you're here, or the fact that you're laying down your over-coat . . .

I swallowed. "To what do I owe the honor?" I asked.

Layla moved to the head of my desk, her thighs brushing against the polished wood. "Well, I've been reaching out to you for several months now, and you haven't returned any of my phone calls—that's not nice, Trey. So I decided to see if you're okay."

"I'm fine," I said, hastily. "And how did you find me any-way? I don't recall providing you with my work address."

"Girl's gotta be resourceful in this day and age," she said, laughing. "Seriously though, Trey, you hurt my feelings by not calling back."

"Sorry, boo—been busy with work and all," I said, arms wide. I stood up, flattened my tie and moved around the table to the couch. I gestured for Layla to sit, and she took one of the upholstered chairs, crossing her legs. The move did not go unnoticed by me. As usual, Layla looked stunning. I controlled my breathing as I looked on nonchalantly. "So," I said, cheerfully, "What's new with you?"

"Missing you." The words emerged from her mouth so gracefully and purposefully that I had the feeling that she had rehearsed it many times.

"I bet," I exclaimed. "Seriously, Layla . . ."

"I am serious, Trey."

She brushed her hair from one side over to the other, a move so blatantly sexual that I had to laugh.

She continued. "I thought that after the last conversation at bluespace, that we were," and here she paused to find the right words, "vibing, Trey."

I nodded. "Yeah, we had some great conversation—"

"No, it was more than great conversation, Trey, and you know it—what we shared at bluespace . . . and what we always had was so different than anyone else—and that's what I miss most—what we shared years ago—that bond, that connection that exists between us. That special something that was on a different plane than everyone else. It was like we gelled in ways that most people don't. I know that now. Having had the years between us has given me the clarity to see . . ."

I held up my hands. "Whoa—Layla—don't you think you should slow down a bit? I mean, we aren't seeing each other *anymore* . . ."

She smiled. And just like that I felt my insides melt. The girl was good—I had to give her credit.

"Trey, I was hoping that after our last conversation we'd start moving toward something, call it a relationship—I don't mean that in the normal sense of the word—us dating—although you know I'd like nothing else. But I thought we connected that night—I felt it, and I know you did too. So I was surprised and disappointed when you didn't call me back."

"Layla—as I said, I've been busy."

"Trey, save that shit for your clients. Okay? This is *me* you're talking to. I know you. The Trey I fell in love with made time for the things that mattered to him most. That much hasn't changed, I know that. So do you."

I was for a moment, speechless.

"Trey, I'm not asking for the world—but I want to be your friend. I see you now, and I can tell that you're hurting. Something is not right in your world. You don't have to say it, but it is there—as plain as day on your face."

"What?" I exclaimed, but I could feel the tension rising, blood curdling beneath my skin. The way she saw through my bullshit was uncanny.

"You need me as much as I need you, Trey Alexander. You know this to be the case. So why are you fighting it—why are you running away?"

I stood up, hand to my baldhead as I wiped away the sweat. Heading to the window, I glanced outward, my mind racing. Turning back, I faced her again.

"Layla—we've been through this before. Things have changed. I've changed. I'm not the man I used to be. You've changed. You're not . . ."

I stopped.

Layla glared at me. She rose slowly as I caught my breath.

"Say it, Trey. Let's stop the charades and get to the heart of the matter." She hadn't moved toward me, but the action of her standing forced me to stay in place. I took a breath and exhaled forcefully.

"I'm not in love with you, Layla. I'm sorry to burst your bubble, but I'm not. I was. Once upon a time. But not now."

Layla waved her hand away.

"Say what you were going to say, Trey. Get it out in the open."

I blinked.

"Let me help you. You're not . . . what? Go ahead—fin-ish that sentence." Layla's eyes had diminished to mere slits.

I sighed heavily as I stared into her eyes.

"You're not the *woman* . . . ," I said.

A pregnant pause.

Five, maybe ten seconds.

Layla's jaw worked. Otherwise she was still.

Her hands found her thighs.

"Not the woman, Trey, or not *a* woman?"

"Layla, please," I said. "Let's not . . ."

"Why stop now, Trey. Why not say what's been on your mind all these years . . . it's not like you were man enough to say it to my face back then!"

It felt as if a punch had been lobbed in my direction. I felt the wind drain out of me. I opened my mouth but no words emerged. My hands clenched as I sucked air.

"You don't want to go there," I said, seething.

"Why, what are you afraid of Trey—I mean, shit—why not bust it all out in the open? Now's as good a time as any. I don't have anywhere to go. How about you?"

I sighed again.

"You know what—I'm not playing your game, Layla—not now. So just drop it—"

"No, Trey, I won't drop it—because this is my life we're talking about—you were the only person who ever meant anything to me—and I lost you—and you won't even talk to me now, or look at me the way you used to, forget touching me, God forbid. What did I do that was so wrong, Trey? Tell me. Was knowing the truth so damn horrid to you, to the point where you would give up everything that we had? That's something I could never understand."

"Yes, Layla—it was," I said, my voice taking on an air of

authority. "Forgive me, but I couldn't live with you after that. I couldn't live with—"

Another pregnant pause.

"Say it, Trey. Don't stop now," Layla whispered.

"Fine," I said. My eyes locked onto hers. "A woman who's not a real woman. There, I said it," I yelled, hand going to my baldhead again as my eyes blinked. "Happy?"

Layla emitted something resembling a laugh. She moved forward one step as she nodded, out and away from the confines of the low coffee table. I remained where I was, watching her silently.

"Not a real woman," she repeated, placing her hands on the tie by her waist. She stared at me—not threatening or with malice—but those eyes were alive, undulating in their own sea. I couldn't help but remain captivated.

Her fingers worked slowly. I followed them with my gaze, silently holding my breath.

"Am I not a woman, Trey?" Layla asked, tugging gently on the string. The effect was that her dress fell away, halves parted, like two hands moving away, revealing her jewels within.

Layla was naked. She wore no bra—none was needed. Her breasts were lying high just as I had remembered them, lovely orbs of flesh that jiggled as she moved. Nor panties—her crotch was bare save for a thin, dark patch of manicured pubic hair. I could see the lips of her sex. They were distended and full. I had always marveled at the shape and form of her cavern—like the petals of a flower, so lovely, especially when drops of nectar glazed the sides.

My jaw had no choice but to drop.

"What does this look like?" she said, legs parted, holding the folds of her dress open so that I could see. I blinked rapidly, as I felt the stiffness in my suit pants. It was an immediate, automated response.

"For once and for all—answer the question you've been longing to answer—and be truthful, with yourself and with me. Tell me what you see, Trey. Look at me . . ."

And I did. I took her all in: the soft, curvy lines of her form, smooth, dark skin, the steep rise to her breasts, the scooping fall of her mid-section, the sensuous expanse to her hips, and slender yet strong legs. Nipples reaching out as if yearning for an embrace, and her sex—the core of her very essence—the draw on me overpowering. I could feel my legs going weak. Reaching out to the window for support, I continued to lock my stare on her lovely features, as I remained silent.

"Tell me what you see, Trey? Is this the body of a woman standing before you? Surely it's not that of a man's," she said. "If your eyes are playing tricks on you, come here and touch me. Take a feel. It's okay, I promise I won't bite."

I cleared my throat.

"I can't," I ventured, my whisper barely audible.

"Can't or won't?" Layla responded, moving until a foot of space separated us. I watched her flesh move. It was womanly flesh. Suddenly my entire being ached—feet to temples, spine to fingertips—and I longed to be swallowed up inside of her, tucked away safely where it was always warm.

The recognition of that feeling made me sick.

"I can't," I repeated, and then mumbled meekly, "I'm kind of seeing someone."

Layla's hands were on her hips. Her breasts reached out to me. They were now inches away. The scent of her was wafting over me, bringing me back to a time that I hadn't visited in ages. I closed my eyes, sucked in a quick breath, allowing the vapors to envelop me, consenting to this delicious sensation that swirled about before reopening my eyes to bear witness to Layla gazing upon me.

"Do you love her?" she asked tenderly. I watched her bite her lip, a response she couldn't control.

Another pregnant pause.

"I don't . . . I've just . . ." I stopped, seeing that any further effort would be fruitless.

"I'll take that as a 'no'." She moved closer still. "Sure you don't wanna venture a feel? Just for old time's sake."

I blinked again.

"No, Layla, thanks."

My eyes were locked in a downward stare—catching her breasts, soft curve to her mid-section, and what lay beneath—all in the arc of my vision.

"There's just the simple question left to answer, then. So answer it," she commanded.

I swallowed forcefully and exhaled. I was fully hard now, my erection making no excuses for what it knew to be true.

I was angry with myself.

Irritated for allowing myself to be caught up in her magic. I so wanted to be dispassionate; hard and firm, but not in the sense that comes immediately to mind—I didn't want her to see me in this state. Just as I was contemplating all of this Layla glanced down, focusing her attention on this thing that jutted out at an ungodly angle from my pants.

She smiled, lips parting before coming together again, the flesh upturned as she reached for me. She brushed my erection with the tips of her fingers, and I felt myself implode—a silent explosion, almost coming on the spot.

"You've answered it," she said, "some things don't lie . . ."

I backed up, instinctively beyond reach, and into the window frame. I needed control. I needed to get out of her space.

Fast.

Layla smiled as she covered herself, the halves of dress fabric crossing over one another until she was no longer bare.

Securing her dress, she turned away from me. I watched the swaying of those luscious hips, seducing me with her hypnotic rhythm.

Layla reached for her coat with one hand and headed for the door. Before exiting she turned, glancing over her shoulder at me as she said, "Some things never lie, Trey. He," she said, gesturing with a nod to my rock-hard dick, "knows a real woman when he sees one. The question is, do you????"

Then she left me alone, pondering the question, and all that it entailed . . .

For the next several days, two thoughts rented out my psyche—Layla and love . . .

I can't help it y'all, but the situation in my office forty-eight hours previously had me thinking about little else.

Layla—coming back into my life, pushing those buttons like only she can . . . hating myself for even contemplating her in that way—I had sworn off her a long time ago—but seeing her like that—exposed and vulnerable, her true beauty revealed—made me ponder some things that I wasn't prepared to deal with.

Layla and I had had our time—we've given it a healthy shot. I was ready to spend the rest of my life with her back then—but that was before she dropped the mother of all bombs on me, and left me changed. Forever.

Or had it?

I no longer could think straight. Nothing made sense to me anymore. I felt as if I was losing ground, slipping into the black abyss of a deep, dark hole, pawing my way to the surface, struggling to breath, straining to get my head above ground.

And then there was the question of love.

Was I in love?

Until Layla had posed the question to me, I hadn't given it a second thought. But after she uttered those words two days ago, I thought about little else.

Was I in love with Giovanna?

And how would I know?

See, this whole love thing was difficult for me. I had been in love before, what seemed like eons ago. Since then, I didn't let myself get attached to anyone. Why should I? I didn't want to run the risk of being hurt again. Besides, most relationships ended in a screwed up sort of way, with folks yelling and screaming at each other, swearing that the last six or nine months of their lives had been one big freaking waste of time.

So I took a different approach.

I didn't let anyone into my space.

Kept them at a distance.

Romanced them, yes, but with the express purpose of getting them into my bed. Sample their wares and then move on!

Don't stay for a second longer than necessary.

Lest one gets hurt . . .

. . . or worse—burnt.

That's my story, y'all and I'm sticking to it!

But over the past few months, everything seemed to be changing.

Giovanna came into my life—a woman who, for the first time in a long while, was my equal. I found someone whom I could vibe with. Yeah, the sex was the bomb—the best I'd had in a long, long time, but beyond that, I dug her company.

Was that love?

I didn't know.

I used to know.

But not now.

I wrestled with these questions in between meeting with

clients, on the commute to and from the office, and at night at home in my crib, the television on but muted, the stereo on, either a Fourplay or a Jeff Lorber CD in the changer, funky jazz permeating the air as I contemplated my life. My *love* life . . .

If Erika were here, she'd tell me the deal.

Set me straight on this love thang.

I even contemplated picking up the phone and calling her—reached for it several times, but always, always ended up putting the receiver down. No, I couldn't just call Erika up out of the blue to ask her esoteric questions about love. We didn't have it like that anymore . . .

Talk to Giovanna?

No, she wasn't the kind of girl you had that kind of discussion with. Not yet, anyway.

Perhaps one day soon.

Once I sorted all of this shit out.

And while I attempted to do that, thoughts and images of Layla bubbled to the surface. The yin and yang of what I was feeling tore at my insides, tugging me in opposite directions. That night, seeing her there, lain open like a ripe grapefruit, ready to be taken, was so overpowering that just thinking about her made me hard. But then the opposite feeling would strike at my center—how could I feel the way I did? How could I even contemplate being stimulated by her after what went down?

The whole thing made me sick.

I shook my head morosely as I steered the Escalade onto River Road. It was a Thursday night, 7:30 in the evening and I was on my way to Giovanna's house. I had called first to tell her I was on my way.

She didn't sound overly happy to be receiving me, but I didn't ponder the deeper meaning of that very much.

I had other things on my mind.

I pulled into the driveway and as always when I visited here, marveled at her home and those in the neighborhood.

To call this house a mansion was an understatement.

Her car, a brand new jet-black Lexus RC, was in the driveway. I pulled up next to it and got out, leaving my ride unlocked.

Who the hell was gonna steal my shit in this neighborhood?

I had to ring the doorbell twice before Giovanna opened it.

I stepped back, surprise written all over my grille.

Giovanna wore a short white mini-skirt, matching top, and fuck-me pumps. Her hair was pulled up, done right, sparkling diamond studs in her ears, and face made up *thick*!

Girlfriend was not playing . . .

"Hey you," I said, reaching for her. I placed my arms around Giovanna's waist and pulled her to me, kissing her deeply on the mouth. She returned my kiss for a quick moment before pulling back and ushering me into the house.

I watched her maneuver down the hallway past dining room and sitting room into an enormous open-air living room. I paused as I always do, glancing left then right at Vince's collection of masks—four pieces, two on each side, their vibrant colors leaping out from the whitewashed walls. Giovanna's attire, however, made me quickly squash any thoughts of Vince Cannon, Jr., and his artwork.

"Damn, baby—check you out all cleaned up," I said, trying to contain the rising tension I felt in my gut. This wasn't home attire, that's for damn sure.

"Hey yourself," she said, her back to me. I watched her ass flex against the taut fabric of her skirt as hips sashayed back and forth. I found myself growing hard. "Destiny just called," she said, "so I'm heading out with the girls. First nice evening in a long time, so they wanted to do a girls-nightout. Kind of an impromptu thing."

"I hear you," I said, but I didn't.

Joining her in the living room, I took a seat beside her on the sofa. She sat, legs together, hands on her lap, eyeing me closely.

"So," I ventured, looking sheepish, "what time you rolling out?" I asked, flashing one of my famous Trey smiles. I immediately sensed that my presentation was weak. These days I lacked the usual effort.

Giovanna checked her watched.

"Soon. Thirty minutes or so."

I nodded. Moving closer. Took her hand in mine, reaching forward, kissing her on her cheek. Tracing a line of kisses over her lips. Probing between the flesh of her lip gloss-covered mouth with my tongue, slipping it inside, sucking at hers like it was a strawberry, hands on her thighs, moving rapidly upward to her breasts, which I kneaded in my palms. Groaning lightly as I moved closer still, hand dropping to her lap, slipping in between her thighs, parting legs as I raced for that sweet spot.

"Trey, stop . . . ," she whispered, turning her face away and leaning back.

"Why?" I asked, perplexed.

"Because, I can't," she said, removing my hand and fixing her skirt. Hands back on her lap. "Aunt Flo is visiting, that's why—sorry baby," she added with a shrug.

It took me a second or two to catch on.

"Oh. You know what—I don't care," I said, moving in, reaching for her face and readying to kiss her again. "I need you so badly right now, baby. Just for a few minutes." I paused. "A few seconds," I added with a grin. "Just let me inside you, girl for a split second—cause I know it ain't gonna take me long!"

Giovanna gave me a stern look, and then relaxed her expression. She grinned at me and I found her so damn sexy I just had to lean back and drink her all in. God, she was stunning, I thought to myself.

"You are beautiful," I said, voicing what was on my mind. "I hope you know just how much you mean to me," I said, taking her hands in mine. Giovanna nodded, but remained silent. She watched me as I spoke, my eyes unwavering as I took in her features. "Truly beautiful," I repeated. Giovanna smiled.

I sucked in a breath while letting my gaze roam over her hard body. My mind was dizzy with thoughts swirling around me, my cock straining against my suit pants, feeling the pulse in my neck thud loudly as my gaze consumed her, Giovanna just sitting there, not moving, but every muscle fiber in her body speaking to me, singing its sensuous song—I wanted her so badly I could barely stand it. But it was more than just sheer physical longing. My eyes quivered along with my heart. So did the rest of my being.

"I think I'm falling in love with you, Giovanna," I heard myself say. Suddenly, it was as if I was a bystander watching the drama unfold from twenty feet away, standing on the other side of the room, staring at us sitting on the couch, holding hands, gazing into each other's eyes, the passion so thick that it was like fog hugging a valley.

The bystander in me observed my breath holding.

Had I just said that?

And where had that come from?

I hadn't fully analyzed my feelings and reached any conclusion yet . . .

Or had I?

Giovanna was silent for a moment. She rose quietly off the couch, disappearing into the kitchen. I leaned my head back, arms at my sides, eyes closed, mind racing.

Did my feelings jibe with my words?

My head hurt as the silence between us deepened.

Giovanna returned with two wine stems filled with Merlot. I accepted one with a smile and took a sip. She did the same and then put hers down on the coffee table in front of us.

"Trey, we need to talk," she began. I sat up and gave her my full attention, while feeling that my legs were like a rickety house of cards, about to blow over. Giovanna wore a strained expression before she continued. "The last few months have been stressful on you. You've lost good friends, at least in the short term, work's been a bitch—I recognize all of that." She paused to wipe a piece of invisible lint off of her lap. She took in a deep breath as she pondered her next words carefully. "Trey, what drew me to you when we first met was the way in which you carried yourself." Giovanna smiled in remembrance. "So cocky, so full of yourself, as if you were the bomb. Some girls might find that offensive and even a turn off—but not me—just the opposite. It was an incredible turn on. To find someone who had the balls to strut about the room as if they were the shit. I so dug that about you."

I nodded solemnly.

"I'll never forget the way you handled my property settlement in New York; the way you spoke with authority; the way you got my husband and his attorney all in a tizzy—you didn't know it, but your performance that day made me so damn wet. I had to run home and take care of business *myself.*"

"Dayum," I uttered, eyes wide.

"Yeah, it was like that. That's why you and I clicked, Trey; that's why I gave myself to you that night in New York—cause you and I were in the same zone—we vibed. We clicked. In case you haven't noticed, I'm a bit of an uppity bitch myself!"

I laughed. She did too. Then her smile died.

"But, let me say this in a way that I hope doesn't hurt you, but I need to say this—over the past months, you've lost that swagger to your step. You're no longer the overconfident, arrogant man who turned me on with his in-your-face attitude."

I winced.

"I want—and I need—the old Trey back. I know you're going through a hard time right now. Lord knows we all have those moments. But I need *that* guy back. Not this one sitting in front of me. You need to get back in the zone, Trey. Need to get back there and join me. Are you feeling me?"

I closed my eyes, and reopened them. Took a sip of wine, a bit too fast, splashing some on my chin. I wiped it away with the back of my hand.

"Yeah, Giovanna," I said, cautiously, my brain sending commands to my mouth and face in way too slow motion. "I feel you."

Giovanna stood. Smoothed out her skirt and rubbed her palms together. She stole a glance at her watch and returned her gaze to me.

"Gotta go, baby," she said, softly. "Feel free to stay . . ."

But when she returned much later on that evening, I had been long gone.

April's rain came down. Seemingly from out of nowhere, it fell with a vengeance, cleansing everything in its path. I drove around in the Escalade, nowhere to go, not wanting to head home and stare at my walls, wallowing in the self-pity I felt right now. So I drove on. Alone . . .

Driving cleared my head. The sheer act of steering and focusing on the road kept me from going insane.

Kept me from feeling sorry for myself.

I had made a mistake.

I had come to Giovanna when I was at my lowest, and reached out for her hand.

Bad move.

She wasn't one to help a drowning man . . .

I think I found that out way too late.

But my words continued to swirl around inside my head. "I think I'm falling in love with you . . ."

In love with you.

Giovanna.

My jaws clenched.

I steered my ride up one street and down another, closed up shops and government buildings flashing by me. The details were lost. I wasn't paying attention.

Once again I found myself longing for close friends. I needed Erika so badly right then. I even contemplated calling her up right that very minute, asking for her forgiveness and womanly advice. After close to fifteen years, she had always seen me through when times were rough.

But this time, picking up the phone to call her was easier said than done. Words had been spoken between us that couldn't be unspoken. And so I stared at my cell phone in one hand, the glow of the screen bathing my forearm with eerie light as I rubbed the polished steel incessantly; flipping it around in my hand, unsympathetic light returning to comfort me, as a Sting song played in the background.

Another thought poked through, but I pushed it back down, safely, for the moment, out of sight.

Across Florida Avenue, then up Georgia heading toward Silver Spring, fast-food restaurants and other establishments passing me by as I drove. My mind on things seven months previous, when life back then was simple and good. A sudden rush of images and emotions: A Caribbean sky—the fiery orange of a Jamaican sky. An enormous hot tub filled to capacity with writhing naked flesh, me in the prime of my existence, flowing from one sensuous encounter to another, dancing in the afterglow of rum-induced passion. Water bubbling underneath our hungered bodies that writhed as we touched, licked, and fed; bodies slicked with water, love juices, and desire as we played under a Jamaican moon; an envious crowd that longed to join in, but didn't dare interrupt this feast. I was the main course. And I had found heaven.

Fast forward in a blinding rush of imagery. Mutha suckas chanting my name as I made way to center stage. Trey, Trey, Trey, Trey, Trey, Trey!!! At that point, everyone knew my name.

Months later, back home—rolling into a club dressed as fly as I don't know what. Women and men whispering as I glide on by. Who the hell is that, they whisper? Oh him—I hear he's some power attorney. Boy is clean, I'll give him that . . .

And then, like a shockwave, I'm thrust back to the present. Two weeks ago, a Thursday night after work—Giovanna and I had been sitting at some bar, sipping a cocktail. Me harboring a serious case of the after-work blues. Giovanna suddenly rose off the bar stool and headed to the ladies room, exasperation painted on her face. I remember thinking to myself; this place is close to capacity in here, and less than five percent of the female patronage were eyeing me like usual. My averages were way the heck down. It was as if I no longer existed.

It was as if these women could sense my discomfort.

It was as if they saw what Giovanna was seeing—that I was no longer in the zone.

Giovanna, I hated to admit, was right.

That thought weighed heavily on my mind.

Back to the present—tonight—the unfortunate here and now—I contemplated going to a strip club, Stadium Club, which I'd just passed a moment ago, where I'm sure some chocolate honey would (for the moment) take my heartache away. But the thought was indeed sobering.

I needed a friendly face—not that of a stranger.

The *other* thought—the one that kept popping up, like a piece of driftwood, refusing to become waterlogged and drown—once more revealed itself to me. And whether it was from sheer exhaustion or just finally being worn down, I do not know. But after glancing for the hundredth time at my cell phone, fondling the glass and aluminum as if it were woman's flesh, I pressed some keys and waited for the phone to connect.

"Trey?" her voice asked, rising in warmth and concern simultaneously.

"Yes," I responded, desperately trying to add some timbre to my volume, but simply lacking the energy to do so. "Caller ID's both a godsend and a mutha sucka," I added, my small attempt at humor.

She did not laugh. I stole a glance at the time. Eleven forty p.m. It was late. Beyond that—I hadn't dialed her number in years . . .

"Is everything okay? You know I'm delighted to hear from you, but frankly, I'm surprised."

A pregnant pause as I considered how to respond. What to say to her? Open up to her, completely? Tell her what's really on my mind?

In the absence of words, I sighed heavily.

"I know it's late," I began, "but can we meet?" A whistle escaped from my lips. " I need to talk."

She didn't miss a blink.

"Of course, Trey. Where are you?" she asked.

"Driving up Georgia toward the Beltway."

"Come here." It wasn't open to debate. She gave me her address. I was approximately thirty minutes out.

"I'll be there in fifteen."

I ended the call, eyes, for a moment boring into the metal like a laser, before I flipped a U-turn in the middle of the deserted street, and headed south.

On my way to see her.

To see *Layla* . . .

Eighteen

When Layla met me at the door, she knew I was feeling down.

She could tell that from just my voice alone.

I would have bet anyone a thousand dollars that Layla would have come to the door clad in the latest Victoria's Secret fashion—something downright scandalous, sensuous, and revealing . . .

Yet she did nothing of the sort.

Layla was wearing flannel pajamas—down to her ankles and covering her forearms. The fit was loose—one could discern her curves, but it was clear that she was wearing these for comfort—and not for turning on a messed-up-in-the-head dude.

"Hey you," I said sheepishly. Layla reached out and gave me a hug. She kissed my cheek. The warmth of her body felt good, but I pulled back, out of sudden discomfort.

How to act?

It was still unclear to me.

As I walked into her home, Layla took my overcoat and led me into a comfortable living room.

It was after midnight. For all I knew Layla had to get up in the morning for work. I sure as hell had to.

"Let me get you something to drink," Layla said, heading into the kitchen. I sat down on a couch. The television was on, BET, concert footage of Sade singing "The Sweetest Taboo." I love Sade—she's one of the finest sisters on the planet, with an oh-so-sweet voice, so I settled back to watch.

"What can I get you? Water, juice, soda, or something stronger?" she asked, her face angling in from the next room.

"Stronger, please," I responded. "Do you have some rum?" I asked, my mind suddenly remembering better times under a Jamaican sky.

"Yeah mon!" she exclaimed, her dancing eyes and winning smile causing me to beam in reply.

Layla returned momentarily with my drink, a tumbler filled with clear ice cubes and dark rum.

"Merci," I replied.

Layla sat next to me as I sampled my drink, closing my eyes, grateful for the liquor that quelled my fears. Layla was relaxed, bare feet tucked underneath her on the couch as she faced me, throw pillow on her lap as she turned up the volume on the TV and began gyrating her upper body to the song.

"I just love this song," she said, and I had to smile at her. For a split second, it was like old times, just her and I, years ago, chilling at her crib, when life was simple back then, not the agonizing constant stress levels of today. I remember that smile—I remember how it used to get to me, make me stop what I was doing and reach for her, regardless of where I was or what I was doing; take her face in my hands, touch her lips tenderly with my fingertips, exploring the surface of her peaks and valleys as if for the very first time before covering her mouth with mine, invading her mouth with my tongue, letting her know just how special she was, just how much she moved me with just a smile.

Her smile.

"Earth to Trey," she said, bringing me back, "quarter for your thoughts."

I smiled.

"Inflation," she added.

"Trey?"

"What?" I feigned ignorance before waving my hand at her. Taking a breath, I said, "It's just, I was recalling how we used to chill back in the day, your feet on my lap as we talked about everything under the sun—sometimes until four or five o'clock in the morning!" I emitted a short laugh; took a sip of my rum before continuing. "Remember that? God—we were silly back then . . ."

Layla was silent for a moment. She glanced away, her own mind wandering before her gaze returned to me.

"There's nothing silly about being in love, Trey," she said, her voice low.

I nodded once and reached again for the comfort of my drink.

Sade's "No Ordinary Love" had come on. She was singing her heart out to a standing room only crowd. Layla gazed at the television for the rest of the song as I sipped my drink, watching closely too. It wasn't until the crowd erupted in applause that Layla turned back to me and said, "So, Trey, tell me what brings you here?"

Until that moment, I hadn't been sure of what exactly I would say to Layla. Did I feel comfortable enough to fully vent, sharing with her the details of my life? As we sat there, Layla's feet curled up underneath her, clad in her flannel pajamas, I suddenly felt that I could tell her my woes—and that she would not judge me. I needed to speak—I needed to vent. Layla was, for now, all I had . . .

So I told her. Everything . . . Starting at the beginning.

Six, seven months ago, when I was on top of the world . . . when Trey was in the zone.

Taking her all the way up until tonight.

Tonight, only hours earlier, when I professed my love to another woman.

"I think I'm falling in love with you . . ."

Layla listened and did not judge. For two hours she let me speak. About Giovanna, Erika, Vince, and Bernard John Marshall. About everything that had affected me, causing me to slip out of the zone. Layla asked questions when what I was saying did not make any sense or required further clarification. When I asked for her opinion, she gave it. But mostly she just sat back and listened, pillow comfortably between her legs, nodding in a sympathetic way, urging me to go on, and to not be afraid of my feelings.

Layla refreshed my drink several times. At some point she poured herself a glass of white wine and twirled the stem between slender fingers as she listened to me.

When I was done, it was after two a.m.

"I messed up by telling her how I feel," I said, draining the last of my drink, the conclusion that summed up how I felt.

"No, you didn't mess up, Trey. You were vulnerable. You needed to be close to the woman whom you've been intimate with. It's natural to say and feel the way you do."

"Is it?" I asked.

"I'd say so. The question you need to ask yourself honestly is this: were your words speaking the truth for you? Are you really falling in love with her, or is it something else?"

"Such as?" I inquired.

"Lust, Trey. Don't mistake love for lust."

I pondered her words for a moment.

Layla had something else on her mind, I could tell. I glanced over and nodded for her to continue. She pursed her lips as she twirled the wine stem.

"None of my business, of course, but I think you need to ask yourself if you are comfortable with Giovanna's response, or should I say, lack of response to your feelings. Are you cool with that? And what does that say about the type of person she is?"

"I know," I replied. "She fully admits that she's an 'uppity bitch'—her words, not mine, but your point is valid."

The Sade concert was long over. The television was still on, muted, to an all music video channel—rap and hip-hop videos dominating the late night hour.

Layla had killed the lights. The window shades were open, and the rain had ceased. Clouds had swept in and back out again, leaving the fullness of the moon to shine down, illuminating the night. Some might say it was a romantic night.

The stereo was on. Playing in the background was a Sade CD—*Love Deluxe*—that Layla had put on because we were both still feeling Sade after the concert. The sounds were inviting, soothing, and comforting. There wasn't much talk between us. It was as if what needed to be said had been said, and dispensed with—we didn't broach the subject that was on both of our minds—when Layla had paid me a visit to my job and bared her all to me.

A woman who's not a real woman . . .

I was glad that issue remained under glass, out of sight, because I wasn't ready to discuss that just yet.

Things were cool between us—the tension that I had felt previously had evaporated. Just sitting there, next to her, was comforting—the silence was a friend. I remembered that about us—how we could go for hours without a sound between us—me on one end of the couch, her on the other, books or newspapers in hand, but some kind of connection between us—an ankle on the other's thigh, the back of a hand on a neck—something that let us know we were still there.

Not going anywhere.

I glanced at the Breitling, suddenly wincing as if in pain. It was very late. I yawned. Layla yawned back. She rose, left the room for a brief period before returning with a thick blanket, some sheets and a fluffy pillow. I yawned again, wondering how in the hell I'd get up in a few short hours for work.

"Don't even think about leaving," she said, shooing me off the couch so she could make it up into a bed. "It's late and you've had too much to drink—you'll stay here tonight."

I eyed her curiously, but said nothing. Once again, she wasn't open to debate.

"And don't worry, Trey—I pledge not to take advantage of you tonight, so don't worry your little head over it!"

I smiled, grateful for her hospitality.

But a sobering thought lingered.

It was exactly my small head that I was worried about . . .

I awoke to the sounds of moaning. They were soft, discreet—the kind of noises that someone didn't want another soul to hear—but that somehow slipped out, while in the fury of passion, escaping like steam from a kettle. I sat up disoriented, cringing as I felt the taut muscles in my neck and back groan.

The sounds were coming from another room. Glancing at my Breitling, I saw it was just shy of 3:30 a.m. I'd been asleep for less than an hour. The lights were extinguished. The shades were drawn, making the room darkened but not

Devon Scott

pitch black. I rose, careful to keep my weight from creaking against the hardwood floor.

Again, noises were emitted. They were soft whimpers, almost animal like in form. Glancing down, I realized I was clad only in my boxer-briefs, black, and form fitting. I stole an opportunity to stretch toward the heavens, hearing my back creak. Suddenly my mind clicked into high gear, as I focused on the sounds and their possible meaning. A tingling sensation grew from my lower body, racing down along my spine.

I inched forward, nose up—stopping for a moment as I cocked my head, first left then right, like a dog sniffing for a scent. I moved on, into the hallway, pausing again to get my bearing. A restroom off to the left. Several rooms on the right. I passed one room, door closed. Braked again a foot shy of an open doorframe—the second bedroom. What I heard was a sharp intake of breath. Then a low, exhaling of breath, almost whistle-like. I filled my lungs slowly and silently before stepping forward into the open doorway.

Layla was on the queen-size bed, fully nude, her legs splayed across the mattress. The lights were off, but a lone candle burned on a nightstand to the left of the bed. Her eyes were closed, her fingers poised at the opening to her sex. Entombed within her was a smooth dildo, white in color. The juxtaposition of those hues—bone white against her chocolate skin was striking—and an immediate turn-on. My heart thumped in my chest. She must have heard it, or sensed me near because Layla opened her eyes, her orbs sparkling as they focused on my darkened form.

The dildo was moving slowly in and out of her, commandeered by slender, dark fingers.

She did not slow her movements on my account. Her stare locked onto mine as her tongue clicked against her teeth. I found that I had to break the stare and glance away—

following the movement of her fingers and that white plastic thing that traveled in and out of her tight cavern. Her nipples were distended, and her breasts swollen. A hand reached up to caress them, fingers gliding over darkened areolas before tracing a line back down, dipping into her navel, traversing the thin patch of pubic hair until she met the rising flesh of her clit.

Her fingers alighted from the dildo, leaving it sunken with only several inches showing as she reached for her nipples. For a moment she closed her eyes, pinching them as she gyrated her hips—and my eyes stayed glued to the plastic within her, watching as it moved in step with her—and there was a feeling that overtook me—not only of intense sensual passion and stimulation, but of admiration—for Layla—and the way she was so at peace, with herself and with me—the mere fact that she could pleasure herself, in full view of me, without missing a beat.

My breath was exhaled through dry lips. I had to re-wet them with my tongue.

Layla's eyes reopened. And she smiled.

"You can come in," Layla said, and I crossed the threshold apprehensively, candlelight flickering onto my taut form. Layla's eyes took me in, her gaze sweeping over my body, stopping when she spied my erection that strained against the cotton of my boxer-briefs. A grin transfixed her lips.

I was unsure of what to do next. Part of me wanted to go to her. She looked so . . . *womanly* . . . just lying there. The other—was terrified. I assumed that Layla would make a snide remark about my engorged state, but she didn't. Instead, her hand snaked back down to her sex, fingers massaging the cleft to her opening as she gripped the shiny white shaft and rotated it inside of her.

"I'm not trying to seduce you, Trey. So, don't be afraid to

come closer." Layla pulled the dildo out excruciatingly slow, until the plastic head breached her lips, wiping the glazed tip against her clit and moist thighs before plunging it back inside with a grunt.

"Ooooh!" Layla hissed, eyes closing for a microsecond before training them back on me, her unwavering stare at cock-level.

I advanced slowly into the room, feeling more alive than I had in years. The yin and yang of emotions tugged at my insides—part of me was on fire—to the point where I felt ready to explode. The other—scared beyond words—this being something I had dreamt about—a nightmare that was suddenly coming true. Face to face with Layla once again—her secret no longer hidden, but bare and all telling, as she was now before me.

And yet, as I stood there, toes curling into the thick carpet that for a moment soothed me, I marveled at Layla's dark writhing form before me. And discovered something that I found remarkable.

I had found myself thinking about Giovanna. And how different she was from the person lying before me.

Layla was sexual in a way that defied description.

It was innate for her—it was natural.

I suddenly realized this, and found that incredible.

Giovanna, with her intense physical beauty and desire to be queen-of-the-damned-sex-*bitch*, couldn't hold a candle to Layla in terms of sexual passion.

She just couldn't . . .

Layla wasn't playing. And she wasn't even trying.

She was just being herself. A woman . . .

Wasn't she?

I stepped closer to the bed, a calm bathing me like sunlight.

My heart was still thumping, yet I was tranquil inside . . .

I was thinking about Giovanna.

I think I'm falling in love with you.

That thought seized me as I sat on the bed, feet folding under my knees. Reclining on my left side, I reached for her. Connected with her ankles, sliding a hand up the smooth skin toward a thigh. Stroking the flesh, feeling her undulate, like a sea anemone, candlelight flickering over our bodies.

We were silent.

Words would have been wasted.

On my knees now, hovering above her, glancing downward at all that she revealed.

Her nakedness and her beauty.

Raw sensuality, unparalleled.

I was more scared than I'd been in years.

And yet, I pressed on . . .

Stroking both thighs, my fingers moved toward her hips, gripping the soft, supple flesh. Remembering with the blow of sudden intensity how good she used to feel.

I think I'm falling in love with you.

Reaching for her navel, ignoring the white rooted inside of her, circling the skin with a finger, tracing figure eights before gliding upward, Layla's eyes alternating between closing and opening, watching me fiercely, the passion in her like a storm brewing.

I think I'm falling in love with you.

Reaching for the mounds of flesh that were her breasts, slowly circling the areolas before giving each nipple my direct attention. As I bent forward, Layla tried to anticipate my movement and arch her back, pressing her breasts toward me. Instead, I allowed my mouth to simply brush against her warm skin for a moment, my lips skirting the edges of the raised flesh that were her darkened nipples before suddenly racing upward and resting my mouth on hers.

I think I'm falling in love with you.

I kissed Layla, softly and tenderly; the years that had sep-arated us seemed to suddenly contract until it was as if we had never been apart. Layla opened her mouth and gave her tongue to me, each of us exploring the other as if we were strangers. In a way we were.

There was no frenzied activity, no loss of control be-tween us.

We each knew what the other was doing.

Layla was remembering . . .

Yet, for me, this was a sort of test, I realized all too sud-denly. A test of my burgeoning love for Giovanna.

I considered this for a moment as I sucked on Layla's tongue. Pulling back, I gazed longingly at her features as I held her breasts in my hands.

I think I'm falling in love with you.

Snaking a hand downward to her core, I brushed against my own engorged sex-wand as I grasped the end of the white object between quivering fingers. Slowly I pulled the dildo out of her, feeling the strength of her fighting against me to keep the plastic entombed. Rubbing the thing against the folds of her sex, stretching her wide, probing her innards before sending the plastic rocket upward, to the smooth rise to her clit, pressuring the bulb as she swayed beneath me.

I think I'm falling in love with you.

That thought was sobering.

Was I?

For a moment I ceased all movement, contemplating my actions as the white dildo rested against her moistened thigh that quivered to my touch.

I'm think I'm falling in love with Giovanna . . .

And I'm readying to make love to Layla . . .

I exhaled forcefully feeling unsure. Layla felt the sudden change in my demeanor. She reached for my face, stroked a cheek with one hand passionately, while reaching for my thick member with the other.

I closed my eyes, the yin and yang tormenting me, like a boxer in a lopsided boxing match. Pummeling me with the back and forth banter inside my head.

I think I'm falling in love with you.

And yet, I am here . . .

Settling against Layla's soft skin, her hands found my ass, gripping me tightly, guiding me as she rotated her hips underneath, her pelvis thrusting against me as my cock screamed against the fabric of my boxer briefs. The head butted against her opening, stretching her, my mouth on Layla's, our tongues now a frenzy of activity, as a single thought coursed through me.

Getting back into the zone.

Getting back into the zone.

That's what it all came down to, I realized suddenly. Getting back into the zone meant getting back to what was real to me.

Feeling like I was before.

Acting the way I used to act.

Becoming the man that I knew I could be.

Again.

I pulled back from Layla, gazing down into her dreamy eyes. She was reaching for my briefs; I felt them slide down my thighs, past my knees and calves. Unencumbered, suddenly free, the passion swelled in me like a monstrous tidal wave, readying to break upon shore.

Getting back into the zone.

Getting back into the zone.

I parted Layla's legs, and with a single arcing motion slid inside of her. She gasped—as I did too—the feeling so out of this world—her sex tightening around me, my flesh quivering inside of her as I began to move, rocking with her, holding her forearms as I made love to her, increasing the tempo and pressure of my thrusting, Layla's head thrashing from side to side as my rhythm met hers, my groove meshing with hers. And suddenly, it wasn't about Giovanna anymore. Nor was it about love. Gone were thoughts of Bernard John Marshall, Erika, and Vince. I ceased to care about those irritants that kept me awake at night.

Suddenly everything lifted away and became calm.

Just Layla and me. Like it used to be.

I made love to Layla with abandonment. Fucked her good, matching whatever tempo she threw at me, sliding back into the warmth of her caress, as I had years ago, when things were simpler back then, when I was in love with this woman.

I fucked the woman I used to love, using long full strokes so she could feel my member's entire length and girth, licking the sides of her neck, gripping an earlobe between my teeth, sucking on her nipple, fingering her clit as she moaned and screamed my name, oh yeah, y'all, Trey was finding his way back into the saddle, doing his thing, hand gliding over her delicious ass, fingers flicking against her asshole, making her flinch, feeling this woman about to cum, kissing, nibbling, massaging every inch of sweat-induced flesh, gripping her ass, stretching that opening, concentrating on each other's breathing, loving what was building as I pulled her off the bed, raising that ass up as I took her *hard* and fast, not missing a single beat, daring her to cum, again and again, the crazed look in my eye and I worked it, toes and fingers curling, breathing strained as I took what had always been mine, drawing strength and power from each other's passion reserves, drinking it all in, delicious wine, intoxicating liquor, sweet mind-blowing drugs that felt so damn good, making one cry out, not in pain, but in pleasure, overwhelming intense pleasure, the feeling so overpowering, the emo-

tion so strong, and Layla holding onto me tightly, riding me
as a surfer rides a wave, hanging on, letting me do my thing,
knowing that we both needed this release, but wanting so
badly to fight the feeling, stem the tide, hold it back, yet
powerless to do so, therefore welcoming it when it did
come, the pressure mounting, the ride accelerating, no stopping this river that raged like a torrent, the floodgates opening until the pleasure was too much, the intensity on way too
high, and there was nothing left to do but unleash as I
screamed, my juice spraying forth, washing into her, coming, insides bathed with my seed as I screamed her name
again and again, Layla, Layla, God, Layla . . .

And her nails bit into my back and ass, a jagged trail of
pain as she too unleashed, oh God Trey this feels so freaking
good—

You got me so freaking tight.

This shit is sooooooooooooooooooooooooooooooooooo
fucking right.

See what love feels like . . .

Both souls exhaling at the exact same time, gasping for
air until our mouths clamped down upon one another, sucking out the screams, silencing our words, her name and
mine, slowing our rhythm, chest heaving, hearts trembling,
eyelids fluttering, lips shivering, bodies pressed against each
other, sweat mingling, oh yes, baby, that shit was good—

You were good

Everything I missed in you and more was good

Every ounce of strength I mustered, ejected, infused into
my baby was so freaking good . . .

My head resting against the warmth of her neck, kissing
the soft spot, licking her earlobe as the frenzy subsided,
heart beats returning to normal and I no longer gave a fuck
'cause I can feel you *clearly*—

That shit of yours is good

And I'm babbling baby
'Cause I'm feeling no pain
Life is about living
And if you ask how I'm livin'
I'm livin' large
Everyting irie with me . . .

'Cause my body is screaming, but not in pain, toes flexing as the tingling ripples about me, lightning striking, from the top of my baldhead, to the base of my feet, and baby, I'm singing to you quietly, can you hear me sing, thank you Lord, 'cause this dude is back, oh yeah, y'all, this bruthaman is back . . .

Layla's words stream into my consciousness, yet I'm having trouble focusing, still woozy, still high, from the Hypnotic, but I can hear music, her music, baby girl singing softly in my ear—

I feel you too.
Withering inside of me.
Like a flower after a sun-drenched day.
Oooooooooooooooooh yeah.
Ahhhhhhhhhhhhhhh right there.
That's it.
That's it right there.
No, like that.
Don't you dare stop.
Baby, keep it there, right there.
Let me feel you, just one minute more.

Her eyes sparkling, begging, pleading for me to indulge her a moment's breath more, for old time's sake, please Trey, please—

Oooooooooooooooooooh.
Ahhhhhhhhhhhhhhhhhhh.
I can feel your heartbeat.
Baby can you feel mine.

Your juices move me.
Your juices flow through me now . . .
And I can't help but smile 'cause this is livin' y'all, her
eyelids brimmed with tears as we nuzzle, both of us crying,
carrying on, 'cause this shit here is for real, and she's nodding and knowing, stroking my neck and shoulders as I
tremble—
Layla knows.
Layla's always known
She can feel me come alive
all over again
still wrapped inside of her
but expanding
filling those sugar walls
until I'm rock hard again
engorged
ready to roll
slow moving now
but accelerating
increasing the force
and the power
as Layla begs me to take her
all over again
up and away
into the zone
where we used to live
where I can live again
will live again,
her repeating five simple words over and over
like a soundtrack stuck on loop
until everything is all mixed up
all good
just gravy
just soup—

see what love feels like
see what love feels like
see what love feels like
see what love feels like . . .

There was a glow to Vince Cannon Jr.'s face that couldn't be denied. Everyone noticed it—Lisa, the counter girl at the Cosi's in Capitol Hill, Erika, his parents, and even the folks at Sipp's Cafe, the new spot Vince frequented in Fort Washington, Maryland because of the hip atmosphere, eclectic clientele, live jazz, and exceptional service. His neighbors had asked about the new bounce to his step. Vince just smiled as he moseyed on up the street, thinking to himself, if only y'all knew . . .

Vince's book, *Finding Nirvana*, had been mentioned in *Essence* magazine last month. With a readership of close to eight million African-American women and men—suddenly, his book was selling out from stores across the country.

Overnight, Vince was in high demand—his seminars were being sold out in several days. Other publications were also calling looking for interviews. And Vince found himself back on the road, heading to Houston, Dallas/Fort Worth, Chicago, and Cleveland in the space of one month. He had five other cities booked within the next sixty days.

But that wasn't the primary reason why folks noticed a pimp in his step!

Nope.

There was a far more important reason . . .

He reached the Fat Boy, wiped her down before donning his helmet, glasses, and gloves, striding the seat, and bringing the engine to life. He gunned it enthusiastically before taking off, in a trail of booming thunder.

Vince took his normal route, steering the Fat Boy across

the Memorial Bridge, down Constitution Avenue past the State Department, Federal Reserve, White House, and museums, then across Seventh Street to Independence Avenue. He loved riding through D.C. on his bike—and here he was, the dawn of spring shining down upon him, hugging his skin like a warm blanket, the feeling of the open air and wind against his dark skin as he rode—something he always found hard to describe. Up Independence, past the sprawling curves of the National Museum of the American Indian, the renovated U.S. Botanical Gardens Conservatory, and the Capitol on the left, speeding by the Library of Congress on the right, loving the Boy as it hummed and groaned beneath him, the Vance & Hines singing their rumbling bass tune in the morning air.

Into Capitol Hill and finally to the place which he continued to frequent several times a week even when it had turned cold outside: The Cosi Coffee and Bar. Vince eyed the Indian motorcycle as he pulled alongside and cut the engine. He felt his chest tightening as he headed for the inside.

When he walked in, Trey was waiting for him.

Vince held out his hand and grinned, but Trey, to his astonishment, pulled him close, giving him a bear hug. They held each other for a moment before they both pulled back, eyeing one another carefully.

"Been a while," Trey began.

"Three months, sixteen days, but who's counting?" Vince quipped.

"Stop your lying! Damn, you haven't changed," Trey replied.

They settled down, Trey on the low couch in back, Vince across from him in a high back upholstered chair.

"My bruh. How ya livin'?"

"Large and in charge," Vince responded. They both grinned.

Lisa, his favorite barista, brought him a steaming mug of coffee—Vince rose, embraced her, and sent her on her way with a quick peck to her cheek.

"You?" he asked, after stealing a sip from his coffee.

"Can't complain—wouldn't matter if I did!"

They settled back into the awkward silence. For a moment they sipped at their coffees before Trey cleared his throat.

"So, it's been a while . . ."

Vince nodded but let him continue.

"We haven't talked in a minute, so I wanted to holla at you. You know, make sure you're still living and shit."

Vince nodded again. He wondered if this was Trey's way of apologizing—if so, this was one hell of a way to start.

"Oh I'm living, Trey. In fact, things with me have been all that!"

"It's like that?"

"Yeah, like that." Vince paused to sip at his coffee. Did he detect a bit of envy coming from his friend/former friend? He couldn't be sure. He pressed on regardless. "*Essence* magazine did a short piece on my book a month ago—now bookstores can't keep copies on the shelf!"

"Dayum!"

Vince grinned. "Yeah. And my seminars are selling out. I mean, it's mad crazy—I've done more traveling in the last two months than in the previous year combined. And my schedule for the next four months is packed like sardines!"

"DAYUM!"

"So, life is good. This is what I've been waiting for. It's not Oprah—not yet anyway, but a brutha can bide his time. Girlfriend's gonna be calling any day now—I can feel it!"

"That's deep. I'm proud of you, man. You always was my dude. My dawg!"

Trey grinned and gave Vince dap. But to Vince, his words seemed hollow, almost out of place. Yeah, Trey was happy for him. But damn it if it didn't appear as if his words were laced with sarcasm. Perhaps it was just Vince walking into this with preconceived notions.

He had gotten the call from Trey several days ago for them to meet. It had come out of the blue—and taken Vince by surprise. His first thought was that Trey was ready to apologize for his actions—well, it was about damn time, Vince surmised. But so far, no apology had been forthcoming.

"You look good, bruh," Trey was saying. "Well rested or something—can't quite put my finger on it—but whatever it is, keep doing what you've been doing, playa!"

Vince laughed as he thought to himself: Wish I could say the same for you, man . . .

They drank some more coffee. Vince watched Trey carefully. He was edgy, shifting in his seat, glancing around the Cosi bar as if he were waiting for someone.

"So, what else is new in your world?" Trey asked quickly.

"Well . . . since you asked . . ." Vince paused, wondering if he should drop this golden nugget on him. Then he thought, screw it, why the hell not? He asked . . .

"I'm in love, man," Vince responded, his eyes unwavering as he stared at Trey, "Seriously in love . . ."

"What???" Trey sat back, putting down his mug of coffee. He seemed genuinely surprised, and perplexed at the sudden turn of events. He'd heard this kind of shit before, but this time, the eyes said it all—Vince was not playing.

"Oh yeah—I'm not even gonna front—this woman's got me hooked, line, and sinker. And I mean hooked for life!"

Trey's eyes narrowed. "WHAT???" His mind was racing.

"Who, bruh? Who is this mystery woman?"

Vince grinned through perfectly straight white teeth.

"A lovely creature named Amber . . ."

Erika was lying in bed when she heard her cell phone ring.

Marcus' bed.

It was late, after eleven thirty on a weeknight. She wasn't used to her cell ringing this late—even work rarely called at this hour.

James . . .

It could only be James.

She shifted onto her side, rubbing against the hard mass of Marcus and his muscular body. He moved in without a sound, pelvis connecting ever so slightly with her ass that was bare. She felt a wave of energy surge through her—that simple action of spooning one another—pelvis to ass, his member finding the soft crack of her flesh, hardening the way it always did when he was within arms length of her, filling, expanding, moving ever so slowly against her caramel skin, heightening the intensity that they undoubtedly both felt, his hot breath on her neck as his hands moved in, wrapping around her thin waist and sliding upward, grasping at her upturned breasts.

She was already wet.

Marcus always did that to her.

And they had made love once already this evening.

But Marcus was insatiable when it came to her. He couldn't have her just once. No, he needed her time and time again.

Like a thirst that soda or juice just couldn't quench.

Erika felt the stirring and longing in Marcus. Heard it in his harried breathing. His frenzied hands. His sensuous yet impatient thrusting. And she gave into him and his carnal desires. Because her needs matched his.

Erika parted her legs, rubbing the head of his penis against her sex, sucking in a breath as she felt him enter her, instantly filling her up, Marcus embedded inside of her, thick stalk in the ground, connecting in a way that she marveled each time because of the intensity, the passion, the *electricity* that they both felt when they were making love this way, raw and primal, but with a tenderness that cut to the bone.

The ringing had ceased.

And then it began again.

And ceased.

Only to begin again.

Erika paid it no mind.

She refused to stop, letting *him* interfere with this thing that she and Marcus shared—for the moment as perfect as perfect could be.

It wasn't until she felt Marcus spasm, cry out, and wash his semen deep inside of her, astonishing herself each time she felt him come, that Erika focused once again on the incessant ringing.

She'd check her phone in a minute.

After the tremors subsided . . .

"James," she began with quiet diplomacy.

"Erika," he responded with guarded reserve.

"I see you called. Several times," Erika said, and then added, "What's up?"

She could sense the frustration in James' silence. He sighed before speaking.

"I thought you'd want to know that the Foundation's making progress on your girl's case."

Erika perked up. She was by the window in the living room, staring out at the skyline. Marcus was in the next room, already asleep.

"Really? Oh wow, James. Tell me!" she exclaimed, trying to contain her enthusiasm.

James smiled. "A great deal of progress, actually." He paused, knowing the silence was killing her. After a few seconds she couldn't take it.

"James, please stop fucking with me. Would you please just spill it!" she hissed as she felt Marcus' seed meander down her thigh. She glanced around frantically for a tissue or something to wipe it with—spying nothing, she used her fingers to scoop it up.

"I wish I *was* fucking with you, Erika," James responded morosely. There was a few seconds of dead air between them. "You there?" he asked.

"Yeah, just thinking about what you said," she answered, moving quietly into the kitchen where she reached for some paper towels.

James exhaled again. "Anyway, here's what they've dug up so far—pretty amazing, I think, considering they haven't been on the case that long." Erika could hear some papers ruffling in the background.

"Your friend, Amber, as you know, was born in Houston. Her maternal great-grandmother, Stella, who died a few years ago, raised her. Rich and Andy who run the Foundation used her as their starting point and worked backwards. They got some information on her estate from county and state records. They were also able to locate a neighbor and friend of Stella's. To make a long story short, they tracked down Stella's daughter, Amber's grandmother, a woman named Lorna. She's still alive and living in Queens, Rockaway, to be exact."

"Wow," Erika said, sitting on the couch as she held a crushed paper towel between her legs.

"Yeah. Lorna was married to a cat named Harold, who is since deceased. Harold and Lorna had an only child, Michelle. Michelle is Amber's mother."

"They were able to gather all of this from records?" Erika asked.

"Yeah, most of it over the Internet, if you can believe that shit! Isn't technology grand?" James mused. "Stella had an executor of her will and for the purposes of probate. That person was her daughter, Lorna. All of that is a matter of public record."

"Damn."

"Yeah. Rich and Andy contacted Lorna in New York. She's an old biddy—nasty as all hell—a real bitch, from what they tell me. Didn't want to give them shit about Amber or the identity of the father. What they did find out was that her only daughter, Michelle, died thirteen years ago in a car accident. She was only 23 when she died. Michelle had problems all of her short life. Seems she got into drugs, alcohol, and God knows what else. She acknowledged that Michelle had a daughter, and that Amber was sent to live and be raised by the great-grandmother, Stella."

"Did she say why?" Erika asked.

"Basically she said that Michelle wasn't capable of raising a child that young. She and Harold thought it was best."

"Okay."

"Moving on—we now know Michelle attended high school right there in Rockaway. Beach Channel High School. She was in the class of 1984."

"Wow—so if they know her high school and graduating class, perhaps they can track down some of her friends—"

"Exactly! That's exactly what they did." James chuckled. "Once again technology comes to the rescue."

"What do you mean?"

"Ever heard of Classmates.com?"

"Of course. A website that reconnects students, class-mates, and teachers from schools and colleges regardless of when they attended."

"Right. Rich and Andy go online. Put in Beach Channel H.S., class of 1984. Guess what? There's like hundreds of former students that are on Classmates.com for that graduat-ing class alone!"

"You're shitting me?" Erika whispered incredulously.

"I shit you not! So, what is Rich and Andy's next move? They proceed to post a message to the entire class—anyone remembers Michelle? And of course they get like thirty re-sponses back!"

"Oh man."

"Yup." James chuckles again. "You gotta love this stuff—I mean, this is coming together like a damn first-rate detective novel. Anyway, they ask some more questions. Anyone remember that Michelle got pregnant? Anyone know whom she was dating? Of course, at this point they are discreet—dealing one-on-one with some of her closer friends. They find one girl in particular, Soli, who was in her class and lived not too far from Michelle's family. Accord-ing to Soli, Michelle was dating this guy from another high school. This guy lived in Brooklyn. Also went to school in Brooklyn. Get this—she even recalls the name of the cat's high school: Brooklyn Tech!"

"DAYUM. What's his name? Please tell me you got a name???"

"Hold your horses, Erika," James quipped. "Soli says that Michelle met this dude at an intramural track meet. You see, Michelle was on the track team—ran the relays. So did old boy, but for Tech. Soli says they met when they were both sophomores, which would make them around 15, and that they had a hot and heavy romance. Everyone knew they were dating. Michelle's mother and father were so incredibly strict, that dating in high school was forbidden. But Michelle didn't care. She was smitten with old boy and took the subway practically every day to Brooklyn to be with him after school."

"James—okay, give me the name. Don't play games any further. What's the dude's name?"

James sighed. "Soli doesn't have a name. Or she can't recall it. But—she does know that old dude had a nickname—what Michelle and all of her friends referred to him by. Rich and Andy says that even with a nickname and a positive hit on the high school, it's a matter of days or weeks at the most before they learn the identity of Amber's father."

"And? The suspense, James, is freaking killing me."

"Okay, precious—I've kept you waiting long enough—the dude's nickname is Peacock."

"Peacock?" Erika yells, "What kind of name is that?"

James was laughing now. "Beats the hell out of me! Soli says old boy pranced around back in the day like he was the shit—like he owned the entire school. Can you believe that? Amber's father was a peacock!" James was in stitches. "Peacock . . . Jesus Christ!" he exclaimed. "Old boy just knew he was the shit!"

Nineteen

E rika was tapping an elderly woman's vein when her co-worker walked in.

"This shouldn't hurt a bit," Erika said to the woman, while sliding the needle under her mottled skin. Setting the I.V., she glanced back at Carmen, who held a bemused look on her face.

"What?" Erika asked as Carmen stood there, arms folded across her chest.

"Nothing. I just want to know what you got?" Carmen said.

"Excuse me?" Erika asked, as the elderly woman's stare panned between them two, trying to figure out what was going on.

"Well, let's see," Carmen said holding up a finger. "You have this very handsome man who just happens to be on Channel Four every single night."

The elderly woman grinned, showing her very stained yellow teeth.

Carmen's second finger came up.

"And you've stolen the fancy of this tall, well-built

chocolate doctor thing who obviously still makes house calls!"

Erika blushed as the elderly woman let out a cackle, slapping her thin hands together.

"And now, to add insult to injury," Carmen exclaimed, pressing her third finger into the air, "you've got this heavenly, and I do mean heavenly man at the front desk, dressed to the nines, holding a bouquet of roses, looking and smelling all good, like one of them delectable Nestle's Crunch bars, and Girl, I swear if you don't get down there within two minutes, I'm gonna head down there myself and take a bite!"

"I know that's right!" the elderly woman yelled, a bit too loud for the small room. Erika glanced rapidly at her watch, and frowned. Close to noon on a Tuesday. She wasn't expecting anyone, she was sure of that. Regardless, she was out the door, and heading for the steps as the laughter of her elderly patient and Carmen echoed in her ears. Just who could it be, Erika wondered?

When she came round the corner, clad in her yellow scrubs and tennis sneakers, she came face to face with Trey Alexander.

A smirk was painted on his face. As Carmen had accurately reported, Trey was dressed in his usual style, well-tailored double-breasted suit, power tie, and lace up shoes buffed to perfection. She ignored the way he smelled: oh so good. Trey was holding a dozen red roses, which he thrust in her direction when she came near.

"I come in peace," he said, one hand to his heart, all loud so that the staff behind the front desk couldn't help but hearing. He then added, "And to fall on my sword if I must— anything, Sassy, to beg your forgiveness and ask for your hand in friendship once again." He ended this with a flourish, raising his free hand to the heavens, as if he were some kind of Shakespearean actor. Every set of eyes was glued to the scene as if this were the daytime soaps.

Erika folded her arms across her chest and shook her head, yet a smile peeked out. After a moment of silence on Trey's part, and a few words of encouragement from behind the desk:

"Get him, girl, go handle your business!"

"I'll take him back, shoot! With his fine self?"

"Testify!"

Erika broke into a grin and went to Trey, snatching the flowers from his hand.

"Trying to embarrass me at my job," she said. "That's low, Trey. Even for you."

"Desperate times call for desperate measures . . ."

"Let's go," she said, pulling on his arm, "Before the entire hospital knows my damn business!"

Erika led Trey outside. The morning had given way to a beautiful cloudless day. The temperature hovered in the mid-sixties, and after a long, chilling winter, folks absolutely loved the springtime air.

"Do you have time for me?" Trey asked, once they had cleared the automatic doors.

"Yes, Trey," Erika responded as if she were weary.

There was a park not too far from the hospital. They found a bench underneath a large tree that was already in bloom, white and pink flowers hanging over their heads. A light breeze hung in the air.

"It's been a while," Erika said, once they were seated. "To what do I owe this honor?"

Actually, she had been expecting Trey's call for a few days now. Erika was well aware of the fact that Vince and Trey had gotten together a few days ago. That had gone well, according to Vince. Trey was making an effort to reconnect with those friends he had pushed aside a few months back.

"What can I say, Sassy?" Trey began, "I messed up with you and Vince. And I'm sorry for that. Sorry, especially, for what I said to you. We go back too far for me to be treating you like that."

"I agree."

"Damn. Are you gonna cut this dude some slack?"

"Maybe. Maybe not! You'll just have to wait and see."

Trey eyed Erika for a moment. She inhaled the fragrance of her roses and smiled.

"These are nice. Thank you for them." Erika leaned over and kissed Trey on the cheek.

Trey's eyes misted up.

"I've missed you, boo," he said quietly.

He blinked away a few tears and used the back of his hand to wipe at one eye. Erika watched him for a moment before nodding and saying: "Me too, Trey, me too."

They sat for a moment staring out at the expanse of tree and grass. A nice image, especially for a city the scale and like of Washington.

Trey cleared his throat. He stared straight ahead as he spoke.

"Things have been really . . ." he paused to search for the right word, "trying for me over the past few months. A lot of shit that I don't understand, stuff that's not making a whole lot of sense. You know?" he said, glancing over at Erika.

"Yeah, I do," she replied. "Life's like that sometimes, Trey. We can't have blue sky and eighty degree weather all the time."

Trey nodded, considered her words.

"This thing with Giovanna's gotten complicated," he said.

"I was wondering if you were still seeing her," Erika responded.

"Yeah, but you don't know the half of it. Giovanna's not even the crazy part. You won't believe me if I told you," Trey added.

"Believe what?" Erika asked, turning her body so that she faced him.

Trey swallowed.

"It's Layla," he said.

"Okay," she said, cautiously.

He glanced over at her for a second before sweeping his gaze away. His chest billowed before he shocked her with his quiet words.

"I slept with her," he admitted. When Erika didn't respond he glanced up and locked his stare onto hers. Neither blinked for a moment.

Erika nodded. Placing her hand on his leg she squeezed it once before grinning.

"See what happens when you diss your friends and end up alone? You do stupid shit. That's what your monkey-ass gets!"

They shared a chuckle over that one.

"Seriously, Trey, you wanna talk about it?" Erika asked. Her voice lowered. "I mean, this is a subject that we haven't spoken of in like *years* . . ."

"I know, Sassy," Trey responded, scratching at his bald head, "Lord knows *I* know."

"Okay."

Trey sighed, and brought Erika up to date.

"The truth?" he said. "No fronting on this one, Sassy—that evening with her left me feeling incredible, so absolutely wonderful, as if we were the only two people in this whole galaxy. She was digging me and I was digging her, and all the negative energy that had been in my life just got sucked out into the vacuum of outer space, you feel me? All that was left was the two of us and this wonderful, most incredibly erotic sensation, which has stayed with me for days . . ."

Trey sighed again and continued. "Does any of this make sense?"

Erika considered his question and his words.

"Yeah," she said. "You loved Layla once. She loved you. And she still does, trust me on that one. So the two of you got together and shared something intimate and special. Nothing strange or mystical about that."

"But . . ."

Erika watched Trey. He was sweating, his hand rising to his baldhead to wipe away the perspiration that had beaded there.

"But?" she asked gingerly. She knew what came next but was afraid to raise the dead.

Sometimes better to let sleeping dogs lie . . .

Trey stared at her.

"There's Giovanna smack in the middle of my life, who for the first time in a long while has me feeling stuff I haven't felt in ages. I'm digging her, Sassy, I'm not afraid to admit it. Feeling her for real—she's good people, we have mad fun, one hundred and fifty percent compatible, and the sex is da bomb! But then, out of the blue, Layla waltzes back into my life, and I can't help it if I'm feeling her vibe too. More than that—the girl's got me thinking about shit that I thought I'd left buried . . ."

Erika nodded for him to continue.

"And then I go to Layla. Shit! I mean, how could I do that?" Trey asked. "Knowing what I know. Knowing what she is/was?"

It was Erika's turn to sigh.

"Trey—"

"No, Sassy, what the hell does that make me? A closet homosexual? Me, Trey Alexander, sleeping with someone who used to be a fucking dude? A freaking *man* . . ."

All Trey could do was hang his head low.

Erika waited for the moment to pass. In her usual consoling manner, she reached over and rubbed Trey's back, attempting to soothe him. She moved closer until their knees were touching.

"Trey—why are you doing this to yourself? You put yourself through plenty of pain and anguish when you first learned the truth about Layla. No one should have to endure the pain and suffering you experienced. I don't think you ever fully got over her and what she did to you. So please, Trey, think long and hard about what you're doing this time."

"Sassy, trust me, I know. But I can't help what I felt that night. I wanted her, Sassy. I'm not gonna even front. I knew what I was doing when I went to her that night. I knew that what went down between the two of us was ultimately up to me and me alone—and yet, I still went to her apartment that evening. Knowing what I know. Knowing that Layla was born a man. And what the hell does that say about what I have with Giovanna? Oh God!" Trey exclaimed, crushing his eyes shut.

Erika held him as he quietly sobbed into her shoulder. She said nothing. Words were not what Trey needed right now.

After a moment, he raised his head, wiping away the tears.

"I'm sorry, boo," he whispered, and attempted a smile.

"For what? Ruining my scrubs?"

Erika grinned and rubbed his shoulder.

"You'll be a'ight," she said.

There was the beginning of a grin.

"Let me ask you a question, Trey?"

He nodded.

"Are you ashamed of what transpired between the two of you?"

He glanced at Erika as if he'd seen a ghost.

"Wouldn't you? If you were a man—sleeping with another man? Men screwing men. Come on, Boo, you know that shit's disgusting."

Erika sucked in a breath.

"Trey, do you remember the conversation we had years ago when you first found out—when Layla told you about her operation? Do you remember what I said to you then?"

Trey was silent, remembering.

Erika continued.

"I said that Layla was no longer a man. Do you remember that?"

"So? What does it matter?" Trey responded.

"It matters a great deal. Why? Because it gets to the heart of the matter. You don't believe that Layla is a woman, and therein lies the conflict within you."

Trey grunted but said nothing.

"Do you?"

"Do I what?"

"What do you think Layla is?"

Trey didn't have to ponder his answer.

"She was born a man," he said, "That's all I need to know."

Erika shook her head.

"I beg to differ. Layla, in my opinion, is one hundred percent woman."

"Please, Sassy, you don't know shit!"

Erika's stare locked onto Trey's.

"Listen to me—when you first told me she revealed her operation to you, I did some digging. I spoke to some folks at the hospital who had experience with this sort of thing. Furthermore I did some research on the Internet. I'll tell you this—actually I tried to tell you back then, but you wouldn't listen—Layla may have been born a man, but when she woke up from that final operation, there was nothing left but all woman. Layla, and there are many others like her, was born a woman inside of a man's body. Surgery can correct those things, thank goodness. And judging from how long you dated Layla, falling in love and loving her the way you did all those years, the surgery went quite well. If you pardon my saying so, it sure as hell fooled you . . ."

Trey said nothing.

"And after all those years of knowing the truth, you still went back a few nights ago. Why, Trey? That's the question that haunts you. That's what keeps you awake at night."

"Yes," Trey whispered.

"Because your mind is saying one thing that differs considerably from what your heart and your own eyes confirm. That Layla is all woman. She's affected you in a way that defies description. She seduced you, in the same way she did years ago—instead, this time you knew the truth—yet you still went to her. You still made love to her.

"Trey, listen up—you need to accept Layla for what she is: a woman who loves you. And judging from your reaction to everything that's happened, I suspect you still love her too."

Trey for a long while was silent. He pondered Erika's words carefully, staring out at the expanse of blue sky, greenery, and passersby. Erika let him simmer in the juices of his silence for a moment. She knew that Trey needed to think this through on his own. When he turned to her, their knees once again touching as she raised her gaze to meet his, Trey took in a deep breath and spoke.

"It's all a mess . . . ," he said, hoarsely.

"Doesn't have to be, Trey," Erika responded.

"Really? I don't see it that way. I'm sleeping with a man. Or a woman who used to be a man. Either way, what the hell does that make me?"

Erika touched his shoulder.

"And where does this leave me and Giovanna? I was really feeling her before I ran into Layla again. Still am . . ."

Erika avoided his last question. Instead she had a question of her own.

"What constitutes a woman?"

Trey stared at her.

"Is it physical beauty? If so, Layla's got that. I'm a woman, and not ashamed to say that Layla is one of the most beautiful women I've ever met. Not only does she possess outer beauty, Trey, but inner beauty as well—you'll agree that she has one of the sweetest hearts around.

"What constitutes a woman, I ask you? Is it those womanly instincts that set us apart from those horrible creatures we have to share the planet with—men? If so, you have to agree that Layla possesses those in abundance too.

"What about those other assorted feminine characteristics: compassion, strength, nurturing, sheltering, giving, loving . . . Layla has all of those and more. She is a woman, Trey. You fell in love with a woman once, and now, years later, you've made love to her once again after being presented with the truth. Why? Because your heart and eyes know what your mind has been struggling to accept. Because you were drawn back into the warmth of that womanly embrace, which once captivated you. She stimulated you then and she does so now."

Trey was silent.

"Close your eyes, Trey—tell me about the night she bared her all to you in your office—what did you see?"

"I'll tell you. Swear to God, Sassy, that night I wanted

Layla so bad I could taste it. I had never been more scared of anything in my entire life—and more turned on! Those two emotions—fear and seduction—two opposite ends of the spectrum—were tugging at me like I was a kite on a windy day. And yet, all I could think about when Layla let the folds of her dress hang free, exposing herself to me, allowing me in to stare at her exquisiteness, was this: As I took in the fullness of her, all inviting, drawing me in like some kind of magic spell, I remember thinking: her entire being is so beautiful and awe inspiring, it had to be carved from the hand of God . . ."

His eyes locked onto hers.

"That was the single thread that raced through my consciousness—her entire being was art—that no man could have created that kind of beauty. No matter what my mind told me, no matter what devilish tricks it attempted to play on me, I knew better. I so much wanted what my eyes spoke to be true. Because my own eyes could not lie—Layla was created by the hand of God. Even in the face of what I knew to be the truth . . ."

Erika nodded solemnly.

"Yes, Trey. You saw a woman who threw herself off a cliff without the benefit of a safety net. You saw in her all of her splendor and rare glory. You saw raw nakedness and striking imperfections spread before you. You were aroused. And finally, when you could stand it no longer, you went to her, and satisfied, what I suspect, was a long-held craving. You took her, all of her womanly virtues, made love to her, in a way that spoke to you, in a way that left the indelible mark of her on you. It's here now, as plain as the nose on your face."

Trey continued to remain silent.

"You made love to a woman. A woman inside and out. Your mind is playing games with you—but you know better,

Trey. Hearts don't lie. Neither do these," Erika said, pointing to his eyes.

"Tell your mind to quit its silly games, Trey," Erika exclaimed, taking his hand in hers. "Take control, show your brain who's the boss, and put this thing to bed once and for all. Layla's all woman, Trey. It's perfectly fine to respond the way you do."

Erika loosened her grip.

Trey's gaze swept up past the colorful flowers that hung in the air to the sky that captivated his attention.

"Never be ashamed of love, Trey," Erika added, patting his thigh twice. "Never . . ."

Trey sighed.

"So where does all of this leave Giovanna? The woman whom I'm falling in love with?" he asked morosely.

Erika waited a half second before answering.

"I think we *both* know the answer to that one . . ."

The next day Erika was back at the hospital racing around florescent-lit corridors in her yellow scrubs and tennis shoes when her pager went off. She swept her gaze down to her hip, reading the number with its 911 suffix, and frowned.

James rarely paged her.

Come to think of it, in the entire time they'd been dating he'd never paged her before.

Erika took the elevator to her station, picked up an available phone and dialed his cell.

James answered on the second ring.

"It's me, what's up?" she asked, heart thumping, wondering what was so pressing that it couldn't wait until after work.

James' response was short and to the point.

"I need you to get to a fax machine. Now. And give me the number!"

Erika's mind raced.

"What? James, what's going—"

"Erika—fax machine. You've got those in the hospital, right?" She glanced around, frantic now.

"Yes . . ." There was one on the far side of the desk. She moved over, reading the number rapidly into the phone.

"Got it," he replied forcefully. "Standby."

"James, what is this about?" Erika asked skeptically. "You're scaring me."

"Erika. Are you sitting down? Because if not, you ought to be. Rich and Andy found your man. I'm sending over the identity of Amber's father *now*."

"Oh my God—who is it, James. Just tell me!"

"My fax is on its way. You'll know in a minute. Besides, you know what they say: A picture's worth a thousand words."

The phone went dead. Erika stared at it, frowned and replaced it as the fax machine rang, making a series of shrilling noises. She moved over to it and huddled close by. Thirty seconds later a single page emerged. Erika snatched it from the paper tray, stared at it: a page from a high school yearbook, photograph circled in thick black ink. Name underneath. Nickname underneath that. Her eyes bugged out as her mouth dropped. The fax fluttered to the cold hard floor without a sound.

"Oh my God!" she howled as her hand flew to her trembling mouth; yet no one was there to hear the anguish behind her words . . .

Twenty

I couldn't understand what all the clamor was about? India Jasmine Jackson had text-messaged me on my cell while I was in a meeting with a client—she rarely did that. She could have just interrupted; hell we were only two floors down in one of the conference rooms, yet she chose to leave me a message.

Because it was personal.

"Erika+Vince Insist U Meet @ Vince Crib 8PM Tonight. 911"

After my meeting I inquired as to what was the emergency.

"Don't know," India informed me. The braids were gone. Instead, she had little twists the color of copper. Actually, they looked quite good. And I told her so!

"Can you get them on the line for me?" I asked, striding into my office. "Either one!" I yelled.

Flinging down my jacket, I checked messages as I waited for India to connect me.

After four minutes, I buzzed her.

"No answer from either one," she informed me.

"Keep trying, please," I issued.

Forty-five minutes later I glanced up from my work, checked the time and buzzed India again.

"Anything?" I asked.

"Not yet. I'll keep trying . . ."

I whipped out my cell and speed dialed Vince first, then Erika.

No answer.

"Damn!" I exclaimed. "What gives?"

Then a smile creased my face.

"Ahhh," I said to the empty room. "I bet I know what's going on," I mused. The two of them are planning a bit of a reunion; just the three of us, for old time's sake. I sat back in my chair, swiveled around so I could face the window and stare out at the Capitol.

How long has it been since we've been to bluespace to shoot the shit and enjoy the food?

I didn't even know.

Too long . . .

Okay, so now I know what the deal is, I told myself.

So relax, and get through the rest of the day.

Which is exactly what I did.

Had another client meeting, finished several briefs, filed a motion with the court, and returned a bunch of phone calls. Billed the hell out of everyone like it was going out of style!

I called Giovanna since I hadn't seen or heard from her in a few days.

The last time we'd spoken was the day after Layla and I had gotten together.

We were supposed to have dinner, but she had called to cancel. Citing not being hungry and too much to do.

Whatever.

I asked her to swing by instead, but she wasn't feeling that plan either. So, I ended up in her crib, spending twenty minutes in her bed having emotionless sex, you know the kind that is just all right, like when it's all said and done, the shit wasn't even worth the effort of getting dressed and driving the hell over . . .

Giovanna didn't answer my call now either.

Damn, were the Verizon and AT&T networks down for maintenance today???

I left the office at 7, wanting to stop by a liquor store to pick up a bottle of wine. Didn't want to show up at my reunion empty handed, ya know?

I arrived promptly at 8. Got out of my car and walked up to ring Vince's doorbell. There was a light breeze in the air. Temp's still on the rise, air still feeling good. Yet something tugged at my insides.

I was still unresolved about being with Layla.

And Giovanna and I seemed to be on the crest of a downturn in our relationship. Lately, I had gotten the distinct feeling that she was losing interest in me.

Didn't know what to do about that.

Getting back into the zone.

Anyway . . .

The door opened and the first thing I noticed was that Vince's smile was strained.

"How ya livin'?" I asked boisterously, giving him dap.

"Trey, come in," he responded.

I frowned as I entered, antennae going up.

Erika got up from the couch and gave me a hug and a squeeze.

"Brought Kendall's finest," I announced, thrusting the bottle into her hand.

"That was sweet. Thank you, Trey."

Immediately my antennae went on full alert. Something here was definitely wrong. I could feel the tension in the air. One could cut it with a switchblade.

"What up, y'all—India said this was important. Everything okay?" I shot a glance between Erika who had taken a seat, and Vince who was standing, hands clasped together in front of him.

I caught the look that the two of them exchanged.

"Seriously, what's up? Erika—your ass pregnant or something?"

"Trey, why don't you have a seat." This came from Vince.

"Okay, bruh. It's your party." I removed my jacket, folded it over the end of the couch, and sat down. Vince took a seat across from me. Erika was to my left. He sighed and began to speak.

"This is kind of serious, Trey. And it's difficult for both of us."

"What's difficult?" I asked, glancing between the two of them.

Erika sucked in a breath.

"Trey—you went to Brooklyn Tech, didn't you?"

I stared at Erika hard.

"As in the high school? Yeah. What of it?"

"You dated a girl named Michelle who ran track for Beach Channel?"

I glared at Vince for a moment, turned my attention to Erika giving her two seconds of my ocular wrath before glancing back at Vince again. Unexpectedly I felt the muscles in my neck constrict. I was suddenly extremely thirsty, as if my entire throat was being baked over an open flame.

"Can a dude get something to drink?" I asked, grasping my throat with both hands in mock strangulation.

"Of course, my bad," Vince replied, rising to pour me a glass of something. "Corona do?"

"Yeah."

I pivoted toward Erika who remained seated, hands

clasped in her lap. She wore a disturbing scowl on her face.
I smiled, attempting to hide the rising tide I felt in my gut.

My Lord . . .

I hadn't thought about Michelle in close to twenty freaking years . . .

Erika's expression remained fixed.

"Michelle," she repeated, as if I hadn't heard her the first
time. Vince returned with a cold Corona topped off with a
sliver of lime. I took my time twisting the lime into the bottle, tipping it over, thumb covering the hole before righting
it, and taking a sip. I swallowed several healthy swigs.

"What is this about, Erika? Vince?" I asked, putting the
cold beer between my legs.

Vince returned to his seat.

"You dated a girl named Michelle in high school." It was
a statement, not a question.

"Perhaps. Perhaps not," I replied in a cavalier tone. "I
dated a lot of honeys in high school. That was over twenty
years ago. You expect me to remember the name of each
one?"

I swung my glare over to Erika whose stare locked onto
mine.

"Only the ones you got pregnant," she replied softly.

Immediately I took a swig of my beer and placed it on the
coffee table in front of me. I said to no one in particular,
"This bullshit inquisition is coming to an end right the hell
now." I did not yell, but there was sufficient depth to my
voice to let everyone in the room know that I was to be taken
seriously.

Neither Erika nor Vince said a word.

"Anybody gonna tell me why the hell y'all are up in my
business?"

Still they were silent.

"Fine." I stood, grabbed my suit jacket and flung it over

my shoulder. "Nice party, Vince. See ya!" I said, strolling for the door.

Reaching for the handle, I heard Erika clear her throat and say: "Peacock. They called you Peacock, Trey, didn't they? Says right here."

I froze. Spun around on my heels and glared at her. Crossed the room to where she sat and snatched up the paper that was being held gingerly between her fingers. I bore my laser stare into it, a faxed page from my high school yearbook. The picture was twenty plus years old. Me with my foot high fro! Trey Alexander. Nickname Peacock.

My expression glowered.

"Hmmn, let's see," I said, holding the paper at arm's length. "Says here 'track team, chess club, astronomy club, debate team. Nickname Peacock. Voted most likely to sue a non-profit organization or government agency!'" I threw up my hands in mock surrender. "You got me, bruh—I can't deny this shit!"

I tossed the paper aside.

"This is bullshit!" I hollered and headed toward the front door.

"You dated Michelle when you were a sophomore," Erika began. "She got pregnant by you in the winter of 1981. She had a child, a girl—"

I spun around.

"YOU DON'T KNOW WHAT THE FUCK YOU'RE TALKING ABOUT!" I yelled, no longer able to contain the anguish. "Just who the hell do you think you are—bringing me here for what? Depose me like a freaking criminal. I don't think so!"

My hand went to the knob.

"For the record, and since you've done a shitty job of fact-finding," and here I spun and glared at Vince for a moment, "both of you suck at this—I'll set the record straight.

"One—Michelle and I did in fact date, not that it's any of your damn business.

"Two—she did in fact get pregnant, but her parents found out, and forced her to have an abortion.

"Three—once she aborted the child, and it is a fact that she in fact aborted said child—she remained in Texas for six months or whatever, finally returning to New York to move on with her life. There was no baby—no child. You are mis-freaking informed!"

Erika stood as I snatched the door open and strolled outside. She once again cleared her throat.

"I'm sorry, Trey," she said softly, but with enough conviction that I had zero trouble hearing her clearly. "It is you who is misinformed. Michelle did have the baby. Her great-grandmother raised the child. She's all grown up now. And she's *your* daughter."

I stopped in mid-stride and turned around slowly as I shook my head so rapidly I became faint.

"No, no, no, no, NO. You're wrong."

Erika moved to the door.

"I'm sorry, Trey, but I'm right. You have a daughter; her name is Amber."

That froze me in my tracks. I glared at her for what seemed like ten minutes. Seconds flew by before I began to grin. Leaning to the side, I caught the stare of Vince who stood behind Erika in the front door.

"Oh, I get it now," I said slowly, nodding my head. "Amber—the one you're dating, right Vince?"

Vince swallowed hard and nodded.

"That's right, Trey."

"I see . . ." I said, but I didn't.

Suddenly the ground felt as if it were moving under my feet. I felt myself sliding and reached out to the doorframe for support.

"So, that's what this is all about!" I snapped, "I fucked your woman, so you're gonna fuck my little girl, is that it?"

Vince was shaking his head, "No, Trey—it's not—"

"FUCK YOU!" I screamed so loud I'm sure the entire block heard me.

"YOU DON'T KNOW JACK!"

Driving straight over to Giovanna's, on my cell the entire time, relentlessly hitting redial, not taking no answer for an answer until I steered the M3 next to her Lexus, and braked to a halt, hard.

I was furious.

I knew Giovanna was home. Her car in the driveway told me that.

She wasn't taking my calls.

I had left her a message, saying it was an emergency.

Then another one.

And another one after that . . .

Pick up, Giovanna, pick up now!!!

Yet, she refused to answer my pleas.

Exiting the car, I hit the steps two at a time until I was banging on the door, ignoring the ruckus I was creating. After a minute and a half I began to yell.

"Giovanna, I know you are in there. OPEN THE DOOR. Giovanna. OPEN THE DAMN DOOR."

A family of four was walking by, their toddlers on bright Big Wheels. I paid them no mind, using the heel of my palm to crash against the stained wood.

Giovanna opened the door and ushered me inside.

"Just what the heck is wrong with you, Trey? Jesus . . ."

I pushed past her, ignoring the artwork on the walls courtesy of Vince Cannon, Jr., and went to the bar, pouring myself a stiff drink.

Three-quarters rum. One quarter ice.

Giovanna followed me into the room, the smoke coming off her head in waves. She was pissed.

No doubt.

I could give a shit.

"What's gotten into you?" Giovanna cried, hand in my face as I downed my drink in several gulps. "Are you wigging out, Trey? Where do you get off coming over here—"

I had poured myself a second and was exiting the room when she paused in mid-sentence.

"Hey—where the fuck do you think you're going?" Giovanna yelled.

"Hey—I'm talking to you!"

Taking the stairs, two at a time, I hit the top floor landing and turned to the right into the master bedroom before Giovanna could figure out what was going on.

I strolled in, taking in the clothes that were strewn over her bed—outfits, undergarments, at least four sets of bikinis—not that I was counting.

She pushed me aside as I stood there in disbelief.

"Get the hell out!" she cried.

"Going somewhere?" I asked slowly, my stare panning over the disarray. I spied travel documents on the bedside table. She followed my stare but I was too quick—scooping up the tickets before she had even moved a muscle.

Placing my back to her, discounting the pummel of fists to my kidneys, I examined them.

Two airline tickets.

Destination—Hawaii.

Her name and her travel companion.

David Morrison.

Departure: Tomorrow morning.

I placed the tickets back where I found them and turned around. Giovanna instinctively jumped back.

"How nice," I uttered.

"It's not what you think," she muttered.

I headed for the open door. Stopped. Spun around. Glared at her.

"All I wanted was for you to support me during my down time. Was that too much to ask?" I said, in disbelief.

Giovanna's hand was at her breast.

"Oh please. Spare me the performance. We aren't having a relationship, Counselor. We're fuck buddies. What part of that didn't you understand?"

I had to laugh.

"And David what's his name? Is he a fuck buddy too?" I exclaimed.

Giovanna didn't miss a beat.

"No, Trey—he's just a friend."

I stood there shaking my head.

After everything I'd gone through: losing my mentor and my friends, my rollercoaster ride at my job, Bernard John Marshall, telling Giovanna I was falling for her, making love to Layla, reconnecting with Vince and Erika only to find out they were backstabbing me, and the latest—that single nugget of critical information that caused my heart to go into palpitations every few moments now—learning the truth about Michelle and our *daughter*—this is what it all came down to.

Fuck buddies.

Fuck buddies.

"I came here to tell you about my daughter, Giovanna," I whispered, trying to contain the rising anger that threatened to spark out of control. "Because I'm scared. And because I have nowhere else to go."

A single tear meandered down my cheek. I quickly wiped it away with my wrist.

"But that's okay. You go on. You and your *friend* have a wonderful trip. Don't worry about me, baby. I'll deal with this shit on my own. 'Cause I'm a trooper, Giovanna. I'll find my way back into the zone. On my own . . ."

Fuck buddies.

I laughed again as I descended the stairs.

The sad part was that Giovanna let me go.

And why wouldn't she?

After all, that's all I was to her, these past few months. A fuck buddy.

Nothing more.

I exited the house, got into my car, and drove away, heading to the only place I had left.

To the only one who would have me . . .

Twenty-one

James and Erika sat facing each other, a bottle of just-opened Merlot between them. The restaurant was Tony & Joes, a seafood place located in Georgetown Harbour facing the water. They had a cozy table by the window, nice view and quiet, away from the din of other patrons.

They picked at their appetizer: lightly fried calamari.

Three days had passed since the time Erika and Vince had "broken" the news to Trey, and neither had heard a peep from him. Their calls had gone unanswered.

Erika was worried, but there wasn't much else she could do.

Vince felt bad also, but he too, was powerless to intervene until Trey came around.

"I can't say I blame the man," James was saying as he squeezed fresh lemon onto the plate of calamari. Erika stared at him. "I mean, come on, I don't like old dude, you know that, but I can't help but feeling sorry for him. You dropped this on him kind of suddenly. Think about it—you've been proceeding along with your life for the past twenty years and then one day you wake up to find you have a grown-up child!"

Erika nodded.

"Yeah, but why take it out on us. We didn't do anything."

James smiled.

"'Cause you're the messenger. In time he'll come around. He's confused right now. He needs time to sort this out—what it means, having an adult aged daughter in his life, and worse, having his best friend dating her. Ouch! I feel sorry for the man!"

Their food arrived. James had the grilled swordfish, while Erika tried the pan seared crab cakes. For the first few minutes, they ate their food in silence.

James broke the silence first.

"It's good to see you, Erika. It's been a minute since we've gotten together."

Erika glanced up.

"I know, James. Work and stuff. You know how it is."

He did.

"But we're here now," she added earnestly.

"That we are—I'm happy for that." He patted her arm and Erika enjoyed the sensation.

She had genuinely missed James. Their respective schedules had them both hopping. Plus, she'd been spending more time with Marcus lately—something she felt quite guilty about—but not enough to stop seeing him.

That was one of the reasons why she was here tonight with James.

Erika stared across the table at her date and once again felt the anguish flood her insides. I'm so confused, she thought.

Sitting right across from her was a wonderful man: intelligent, confident, and good looking. Great job, stable, and let's not forget wonderful lover. Most women would give their right ovary for a man like James. And yet, Erika felt unfulfilled by their relationship.

And then there was Marcus—tall, muscular, handsome, a woman's true fantasy. A wonderful lover in ways that defied description. Also intelligent, confident, with a great job, and stable (well, that remained to be seen).

So what was the problem? Most women struggled to find and keep one man, let alone two. Here she was, nitpicking over two men and their sometimes seemingly inconsequential issues.

Still, she couldn't help feeling the way she did.

Erika was never one to just brush aside her emotions.

An intense shoot-from-the-hip kind of gal, Erika had always trusted her instincts—and for the most part, they hadn't steered her wrong yet.

So what did her instincts tell her about James? And Marcus?

That was the part she was unsure about . . .

James' fingers were lightly tracing figure eights on the back of her hand, following the path of opaque veins that glided beneath the skin.

Erika watched him silently, feeling the tickles transmit pulses of minute pleasure bombs that were discreetly going off inside of her. She crossed and uncrossed her legs absentmindedly.

"Erika, there's a party tonight north of Baltimore that I'd really like to check out." He glanced up, his eyes meeting hers.

"Where? What kind of party is it?" she asked. "I'm not really dressed for a party, James."

He smiled.

"Sure you are. It's not that far from the Inner Harbor. And it's a party thrown by some friends of mine."

James could read the indecision on her forehead.

"It's a *fetish* ball, Erika," he added. James let the words sink in before venturing forward.

Erika had been poised to fork a piece of crab cake into her mouth. When she heard the word "fetish" her hand froze, stopping all action in mid-stream.

"WHAT?" she exclaimed.

James glanced around.

"Erika, keep it down."

"James—please tell me this is a joke."

James sighed.

"No joke, Erika. What's the big deal? It's a fetish ball, where some folks get dressed up in various outfits. Some go to check out the toys. Others go to just watch. Regardless, it's harmless fun for consenting adults. It's something I've been meaning to check out for some time, if you don't mind. We wouldn't have to stay long."

"Let me get this straight. You want to take me to a fetish party? James, you know I'm not into that shit. Come on, what am I supposed to do while a bunch of S&M-loving freaks get it on. Are there going to be swingers there?"

"I don't know. There probably will be some, but that's not why we're going."

"Jesus!" Erika said, exhaling loudly.

"You know what, Erika? Forget it!" He sipped his wine and then added, "I really don't understand you!"

"What do you mean?"

"This," he exclaimed, holding up his hands. "For the entire time we've been dating we've been doing what you want to do—I'm always the one who compromises. I'm always the one who seems to be adjusting this or that in order to make sure you are happy. I'm not complaining, but I thought relationships were about compromises—on both sides. Therefore, is it asking too much for you to bend and do what I want? Just this once, can you indulge me, instead of the other way around?"

Erika opened her mouth to spew a retort, but quickly shut down.

James, she mused, was right.

"Okay James. Tell me this—how am I supposed to act at one of these things? It's not as if I'm an expert in this kind of activity. I don't practice this stuff every day!"

"Erika," James said, smiling, seeing he had won some ground, "It's okay. Just be yourself. No one's going to force you to do anything you don't want to do. Just come with me and keep an open mind. Okay? Maybe, just maybe you'll actually have a good time. And maybe, you'll get turned onto something that you've never even dreamt of before . . ."

Doubtful, Erika thought, but kept her comments to herself . . .

It wasn't forty minutes. It was more like an hour forty. Or that's what it seemed like to Erika. When they arrived at the party, she was ready to exit the car and go anywhere—just not a fetish ball.

They found themselves in some kind of warehouse district. Lots of huge windowless buildings out in the middle of nowhere, low lighting, trash strewn about the sidewalk, the smell of piss suspended in the air. A lot of cars parked on both sides of the wide street, which was a good sign.

But that didn't change the way Erika felt.

They entered the non-descript building on the first floor, paid the cover and were immediately assaulted by the heavy bass of house music. An enormous dance floor was littered with partygoers—most dressed in various stages of undress or leather, others completely nude or adorned only with body paint. Erika held her tongue as she followed James to one of a half dozen bars edging the dance floor. She spied a tall Amazonian black woman with flaming red hair down to her ass dancing in front of two men with dog collars—and she was holding both leashes; women wearing leather lace up corsets skirted against others in baby doll outfits; a few pre-op transsexuals wearing PVC dresses or short skirts; men wearing only thongs and pouches, rubber vests; and the list went on and on . . .

Erika pulled at her Corona as they took the wide metal stairs to the second floor. Mid-center on a raised platform there was an auction taking place.

A human auction.

Both scantily clad men and women, black folks along with whites, Erika noted, were being auctioned off to the highest bidder. Audience participants were huddled close to the stage, holding up their hand when they wanted to bid on human flesh.

Erika was shocked to see a throng of black people standing by the front row, hands constantly erupting into the air as if they were at a rap concert.

James stopped to make introductions to several people and a few couples. Erika smiled automatically and shook a few hands—feeling out of place in her non-descript black dress and knee high boots. James had chosen a pair of black leather pants and a tight sweater for this evening's activities. Now Erika understood why he had dressed the way he did.

Moving onward, they passed what could only be described as a field of pup tents—over two dozen set on this plot of warehouse floor half the size of a football field. James maneuvered past them like a serpent, while Erika to her chagrin noticed that there were couples inside, having sex. Voyeurs stood outside the tent flaps, their mouths agape as they watched the various love scenes unfold. Some of the inhabitants chose to close their tents in order to make their copulating private—or as private as one could get here, in the midst of this tent forest, while the pulsating sound of techno invaded every space.

James led Erika to the third floor. Thankfully, it was quieter here. A few couples were paired off in dimly lit areas with curved walls, showcasing their talents. A small crowd had formed in front of a pair of performers, watching in silence as the man fitted his woman with a leather hood, restrained her hands and feet with gleaming handcuffs, and then proceeded to flog her with a leather-studded paddle. A second performer twenty yards away was demonstrating the proper use and fit of cock rings, aided by his large-breasted assistant who jerked him incessantly, a thick tube of KY Jelly in her left hand. James didn't seem to show much interest in these kinds of activities, so they moved onwards. Further ahead was an Indian or Pakistani vendor selling adult movies in VHS and DVD formats. An entire wall of product, Erika observed. James perused the selection while Erika hung back, nursing her Corona, other folks wandering by, attempting to catch her eye, especially the women. Thankfully, they moved on when Erika didn't acknowledge a single solitary one.

Off in the distance, Erika spied what appeared to be a mock jail cell. She whispered to James that she'd return in a minute. Walking off, moving closer, she noticed the twenty-foot-square cell situated against one wall of red brick. The bars appeared to be made of steel and ran about eight feet in height. Inside, sitting on a lone wooden bench by himself was a muscle bound black man. He was as dark as midnight, smooth black skin that reflected not a wink of light. He was fully nude, sitting there in his lone cell, a single naked light bulb hanging over him, light cascading down like an invigorating shower, highlighting his long black cock that he held between thick fingers.

Erika moved to within spitting distance of the cell door, acknowledging the thick metal padlock on the outside, and paused as they made eye contact. He was stroking himself, and when he spied Erika he neither smiled nor changed his expression. Nor did he miss a single stroke. The only subtle change was the increased pressure of his hand around his dick, and the change in tempo.

She swore she sensed him beginning to move faster.

Erika continued to watch him, taking slow swigs of her Corona as he masturbated for her. After several moments he was fully hard and over eleven inches in length. Erika was enthralled. She watched his eyes for a moment that were locked onto hers. They were sad eyes. Erika felt sorry for him. Yet she couldn't pull herself away.

Erika felt a tug at her side, turned to see James in her space, watching her silently. He gestured for them to go, but she shook her head. She returned her gaze to the man who tipped his head up to the light bulb for a moment, eyes squinting before settling back on Erika.

James, she could tell, was bored. He shifted on his heels, but Erika was determined to see this through . . . to completion.

And she did.

When the black man came, he groaned, spurting his hot liquid onto his smooth dark stomach. Erika watched with a detached sort of fascination—the act didn't turn her on, not exactly, but she knew that she was instrumental in helping him get off. And that brought a wave of satisfaction to her.

With his hand in the small of her back, exerting an increasing amount of pressure, James moved Erika along. They passed another bar against a wall, tended by a thin Asian woman with the largest set of fake tits she'd ever seen. Cold Coronas in hand, they moved off toward the opposite end of the floor.

And came to an area made up of large drab green army tents.

Tent city.

Each tent was the size of a small room, and they were placed together in rows, with little more than a foot or two between them. James led Erika over to one, pushed open the flap—empty; moved on between a row of tents to a second row standing in the shadows of the first—they stopped in front of another, hauling back the flap—spied a white woman in a Super Girl costume astride a nude black man on an army cot.

He was facing away from her, ass up, his face buried in a thick white pillow.

She wore a strap on, and was thrusting the thing into his behind.

Immediately Erika could feel James tense up. He dropped her hand that he had been holding and sucked in a breath.

This is what he had been after.

The woman's face turned while in mid-stroke, and a smile formed on her lips; she mouthed something to James and he nodded once, then took Erika's hand and retreated quietly.

Erika stood outside the tent, wide-eyed.

"I've seen enough, James. I want to go home."

James had a glazed look in his eyes. Erika had seen that look before.

Once before.

"Not yet, Erika. Just a few minutes more . . . ," he said, almost groggily.

Erika stood, arms folded as she eyed him.

"Just what's going on, James?"

"I want you to meet someone—"

The rest of his sentence was cut off by the high-pitched scream coming from inside the tent.

Erika noted with certainty that it had emanated from the male. She took a long swig from her beer, glanced at the empty bottle as if she'd just witnessed a carjacking and said, "I think I need another."

Walking away, leaving James in front of the drab green tent alone, she wondered just what had possessed her to come. She knew she was trying to compromise, but this shit took the cake. There wasn't a single individual inside here that turned her on—okay, that wasn't exactly true—there were a few nice looking dudes she'd eyed downstairs on the dance floor, but they had their sights set on other dudes!

What a waste!

She found the Asian chick with the big tits a moment later, paid for a fresh Corona and leaned against the bar as she pondered her next move. She couldn't very well leave. She had come with James. It was his car that was parked outside. Hell, she had no idea where she was; let alone how to get home. A burning anger rose inside of her. Would Marcus put her in this kind of position?

Absolutely not . . .

She turned back to the bartender, eyed her silently, pondering if making small talk was a smart move, then thought better of it.

Bet she's a dyke, Erika mused.

On the other hand, I'm not feeling that vibe.

She spun around.

"Some freaky shit up in here," Erika barked, attempting to break the ice.

"Yes and no," the bartender answered, reaching for her water with a lipstick-painted straw, "depends on the kind of shit you're into."

Erika grinned.

"I guess. But what happened to straight sex, no onlookers, just you and your man?"

"Or your woman . . ." the Asian added with a grin, "not that I'm down like that, just so you know . . ."

"Naw," Erika exclaimed, "never crossed my mind!"

"Yeah right!"

They made small talk for ten minutes. Erika finished her beer and ordered another. Instead the Asian offered to make her a specialty drink, on the house.

The chick was bored.

So Erika got something called a Hummingbird, which turned out to be one fine tasting beverage.

They conversed for a few moments more before Erika slapped a ten on the bar and said she had to go find her man.

"God knows what trouble he's getting into," she said with a wink.

The bartender pocketed the tip, thanked Erika, and told her it was probably way too late for that.

Erika headed back to tent city thinking, I'm gonna find my freaky-ass man and haul his high-yellow ass home! That's what I'm gonna do!

She came to the first set of tents and maneuvered her way over to the second row where she had left James. The particular tent where they had stopped before was closed. Erika reached for the flap and pulled. What she saw caused her to almost faint.

James was on the cot, face up, and naked. He was holding his knees in his hands. The woman in the Super Girl outfit was sitting on the floor behind the cot, facing Erika. In her latex glove-covered hand she grasped a slender dildo. The dildo was half embedded in his ass. James' eyes were closed. When the woman paused her tender thrusting, James opened his eyes and turned, seeing Erika. The woman beckoned for her to enter. Yet she just stood there, unable to breath and to move a muscle.

"It's okay, honey," the woman offered softly in her down

home Southern drawl that made Erika's skin rise, "He's been waiting for you." The woman gestured for Erika to move forward, and Erika felt her feet move slightly. Suddenly she found herself sucked inside the tent, flap caressing her back, standing less than ten feet from the prone form of James, her boyfriend and local television anchorman, and this stranger, with a dildo stuck up his ass. She glanced down. That's when she noted that James was fully hard. In fact, she had never seen him harder. His cock seemed to be expanding as she stared at it.

An optical illusion she hoped, but the effect did little to settle her almost burnt nerves.

The woman's hand returned to the dildo, pressing it forward. James grimaced for a moment; head coming forward in an automatic reaction before settling back and closing his eyes with a sigh.

"Come forward," the woman intoned, eyeing Erika, "help him get off."

The woman jutted her chin toward his hardened member.

Erika shook her head imperceptibly.

The woman gestured her chin toward his belly again.

Erika stood her ground.

The woman shrugged. Reached for James with one hand, the other holding the dildo, rotating it clockwise, then counter, tugging on it gently until several inches emerged before plunging it back inside with fury. Wrapping her fingers around his member's girth, she proceeded to commence jerking him off, slowly at first, then with an increased tempo, her two hands operating independently in the beginning before finding their groove, a rhythm, becoming coordinated and synchronized, a symphony of erotica.

Erika was too far-gone to notice.

She stared at the scene unfolding before her, feeling her heart race. At this point she wasn't really seeing . . .

Hands and knees began to move in a flurry of activity, James's caramel skin and the woman's white hands, the vibrant blue and red of her Super Girl's suit, tits jiggling in the tight top as James's chest heaved while he moaned, pressure and intensity increasing until he cried out, sputtering like a car running out of gas, the woman ceasing her movements, opening her hand, latex covered palm up toward the ceiling, like in offering, his cock spasming against her warm flesh as he came, hot liquid shooting onto smooth caramel skin.

It took several more minutes for James to complete and wind down, painful, agonizing minutes as Erika clutched her dress, listening to his rapid breathing and decelerating moans, watching his toes twitch like a chicken without a head, dead and unknowing, still believing there's a bit of life left. Finally, James came to a rest, opened his eyes, turned toward Erika and presented her with a satisfied smile.

Erika could only watch on in horror, realizing in that second with absolute clarity that she had never witnessed James in that kind of blissful peace before.

He had never been this happy.

The thought cut straight to the bone, racking her like a spasm; the truth appalled her.

Suddenly Erika found herself clawing at the cloth of drab green tent flap, racing away from the tent city throng, past the Asian with the big tits who winked as she flew by, her breath stinging in her throat, wide-eyed like a terrified child, down a dank corridor that led past the cold steel cell with its midnight black inhabitant, down the metal staircase, cell phone out, clutched in hand as she passed the mob of semi-naked partygoers, out the front door, the damp rancid air catching in her throat as she refused to look back.

Not even once . . .

* * *

It wasn't until she was speeding away in a cab that Erika slowed her breathing. She had been on her cell, trying frantically to reach Marcus. She left messages at home, on his cell, and even had his service page him. But Erika never reached him that night.

James, on the other hand, had called her a million times, frantic and out of breath.

She refused to take his calls.

Three days later, Marcus finally returned hers.

Some lame excuse about being out of town.

By that time, Erika had made up her mind.

Both men in her life were *history*.

And this time, she made a promise not to look back.

Not even once . . .

Twenty-two

The structure stood majestically in the dizzying brilliance of a summer sun against a yawning line of dark poplar trees. From the log cabin exterior, with its thick deep brown and beige polished woods, to its expansive upper deck that skirted the entire length and faced the setting sun, its size was deceiving. For once one ventured inside, their first reaction was to marvel at the enormity of the great room, with its huge stone fireplace, high ceilings with thick blackened cross-beams, and the four spacious bedrooms.

He had done so the first time he'd set foot in this space close to three months ago.

Outside, to the right of the cabin, if viewed from the waterline, was an enclosed area, where firewood was stored. As large as a two-car garage, the space was filled to the ceiling with seasoned split wood. But that did not stop him from rising every morning to stoke the still-burning wood stove in the kitchen, brew his first cup of coffee before donning his frayed jeans, worn tee shirt, and black boots, to spend forty minutes to an hour outdoors halving logs with an axe.

The work was hard and tedious, and not at all needed. It

was late June, seasonable and quite warm. Regardless he followed this regiment to the letter. The result was a honing of his upper body; muscles, which had lain dormant, rose to the surface like a submarine, giving way to sinewy forearms and a ropy back. The tattoos shown like neon on a darkened street. He actually considered more ink, now that his body was being ground into shape.

Perhaps he would.

Behind this wood shed that was cut into the cabin was a garage. A single vehicle in width. It was here that he kept his auto, free from the sun's penetrating rays.

To the left and right of the cabin were stands of apple trees, their scent hanging in the air. Frequently, he'd pick a half-bushel, disappearing into the kitchen to bake pies that he was never able to finish.

Directly in front of the set of French double doors that opened out onto the narrow patio, and several yards down from where the last flagstone ended, lay a motorcycle in various stages of disassembly. The front and back tires were off. The fenders and tank had been dismantled and were sitting together on the grass under the sun. He had just gotten them back from being repainted—a vibrant reddish orange with singes of bluish flames at the edges. Later on today, he'd put the machine back together. Tomorrow perhaps, he'd put on the new set of Sampson pipes. By the following day or the day after that, he'd be feeling the wind on his scalp once again.

Of course, he was in the midst of a fine book—several actually; he'd turned into a voracious reader during the past few months, especially the classics—Charles Dickens, Bram Stoker, James Baldwin, Jack London, Alexandre Dumas, Mark Twain. So perhaps the schedule he'd outlined for himself would slip. It didn't matter. Time was something he had plenty of out here.

Looking out from either the upper deck or French doors, one was assaulted by the expanse of lake that was reached by a thin line of weathered dock. This rickety contraption that was used to tether a seventeen-foot skiff had been hand built almost ten years ago. Sections were in disrepair and rotting. Others sported fresh dark wood that lacked the gray-ish washed-out expression of its neighbors. Regardless, he'd sit, sometimes for hours, at the end, toes dipping in the dark water, watching the sun go down, or counting the stars, imagining if there are worlds beyond our reach, or simply wondering what was lurking beneath his feet.

The boat he was in lay less than two thousand yards from the cabin, in deep water, cool to the touch. It was motion-less, motor off. He was fishing or napping or reading, de-pending on when you chose to glance his way—the pole was in the water, and he was reacting to the nibbles every few minutes. A leafy novel lay at his side—Herman Mel-ville's Moby Dick, fingers tracing the curled edges of acid paper—khaki waterman's hat with the wide brim sheltering his eyes from the relentless sunbeams. What time it was, he could not tell; no timepiece adorned his wrists. But he knew in general terms, by noting the location of the sun.

Way past the noontime hour, less than half way toward the horizon to the west; close to three or four o'clock. That was when he spotted the glint coming from the vehicle as it rounded the gravel road. As it ground to a halt a second ve-hicle appeared. Both were Jeeps or SUVs—it was difficult to discern the details this far out.

He watched, almost in a detached, amused kind of way, neither shifting forward nor bothering to stand up. He wasn't expecting visitors and he had no friends. Not here in West Virginia anyway. He watched a form emerge from the lead ve-hicle, tall, male, and black. Something made him sit slightly forward. A second form, definitely female, emerged a moment later.

His chest began its slow tightening.

He squinted his eyes, attempting to see more clearly.

Finally, he gave up, stood and stretched, while holding a tan forearm to his forehead.

He glanced down, his two pails almost full with fish, gills still flapping—a good day, he mused as he regarded them silently—and decided to bring it on in.

As he got closer, he made out the appearance of Calvin Figgs, Esq.

It was as he had remembered, he noted as he pulled up to the dock, tossing a bowline silently—infectious smile, low cropped hair and thin beard peppered with gray.

Still looking good.

Still the fire in his eyes.

Erika stood behind him, the radiance from a picturesque blue sky doing little to diminish her beauty.

Behind her, Vince Cannon Jr., watched silently.

He cut the motor and stood, feeling the boat shift lazily under his weight. He wore, they noted, torn jeans, black boots, a faded blue bandanna tied tightly against his bald head. His upper body was bare, tanned, and well developed. Erika was amazed at the transformation. But what was most noticeable, she considered, was his eyes—he wore a look of completeness about him—he was not the person she remembered and last seen months ago: shifty, nervous, seemingly out of place—no, here he was at peace.

He was home.

Passing Calvin the pails of fresh fish, he accepted the proffered hand, climbing onto the dock, and staring silently at all of them.

Calvin broke the silence first.

"You're a hard one to track down."

"Some don't want to be found," he replied.

"But found you we did. So, you gonna stare us down for the rest of the afternoon, son, or you gonna give us our proper greeting?"

And for the first time, Trey smiled.

He reached out for Calvin's hand, but Figgs shook his head angrily as he grabbed him, embracing Trey in a bear hug.

"Good to see you, son."

"You too, sir."

Erika stood holding her hands in front of her. She wore an uneasy expression; Trey stepped up to her, stared for a moment, before he broke into a grin as he stretched out his arms. She went to him and hugged him tight.

Vince was next. They embraced silently, words not needed.

Trey moved back, allowing everyone to stare at each other.

Trey settled his gaze upon Calvin. It was clear he was the leader.

"How'd you find me?" Trey asked.

Calvin nodded in Erika's direction.

"Ask her. She's the one who did all the dirty work—been at it for close to a month—tracked you here even though you were as slick as they come—as you said, some people don't want to be found."

Trey was staring at Erika.

She wore a painted-on smile that she shot back at him.

"Resigned from the firm, condo locked up good and tight, bills paid through the fall—nice move, especially not telling anyone where you were going . . ."

There was a sparkle in her eyes.

"But you messed up, son," Calvin declared. "Yes indeed—giving that woman at the Nona E. Taylor Women's Center a P.O. Box where you could be reached in an emergency—like Erika here wouldn't find out sooner or later? Sloppy!"

Trey sucked his teeth as he scratched his bald head through the damp bandanna.

"Why are you here?" he asked.

Calvin's face turned serious.

"Because an intervention was needed."

Trey's stare wavered between the three. For a moment they were all silent.

"Intervention?" he asked cautiously.

"I'm here, Trey, because you've lost sight of those things that are most important to you."

Trey glared back at him. "I suppose you're going to tell me what those are?"

"Don't catch an attitude with me, son—I may be old, but I can still kick your ass—you forget I'm the O.G.—Original Gangster!"

Erika attempted to contain her laughter.

Calvin continued.

"Life, when it comes down to it, Trey; when you strip away all the bullshit—what's *only* important is family."

Trey nodded.

"You say you understand, but do you?" Calvin asked. "Do you grasp the significance of these people standing before you? I wonder if you've forgotten."

Trey sucked in air to speak. He glanced down at the weathered wood of the dock, the ripples in the lake, and blinked. Calvin forged ahead.

"Doesn't matter, son. I'm not here to pass judgment on you or anyone else. I've driven the three hours with these folks because I believe in family." He looked at Erika and then at Vince. Reached out to take their hands. "And this here's your family, Trey. I'm here because today, the past disappears into the past, and what's only important is the glorious future. A future with the folks standing beside me who love you and care about you, just as I do. As my daughter is fond of saying, ya feel me, son?"

Trey's eyes watered. He nodded once. Then nodded again.

"Yes," Trey replied softly, showing his white teeth, "I feel ya!"

"Excellent!" Calvin quipped. "My job here is *almost* done."

Trey's stare went to him.

"Almost, sir?"

Calvin smiled and turned toward the second vehicle. Trey heard the car door slam. He glanced up, past Vince and Erika, who parted so that he could see.

A figure emerged, a shock of lovely brown hair and auburn skin caught by the sun, illuminating the space around her like a halo. Trey shook his head as if to ward off the aberration. She moved toward him in slow motion, and Trey inhaled a sharp breath, witnessing his daughter for the very first time.

They met at the dock's edge where hard wood met soft grass. She glanced up into his eyes, searching for recognition as he removed the bandana from his bald head. He smiled, and she found it.

"Hello baby," Trey ventured, his arms spread wide.

She stared for a moment.

"Can I call you 'daddy'?" she asked hesitantly.

Trey pulled Amber to him, wrapping his arms around her body, engulfing her with all the warmth and love he could muster. At that moment, all emotions were funneled into the sheer joy he felt at holding his little girl for the very first time. He kissed her tear-streaked cheek as his own tears fell.

He took her face in his hands and stepped back, staring long-ingly at her beautiful features. Trey touched her cheeks, ran a finger along the bridge of her nose, and felt her eyebrows. He pressed her against him, stroking her hair and whispered, "You're beautiful, Amber, and you're my baby girl . . ."

Amber sobbed loudly, but Trey held her until her quivering stilled. Erika and Vince hovered around them and together, all four people reunited, arms and fingers intertwining until it was difficult to tell where one ended and the other began.

Amber wiped the underside of one eye with a fingernail and Trey took care of the other. He stared at her, smiled, and said, "You remind me completely of your mother. Would you like me to tell you about her?"

Amber beamed as she nodded her head.

Vince cleared his throat. As he patted Trey on the back he said, "I knew from the very first time I laid eyes on this lady that there was something vaguely familiar—something about her that reminded me of something or someone—it took me a while to figure out just what it was." He paused, locking eyes with Trey before saying, "It's you, Trey. Amber has your features, especially your smile. Can you see it, Erika? Can you see it in their eyes?"

"Oh yes," she said. "A wonderful smile, just like your daddy's."

Calvin cleared his throat as everyone turned.

"My job here is done," he boasted, arms held wide. At that moment he felt like a preacher after a heartfelt sermon on a Sunday morning. He flashed a warm smile as he smacked Trey on the shoulder. "Just one thing, counselor, if I may?"

"That's ex-counselor if you please."

Calvin ignored the comment.

"Well, I don't know about you, but driving three hours

makes me damn hungry. What you got to eat up in this piece?"

Trey grinned showing his vibrant white teeth.

"Anyone for some fried fish???"

They ate until well after sundown. Actually, the rest of the afternoon and evening turned into a celebration as they ate, drank, napped, and ate again. For Trey, it was a dream come true. This morning he woke up thinking he would be spending his day quietly fishing, doing some reading, working on the bike or perhaps spending time in the kitchen concocting some new recipe—instead, he was reunited with his family, seeing his little girl for the very first time. Amber, he was convinced, had similar thoughts and feelings about this special day.

Vince and Erika knew that things between him and Amber were going smoothly. As soon as they had settled in, Trey had asked Amber to assist him in the kitchen. While Erika and Vince were shunned to the dock to gut and clean the fish, Trey supervised Amber cutting up vegetables. Pretty soon there was laughter and carryings on emanating from the kitchen. Vince and Erika kept coming in to check on things, but they were shooed away—first by Trey and then by Amber.

"Vince, leave me alone!" she said, as she cut up potatoes into thin slivers for later. "My daddy is schooling me and I need to pay attention!"

"That's my baby girl!" Trey added with a chuckle.

Vince just shook his head and left.

They ate in the Great Room, on couches, comfortable leather chairs, and on the floor in front of the stone fireplace—fried fish that Trey had caught in the lake that day, scrambled eggs stuffed with onions, ham, and cheese, and potatoes, cut sliver-thin and deep-fried in oil. After nightfall, Trey lit a fire—not that one was needed, but the effect of having one going after the sun went down was too good to ignore. He pulled out a bottle of Johnnie Walker Black and poured a round of drinks before serving hot apple pie baked from the apples they had picked that very afternoon.

"Are you legal?" he asked with a smirk as he held the bottle in front of Amber.

"Yes, Daddy! Please!"

Calvin made the toast once everyone held a glass.

"To family and good friends. May they both be in our hearts forever."

"Oh my God this pie is soooooo good!" Erika exclaimed after taking a bite.

"Compliments to Amber—she made it!" Trey quipped.

"With your help!" she quickly added.

They settled down to talk and reflect on the past year.

"Why did you resign from the firm, Trey?" Erika asked as she sipped her drink.

Trey was lying on the floor, his head on an oversized throw rug. Amber's head lay in his lap.

"I got to the point where my work was no longer engaging or fun. And that felt wrong to me. I was spending far too much time thinking about negative things—what I'd say to my boss the next time he barged into my office, how I'd structure my appeal letter to the EEOC, stuff like that. I woke up one morning and said—Trey, no more!"

Calvin nodded.

"So, what are your plans now that you are no longer working?" Vince asked from the couch.

"Honestly, I don't know. I came here to figure out just what my priorities are. I didn't put myself on a time schedule. I knew that when I was ready to go back to work and home, I would. I've got enough money saved to keep me

here for a year or more, if need be. When I go back I'll figure out what I want to do. Whether its law or something else,
when the time is right, I'll know."

Vince grinned. "Your head is on straight, and that is what
matters most. I applaud you for recognizing when it's time
to move on—most folks just stay in a dead-end job, a marriage, or what have you until they are so damn bitter they
just give up on life or go postal, whichever comes first!"

Amber turned to stare at her father.

"I have a question."

"Shoot."

"Any females in your life?" she asked. "Love life I
mean," she added.

Amber was asking the question everyone else in the room
dared not ask.

Trey cleared his throat and smiled, sitting up.

"Not at this time," he responded, his eyes clear and unblinking. "Part of why I came here was to take control of my
life—get back to where I was before—to regain what I had
lost along the way. I think that in the past year I've spent too
much time focusing on the wrong things, instead of what's
truly important. Right Erika?"

Erika grinned.

Vince and Calvin nodded in unison.

"There was someone special in my life. But what we had
was complicated. I need time to figure out just what the future holds, if there's a future for us. I think there is, but I
need to be sure."

Trey took in a breath.

"I felt that I needed space to contemplate all of this—
alone."

They were silent for a moment before Amber opened her
mouth and spoke.

"I feel you," she said, returning her head to her father's lap. "I was just wondering—I mean, if Vince over there can get a girl, surely you can too!"

The fire had been reduced to simmering coals that sparked a warm red-orange glow. The five of them, Trey, Vince, Amber, Erika, and Calvin had consumed more liquor in one night than Trey had drunk in the entire year! Additionally, they finished off the rest of the apple pie until each of them lay around the Great Room holding full stomachs in hand as they frowned and groaned.

Erika lay in front of the fire asleep. Calvin was in a chair engrossed in a novel he hadn't read since college.

Vince gestured for Trey to follow him outside onto the upper deck. They toasted one another as they stared at the stars. Out here, with no lights from the city to impair their vision, the night was crystal clear and the stars brilliant, almost dizzying in their intensity. Vince stared for a moment, engrossed with how black the sky had become. The lake was still and ink black too—eerie, yet hauntingly beautiful.

Trey broke the silence first.

"How ya livin'?" he said simply.

"Having you back in my life, and Amber too—man, I'm living large. And that's no lie!" He eyed his best friend. "It's good to have you back, Trey. I missed you, bruh."

Trey gave his friend dap and nodded.

"I feel the same," he uttered.

"There's one thing I need to ask," Vince continued quietly, glancing back through the glass at the Great Room and its inhabitants.

"Anything," Trey said.

Vince leaned forward and whispered in his ear.

Trey listened to his best friend, nodded and turned to him, considering his words for a moment before rewarding him with a smile.

"Nothing would please me more, man," he said, and reached over to give him a hug. They embraced silently. Vince had tears in his eyes that Trey could not see.

"You know what this means," Trey added with a gleam in his eyes.

"What?"

Trey leaned in and whispered. Vince's eyes rolled back in his head as he laughed out loud.

"Oh Lord!" he exclaimed, "I sure as hell didn't consider that!"

"That's right," Trey boasted, raising his glass to the heavens, "I'm gonna be your freaking *daddy*-in-law!!!"

"There's way too much mischief going on out here!"

They both turned, and saw Erika joining them on the deck. She had wrapped herself in a blanket, the same one she had covering her by the fire. Only her hands were visible, and one held a fresh drink. She nuzzled between Vince and Trey and stared out at the stars.

"God, it's beautiful here. I can see why you came."

"It does wonders for cleansing the mind," Trey said.

"No question."

Vince rubbed her back while Trey draped an arm around her shoulder. The three of them stayed like that, no one speaking for a while, the trio enjoying the warmth and love that radiated from this place.

Erika raised her glass to the others.

"I want to say something. You two are the most important people in my life. You are my family. We've been through shit and thin together and we're still standing strong." She gazed upon Trey for a moment. "And we've had our share of troubling times—but regardless, we were always there for each other. That's what best friends do—they never turn their back on each other."

Trey and Vince nodded.

"I want for us to pledge right now that we will forever and always be here for each other—in sickness and in health . . . you know the drill, so raise your damn glass!"

Vince grinned.

"Well said."

"I'll drink to that," Trey said.

And they did, on a warm summer night, somewhere in West Virginia, nuzzling against each other as they held their glasses high.

They had gone to bed—finally unable to keep their eyes open a second longer. It was way past one a.m., Erika had crashed a while ago, and then Amber turned in followed by Vince. Trey remained awake, unable to sleep. He stood on the deck by the railing, observing the stars. The remains of a drink lay in his palm. He swished the contents around, over and over in a circular motion, the action repetitive and comfortable, before tossing the remains over the rail.

Calvin joined him on the deck, bringing him a fresh glass of Johnnie Walker Black.

"Thought you could use a nightcap."

"Thank you, sir."

They sipped at their drinks in silence before Calvin set his down on the wooden rail. He turned to Trey.

"You have a wonderful family, Trey."

"Yes, I do."

"Don't forget that," he added.

"I won't."

"Good."

They drank a moment more.

"Trey—concerning your law career."

"Yes, sir?"

"I've started a new firm." Calvin's eyes reflected stray moonlight.

Trey's jaw went slack.

"I thought you were retiring—that's what you told me!"

"Yes—and after a lengthy trip with the missus and way too much time at home, it became apparent to both of us that I needed to get back to work! So I decided to start my own firm. I want to specialize in high-profile clients and cases, the kind I've spent my career negotiating."

Trey nodded, waiting for what came next.

"I'd like for you to come work for me, son—I want you with me."

Trey exhaled forcefully.

"Sir, I don't know what to say." Trey beamed. "Thank you, sir, thank you for thinking of me."

Calvin waved him away.

"Counselor—I've always been one of your biggest fans, you know that. You do great work, that is when your head isn't in the clouds, or up someone's skirt!" He gave Trey a wink. "Seriously, I think you'd be a valuable asset, especially with the contacts you have in Washington."

Trey grinned, shaking his head. Suddenly, everything was falling back into place, right where it belonged.

"I'm not going to lie to you, son—it'll be hard work— we're starting from scratch—I can't pay you what you were making before you resigned—but the money will come in time. Just keep your nose clean and work your ass off!"

"I will, sir."

"One thing, Trey—and this is vital, so pay attention." He

pointed a finger at Trey's nose. Trey put down his drink and gave Calvin Figgs his utmost attention.

"Take whatever time you need to consider my offer, but get your family in order first. When you come work for me; that is if you decide to work for me, I want no less than two hundred percent from you. I won't accept anything less. Do I make myself clear?"

"Understood, sir," Trey responded.

"Good. Remember what I said, Counselor—take your time but get your family in order first—then come, ready and willing, and together we'll kick some serious ass. Bernard John Marshall be damned!"

Trey grinned and held up his drink.

"With all due respect, sir, fuck Bernard John Marshall . . ."

Calvin finished the sentence for me: ". . . And the horse he rode in on!"

Epilogue

(One year later . . .)

I can't begin to tell you just how wonderful Vince and Amber's wedding day turned out to be. Simply put, it was one of the most incredible moments of my life!

My little girl, Amber, was dolled up in this fabulous wedding gown, hand-beaded with sequins and pearls, intricate lace and matte satin, with a flowing train and matching headpiece. Her brown hair was straightened and worn long, makeup flawless, skin beyond radiant as she emerged from the white limousine on a cloudless day in June to stand in front of this majestic black church in Northwest D.C. Oh my God! I took her hand, me looking dapper, funky *fresh* in my tuxedo, oh yeah, y'all, the honeys were clocking a dude, and why wouldn't they as I walked her up the steps and down the aisle.

Yours truly walked my baby girl down the aisle!

There was so much pride in me that day as hundreds of onlookers turned in their pews to watch this icon of loveliness, my baby girl walk to her husband, Vince Cannon Jr., my best friend. Vince was looking as fly as he wanna be in his tux, GQ-*down*, you hear me, waiting to say, "I do!"

I don't mean to get choked up, but this is my baby girl we're talking about.

The ceremony was wonderful, not too long, and filled with singing, music, and spoken word—oh yeah, y'all we got down like that, for real!

Black folks in the house! So holla if ya hear me!

Get this—everybody that was anybody in D.C. was there—I mean, Vince's parents, Dr. and Mrs. Vince Cannon, are well connected, so the elite were all up in this piece! But more importantly, all of our family and friends were there to support us on this most auspicious day.

A wedding invitation had gone out to Amber's grandmother, Lorna, but as expected, she had declined to attend. Soli, her good friend from high school made it down with a few other high school chums in tow.

Amber was also successful in reconnecting with some of her friends from Houston, and a contingent of ladies came to D.C. for the wedding. Amber couldn't have been more pleased.

It was great to finally meet Angeliqué, Vince's old flame. She came and stayed an entire week, seeing how she was one of the bridesmaids.

Erika, it turned out, was the Maid of Honor. She, too, looked radiant, but of course, my boo always does.

Always has—always will!

Guess who else was in the wedding party?

Okay, I've made you wait long enough.

You guessed right.

Layla!

My girl!

My boo boo!

Damn that woman looked so fine in her sensuously tight bridesmaid's dress, I swear to God I couldn't wait to sex her after church! But let me get back to moi!

I held the dual role of being the best man and giving away the bride.

How cool is that?

Plus, I had fine-ass Layla on my arm so you know I was the man that day, prancing around like some spring chicken, all cocky and shit, like a peacock—yeah, I said it!—y'all know by now how I do, this dude's back in the zone, way up in the oooooooooo-zone!

I gotta tell you this, though, the absolute highlight of the day/evening, was at the reception when guess who strolls in???

(Drum roll, please.)

Yup, y'all guessed it.

Giovanna!

That heifer had the nerve to show her face on Amber's wedding day. Check this—I hadn't heard a peep—and I do mean peep from girlfriend since April of the *previous* year! After she went on her trip to Hawaii with old dude—I cut her ass loose.

Had to!

You know you can't pimp this dude here and get away with it!

Months later she did try and contact me a few times, but by then I'd had enough of her shit.

If I wasn't good enough for her then, I surely didn't want any part of her now!

Anywho, back to the story—girlfriend rolls in, looking, I must say, as tasty as one of those Hostess Twinkies! I mean, she was not playing in her tight-ass dress, fuck me pumps, hair done all up, like she owned this mutha sucka!

Listen, I may be in love, but I damn sure ain't blind.

I had to give girlfriend credit—she was trying to make a scene and *succeeding*, with her fine self, every mutha sucka turning in their chairs, straining their necks, trying to get a closer look.

Vince just shook his head and sighed.

The truth is, next to my girls—Amber and Layla—Giovanna ain't shit!

At the reception I spotted her out of the corner of my eye. I did a double take (I'm not gonna even front), and decided to pay her ass no mind!

Later on, when folks were dancing, I got up from the head table to go to the bar. Guess what? She was clocking the hell out of me—and I just tipped my head back and laughed out loud!

She actually had the audacity to join me at the bar, away from the stares of Layla and Vince, where she could say her hello.

"Damn, Trey, you are looking *foine*. I guess a girl really messed up by letting your smooth ass go," she began, and I just stood there, tugging at my mustache, while she proceeded to brush invisible lint off the lapel of my jacket.

I was grinning like my numbers just came in!

"Yeah, you sure did mess up," I said, as I flashed my best Trey-smile, "but it's all good, girl, so enjoy the party, 'cause I'm sure gonna!" And then I waltzed away, fresh drink in hand, snickering my ass off.

Giovanna's hand reached for my shoulder and spun me around, whispering low, eyes wide, "Trey, you can have this," her stare dropping seductively to my crotch, "why don't you take this, for old time sake—

My pussy is wet,
my sex box is hot,
you got me twitching,
like an addict on rock . . ."

Cocking her head to the side, gesturing upstairs to one of the private rooms, she told me, "You can take this right now, wedding day be damned, I'll let you hike up my dress, and you won't find any panties to get in your way . . .

"Remember that, baby? Do you???"

I just smirked as I walked away.

I didn't even give her the satisfaction of responding.

End of story, y'all.

Poof! Giovanna's gone . . .

Later, as I sat with my woman drinking champagne, Layla's elbow resting comfortably in my lap, teasing my fly in a luring yet tasteful kind of way, I pondered the past year as I watched Vince dance with his new bride.

I had regained my friends.

I found my family.

The job was going remarkably well—better than expected—we had pulled in some big name clients, and in the short time that we had been in business, Figgs & Associates had created quite a stir within the D.C. community.

And—

(Another drum roll, please)

Layla moved in with me!

Yeah, you heard right. Okay, y'all can get up off the damn floor now, 'cause I ain't playing. Your boy, Trey decided, why the hell not—I mean, I'm feeling her something terrible—actually, she's the best thing that's ever happened to me, other than finding my daughter, or should I say, her finding me.

Simply put: I'm in love, y'all, and I'm not ashamed to admit it!

Dayum.

I guess momma was right.

You can teach old dogs new tricks . . .

Vince's book, *Finding Nirvana*, has been on the Essence bestseller list for the past nine months in a row. That dude's seminars are sold out wherever he travels to; he's working on a sequel to the book, and is frequently on television and radio shows. He's waiting for Oprah to call any minute now . . .

You go boy!

Vince is livin' large!

Angeliqué's art show took to the road to rave reviews. After doing a short stint in Dallas and Atlanta, she came to New York where her vibrant, colorful, live show featuring Amber, Jacques, and a handful of other nude models covered in veve netted her a feature in *Heart & Soul*. Turns out, a very successful video director saw the show while it was in New York, and fell in love with Amber's looks. Next thing we knew, my baby girl was cast in several of his video projects.

All of a sudden, Amber's face, wonderful smile, and body were gracing the screens of BET and MTV.

My girl, Erika, too, is doing quite well.

After kicking both James and Marcus to the curb, she took some time off to be alone—to chill, and enjoy being by herself.

After her experience with the foundation run by Rich and Andy, she decided that she wanted to start her own not-for-profit group to assist people of color with finding their birth parents.

So, homegirl put her head down and started her own shit! It takes up all of her time, we barely see her ass anymore, and then only at fundraisers, but she's doing her thing, and she's happy. Girl's finally found her passion—and y'all know just how important that is!

I'm damn proud of my boo!

She's an independent black woman doing her own thing, in control of her own destiny! And nobody's gonna get in her way!

By the way, Sassy came to the wedding with this dude she'd just started dating—this local author, tall, bald, light skinned, thin goatee; guy by the name of Devon Somefuckingbody. Okay the brutha's good looking, I'll give him that. I expected him to bend my freaking ear with talk about his novels like he was Eric Jerome Dickey, but he didn't. He was way cool. We spoke for a while about all kinds of eclectic stuff: jazz, politics, classic literature, the rebuilding of Iraq, funding for NASA explorations to Mars—the dude's quite deep! And I must admit he and Erika do look good together.

Hmmn . . . I might have to start hanging with him . . . you know, two good-looking baldheaded bruthas with an intellect and something to say—oh hell no! But I digress . . .

Let's see—what else can I tell you?

Oh yeah—India Jasmine Jackson followed me to Figgs & Associates. And of course, she's working out great. She's keeping my black ass in check every single day!

Quentin Hues, who incidentally was traded to the Miami Heat, also followed me to my new firm. We still see each other when he's in town, we stay in touch, and I'm still his lawyer for any mess he finds himself in.

Aponi—I left that fine shit alone.

I'm still doing my volunteer thing at the Nona E. Taylor Women's Center—I try to get there every other month or so, since work's been taking up most of my time. It's always a pleasure to cook for those ladies, and Yolanda Taylor hasn't changed a bit! She still hugs me to death whenever I stop by, and we can sit for hours just shooting the shit and telling lies.

She's good people . . .

I ran into Allison some months back at a reception held at the D.C. Convention Center—real hoity toity affair—spied her at the bar—didn't go over—didn't want to make a scene—she saw me, though—our eyes connected and locked, I winked and she didn't smile back—so I went on my way!

Get this—I also ran into Bernard John Marshall a few months ago at Angelo's & Maxi's. We both were there dining with our respective clients. He was leaving when I was coming in, and he had no choice but to shake my hand and ask how things were going. You could see the seething anger dripping from his fangs when I told him about a high-profile client I had just nabbed—a client I had actually stolen from the old firm! It was so good to see him outside of work, where he no longer controls me.

My how things change . . .

So, here I am, standing with a champagne flute in my hand, Erika and Devon sitting to my left, engaged in some serious conversation about God-knows what; Sassy hanging on every word this baldhead dude utters, head tipped back as she laughs at his corny-ass jokes. My boo boo to my right, eyes sparkling like diamonds, dress fitting her like driving gloves, her plunging neckline, curvy hips, and heart-shaped ass speaking to me in volumes; her loveliness shining like a beacon so damn bright that I have to resist her potion with every ounce of strength I can muster. Amber and Vince slow dancing a few feet away; her eyes and mine connecting, her mouthing over the din of the slow jam, "daddy, I love you," and my eyes watering because it's at times like this that I realize that I'm the luckiest damn guy in the world . . .

And I think to myself, back when I was in Jamaica, a time now that seems like eons ago, down among the throng of naked partygoers, I thought I'd died and gone to heaven. But now, as I stand here tonight, my family and close friends all around me, I realize that, naw bruh, you were wrong.

DON'T MISS THE FIRST BOOK IN
THE SEDUCTION SERIES

Complications

On sale now

One

Four a.m. came way too fast! The alarm shook my ass out of bed as I struggled to keep myself from falling back into the warm confines of my comforter. But today was not a day to reckon with—no, today I couldn't just lie there and hit the snooze—not on this day. Today I was going on vacation!

So I held my head that was smarting from the buzz of the alarm clock and ran the shower. Then quickly got into my normal routine—teeth brushing and shaving my face and bald head with the Braun, and trimming my thick, dark goatee. I was turning toward the shower but then thought about it for one quick second—I was heading to the islands to play, so I should spend a minute more on grooming, 'cause things like that were important to me. So, I buzzed off what little chest and stomach hair I had, used the clippers (with guard!) to trim my pubic hair down to a thin layer just the way I liked it. Then got in the shower after admiring my taut form in the mirror. I liked what I saw. Firm, bronze-colored body, tight upper body with a hint of muscles, but not overdone, like some jarhead. Tattoo-adorned—a thin tribal band on my left arm above my elbow; the colorful face of an Indian chief on my right shoulder—feathers from his headdress meandering down my arm to just below the elbow; and my latest acquisition—a five-pointed star, almost snowflake-like in form, sitting on my chest above my left nipple. Well-defined legs and a tight ass that sent the women wild (I'm just repeating what they tell me, so don't hate).

The water running down my bald head, face, chest and arms felt sooooo good, I could have stayed there for an hour. But Air Jamaica was calling my name, "Trey, everyting irie, so get ya ass down here, mon!" I wasn't about to miss out on any of that. It had been too damn long, ya hear me! Over a year since a real vacation for me. I mean, I've been traveling on business, don't get me wrong, but it isn't the same. This was the vacation that I'd been waiting for all year long. And today was the day. By noon I'd be on white sandy beaches! I couldn't wait.

I glanced down at my flat stomach and dark cock, grabbed the razor and the bar of soap, and went about cutting off the hair around my package. I loved that feeling of little to no hair down there . . . and the ladies loved it as well. I'm not sure if it was the fact that it made me more sensitive or not, but all I know was that it felt good to be sexing with smooth balls. With each scrape of the razor I thought about the possibilities awaiting me on that island—all of those dark and lovely honeys . . . six wonderful days . . . my dick began to swell as I thought of the delicious possibilities . . .

While toweling off, I recalled the conversation last night with my boy.

"Speak!"

"What up, bruh? How ya livin'?"

"Living large and in charge," I replied to the routine that hasn't changed in over fifteen years. Vince and I are best friends, homies from way back! He's my man, the one person I genuinely look up to and love like a brother.

"So, my man, you ready?"

"Hell naw, what you think? I got my shit all over this mutha sucka—looks like a cyclone hit this place. But don't worry, my man, I *will* be ready!"

"I hear that."

"True dat!"

"So, my man, seriously, you gonna go down there to relax, right? Find your flow and do some soul searching?" I could hear Vince through the phone cracking up before my response was forthcoming.

"What you think? I'm gonna tag every piece of ass that winks at me . . . I'm not playin'!"

"Dude, listen to me—what you need to do is take it down a notch, find yourself one of those fine-ass Jamaican women, like Rachel on BET, remember her, with the long, dark hair, and thick like I don't know what, and romance the hell out of her. Do your thing, man, and she'll be like putty in your hands. Then bring her ass back up to the States and make her your wife!" He chuckled but not more so than I did.

"First off, this is *me* you talking to! Why you trying to play me like that? You know that ain't me. Shit. Wifey??? Screw that, V. That's you, and listen, I ain't mad at ya, but that, my bruh, ain't me. Wife," I said again. "Negro, please!"

It always amused me how two grown black men with close to seven years of post-graduate work between us still talked like we were from the ghetto—hoodlums, like rap stars or something. That's one thing I loved about Vince— put him in a work situation and he was all professional, like another person took control of his voice—the way he said things, the manner in which he gestured; and his inflection sounded so damn *intelligent* and I dare say, *prophetic*. He was good at that stuff—I mean, to a certain extent I am, too—I have to be in my line of work, being an attorney and such, but I'm not like Vince. He's 'da man when it comes to stuff like that. I guess that's why people pay to hear him speak! Anyway, some things never change between us, and this was one of those things—the way we spoke and vibed when we were around each other.

"I'm just saying, if it were me and I was heading to Jamaica for six days, I would be on the lookout. There's something about the islands that gets my juices flowing . . . when I'm around those beautiful beaches and sunsets it makes me feel all romantic inside. Make me wanna grab a honey and wine and dine her all night!" Vince was laughing now, but I knew his words were speaking the truth. That was the major difference between the two of us—the way in which we viewed the world. Vince was a serious romantic through and through—he still got plenty of play, but his approach was totally different than mine. Me, well, I'm just a stone-cold playa! I'm in to pussy, for real! The punany, plain and simple. I don't screw around—when I see something I want, I go for it—no long-term romancing allowed! Just not part of my rules, ya see!

"I promise you this, Vince," I said, as I closed my garment bag filled with clothes for every possible occasion— my favorite dark, Italian-cut, three-button suit for the club; black, tight leather pants and stretch muscle shirt; a few button-downs, a thin pullover in case it got chilly; assorted jeans and shorts; and loafers and two pairs of sandals—black and tan. An unopened box of Lifestyles condoms (lubricated) lay in the upper right compartment of the garment bag. "I'm gonna relax and I'm gonna chill, but I *will* tag every fine piece of ass I see. I ain't playing. This ole dick of mine is gonna get itself a fucking workout! Ya hear me!?!"

"You mean *more* than normal?" He laughed some more. Then we hung up after saying our goodbyes. I had to finish packing a second bag . . .

Both bags along with my leather carryon were currently sequestered in the trunk of my black M5. The engine was running and humming as I prepared to leave. I was dressed casual—over-dyed jeans, polo shirt—robin's egg blue, black leather jacket, and my favorite Under Armour running shorts, blue-tinted sunglasses perched atop my smooth dome—yeah, casual, yet stylish and fresh as only I could be—this I'm thinking to myself as I checked myself out in the full length mirror in the hall before setting the alarm to the crib and jetting—after all, as I'm fond of saying—image is everything! No need to have the panties flying just yet. I mean, it wasn't even daylight yet. Yeah, mon!

Fast forward six hours. I was forty-three thousand feet in the air and cruising above Cuba at five hundred forty-five miles per hour. How do I know? 'Cause I'm a gadget freak and brought along my Garmin GPS. I pointed that bad boy out the window (I was in the aisle seat with nobody beside me), got a fix on a handful of satellites (my device has a twelve-channel receiver!) and bam! My position was instantly calculated and displayed on a small LED screen. Kind of nice to know just where you are at all times!

Anywho . . . we'd been flying for several hours and the flight had been uneventful. Security at Baltimore-Washington International had been tight, but nothing overbearing—my designer belt buckle had set the metal detector off (even though I was TSA Precheck and they told me not to take off my belt or shoes) and then they went through the pockets of my leather jacket because my Beemer key looked suspiciously fat under the X-ray machine. (Don't any of these

TSA chumps drive a *luxury* car???) I was frisked by an elderly white guy (hourly employee, no doubt!) under the watchful eyes of a pair of TSA supervisors or whatnot. After that I chilled at the gate until boarding time, looking around like a hawk at my fellow passengers, trying to see if there were any fine honeys that I might get next to. Alas, no such luck. That was cool with me—I needed to save my strength for when I arrived in Mo Bay, ya know? I decided to call my other best friend, my boo, Erika, a.k.a. Sassy, even though it was before seven a.m. Damn, she hadn't even called me last night to give me a send-off, so screw her if I wake her black ass up!

"Sassy, what's up, girl?" I said, booming into my cell.

"This better be a goddamned emergency, I swear to God." I could hear her turning over in her bed. *Good, I got her at just the right time.*

"What up, boo? You forgot about your main man or what? Gonna let me get on a plane without any goodbyes? You know that ain't right!"

A stream of expletives escaped from her mouth, and I just had to laugh out loud. I loved it when she talked dirty to me. Erika and I have been down since I don't know when. At least as long as Vince and me. Actually, we had been friends since our college days, staying tight and sharing with each other the kind of things usually reserved for same-sex friendships. But Erika was down. She was cool. One of the fellas. I let her know that every chance I got.

"Look, baby girl, sorry to wake you, but I just had to holla at you before I go."

"No, your dumb ass just had nothing else to do while waiting at the gate! Am I right?" Erika responded.

"See, now I'm hurt."

"Well, screw you!" She laughed. "Trey, I only got one

thing to say to you, since you never listen to me anyway—are you listening?"

"Yeah, Sassy. Fire away."

"Trey, use protection. You hear me???" I laughed loudly as I grunted, and disconnected her dumb ass . . .

Okay—here I am just ranting and raving, going on and on about this and that, and I haven't even taken the time to properly introduce myself. Where are my manners? My mother would not be proud! So, here it goes . . .

My name is Trey Alexander. I'm thirty-three years old, living in Chocolate City (that's the nation's capital, D.C., for all of you who are not in the know!) I'm a divorce lawyer, admitted to the bar in D.C., Virginia, and New York. I work for a prestigious law firm in D.C.—and, no, I'm not going to tell you the name, 'cause some of you bitches just might Google me and try to get my digits—I'm not having that! I'm originally from New York, Brooklyn, to be exact, and yes, that totally explains my cocky, in-your-face attitude and demeanor (screw you, very much!) But to paraphrase what I've said habitually, "Don't hate the playa, hate the game!"

I've been in D.C. for about ten years—I came here to go to law school, Georgetown, thank you very much, and been here ever since. I love D.C.—love the atmosphere, the people, and most of all, the *ratio* of women to guys! When I got here I said to myself, "This is soooooo me!" And I'm still here, dammit! For real!

Anyway, I've lived in D.C. the entire time I've been here—right now I've got myself a stylish crib off 15th and U, a two-story condo with, check it—a doorman! Yeah! I'm moving on up, to the East side . . . you already know what I drive, but in case you haven't been paying attention, my ride is a sexy ass, black M5, courtesy of the firm. Yeah, late last year I won this high-profile divorce and child custody case for a prominent, McLean plastic surgeon. The case was very complex and extremely nasty, so the Beemer was my bonus for winning. Listen, I love the ride and all, but to be truthful, when I think about it, I billed close to one hundred thousand dollars on that case alone, so that's the least they could do!

Let's see—what else can I tell ya—last year I cleared $298,000 in salary. I'm not a partner, and that used to be a sore subject for me, but in the last nine to twelve months I've come to grips with the fact that Trey here does not intend to put in the hours that are demanded of an up-in-coming partner-to-be. My motto is and has always been—"work hard, play even harder!" And I live that maxim every day of my life. The firm gets its money's worth out of me; don't get me wrong. But when my workday is done, it is done, and don't talk to me about my professional gig. At that point it's Miller time, and Trey is ready to party! So, I'm cool with the salary and bennies they give me, my phat ride, crib in the city, and plenty of punany to chase after and keep me hoppin'! Now, I know the next question on your mind, so let's dispense with it right now: Girlfriend? Wife? Significant other, you ask? Not only "no" to those questions, but "hell naw!" Does that answer your question???

Less than an hour later the clear, fresh aquamarine waters of Jamaica rolled underneath the belly of our jet as we approached Montego Bay. The lush hills of the island slipped beneath us as we landed into the wind. An ancient jeep that was painted just like the one on *M*A*S*H* (for those of you old enough—like me—to remember that show) stood off the main runway by a tin-slatted hut. As we deplaned onto the tarmac, the heat hit me square in the face and chest. Hard to believe that less than six hours earlier, I had been in forty-degree weather. "Welcome to Jamaica," a sign proclaimed as we made a right turn and headed for the terminal and (I hoped) air conditioning. I was here. The vacation was beginning! Ah yeah!

I'll dispense with the details. Suffice it to say, it took me close to two hours by bus to get from Mo Bay to my resort in Negril (located on the western part of the island). It was hot as hell and the roads were—pardon my French—fucked up! I mean half that island was in disrepair and the roads were in the midst of a serious reconstruction. That meant that every few minutes or so our Jamaican driver would have to downshift and maneuver around pot holes large enough for a horse to lie in. Along the way we saw some interesting sights—cows and/or steers (I don't know the damn difference!) grazing on the side of the road; a Pizza Hut and KFC that our driver was so damn proud of, he had to slow down and get on the P.A. system to announce; fishermen on the side of the road carrying fresh fish on a line; sellers of assorted fruits, beer, Bob Marley hats; bicycle tires or perhaps steering wheel covers (carried around their dark necks), and of course, ganja—yeah, these dudes actually ran alongside of our bus as we went through intersections trying to sell us this stuff; a guy barefoot carrying groceries on top of his head . . . I thought I had died and gone to Africa!

There were five of us on the bus—two black dudes from Chicago who had gone to Howard and were therefore familiar with the D.C. area. And a nice, chatty, young, white couple named Lance and Chris from Louisiana. We got through the introductions and the normal chatter—first time to Jamaica? First time to this resort? Yada yada . . . But finally, we turned into our hotel complex and I breathed a sigh of relief. We were finally here. Yes, Lawd!

I thought check-in would be a breeze, but guess what? Our rooms weren't ready. I guess some things never change, regardless of what part of the world you are in. They invited us to leave our bags out front and relax in the dining room where a lavish buffet was in full effect. I was totally down with that. I sat with the H.U. bros and scanned the room for honeys as we ate . . . saw a few that definitely caught my eye. Everyone but us was clad in tee shirts, bikinis, colorful sarongs—sunglasses adorned their heads—carrying plates loaded with food to rounded tables. Open bar (this was an all-inclusive place, and I was not mad at anybody, you hear me!), so the Jamaican rum and other top-shelf liquor was flowing! An hour later we were stuffed, and I was ready to lose my jeans, running shoes, and jacket, find a spot on the beach under one of them palm trees with plenty of shade and catch a snooze—after all, I'd been up since four.

I sauntered over to the front desk where my H.U. boys had already checked in and were following the bellmen to their room. I waved goodbye and waited my turn. Come to find out, there was a problem with my room reservation. Now listen, don't mess with me after I've flown close to fifteen hundred miles and put these six days, five nights on my Visa—I had all the proper paperwork and documentation in my leather carryon—just give me a minute to get to it. No, that wasn't it, I was told—the crux of the matter was that the resort was under renovation. Funny—no one (Orbitz where I had booked my trip) had mentioned that *minor* point to me . . . an entire section of rooms (ocean view—*my* ocean view room, btw!) was closed, in addition to the main pool and club!

Okay . . . here we go! It's about to get ugly up in here! OH HELL NO! I put on my best "don't-mess-with-me-I'm-an-attorney" face and voice, kept my composure but told the cute, but tight-lipped Jamaican woman behind the desk that she (and this place) was about to have a serious problem if they didn't produce a comparable room ASAP! She ducked into the back, presumably to consult her manager since the computer terminal at the front desk wasn't telling her squat—came out a few moments later (okay, more like five to ten minutes later), smiley face painted back on just right. This was what they were going to do—they had a sister resort literally right next door—she genuflected with a smile like she was Vanna freaking White—and it had some very nice ocean-front rooms that were available—I'd be transferred there—I'd retain the use of the privileges at this resort for the entire week, if I'd like—and, here's how they got me to ease up on a sistah pronto—for my inconvenience, they would comp me three days to be used the *next* time I came back here to Jamaica and to this resort!

Hmmm, three days . . . suddenly things weren't looking that bad . . . but hold up—tell me more about this other resort, I inquired. I mean, what kind of place was this; what kind of amenities did they have? The Jamaican woman with her dark, perfectly smooth skin smiled a seductive smile as she leaned in toward me, knowing that she now had my full attention. Here's the thing—this place next door was really nice—and (she just *knew* from looking at me that I'd love this part), they had a nude side and a prude side . . .

Nude side! Did someone say, nude side!?! My mind raced for a nanosecond—let me see, does that mean nude honeys flocking by my open window as waves crash onto the white sand every few moments, I wondered??? Hmmm, tell me more, baby, don't let me interrupt you . . .

Pause—since y'all don't know me that well yet, let me say this right up front—I've never been an exhibitionist . . . okay? I mean, this dude is comfortable, *very comfortable* with his body, but that doesn't mean I get into this naked, holistic, I'm down with nature, let my stuff swing free, au naturel shit! I've been to a nude beach before—hasn't everybody? Actually, when I was growing up in NYC, my parents took me to Jones Beach one day and I wandered over the

Awakening

Taj has a successful career, a loving fiancée, and a life full of promise. Cheyenne has all the security money can bring, thanks to her powerful husband, and her own soul-stirring talent. But one chance encounter during the holidays sweeps these two back into a wrenching past they thought they'd put behind them. As they desperately try to face down a secret they've never dared share with anyone else, the desire that saved their lives reignites. And it's tearing apart everything they've achieved, revealing unthinkable truths, and sending their perfect lives into a nightmarish tailspin . . .

Now the only way Taj and Cheyenne can fight their shattering ordeal is to go back to where it all began. And letting their passion consume them may be their only chance to put the past to rest—unless it burns too hot to survive. . . .

Illusions

David Sands has just moved into a spacious new loft when he spies a beautiful woman in the window of the vacant house facing his. Her dancing mesmerizes him, and when she shows up at his door, he succumbs to her erotic moves. In the morning, she is gone, leaving Sands with an empty feeling that just won't go away. But when he seeks her out, what he finds shocks him—Nona, this mystery woman, died years ago at the hands of her abusive husband. Or did she? David Sands is dying to discover the truth . . . and what he finds just might kill him.

AVAILABLE WHEREVER BOOKS ARE SOLD

Enjoy the following excerpt from *Awakening* . . .

One

The snow drifts lazily to earth, the way leaves flutter to the ground caught in an autumn breeze, descending in a haphazard fashion, see-sawing back and forth, each over-sized, water-laden snowflake following its own course immune to the path of others. Taj presses his nose and cheek against the dual-pane window and exhales gently, observing his breath fan out across the sheet of cold glass before fading quickly, as if an aberration—a bubbling well in a sea of sand dunes. He glances down forty-something stories to the Manhattan street below, which one he isn't exactly sure; they are staying at the W hotel at Times Square—it could be West 47th or Eighth Avenue. Taj never has possessed a keen sense of direction. One thing is clear: it isn't Broadway that he is staring at. He is certain of that.

Taj presses his cheek again to the glass. The cold feels good on his smooth dark skin. He glances upward, marveling as he does each time he returns to the city at the diversity of structures and their architectures—like the city itself, a microcosm of multiplicity—granite, steel, brick, aluminum, old and new in peaceful coexistence, like hip-hop and jazz. He never grows tired of exploring her structures—the details, fine lines, and craftsmanship that speak to him of art, creativity, and a way of constructing things long since retired. He subscribes to this mode of thinking, this way of life.

"These are some big-ass snowflakes," Taj remarks softly. He turns slightly, taking in the brown couch, low coffee table, wall unit, and entrance to the bedroom. A single lamp by the couch is illuminated. Soft music emanates from the clock radio in the bedroom. The two-room suite is small, yet comfortable. Perhaps the mood has something to do with the snow—the way hundreds of flakes each second collide with the tall windows, opening up, smearing their contents on the glass.

"Please. I hate it when you talk like that."

"Like what?" he asks, already knowing the answer as he turns toward her. He stares at Nicole. She is on the couch, her legs folded underneath her, shoes off, with thin square-frame glasses perched atop a perfectly shaped nose. Her dark eyes, enhanced by brown caramel skin and rosy cheeks, flick over to him briefly before turning quickly back to her book—a leafy hardback, James Baldwin no less.

"You know, trying to talk like that. 'Big-ass?' It doesn't become you." Taj runs a hand over his chocolate baldhead and smiles. He loves his woman. Precisely at such times he knows this with the certainty of a Swiss quartz timepiece— watching her the way he is just now, thinking to himself how lucky he is to have someone like her in his life. And so Taj sighs, captures her wink, and turns away. As he returns his stare to the window, glancing down once again at the street, the stream of traffic, and warmly dressed people, he feels a sudden urge to be out among them.

* * *

Taj and Nicole walk hand in hand (more accurately, glove in glove), the two of them bundled against the deepening cold. Nicole's wool ear warmers keep her head somewhat shielded; her red ski parka seems to attract snow the way a summer barbecue attracts mosquitoes. Taj wears a long dark wool overcoat, collar turned up, that reaches nearly to his ankles, and one of those Russian military-style hats that submarine captains wore during the second world war, with real fur that peeks out as if a squirrel or rabbit were seeking refuge underneath. The snow is swirling around them, attacking from all angles, getting into their nostrils and eyes, pelting their heads and thighs. Nicole reaches for Taj's arm and intertwines hers with his, enjoying as they always do the closeness—the warmth that can be felt even now, on this bitter, New York evening. It is eight p.m., several weeks until Christmas. The streets are lined with holiday lights, decorations, and shoppers: courageous souls like them who have braved the elements in search of a sale or last minute gift item or, in the case of Taj and Nicole, have a chance to walk in one of the greatest cities in the world (just ask anyone in Manhattan!), marvel at the architectures, take in a museum or two, or just enjoy the magic and romance of this snow-covered evening.

The sound of music is everywhere, emanating from speakers hung on lampposts every hundred feet. Christmas favorites are cycled, ones that they sang as children, and Nicole can't help but hum along as Taj points upward at the carved molding on the top edge of an Eighth Avenue apartment building or co-op. Intricate patterns carved in stone are interspersed with decorative corbels; eighteenth-century faces gaze downward. An unending sea of taxicabs glides along choking the entire avenue, and Taj notices that not a single one is unoccupied.

Going nowhere in particular, they turn right at the corner and dash into a coffee house, as much for relief from the cold as to get something to eat and drink. They settle into a high table by the window, amazingly vacant at this exact moment, after ordering a pair of lattes and jelly-filled pastries. Nicole removes her ear warmers, shakes the snow from her thick hair with a quick zig-zag movement of her neck, and attacks the pastry with her fingers, tearing at the flaky bread as though it were wrapping paper. She watches Taj closely, reaching out as he removes his hat and wiping the moisture from his smooth dark head with her hand. His eye begins to quiver—again; the third or fourth time today (that she's noticed), the lower eyelid trembling as if to its own eclectic beat. She passes her fingers over it to cease its movement. He catches her left wrist as she pulls back, brings it to his mouth, and gazes at the ring silently before kissing her fingers gingerly. Nicole blinks back tears and stares at Taj for a long time. Their eyes are unwavering before movement outside their window releases their concentration on each other.

Nicole is speaking about *Giovanni's Room*, Baldwin's acclaimed novel set in Paris in the 1950s—a young man grappling with his sexuality and the pain of choosing between a man and a woman, and how she intends to weave next week's reading into a discussion with her students on sexuality in literature. Taj listens intently, watching her eyes animate as she speaks of her work—associate professor of American literature at Howard—adding Baldwin to his already extensive to-do list.

Redressing in their coats, hats, and gloves, the two reemerge forty minutes later, appetites satisfied and freezing limbs thawed, ready to brave the elements once again. They cut across the street during a momentary lull in traffic, Nicole in tow as Taj heads for a brownstone with a lone sign in the shape of a saxophone, pulsing blue neon. They stand for a moment discerning the jazz that escapes, deciding whether or not they wish to check it out. In the end, they decide to move on, still warm and cozy from the coffee and pastry, feeling the night air, the temperature seemingly on the rise.

Onward . . . past Christmas lights and the serene nativity scenes in store-front windows, then on to the neon madness and excessiveness of Broadway. Taj just shakes his head, attempting to quickly calculate how much power is expended in this four-block radius on signage alone. He gives up, recognizing it is of little consequence to him or others.

Back onto side streets where life seems to move at one notch back from normal—third gear instead of fourth—down tree-lined blocks whose canopies are blanketed with fresh snow. Past residential homes that sport fully decorated trees in their parlor windows, each one more beautiful than the previous, as if the whole spirit of Christmas has been reduced to a competitive sport. Taj and Nicole walk hand in hand, drawing it all in, like smoke, inhaling the scent and the vapors—the very essence of the city.

They come to a dark stone church on the corner of a busy intersection—a three-building structure that is out of place among the steel and aluminum skyscrapers that tower toward the heavens, their top floors obliterated by the falling snow. The church is eighteenth century, Gothic in its design, embellished with cathedral spires and thick wrought-iron gates. A crowd of onlookers stands on the stone steps leading to enormous oak doors that are held open as though they are wings or outstretched palms, the bright warm lights inside inviting. Song can be heard spilling out into the night—Christmas carolers singing "Silent Night." Nicole turns to Taj and grins. He leads her up the stairs, past the onlookers, and into the sanctity of the church's interior.

Inside it is warm. Nicole shakes off the snow and Taj respectfully removes his hat. The pews are intermittently filled with folks who have come to hear the choir sing. They are diverse: blacks, whites, Asians, Africans, young and old, each putting aside their cultural differences on this night to sing songs that toll of the night Jesus Christ was born.

Crowds of people gather at the rear end of the church, as if afraid to move closer to the singers, or still deciding whether to stay or go. Taj leads Nicole past the throng, thick coats and jackets covered with melting snow that runs down the fabric and pools at their feet. Inching closer, Nicole behind him, his hand clasped in hers, fingers intertwined, they move past folks who have joined in with the carolers singing "O Holy Night," the sweet sound reverberating off of domed ceilings and stained glass windows. And then, as Taj is consumed by the sights, sounds, and smells within this church, his ears discern one strain that is unique and stands alone—and he pivots to search for the source: a woman's voice—distinctive and hauntingly familiar—sensual in its smooth delivery, a soulful melody that interlaces itself amidst the choir's song. Taj turns, first 180 degrees, then in the opposite direction. Nicole senses the change in him, like a flame extinguished from a sudden change in pressure, and asks if everything is okay. Taj ignores her, not in a disrespectful way, but some things can only be dealt in a serial way, one at a time, in order of priority. And so, Taj gives *this* his full attention.

Before the first row of pews is a black couple facing forward, their backs to the others. The woman, with her thick twisting hair tied back and head moving to an unknown beat, is accompanied by a tall, bald gentleman wearing an expensive camelhair coat. Taj is certain this woman is the source of the familiar melodic strain. Taj moves parallel with them and turns, releasing Nicole's hand as he does, looking past the man and observing the woman in profile. He watches her as the words of the song waft from her lips. A tidal wave of recognition rises up and crashes onto him with a force that stops his heart cold.

Twenty years.

Can that be right?

Yes.

Twenty years.

His movements are now beyond his control. He is being choreographed and flows along, his mind outside of himself as he shifts closer to the couple. And then without conscious thought, Taj opens his mouth, leans in, and says softly, "Jazz, look into my eyes . . . focus only on my eyes . . ."

Cheyenne is raptured by the sound, the way this choir has come together and filled this holy space with their sweet voices. She raises her head to the vaulted ceiling overhead and closes her eyes, matching their words but with a melody all her own. When Cheyenne is singing, she is in her element—it is what she is passionate about, what moves her, what makes her blood course through her veins with a sudden rush. She spies her husband Malcolm quickly glancing at his Movado. Yes, she knows they need to watch the time—there's a CD release party later on that evening at one of the city's hottest clubs. Malcolm, record executive and producer *extraordinaire* and currently one of the hottest and most powerful forces in urban music today, needs to be there at precisely the right moment. Cheyenne knows this all too well, the routine repeated many times during the last year. Not that she's complaining. The life they lead is storybook, no two ways about it. And yet tonight, what is most important to her right now is completing this song, singing these words that take her to a special place—many, many years ago, before she grew up and when her mamma was still here.

She leans into Malcolm, rubs his arm as he turns to her and smiles. He loves to hear her sing. It brings him comfort and joy. And so he reaches for her, placing his arm around her waist as he flashes her a smile, and he reminds her that they need to be going soon. Cheyenne silently nods.

"Jazz, look into my eyes . . ."

When she hears those words, uttered from behind her, the color drains from her face. Cheyenne ceases to sing. Her mind is racing, connecting thoughts with long-filed-away images.

" . . . Focus only on my eyes . . ."

She is already turning, a mixture of pain and pleasure filling her so quickly that she fears she will drown. And in an instant she is facing *him*. She raises her eyes slowly, as if not wanting the confirmation that is sure to come. But then their eyes meet, and she *knows*. One look at the eyes tells all. It's Taj.

"Oh–my–God," she mouths, so softly that no one, including her husband or Taj for that matter, can discern a single word. Tears freefall down her beautiful face. Never in a million years did she ever expect to see him again. And yet, staring into those amazing eyes, the ones she recalls with sudden clarity—hazel colored (the yin/yang of *that* color against his dark skin), their piercing yet calming intensity and almost magical qualities—Cheyenne is speechless. Suddenly, the air is being drawn out of this enormous room and she is finding it difficult to breathe. She is dizzy. Her husband turns back and flicks his stare between his wife and this stranger standing far too close.

"Baby?" he says, reaching for her. "Are you okay?"

Behind Taj, Nicole is watching the scene unfold. She hasn't heard the words that he spoke to this woman, but she has witnessed the reaction. Nicole, like Malcolm, has figured out (in the short time that has elapsed—five or six seconds) that something is not quite right.

Cheyenne continues to stare at Taj.

Taj silently returns her stare with his.

"Baby?" Malcolm says, louder this time as he turns to Taj. Malcolm and Taj are roughly the same size, Taj being a half-foot taller, but both possess similar characteristics—baldheads, dark-skinned complexions, and piercing stares.

Nicole reaches for her man, tugs at his shoulder as Cheyenne sobs louder. Taj waves Nicole off with a shrug and reaches for Cheyenne's face. He strokes it (cheek to chin with a single finger), smiles, and asks softly, "Have you remembered our pact, Jazz?"

Cheyenne opens her trembling mouth and responds, "Yes."

Taj smiles. "Good. I see life has treated you well." Cheyenne readies to respond, but Malcolm has wedged himself between his wife and this man.

"Look—I don't know who the hell you are," Malcolm says, his face twisted into a snarl, "but I don't appreciate your stepping to my wife like this."

Cheyenne steps forward and pulls on Malcolm's coat as she momentarily loses sight of Taj. "Honey. Don't!"

Taj, on the other hand, remains still with eyes forward, his gaze boring into Malcolm's forehead. Nicole reaches for Taj's elbow again, connects with it, and tugs him backwards. Taj continues to smile.

"Are you well?" he mouths. Cheyenne nods and sobs harder.

"Taj? Taj?" Nicole yells, pulling harder on his sleeve. "What is going on?"

Malcolm shrugs off Cheyenne's attempt to control him. He steps forward, this time inches from Taj's face. Beads of sweat have appeared on his forehead and baldhead. He wipes at his head forlornly.

"Listen, asshole. Who the fuck are you, and why are you calling my wife Jazz?"

Taj breaks his stare with Cheyenne and locks onto Malcolm. He remains silent.

"I'm talking to *you*, asshole!" Malcolm's finger juts twice into Taj's chest.

Nicole's voice is behind them, rising in pitch and intensity. "Taj, what's going on? Taj, tell me what's going on!"

Taj looks down slowly at Malcolm's fingers, then back up. He considers his surroundings and steals a glance at Cheyenne, who is pulling on her husband with one hand while wiping her eyes with the other. Mascara is smearing along her full cheekbones. Taj feels a sudden twinge of sadness and turns to leave.

"Where do you think you're going?" Malcolm says loud enough that some of the carolers cease their singing and begin to crowd the space, wondering what the commotion is all about. Seeing that Taj is not paying him any respect or attention, Malcolm grabs for his elbow. Nicole has gripped the back of Taj's coat with her hand.

Taj spins around so suddenly and with such intensity that Nicole has no choice but to loosen her grip on his coat. Again, he bores into Malcolm with those hazel eyes and leans into him until mere inches separate their faces. Taj opens his mouth and whispers to Malcolm: "Don't ever touch me again," he hisses. "You have no idea who you are dealing with. You need to be fearful and walk away."

Cheyenne has attached herself to her husband, pulling and begging him to back off. Nicole is yanking on Taj and becoming frantic. Both men refuse to budge, but Malcolm blinks first.

"Be fearful," Taj repeats, lowering his voice a notch further. "Walk away." Taj breaks his stare with Malcolm, rotating his head slightly so that he can see Cheyenne.

Their eyes meet—briefly.

They lock—then disengage.

And then, Taj turns and leads Nicole through the crowd.

Malcolm remains where he is, nostrils flaring, chest pounding, recalling the intensity of his adversary that has suddenly chilled him to the bone, wondering as he collects his wife and stares her down, *who* was that man?

Two

The thing Taj recalled first—when he dug deep into the recesses of his mind—was the heat. He remembered the terminal, Norman Manley International, a place so small and backwater that he knew for sure he was in a foreign country. Well, yeah, what did he expect?

Here he was, in Kingston, Jamaica, just landed after flying nearly two thousand miles—a journey that took him from the Eastern Shore of Virginia north to New York. He and his pop had looked in the encyclopedia he had borrowed from school to get a sense of where he was going—and where he was going was south, not north. So why then, did he have to travel by air from Norfolk, north to New York's Kennedy, only then to head south? It never made any sense to him.

While deplaning in Kingston the heat had hit him fast; as he walked down the metal stairs from the jet's belly to the tarmac, the heat had smacked him dead in the face so hard that it took his breath away. This wasn't a little bit of heat—this stuff was downright oppressive!

The second thing that Taj recalled, which had always

*stuck in his mind, was the soldiers with their weapons—
large, black automatic rifles and semi-automatic hand-
guns—big, bulky things that would scare the shit out of any
sixteen-year-old—especially one who hadn't been raised on
guns.*

*He was from the Eastern Shore of Virginia, a narrow tract
of land between the Chesapeake Bay and the Atlantic Ocean.
His father was a waterman. His father's father had been one
too. They didn't play with guns or associate with them. Didn't
have the inkling to. Handling fish was what Taj's family did—
day in and day out.*

*In the shade of the terminal lobby, a corrugated alu-
minum building with Coca-Cola signs displayed every hundred feet or so (the branded red and white logo that is
internationally recognized), Taj waited among the hordes of
Jamaicans—black people with downtrodden eyes. Taj had
seen blacks before—his father and relatives are dark-
skinned as well—but here there was a sea of them. A few
stared back at him, a few nodded silently, their long dreads
swaying as they moved, but most ignored him. Which was okay
with him.*

*Taj's very first plane ride had gone fairly well. He had
been scared—had talked to his pop about it—asked him the
night before he was to leave whether there was anything to
worry about. And Pop had looked him in the eye and said no,
there was nothing to fear. Taj nodded, considered his pop's
response for a time, and then asked if he had ever taken a
plane. Pop regarded him silently for a moment before shaking his head.*

*They had encountered some turbulence just past Miami,
up around 37,000 feet. The plane had been buffeted around a
bit, not very much, but enough to scare Taj into thinking he
was going to die—until the woman sitting two seats away (a
quiet white woman with glassy blue eyes) reached over and*

patted his tense knuckles, told him that what they were feeling was normal, and that everything was going to be alright.

He felt like kissing the ground when they finally touched down in Kingston, but as he headed for the tarmac the heat had slapped him silly. Then he suddenly was aware of the guns and soldiers. Well, he momentarily forgot all about turbulence and that kind of nonsense.

Taj was part of a church mission, a small group of folks who were heading to the mountains of Jamaica to help build a community. He had been selected from hundreds of teenagers in his congregation. Why, he never really knew—but he was honored to be going. His guidance counselor at the high school had told him that this was indeed a once-in-alifetime opportunity to see how other people in a different part of the world lived. Okay, he wasn't traveling half way around the world, but Taj got the point.

A very small group was to go on this trip and remain for a month. Taj had very much wanted his pop to go with him, but that just wasn't going to happen. Pop couldn't afford to be off from work for one single day, least of all thirty. Besides, in New York they would be joined by four other individuals—two other high schoolers, like himself, and their guardians from their respective churches. In addition, there were supposed to be a dozen or so folks already there in the mountains. Taj and these new people were cycling in; others would be cycling out over the course of the upcoming month.

Sitting in the terminal, wiping the perspiration from his forehead (wishing like hell he had had the forethought to corn roll his afro), his knapsack and oversized suitcase beside him, Taj glanced around, trying to ascertain which folks were in his group and making the final leg of the journey with him.

And then he saw her—coming around a corner, a shiny

blue Samsonite trailing behind her, bell-bottom jeans, san-dals, and a flowery patterned shirt that accentuated her bur-geoning breasts. She was about five seven, with a thin waist, a golden bronze complexion, and thick frizzy dark hair that hung halfway down her back. He put her at no more than sev-enteen—Taj had never seen anyone so beautiful in all of his short life. He sat there, enthralled, watching her, unable to move, his limbs glued to his sides, feeling the adrenaline surge through him. His mouth dried up, even though he had no intention of speaking.

She walked with an older woman who Taj guessed was her mother (who was shorter, a bit plump, and wore her hair in a much more conservative, shorter style) but had the same face—half Indian, half something else—probably black. The girl was beautiful like he had never seen before, with high cheekbones, a thin nose, and sculpted features—a hint of American Indian, but with a skin tone that told Taj she was mixed.

Taj spent the next forty-five minutes watching her every move—the sketchbook that he had brought with him laid in his lap, untouched. (Taj knew that he wanted to be an archi-tect, so he carried a sketchbook with him wherever he went, capturing ideas on the white pages.)

By the time they announced his flight (he overheard some Jamaicans call it a puddle jumper) he had completed three separate fantasies with this stunningly beautiful girl as his co-star. Of course, Taj never spoke to her—he couldn't actu-ally go to her and just say something. Taj wasn't confident around girls, never had been. He was well liked in school, but never found the right words to say to girls—so he, for the most part, left them alone.

And then she was rising along with her mother as they called the flight—his flight—and Taj felt his stomach burn. The same queasy feeling that had come over him at 37,000

*feet returned—yet he was on solid ground. He watched her
as she gathered her things and headed for the plane. He followed slowly, his mind and heart racing, mesmerized, like a
lamb to the slaughter.*

The tarmac was on fire—or so it seemed. The asphalt appeared to be smoldering. Taj guessed it was just the heat.
Beyond the gate was a Beech King Air Turbo-prop. As he
trudged toward it, his bags trailing behind him, he watched
the girl—the sensual way her hips swayed and the way she
ran her hand down the side of her face, pushing her thick
hair behind her ear. It would remain that way for a good
half-minute or so before falling out of place again—and just
that simple act, of raising a bronze arm to her face, was
driving Taj crazy. What it was, he couldn't figure. But it
made him feel . . . very good . . . .

The plane wasn't large—Taj counted five round portholes
on the side of the white fuselage with red and black trim, so
he figured it would seat a dozen passengers at the most. He
glanced behind him and saw no one else except a Jamaican
with long black dreads held down by a yellow bandana, carrying a single black bag, slowly limping toward him. A thick
black walking cane was used for support, and Taj noticed
that the handle was intricately carved; the bottom, however,
was as smooth as a blade of grass. The man wore an expres-
sionless face behind black sunglasses. The pilot, Taj
guessed, was already on board.

At the doorway, a dark woman with bright teeth smiled and,
in a thick accent, directed everyone to leave their bags by the
rear of the plane. A well-muscled Jamaican was stowing those
in the cargo hold.

Taj reached the tiny steps that were built into the fuselage. He climbed slowly, conscious of his head—he was al-

ready over six feet tall. The stewardess smiled and motioned for him to take a seat. Taj glanced around the tight cabin, saw that the girl and her mom had taken one set of cracked leather seats two rows up from the door. She was reaching for something in her knapsack when he entered—and glanced up momentarily. Taj stopped, sucked in a breath, as her gaze roamed over him, stopping at his eyes. He decided to smile after some slight deliberation and gave her a weak one, but the girl neither returned it nor held his gaze for a moment longer. She went back to what she was doing—rummaging through her knapsack, as if he weren't even there.

Deflated, Taj took a seat at the back of the plane and next to the window, pushing away thoughts of this girl, replacing them instead with thoughts of his pop.

Connect with

Us

Visit us online at
KensingtonBooks.com
to read more from your favorite authors, see books
by series, view reading group guides, and more.

Join us on social media

for sneak peeks, chances to win books and prize packs,
and to share your thoughts with other readers.

facebook.com/kensingtonpublishing
twitter.com/kensingtonbooks

Tell us what you think!

To share your thoughts, submit a review,
or sign up for our eNewsletters, please visit:
KensingtonBooks.com/TellUs.